The Desert Between Us

The Desert Between Us

A Novel

Phyllis Barber

UNIVERSITY OF NEVADA PRESS *Reno & Las Vegas*

University of Nevada Press | Reno, Nevada 89557 USA
www.unpress.nevada.edu

Cover art: Vischer's Pictorial of California (1870), View No. 47
Cover design: Iris Saltus

LIBRARY OF CONGRESS CATALOGING-IN-PUBLICATION

Names: Barber, Phyllis, 1943– author.
Title: The desert between us / Phyllis Barber.
Description: Reno ; Las Vegas : University of Nevada Press, 2020. | Includes bibliographical references. | Summary: "The Desert Between Us is about the beginnings of Route 66—a military road called The Great Wagon Road, built from Albuquerque, New Mexico, to the Colorado River in 1858—and the men and camels who helped hack this road out of the wilderness. After completion of the expedition, one of the roadbuilders falls in love with the third wife of a polygamist in St. Thomas, Nevada"—Provided by publisher.
Identifiers: LCCN 2019053415 (print) | LCCN 2019053416 (ebook) | ISBN 9781948908566 (cloth) | ISBN 9781948908573 (ebook)
Subjects: LCSH: Frontier and pioneer life—West (U.S.)—Fiction. | Camels—West (U.S.)—Fiction. | Mormons—Fiction. | United States Highway 66—Fiction
Classification: LCC PS3552.A59197 D48 2020 (print) | LCC PS3552.A59197 (ebook) | DDC 813/.54—dc23
LC record available at https://lccn.loc.gov/2019053415
LC ebook record available at https://lccn.loc.gov/2019053416

The paper used in this book meets the requirements of American National Standard for Information Sciences – Permanence of Paper for Printed Library Materials, ANSI/NISO Z39.48-1992 (R2002).

FIRST PRINTING

Manufactured in the United States of America

This is a work of fiction. All incidents and dialogue, and all characters, with the exception of some well-known historical figures, are products of the author's imagination. The author has followed historical outlines closely to convey the happenings of the period, but the characters have been enhanced by inventiveness.

To all the Sophias and Geoffreys

Contents

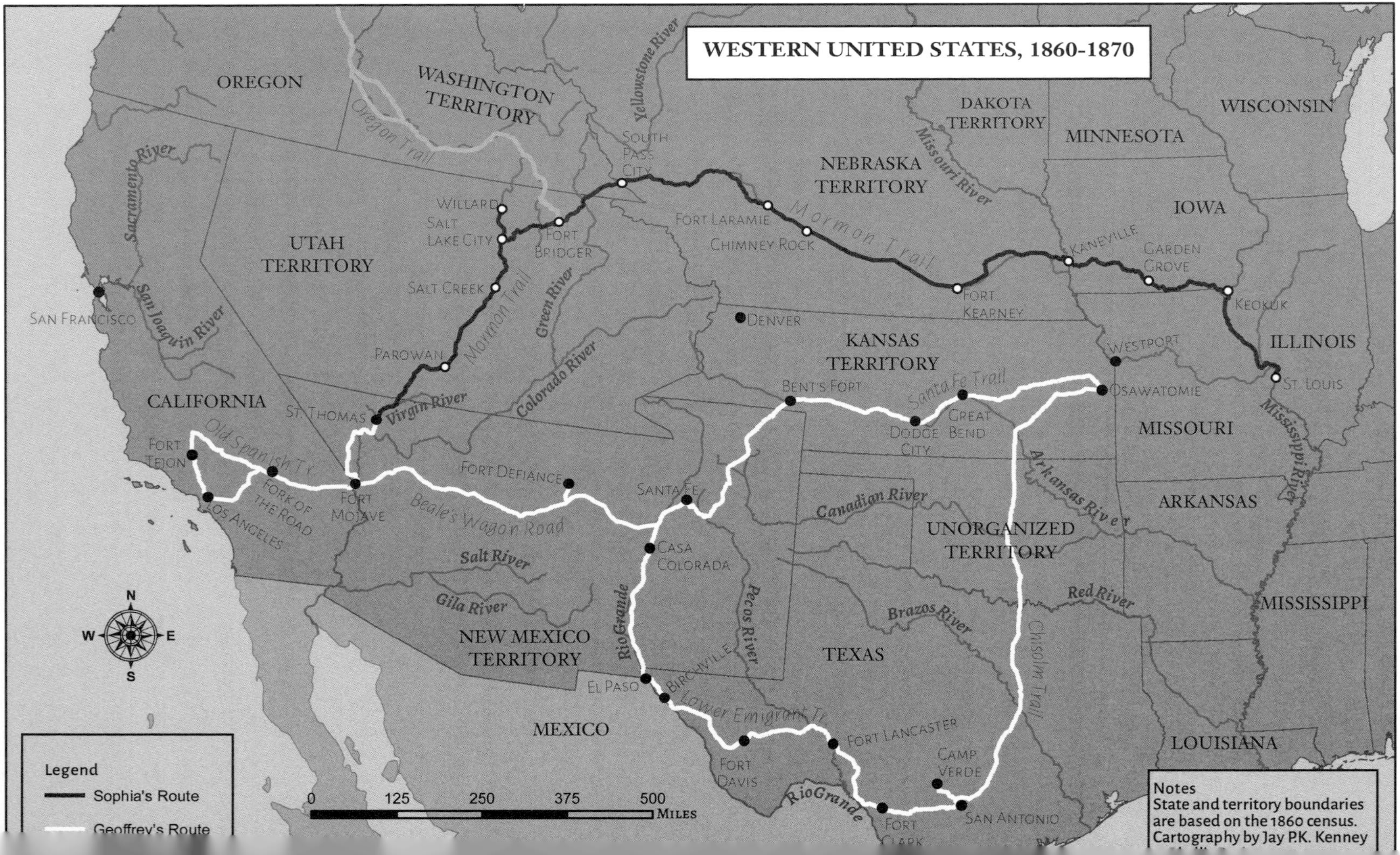
WESTERN UNITED STATES, 1860-1870
OREGON
WASHINGTON TERRITORY
Oregon Trail
Yellowstone River
South Pass City
DAKOTA TERRITORY
MINNESOTA
WISCONSIN
NEBRASKA TERRITORY
Missouri River
IOWA
Sacramento River
San Joaquin River
San Francisco
UTAH TERRITORY
Willard
Salt Lake City
Fort Bridger
Salt Creek
Mormon Trail
Green River
Fort Laramie
Chimney Rock
Kaneville
Garden Grove
Keokuk
Fort Kearney
Denver
KANSAS TERRITORY
ILLINOIS
Westport
St. Louis
Osawatomie
Parowan
Colorado River
Virgin River
St. Thomas
CALIFORNIA
Bent's Fort
Santa Fe Trail
Great Bend
Dodge City
MISSOURI
Mississippi River
Fort Tejon
Old Spanish Tr.
Fork of the Road
Los Angeles
Fort Mojave
Fort Defiance
Beale's Wagon Road
Santa Fe
Canadian River
Arkansas River
ARKANSAS
UNORGANIZED TERRITORY
Casa Colorada
Salt River
Gila River
NEW MEXICO TERRITORY
Rio Grande
Pecos River
Red River
Brazos River
TEXAS
MISSISSIPPI
Chisolm Trail
El Paso
Birchville
Lower Emigrant Tr.
MEXICO
Fort Davis
Fort Lancaster
Camp Verde
LOUISIANA
San Antonio
Fort Clark
N
W
E
S
Legend
Sophia's Route
Geoffrey's Route
0
125
250
375
500
Miles
Notes
State and territory boundaries are based on the 1860 census.
Cartography by Jay P.K. Kenney

CHAPTER ONE

THE VISIONS

AUGUST 1867

Geoffrey Scott does a double take. Is that what he thinks it is?

He's left Fort Mojave behind—buildings, stockade, new fence—and wandered into the desert to the tune of a few cicadas repeating their crrr-ing call. The night is lit by a fingernail moon and more stars than he's ever seen before. Millions. Billions. But there's an outline against the night sky. A bizarre repeat of something he's seen before. Head raised high. The hump of a back and the arch of a neck accentuated by moonlight. That silhouette looks like *Attah Allah* standing in an outcropping of rocks but looking more like the carving of an animal king looking down from a high place. Tonight it's not foraging. Perfectly still against the backdrop of a starry sky in its kingdom of sand and bush.

It takes a few steps. Geoffrey Scott takes his chances.

"Adababa," he yells into an almost empty desert.

No sound. No answer.

But now he's sure. That silhouette is the camel he rode next to on the first expedition from Texas. The one he'd ridden to the Colorado River to get supplies to Beale. Untethered, unhobbled, and uncoralled. The Civil War's over and Jefferson Davis, the main honcho for bringing the camels stateside, well, he's gone. What a joke. But what's Adababa doing here? Tonight?

Geoffrey Scott feels a sharp wind cooling his backside. He lifts his shoulders as high as they'll go, rotates them backward and forward to ease the stiffness, then reaches for the thin roll of blanket tucked into his pack. What does this all mean, he wonders, then shakes himself from the allure of pies in the sky. He'd better get the animal back to the fort where it belongs.

Tossing the blanket over his shoulders, he stumbles through the scattered rocks and approaches the camel. He shakes his head. Frustrated. When he looks closely, he sees that no one has tended to the animal's well-being.

"Hi there, Baba. What you doing out here, no hobbles on your feet? You run away?" Adababa nuzzles into his shoulder and groans, a familiar sound Geoffrey Scott's heard before.

The army's been careful with their valued cargo from the Levant, even brought their own handler with them over the high seas—Hadji Ali—the man who'd taught Geoffrey Scott how to get a camel to do what a man wanted, something most of the military never bothered learning. Few soldiers are interested in the camels or their handler—a man who speaks foreign gibberish, they say. A believer in Mohammet.

Geoffrey Scott's glad he never signed up for the uniform. Never wanted to. The idea never settled well with his congregational/abolitionist sensibilities anyway. Thank the Lord Above, he knew how to build things. Keep himself employed and away from the enlistment office, but uniform or no, he's helped carve the Great Wagon Road out of his bone and blood. Under Lieutenant Beale. A military road even if most of the builders were just plain working men. An accomplishment not small in anyone's memory. Then he's hung around Fort Mojave to help build its walls and repair its leaks. But now, as of last week, the government's claimed the Mojave's land. Told the tribe who knows best. He's had enough.

He takes a long look at Adababa—alone in the desert, free as a wild animal and yet not wild. No one's tending him. No hobbles. No broken rope around his neck. Property of the US Government, even if soldiers've been pushing some of the camels over cliffs. Favor their horses. Put off by exotic animals. But he knows this particular one. He's ridden on its back: ten feet tall when his head's straight in the air, about nine feet long and five feet wide, probably a ton. A camel can outlast and outpack any horse or mule in the Mojave Desert. Adababa's his camel as much as anyone's.

Geoffrey Scott scratches his nose with the back of his hand. Impulsively, he decides. He and Adababa will head north. Together. On the Old Spanish Trail that the Mormons have turned into the Salt Lake Road. Look for that salt mine Kwami's told him about. Find pieces as big as a man's fist. Pure, clear, more valuable than diamonds. People will pay for salt. That's what this night is all about. This camel. This vision. God's gift indeed.

* * * * *

The crescent moon. One side of a parentheses, he laughs to himself. A future open to him. Geoffrey Scott, from Osawatomie, Kansas, reaches over his shoulder and pats himself on the back. He has a partner now. A camel. He's about to become something more important than he's been. He smiles, the full moon itself. Too bad his mother isn't alive to see this. Then he shuts his eyes to escape the memory of blood haloing her head, pooling on the floorboards of the porch in Kansas, her stillness.

Wherever the souls of his parents are, he'll make them proud, though he'd best not forget his father scoffing at pride. That man never had hopes—high or low—pushing his only son out the door when his mother was killed. How he, Geoffrey Scott, came to be, he'll never figure because that coupling was unimaginable. He never saw tenderness of any kind. Or nakedness. Those parents had moved to Kansas from Massachusetts to cultivate fertile land, to live wide-open, and to help protect the territory from the spread of slavery. But then, something called Bleeding Kansas happened. Porous borders with Missouri. Slavers who hated anti-slavers. Slavers with their shotguns and their moonshine. His mother said no goodbye at all. She'd been so kind to everybody, no matter who. Even to his cantankerous father—the man he both loved and feared. He could still hear the man's crazy talk in his head.

He ties Adababa to a bush with a long rope from his pack, uncoils the horsewhip he's carried from Kansas, and forms it into a circle on the sand. He takes his blanket off his shoulders and lays it inside. Snakes won't cross that line.

While Geoffrey Scott sleeps, dreaming about salt mines and the people who'll pay top dollar, Adababa eats the first, the second, then all the branches on the bush to which he's tied, mashing the brambles and thorns in its teeth. Then the camel wanders into the desert, snaking the line tied to his neck, forming a myriad of sand patterns, unmindful of his business partner sleeping inside the circle of rope. He grazes from bush to bush, from yucca spike to creosote leaves, and then stands still as a statue on another hill—this time for the eyes of Kwanyumai, the Mojave, who never sleeps by the fort at night even though he walks and hammers on its rising walls by day. Geoffrey Scott came across him about three years ago. On the other side of the river. Gave him yellow medicine for his chills and shivering.

But tonight, the stars are legion. The sky is alive. Kwami is alone, unseen by Geoffrey Scott. The camel strolls into the night with no invitation and no capture—*Attah Allah*, as the Arab has taught Geoffrey Scott and as he has taught Kwami. God's gift. The Indian, if he spoke of such things, would use other words and say the camel is a gift from *Mutavilya.* Alone on the hilltop, the animal must have come for *Mutavilya*'s reasons. Kwami moves quietly through the night, his moccasins soft in the sand, then catches hold of the rope hanging loose from Adababa's halter. He reaches up and rubs the side of the camel's nose with two fingers. Good animal. Strong. Taller than Kwami. Almost two Kwamis for one Adababa. Together, they walk toward a shallow cave where the Mojave hobbles the camel by his side. This camel belongs to him now. It is a gift. He rolls into his own blanket and closes his eyes for the night, all of this while Geoffrey Scott tosses in his own bedroll, dreaming of Adababa close by.

* * * * *

Rising before the sun, Geoffrey Scott witnesses the emptiness. He panics and coils his rope and whip, tucks them into his saddlebag, and follows the trail left by the camel and the rope. At first, he only sees the unusual footprints and snaky imprint of the dragging rope, but then there are human tracks to the side. Over rocks and mesquite, Geoffrey Scott follows these prints to the cave of red sandstone, which is more indentation than cave—a windbreak. On a bed of sand cradled next to a rising wall of striated sandstone, he sees Kwami wrapped in a blanket, his long black hair freed from its usual band of deer leather and fanned out across his cheek. Adababa dozes beside him, his legs stretched in front and a rope tied around his back hooves.

The light of dawn works its fingers through the myriad of rock formations, the deep shadows paling to an indistinct gray. Geoffrey Scott finds a long branch to tease the black hair away from Kwami's cheek.

"Wake up, you lazy Injun."

Kwami wakes. He's startled to see Geoffrey Scott standing there, so far away from Fort Mojave where they usually meet.

"What are you doing with my camel?" Geoffrey Scott asks.

"He comes to me," Kwami says. "Last night."

"You got it wrong. He came to me."

"No. To me. His shadow against the moon."

There is no arguing with Kwanyumai's certainty, but Geoffrey Scott believes the Indian doesn't understand the order of things. "You don't believe in ownership anyways. I had him first." Chin talk.

"I did." Raised-fist talk.

Adababa remains seated, unable to rise with the hobbles on his back legs. His luxurious eyebrows magnify the handsomeness of his face, long, thick eyelashes brushing the air, opening and closing. Looking wise, impartial, and imperial.

"I could shoot you." Geoffrey Scott puts his hand on his gun, which has never been aimed at a human being or even an animal. "But then," he tempers his initial impulse and folds his arms. His bravado turns to gest. He laughs. "I guess you could pierce my side with an arrow." He points to Kwami's quiver and the arrows bundled inside. "Where's this argument leading anyway?"

Something diffuses between them. The anger dies a simple death. Maybe because the two men are friends. They've been learning each other's language back at the fort.

"We'll be business partners," Geoffrey Scott says. "How about that?" He offers his hand, though he isn't sure Kwami understands business the same way he does. He isn't sure if his deal with Kwami can be decided with a handshake.

And Kwami, on his part, keeps close watch on Geoffrey Scott and Adababa, as if he's making sure neither of them goes too far away. Mr. Scott is not a man of Kwami's tribe, after all. He has light eyes and strange skin. And the camel has been given to him by *Mutavilya*.

SEPTEMBER

"You better make yourself scarce," Geoffrey Scott says to Kwami, the river roaring in the background. "Your kind's not too popular around here."

Kwami ignores him, squatting, tossing rocks into the roiling current. Fast. Savage. Powerful. He seems spellbound by the river.

"Hey. You hear me? You better get while the getting is good."

No response, only another rock sailing through the air and disappearing into the fast-running water.

The canyon walls are pressing tighter here. The river's grown preposterously huge arms to wrestle the channel making its way south. Broad. Brackish. Red with sands picked up along the way, turning over and over, red sand rolling.

Geoffrey Scott knots the rope attached to Adababa's halter and takes a long look at the ferry that crosses the river. Hardy's Landing—a hefty line of woven hemp stretched across and a flat-bottomed boat waiting on the other bank. But then, suddenly, Adababa spits, startling both Geoffrey Scott and Kwami. Then the camel turns and twists as if it's swallowed a jumping bean.

"Whoa," Kwami shouts and jumps to full height. Then, he pulls his shoulders down and rolls his head around to straighten it. "Baba," he says in a low voice. "You don't spit."

Geoffrey Scott tries to stroke the camel's neck, hoping to calm the nervous animal, but Adababa's acting like the water is an enemy, maybe remembering the way it swept the horses downstream the time they all crossed. It skitters sideways, then spits again and swings its neck, threatening Geoffrey Scott because it could crush him against a rock and squeeze his life out in not much time. Adababa's one perturbed, unpredictable creature.

Kwami quietly works his way to the camel's side and reaches out to squeeze its thigh gently. Then, best as he can, he strokes the camel's neck. It's riled up big time, showing another side of itself the two men have never seen before.

"Settle down, Baba," says Geoffrey Scott, jumping back to keep his distance from the kicking hooves. "We're not crossing this beast today. When'd you start spitting and kicking anyway?"

Adababa turns its back on the water and on Geoffrey Scott, pulling on the rope and prancing angrily on its dinner-plate hooves.

"Temperamental thing, aren't you now?" Geoffrey Scott says. Adababa keeps overworking his tether. Deaf to any reason except his own.

"It won't do you any good to be ornery." Geoffrey Scott holds tight in this seesaw battle.

Kwami steps closer, then puts both of his large hands on the animal's side and mouths a few words, indiscernible to Geoffrey Scott. Maybe some Indian words. Some chant to remind Adababa he's among friends. Gradually Adababa settles, not yanking the rope so hard.

"That was a tantrum," Geoffrey Scott says to the camel who's now chewing on the branch of a tamarisk as if nothing had happened, a committed sampler of anything with leaves. "Hey. Kwami. You ever seen Baba like this?"

Kwami shakes his head then walks back to the edge of the river and squats.

"Easy for you to say now he's calmed," Geoffrey Scott calls after him, envious of the nonchalance of the man.

"Adababa understands. My words. We are like brothers."

Geoffrey Scott thinks he hears what Kwami is saying, but there's too much background noise from the river. Maybe Kwami thinks Adababa's more in tune with him for some reason. Foolish thinking. He looks back to the river and squints his eyes at the narrowing of the canyon. The Colorado is large. Humbling. Domineering in a land of mountains of stacked, dried mud and valleys of rock and dirt. Kwami seems to be listening to the subterranean roar of water over rocks—the unseeable forces submerged. "*Aha Kwahwat*," the Indian says out loud, as if the water's a fire that needs close watching.

"Colorado. The Red River," Geoffrey Scott says, smiling, tilting his head back, and proud of the fact he's speaking both Spanish and English. Kwami, however, seems more interested in the water. But no matter how big the Indian is, Geoffrey Scott thinks, he's still diminutive next to that big-ass camel that could hurt a body if it had a mind to. Wouldn't want to be on the wrong side of the fence when that animal's ire is up and running. But then he wonders again about Kwami, who seems to understand the animal better than Geoffrey Scott does even though he doesn't believe that for one minute.

When they'd first met, the Indian had been shaking like a leaf. Pitiful with ague. After the medicine and more than one painful grimace, the Indian wrapped himself in the blanket Geoffrey Scott had given him and sat by the fire into the night. A year later, Kwami appeared again, the same man, but this time a painted warrior dressed in loincloth and warbonnet, pointing an arrow at Adababa's heart while it carried Geoffrey Scott to get supplies to Lieutenant Beale stranded on the other side of the river. Both of them could have died then. No more pulse. Heartbeat. Nothing. Painted men running in every direction, the situation a mad scramble. And now, he's squatting next to the river, quietly contemplating its fury, maybe even its blessings before the three head north. How his father would have loved the irony: the son of an abolitionist, a camel, and a Mojave Indian.

"Time for you to skedaddle," he says. He looks carefully up and down the banks, wary someone might be watching him talking to a red man, which was trouble to most minds. "Get yourself out of here. Now." He hands the rope to Kwami.

Kwami starts climbing with Adababa, but then turns his head back and points to the cliffs. "Mojaves know secret places in rocks."

Somewhere, in the myriad of chats he's had, Geoffrey Scott's heard of a rocky labyrinth near the river carved out by the Indians. How the natives scramble over tortured rocks, tunnel through, negotiate this cobweb to travel from south to north. Hiding from those tribes that would pursue them or seeking shade in this hostile land. But this is the first time he's heard mention from Kwami. "You know about those?"

"Some."

"Would Adababa fit?"

"Some."

Kwami starts to climb again, Adababa behind him. He never smiles, and in this way reminds Geoffrey Scott of the very wooden Indian someone had carved and placed at the temporary entrance to the fort—a cockeyed notion of a red man. Kwami is silent most of the time, though Geoffrey Scott knows him for more than this. If there were such a thing as blue ribbons given out in a competition for learning English, Kwami would win. By a long shot.

"Time to be gone, you two."

The Indian pulls Adababa carefully by the rope around its neck. "Follow your master, Baba."

"Master?" though Kwami is beyond hearing his response. Geoffrey Scott can't believe what he's just heard. "You gotta be joking with that one." Then he shouts. "I need to get more information about where we're going. Take care with Adababa's feet. He's been complaining."

Never mind what Kwami thinks, he says as he trudges off to Hardy's

Landing, sinking below the surface in the unreliable sand, some of it filling with water after he steps, but he's glad his companions are headed where they'll be invisible. Somebody could ask questions. The camel's a circus, hands down. Everyone's always curious, military or no. "What in the hell's a camel doing in these parts?" people usually say. And everybody's frantic about Indians these days. Without those two, Geoffrey Scott might get a good meal. His provisions are smelly from the heat even though Fort Mojave is not that many miles away. But 110 degrees is too hot for anything. The soles of his once-strong boots are thinning. No one can walk far before they'll fry like bacon—the sun sizzling skin and bones. The sand a griddle. And rocks. Eternal rocks.

With Adababa's ability to survive in waterless places and Kwami's knowledge of the land, he thinks, as he negotiates the terrain toward Hardy's Landing, they might be able to make it through the fire-and-brimstone rocks and cliffs and skirt the worst canyons. Maybe they should take the rough military road he's heard about. The one carved out by surveyors, boatmen, geologists, engineers—curious types figuring how to get from the Gulf of Mexico upstream. Adababa would do best without rocks, that's a given. The Old Santa Fe will most likely be best, though he'll ask at the settlement just ahead, complete with a store, billiard room, dining saloon, a blacksmith, a warehouse, and several houses, or so he's been told.

After scrambling over a small cliff face, Geoffrey Scott sees a lone man washing clothes. He pulls on his groin, absentmindedly remembering the grains of sand turning his private parts red. Sandpaper in his britches. He pauses and sips the too-hot water in his canteen, careful to ease the scalding liquid over his tongue. It's September. Indian Summer. Way too hot. The man doing the washing wears no undershirt, his bare feet cooling in the harmless eddy. Geoffrey Scott also sees a soldier on the porch of the main building, this one fanning himself with a military cap, leaning against the adobe wall in a cane chair. No use for discipline in heat that keeps a body from going anywhere or doing anything.

Hacksaw military, Geoffrey Scott thinks to himself. Drifters with nothing else to do. Bludgeons with dull knives trying to be a part of something that's not anything yet. The whole endeavor of trying to get organized, though nowhere resembling organization yet. But damn, that Kwami'd be a tough one to round up, so soldiers, don't get ideas.

The last stretch of sand, damp and deep, requires heavy walking. And heavy thinking. Adababa might be the property of the U.S. military, Geoffrey Scott tells himself, but who cares whether or not the camel's stolen or discarded property? It's traveling with us now. And nobody's going to change that. Me, Kwanyumai, and Adababa are on our own. Not an expedition, military or otherwise. Just a crazy troupe of travelers.

He feels like he's getting nowhere as his feet sink in the endless sand but nevertheless keeps an eye on the half-dressed soldier nodding off on the front porch. Everything's slow. Heat like thick molasses. Hot wax. No shade. No escape. Fort Mojave wasn't like this. Many more soldiers. Lots more activity to protect the military and the emigrants. But it's no small irony the fort's been given that name. Replacing the Mojaves like it is. Geoffrey Scott shakes his head and wonders how anyone can tell someone else what they can't do. Where they can live. What they can eat.

He battles the last few sandy steps and finally reaches the porch of Hardy's headquarters.

"Howdy," he says to the soldier who's half dozing. "Mr. Hardy anywhere around here?"

"Inside." The man says, then closes his eyes again, not inclined toward conversation of any kind.

Geoffrey Scott climbs the stairs of the main building of Spanish adobe. He opens the door, then hears his footsteps echoing on the red tile floor, the sound larger than the room. Cooler interior, thank God. A relief. More footsteps. A hallway.

Hardy is huddled over a desk in a back office—a man parched and dry from the desert like everyone else who comes here. His face is tanned the color of a kidney bean, almost a dark red, and he wears a battered straw hat that seems more a habit than something to shade him from the unmerciful sun. It's set back on his head at a tilted angle.

Geoffrey Scott knocks on the half-open door. "Excuse me sir," he says, pushing the door enough to be seen. "I'm on my way north. Thought you might have some suggestions."

"I might know a few things," Mr. Hardy says, half-attentive, thumbing through the papers on his desk. He finally looks up to see who's talking. "The best advice is to keep goin'. Take the Old Spanish Trail. You can follow the river best you can, but that would be a trial you wouldn't want."

With his finger that's been separating paper, Mr. Hardy tips his hat even further away from his face and makes more of an effort. "Bring yourself inside. Couple of settlements north of here. Semi-farmable land, if you're not afraid of the Mormons. St. Thomas. St. Joe. Mormon towns. Even Callville at the fork of the Muddy and Virgin. Tryin' to compete with me, think of that, but they'll never succeed with the river like it is."

He straightens the few papers into a neat pile. "Keep goin', young man. Those Mormons are clannish and maybe you won't get past that. But you might. If that don't work, there's a road goes through Las Vegas Meadows into California. Or you can head east to Colorado Territory. Wide open about now. Everybody and California and gold, though the Indians are testier than ever. Watch out for them. Military's rounding them up where they can be watched. Look out for them. Trouble. That's what they are. Think this is their country. We'll grab them and turn 'em over to the military if they come here."

Geoffrey Scott says nothing in response.

"Always hungry. Thieving. Stealing."

Geoffrey Scott still knows more than he's hearing and isn't about to divulge the hiding place of his traveling companions.

"Why don't you have a bite to eat before you go?"

"Suits me," he finally answers.

"Got a cook'll rustle something up for you. Excuse me from joining you. Work to do."

Questions. Answers. Supplies bought. A hot meal. Over an hour before Geoffrey Scott is climbing the same slope as the camel and Indian had done before him. Looking for his compatriots and hoping Hardy or the soldiers don't catch sight of Kwanyumai or Adababa passing Hardy's Landing at the tops of the cliffs, making their way north.

OCTOBER

Geoffrey Scott stands with a pack on his shoulder in what passes as a backyard with its crooked fence of mesquite and leggy creosote. Unknown to him, this man in a dusty cap with an emblem of crossed rifles fastened at the front, this wearer of a pair of nondescript pants and shirt that was crisp and new once upon a time—is interrupting someone's weekly ritual.

The locusts sing their predictable song, no cloud hovers anywhere in the too-blue sky, and everything loses color in the heat. The heat, its oppression and everywhereness, is strong. He wipes his brow with his much-used handkerchief and stares at this ragtag town. A few mud houses, makeshift tents, and the skeletons of houses to come—signs that the settlement's working toward respectability. Then his eyes focus on the woman in the yard dressed in a long skirt and soiled blouse. He watches her biting down on the clothespin between her teeth. She wipes the hair from her face and the perspiration from her cheeks.

"Must have been wandering too long," Geoffrey Scott calls out, touching the brim of his sun-bleached, barely blue hat as he comes closer. "You some kind of vision?"

"YOU are the apparition," she says, startled, a slightly nervous laugh at the edge of her response. She wipes her abused hands on her skirt and hides them in the pleats of the fabric. She's ashamed of them, he thinks. Probably doesn't have any glycerin to soften them or ease out the redness. "A dust devil. A soldier. What are you?"

"The name's Geoffrey Scott, Ma'am." He tips his hat. "I use both names."

"Sophia Hughes," she answers. "Madonna of the Muddy." She laughs, seeming suddenly conscious of her English accent and maybe aware that her response could seem strange.

She has an odd sense of humor, Geoffrey Scott decides. But she's fetching. That's for sure. "Where you from?" he says, shifting his weight from one foot to the other. "You talk different. Say something else."

The blood rises in her face, lifts to the high point of her cheekbone. He wonders if she's ever seen a stranger, especially as dusty a one as he is, even though the settlers of this place must have seen a little dust in their time. But he can tell she'd like to check herself out in a looking glass, the way she's adjusting her hair. Almost primping. He hasn't seen a woman primp in some time.

"You look like the desert floor itself, sir," she says, patting both sides of her bun. "You're probably starved."

"You know something I don't?" He laughs a wheezy laugh, his lungs coated with more silt than he can measure.

"I baked three days ago. There's a bit left. Of bread."

But then Adababa appears over the small desert rise behind the woman's house, which is built out of sticks and stones and slathered mud. To her, the camel must look like a misshapen horse with a malignant tumor on its back and a head too high for good confirmation. Her eyes widen. She sniffs. "Oooh–fh," she says, twisting her face.

"I know what you mean," Geoffrey Scott says, moving toward Adababa to reassure him with an outstretched hand. "This here's Adab Abib. Better known as Adababa. My business partner who could stand a good currying. I was counting on him staying behind that hill."

Adababa peers down its nose at Sophia, who stands in her barren yard in mended clothes and hands buried in their folds. A haughty look, actually, dwarfing Sophia and the slanting, sliding, oozing hills of dried mud all around, baked stiff into place. She reminds Geoffrey Scott of an actress playing her part on a stage filled with nothing but these hills split down the middle, their parched cracks leeched of any moisture. A strange and powerful beast has appeared out of one of these cracks, the likes of which she has never seen before. And it has the exceptional gall to look down on her with arrogance.

"A descendant of Ali Baba?" Her lips twitch. Is she smiling or is she nervous, Geoffrey Scott wonders, remembering the señorita in Santa Fe, the one he would have chosen if they hadn't had to leave so fast.

"Absolutely not. No thief, this one," he says, slapping the camel on its hindquarter and sending it to the closest creosote bush. "Eat those leaves," he says, then turns back to Sophia again. "Adababa's gotten me through some rough spots."

"An odd way to speak of an animal, I would say. But Ali Baba is not a thief as you imply. That term is a password. That's how the story goes anyway."

He shrugs his shoulders, not caring much one way or another.

Sophia keeps her distance from the woolly animal and its smell. "That camel has long eyebrows and eyelashes."

"The best part is that Adababa can eat anything, I tell you. Cactus and thistles. Thinks the desert's his personal banquet."

"How did you come to be traveling with a camel in Utah Territory?"

"Begging your pardon, Ma'am, but this isn't Utah Territory."

Because Adababa keeps wandering close to their conversation, Geoffrey Scott puts up his wait-a-minute hand to Sophia, ties the camel's front feet together, and tells it to sit. "Only Brigham Young's grand vision for himself and his followers," he continues. "This here's Arizona Territory. Might even be Nevada before you know it."

Geoffrey Scott's been told, just last week, that the Arizona Territorial Legislature sent two delegates with an invitation to send a representative from St. Thomas to the next session. But, besides that, he's heard talk that Nevada, the new state, is anxious to claim the town for itself. Needs cash and population, though there isn't much of either he can see. Sophia best catch up on the news. He knows what he's talking about.

"I have read about the three wise men in the Bible. Their camels," she says, a hint of mischief in her eyes as she skirts the topic of St. Thomas belonging anywhere except in Utah Territory. "But they belong to another part of the world entirely. Africa. Persia."

"Think again," the man says, the camel now settled onto the ground, content to chew on the branch that droops close to its nose. "This here's a Dromedary, a one-humped camel. Bona fide property of the U.S. Military. Seventy-five in all, shipped from the Araby. Old Jeff Davis worked Congress over to get these animals sent to Texas on a steamer."

"Jeff Davis? Wasn't he a Confederate?"

"Not only that, Ma'am. He left Congress. Resigned everything to lead the Confederacy. Sorry man, in my opinion. Except I've grown fond of camels, truth of it. But no one knows what to do with them now. Horsemen don't like them one bit." He pauses for a beat, but not a long one. "Don't know what to do with the freed slaves either. Even the freed slaves don't know what to do with themselves."

"Camels brought here for the military?" she says, again sidestepping the subject at hand. You jest."

"No joking here."

Sophia laughs as if laughter could cure the confusion she must be feeling this morning, but, to Geoffrey Scott, something seems out of whack. Maybe he's lonely for somebody who reminds him of his mother. Or, maybe, the demanding sun is sucking her brains dry. It sucks everything dry—even plants the woman's trying to grow. He notices how straggly and starved the seedlings look in the brick-like clay soil. The sun is amorphous, the way it leaks heat and bleeds light beyond its circumference.

The autumn sky seems a mere stage for glaring yellow sunlight taking up too much room.

"This desert is so unlike my birthplace in England," she continues, wringing her hands. "Skies are always leaden there. Clouds block the sun. Rain. Mist. Drizzle. A blissful haven from a mad, brazen sky like this one."

He decides he'll let her talk. She needs an ear to listen. He removes the pack from his shoulders and parts his lips in a lopsided smile. He's seen better days but knows he's still young and vital. He tips his Union-style cap, which doesn't match the nonmilitary clothes. His pale green eyes assess her, and, even though he'd rather not, he's more attracted to her than he'd like.

"Your eyes are green," she says. "My husband, Charles, has brown eyes, and Mr. Milhaus…had brown eyes, too." She pauses as if in a trance, her head slightly swaying. "But he stranded me in Salt Lake City, he did. Left me by myself—a hatmaker in the midst of a passel of practical women. Some thought me self-satisfied and disinterested in furthering the Kingdom of God. All because I love to make hats."

"Where's your husband right about now?" he asks.

"He's helping dig a canal," Sophia says. "Water, you know. He's usually off on one of his mail runs. You've heard about the mail and how it's supposed to be delivered, rain or shine."

She looks off into the distance, a hint of loneliness in her eyes, and Geoffrey Scott tries to fathom what it must be like to live so much of the time alone in the middle of nowhere. But he's starving. First things first.

"Excuse me, Ma'am," he interrupts her reverie, shifting his weight from one foot to the other. "You mentioned bread?"

"Oh, of course. Forgive me. Your arrival unhinged my mind, and the shock of a camel in my yard! Please forgive me." Her hands flutter through the air like two delicate wings. "You must be ravenous."

"You're pretty," he says, looking at Sophia too directly, his expression almost wolfish. He's been without a woman for a good, long time, since the early days of Fort Mojave at least, and the few women supplying the fort were usually passing through, never to be seen again.

She turns away, as if to hide her response. Maybe she hasn't heard those words for a while. Maybe she wants him to say them again. She pulls a wet hand towel out of her clothes basket and folds it over the line of rope secured between two mesquite bushes.

"Excuse me, sir," she says, collecting herself. "I have to hang the last of this wash before it stiffens into boards. Then I'll secure some bread for you. But remember, real bakeries do not use mesquite bean flour like I do."

"I have time," he says, resting one leg on the highest sandstone step and checking through the contents of his pack. "One thing I have plenty of, though I am hungry. I see my camel has found a few bites." Adababa has reclined in the shade of a greasewood bush and chews its branches, seeming content.

"This task will be brief," she says. "I promise." She reaches into the cloth bag she uses for clothespins and draws out chunky, notched pieces of mesquite about four inches long. "Look at what my husband made for me. He's carved these heads. See? A woman with long hair like my own, and a man with a beard wearing a bowler hat. I felted one for him just like that one. Sometimes they have conversations. But you must think I am dazed in the head when I tell you things like that. I get hungry for good conversation. I do."

When will her husband be back, Geoffrey Scott wonders. Hopefully he'll appear soon out here in this conglomeration of mud huts and lean-tos, though who am I to judge conversations between two clothespins? He closes his hand around his mouth to hide his grin.

She pulls out pieces of the wash and then tucks a two-legged something that looks like long underwear back into the pile quickly, as if to hide it. She rolls the remaining wash in a kitchen towel and puts it back in the basket, which she leaves on the ground. "Forgive me," she says. "I should not keep you waiting. I have quite forgotten my manners."

"I'm obliged, Ma'am." The dusty, wrinkled, road-weary Geoffrey Scott is nimble, and there's no sound of creaking knees when he stoops to a sit. She disappears behind the burlap curtain hung across the door.

Seated on the step, Geoffrey Scott looks at his rumpled clothes. He's worn them for sleeping, riding, walking for many days, and there are stains across the front of his shirt. His boots are no longer stiff and strong. The toes curl. The sides are loose. He realizes he's no prize at the moment though he's strangely drawn to this woman.

She returns to the doorstep with a chunk of the tough, crumbling bread in hand, and a wrinkled napkin. "The best I can do, sir."

"I'm obliged, you'll never know how obliged."

"I wish I had strawberry preserves," she says, handing the food to Geoffrey Scott. "Honey. Tea. Lemon curd. Some shortbread. High tea. Where have you come from? You have been traveling for days, it would seem." Folding her arms tight against her chest, almost as if she is hiding her feminity, she stands and looks down at him while he gulps the bread.

"Originally hail from Kansas, Ma'am." He eats the bread with two hands, almost as if he's playing a harmonica. Sophia smiles though she keeps her lips pressed together. "More recently, I had to get away from Fort Mojave, about a hundred miles south of here. Back home in Kansas, the Border Ruffians attacked anybody resembling an abolitionist before the War, especially when they were roaring drunk, which was most all the time. I left in '58. Helped build a road from Fort Defiance clear through to the Colorado River. Two years we worked, readying it for travel. That's how I ended up south of here." His face darkens to black space. He pauses for a long time. "Important to guard the Indians from their own land, you know," he says, then laughs from deep in his throat. "Of course, the white man will take better care of the property than the primitives. That's the better part of wisdom these days."

Sophia listens attentively to his sarcasm. "I always thought those people were too basic for their own good. More advanced techniques might be good."

He doesn't respond to her comments and points to Adababa mashing mesquite with its teeth and long tongue. "This here's my mount. Everyone in this idle-not-and-work-hard-all-and-every-day community will be curious to see him. In fact, I'm surprised they haven't shown up already."

But a few bodies are peeking out of canvas and screen doors even if they haven't revealed their faces. Geoffrey Scott has seen the movement behind doorways and wonders when one or two inhabitants of St. Thomas will be brave enough to come to the sideshow. There's not much here in this place to brag on. Or probably even talk about. These people seem to be beginners at living, squirreling away from the sun. But he's mesmerized by Sophia tenting her hands beneath her chin and smiling at the sight of this animal in her backyard, a folded blanket across his back, a rough-looking saddle with a horn at the front, and the black, haughty eyes. Its split lip is manipulating the thorny branches as if they were supple fingers, unbothered by the sharpness of thorns against the roof of its mouth.

She cautiously takes a few steps toward Adababa and holds out her hand for the animal to sniff, though she backs away when he does. Adababa is gigantic compared to her. This time the camel looks up at her, calmly, still. Even seated, it seems to be the king of some exotic desert palace with no appreciation for commoners.

"Adababa?" she says its name, then turns back toward Geoffrey Scott. "From Fort Mojave? I have never heard of such a place or heard Charles mention it. I thought we were the only ones touched enough in the head to try and survive in this inhospitable desert."

"Military post," he answers. "About a hundred miles south of here where the Colorado's more predictable. *Aha kwahwat.* That's what the Mojaves call the river. And, believe this story, Adababa swam across once to get to California, then later rode me past a slew of Indians so I could get supplies to Lieutenant Beale. With rubber rafts, you know. Natives still live on both sides down there, even though the military's been rounding them up. One of them is trailing me now. Kwanyumai. Means 'warrior.' I call him Kwami. Thinks Adababa's his as much as mine, though he makes noise about nothing belonging to nobody."

Sophia claps her hands against her cheeks, as if all of this is too much to take in. "I should not ask, but are you on the wrong side of the law? A deserter maybe? Forgive me for asking, but you're like a genie from a bottle."

"You have a big imagination, but maybe I could bother you for water?" he says, still chewing on the tough bread.

"I'll see what we have."

She picks up the basket and balances it on her hip. "I've got to get this laundry inside before it turns to a wadded crumple." With one of the hands she's kept hidden from him, she pushes aside the canvas flap, enters, and Geoffrey Scott can hear her moving dishes in the kitchen. Then she's on the porch again, carrying half a cup of water in a cracked cup. Geoffrey Scott watches it slosh as she balances on the uneven steps, though not enough to spill over the sides. He wonders who this woman is. What she's all about. Not someone he expected to find here. So vulnerable. Fragile even.

CHAPTER TWO

THE DISRUPTION

Charles should be home any time now, Sophia thinks. She sits on the stairs next to the stranger, more than aware of avoiding appearances. Everything needs to be aboveboard. Which it is. She measures the amount of space between them, sits back, and, while Geoffrey Scott eats the miserable bread she's baked and sips the too-little water, she wonders about his connection to Fort Mojave. To the military. One can never be sure. She has heard stories of the military spying on the Mormons, convinced those settlers and the Indians are plotting war. And the government did send troops, though the Utah War, the "Mormon War," while real with its intimidation and rock walls, was ultimately not much more than its name, thank goodness for those who kept an all-out battle from happening.

Geoffrey Scott chews her mesquite flour bread with pure relish (God save the man from his bad taste, she comments to herself, though to be fair, he is famished). She folds her hands under her apron, worried about the obvious split in her index finger, and advises herself to keep from questioning the stranger. She pretends interest in the scenery around them.

James. On her mind again. But no more thinking of him, she warns herself, and puts her feet together on the sandstone slab beneath the one on which she sits—parallel, precise, two feet. James was a fool, a scoundrel, a meat plucker. Whatever he was. But things about the man who's chewing next to her—the intense eyes, his supple body, the almost paper-doll handsomeness, though he could stand a once-over with a hairbrush, straight edge, and a bath—remind Sophia of James.

They were Brother and Sister Milhaus when they arrived in Salt Lake City in 1857, just in time for Brigham Young's proclamation of martial law. "Everyone will be given passes," Brigham announced at one meeting, his voice rising. "And everyone," he pointed his finger at the congregation, "will use them." The Milhauses were caught in the middle of a huge preparation for a battle that never happened, participating in the Grand Move. Sophia shivered, even in the heat, when she remembered the leaky fort south of Salt Lake they lived in for protection. Never warm. Never dry. Basically squalid with unsafe walls that sometimes caved in. Everyone abandoned their homes, knowing the city might be burned, and those soldiers must have been doubly surprised when there was nothing and nobody to conquer. Luckily, war failed to materialize, but there was one discussion from that damp fort she had not forgotten: Utah Territory should have been called the State of Deseret. The land of milk and honey. Who is jesting whom? Brigham petitioned Congress for that name and proposed borders with his pencil and his hopes. Huge hopes, in fact. Despite his dreams, the government shrank those boundaries and named a much smaller piece of land Utah Territory in 1850, named after the Utes rather than the Mormon ideal. Her husband James had called Brigham greedy, though that particular adjective did not suit her taste.

She straightens her dress around her ankles and pulls the seams at right angles to the sandstone. Must not appear anything other than orderly to this stranger, even though she wonders what he might be thinking other than "Thank the stars for people!" But on this excruciatingly hot and windy day, she is unsure she has made the best decision about anything. She is alone most of the time. She's marooned here in the Vast West of Everything. "Stop, Sophia," she whispers to herself. "You have promised to follow the Prophet's word. That is what brought you from England in the first place." But she still feels the wistfulness that comes of questioning one's worth.

Sophia checks on Geoffrey Scott looking content as he soaks up the dry sunshine. Not a care in the world right now. Part of his shirt is unbuttoned. The hair on his chest pokes through the open top, curling even, and, for one blind second, she is tempted to wrap it around her finger as she used to do with the hair on James' chest. But then she forbids any foolish coquetry from entering her thinking. She will not disturb him in any way.

James had his fill of authority before he was born, it seems—a man unwilling to give over to something greater than himself, to the simple act of listening to the words of Jesus. "The military," James had said, disgusted when he realized men were building a fortress on this last leg of their route to Salt Lake City. "We haven't traveled all this way to wage war," he said. "We came to gather the pure in heart. That's what we were told."

That had been ten or so years ago, among the tall grass and the dry dock standing like swords on the back side of the Wasatch Mountains, just east of Salt Lake City. She and James had seen the battlements being built—the boulders, the embankments, the heavy stones rolled into place. But now she knew it was mainly rumor that had kept this war alive. Senators in the nation's capitol saying: "We're going to get those outlandish Mormons, those disobedient and disloyal people in Utah Territory who are heedless of the government." Saints in Utah Territory were not talking much different: "Mormons are not going to be run out of anywhere anymore, not going to relive massacres, extermination orders, or more martyrdoms." People and their tongues.

Except James had a forked tongue, she needed to remember that. Why had he been so insensitive when Franklin Giles, the blind harpist they met on their trek across the plains, lost his family to dysentery? Why had he not believed God would help that brother live, especially after his wife and child had died? Oh, ye of little faith, Mr. James!

Sophia changes elbows as she sits beside Geoffrey Scott on the sandstone, her hands still secreted beneath her apron. She notices her shoes on the bottom stair are unpolished, their wear and insufficiency staring up at her. She hides them beneath her skirt. So many things have fallen apart.

She had tried to make herself clear to James that no one's pillows were that comfortable when people were up to their necks with worry about soldiers crashing through doors. If only the world could understand how the Saints would shape things, given the chance. She tried to explain to him. "No war would be necessary, James, if everyone loved as they have been taught. 'Love one another as I have loved you.' The bulwarks built at Mormon Flats, the territorial passes, the words flying through the air, all symbolic of muscles being flexed. The military is secondary to the Gospel. It is," she almost whispers out loud, the argument still alive in her. "Brigham Young may be human, but someone has to do the job of leading and believing in The Director Up Above."

Geoffrey Scott leans forward and reties his boots. "Sure good to have something to eat," he says, though signs of fatigue are still evident on his face. "I'll just lie back on my elbows for a minute if you don't mind. Rude of me, maybe, but some shut eye would do me good. Long enough to savor the fact I've arrived somewhere. Okay with you?"

"Of course," she laughs, though she is ready for his rest to be over. She wants to know more about this man. "It might take some time for that bread to digest."

He tilts his face to the sky, surveys the horizon, and the afternoon shadows lengthen toward his toes. He stretches out, legs and all, and rests his hands over his abdomen. "Sure is nice to have nothing pressing on my backside except good old stones from the ground. Thanks for this respite, Mizz Sophia," and then his eyes close.

Miss Sophia. She hasn't been called that for many years. She has been married twice. Two times. She is no Miss. Never will be again.

Even after Sophia and James made it through The Great Reform—the rebaptisms and recommitments of the Saints in that cold winter when they were told to leave the city ready to burn—James decided he had been through enough. "I can no longer believe Young is guided by God. He's human. Furthermore, he lacks sane judgment." Even when the military bypassed the city and built its fort southwest by Utah Lake, James did not change his mind.

"I am returning to England." His words came before bedtime one night. While she was sitting on the edge of the bed braiding her hair. A vivid picture—his head resting in both palms, his fingers curling beneath his ears, his elbows planted on the desk he had built from loose boards. Then he sat up as tall as he could and shook the backs of his hands toward her. His fingers soon cramped into fists, almost as if he were a desperate preacher. "Don't try and change my mind. Don't."

Sophia was shocked. She stopped weaving her hair. "How can you talk like that, just when we are getting on the right footing here?" Her voice quavered though she tried to keep it even. "Think about it differently, dear James. You must trust in the arm of the Lord. Believe in all that is good. Jesus Christ's very own gospel has brought us here. Don't you care anymore?"

He bowed his head, two hands on the crown of his skull, maybe trying to push will into himself. "I'm afraid I do not, my dear Sophia, but I know you believe." He sat back and folded his arms. Resolutely. "I must go. There are too many high jinks here. Too much loose talk. Too much posturing. Believe me. I don't wish to stand in your way. That is not what I want to do."

"No, James." Sophia had covered her ears with the flats of her hands. "You cannot go. I'll be without you. You are my life."

"But," he whispered, "you must uncover your ears, my little one." He gently pulled her hands away from her head. "The Gospel IS your life." His face closed in on hers. Deep eyes looked into hers, the same ones that reminded her of Geoffrey Scott's eyes. "Respect that truth, my Sophia."

"But you are my beloved, my husband, my companion." Copious tears wet her nightgown while one side of her hair fell loosely over her shoulder. "We can make everything all right. You and me. If we keep trying, I know we can. Just remember that the war never happened, did it? Does that not prove God's hand was present? Thomas Kane? Friend of Brigham's? Friend of the Mormons in that den of senators who knew nothing but rumor? Thank God and Thomas Kane for making fact out of fiction."

"I no longer believe in the Mormon way, Sophia, no matter what happens in Washington. I. Do. Not. Believe. Can you hear me?"

She had wanted to bind herself like a mummy from Egypt. Keep all sound away from every crevice in her body. But he continued. "The Mormon Way is lived, inhabited, and conducted by mere mortals with fancy ideas. You do not share my thinking. It's impossible for me to ask you to forego what I consider a tangled, off-the-mark cause. I want you to stay by my side, but you believe with a capital B. That I understand."

She does not want to think of this anymore. She has a guest by her side who is dozing in the afternoon sun. She crosses her ankles, then uncrosses them. She sighs a big sigh. She spreads the two sides of her hair flat. No hat today. No bonnet, even. How far she has fallen in keeping herself up but maybe there's nothing to keep herself up for. The split in her finger bothers her, and she wants to throw her hands away if only she could. She re-tucks them beneath her apron.

It is true. She believes in the Restored Gospel–the church as it was when Christ was alive. Its perfection. Its true teachings. She cannot give up everything she has given away to leave Zion. She could not return to England then and cannot now, although she was heartbroken when she awoke the next morning and James was nowhere in sight. Gone. Disappeared without a good-bye.

"Coward." She makes no sound with her lips. She glances to where Geoffrey Scott's head is bent back and listens to his soft snoring. The sun lights the tops of the mountain peaks over which it disappears a bit earlier every day. Winter, or at least something that's supposed to be winter, is coming, thank goodness. This man or Charles will never know about James. That he was a deserter, an opportunist, a charmer, a snake charmer even. That she sometimes calls him a coward. He has his own principles, old James. Not hers though.

Sophia feels the increasing flatness of the sandstone, its unyielding nature, and knows she needs to stop rehashing the past. She likes Geoffrey Scott's face, and his bearing, shabby as he seems. His eyes, when they are open, remind her of evaporating pools in the cradles formed by rocks exposed to sun, mysterious even. She is feeling poetic today. Something about a new face. About change. Beneath the covering of dust, there is something fresh about him. An adventurer. A man accompanied by a camel.

"Ma'am." Geoffrey Scott opens his eyes, sits up, and wipes his face to make sure there are no crumbs left. "Can't tell you how good that tasted. Been a few days since my provisions ran out." He looks like a young boy after soaking up sun on a spread blanket. He claps the palms of his hands on his knees and rubs them, fingers splayed. "I could holler 'yippee.' I could."

"I would have given you more," she says, smiling, comforted by his elation, "but food and water are scarce here. Charles brings water by horseback from a spring about fifteen miles away. We wash with river water, but it leaves half an inch of silt in whatever container we put it in. It turns our clothes pink. And by the way, do not take your camel out on those sandbars. Quicksand. I've seen one or two large animals disappear."

"I'm eager to wash up. Even if I turn red. I'm eager to explore what there is of St. Thomas. We'll find more to talk about later, but maybe, because of those sandbars you talk about, I better leave Adababa where he is. Okay with you?"

"That is not a problem," she says, but then, after he has disappeared, she is not sure of her hasty acceptance. A stranger associated with the military. And Indians. Not a good sign. As she checks on the camel sitting quietly by mesquite, she is of two minds.

She has agreed to Geoffrey Scott's request to watch him, but Charles will probably be undone by the sight of a such beast. Uncomprehending at the least, but probably angry, his usual response to most everything. His life has been interrupted after all. And he has a short fuse.

* * * * *

A crowd is gathering, people from St. Thomas gawking at Adababa, people who have probably been watching longer from the safety of their shelters.

Some creep closer, maybe afraid their noise might disturb the animal, yet wanting to see a sight they've never seen before. Sophia wishes she could disappear herself until this interruption is past. A soldier and a camel in her backyard when all she is supposed to accomplish today is to finish the wash, put the last stitches on an almost finished quilt, and find something to make for dinner. But there's one face she's happy to see: Almira. Almira Marshall. Her best, and by far, her main friend.

She gathers her skirts and runs to Almira to give and receive a hug. "So glad to see you, Friend," she effuses.

"What's going on over here today?" Almira asks. "You got something you need to tell me? Some deep, dark secret? I hear tell you've got a camel in your yard. Tell me I'm full of beans."

"You won't ever believe all of what I have to tell you, but," Sophia looks at the gathering crowd and, though she scolds herself for such thoughts, thinks of moles coming out of their holes. Little eyes. Careful. Watching. "Can you believe this?" she asks Almira. "A camel and a dusty stranger all in one day. The curiosity is more than I can comprehend."

"That's a big animal," Almira says, backing away from Adababa after she examines the exotic creature as closely as she dares. "Where's its owner?"

"Down at the Muddy, washing up. He'll be back soon, but wait until you meet him, Almira. I swear he's a mirage."

"I hope he's good looking is all I can say. My eyes are tired of looking at so little."

The two of them laugh as if this is the first thing worth laughing about for a long time, these two women who came to St. Thomas together. Rode in a wagon train together. Wondered if they'd ever make it together. They've faced the same ordeals—the difficult road to this place, the many crossings of the Virgin River, the red sand in the water, the dysentery, and then the death of Sophia's first and only child. Sophia's shared her regrets about her lost daughter and her temperamental husband, but luckily, Almira's a friend who can make her laugh when the impulse is to weep.

"And where is your ornery husband?" Almira asks, raising her eyebrows, an all-knowing smirk on her face.

Sophia does her best to ignore the look on Almira's face. "Helping dig that canal everybody has been talking about. You know they keep trying to keep the sand at bay."

"Fat chance of that happening," Almira says, then they both laugh, happy to be with each other, happy to be laughing in this place that's mostly work and little play.

"What's that animal doin' out here?" Sister Davis blurts out as she and her son close the distance between her place and Sophia's. She's positioned one hand on her hip and the other is holding tight to the shoulder of her eight-year-old son, not quite sure of what they're seeing. Her John has come without his shoes but doesn't go anywhere without his hat.

"How'd a camel makes its way from the Araby?" someone else from the crowd asks. "Only seen one of them in Bible pictures."

"What's it chewing?" John Davis asks, and Sophia wonders at the awe on his face as he moves closer and nearer than the others. "And look. It don't have any front teeth on the top. Like goats. See that?" Always a daredevil, Sophia thinks, then raises her eyebrows and flashes a 'can-you-believe-this' look at Almira. His mother follows behind, straightening the straw hat on his head supposed to cover his home-cut head of hair. She mashes him against her apron.

"Why's it sit that way?" John pulls away to ask Henry Maudsley, a slightly older boy who leans on the hoe he's brought with him. "You'd think that'd hurt with its legs folded like that." He picks up a stick and looks ready to test the camel's temperament.

"Your guess's good as mine," Henry says, "but I'd keep my distance if it was me. That's a big animal."

Adababa doesn't seem to notice anyone or anything. He mashes impossible thorns with his teeth and thick tongue, the palate of its mouth seemingly impervious to the sharp barbs. He closes his eyes as if he were in a land far away, blissful at the thought of such delicacies, and content to chew on food most would consider out of the realm of possibility. But the crowd gasps when the camel turns its head and blinks its long eyelashes slowly–a dramatic actor on the stage, holding an audience in rapture with its pause. Then it turns its head away and recommences its chewing. No time or thing seems to matter to this creature except for its meal. People can say what they want, but everything but the joy of mastication is closed for consideration.

"How can it chew anything like that?" John's mother asks her son, who keeps creeping closer, maybe too close, and Sophia wonders if this crowd is something Geoffrey Scott would want, let alone Adababa. What should she say to keep them at bay? To keep them from frightening the camel who's been so content?

Suddenly, in this melodrama with no curtains or wings but a backdrop of rugged mountains, a giant of an Indian appears wearing beads on his bare chest and a loincloth tied at the waist with a leather thong. Majesty. Mystery even. At least six and a half, probably seven feet tall, and almost a foot taller than anyone in the crowd. Sophia feels the collective fright of those moving out of sight. "*Kwichkamaduum*," she hears him saying, the word foreign to her way of hearing. She doesn't answer, of course, dwarfed by this man who is both varnished and unvarnished like the rock in this country. Sharper. Accentuated. More extreme in the way he moves. He is not like the Paiutes. What could he want here in St. Thomas, this man of cacti and Joshua trees? He is more than a man in the usual sense, but then, what is a man? Sophia wonders.

"Geoffrey Scott? Where is he?" No one responds to the Indian's question. "Tell him Paiutes have village close by. I will sleep there. Tomorrow I will take him to salt in big mountain," he says, pointing in a southwesterly direction.

"You know about the salt mines?" Sophia cannot keep her surprise to herself. She and Charles go there for entertainment on occasion.

"Much salt in big vein running above ground. For many years before these people come," he gestures to the crowd mostly hidden from view by now, the crowd walking quickly back to their homes, cringing even, hoping he won't notice them. "Paiutes have been mining for many years, enough for every man. We will carry much salt when I return."

He speaks better English than some of the settlers, Sophia thinks. Where has he learned to speak the language?

And then he is gone, his legs carrying him away. He is no longer a man who takes up an unusual amount of space, except his absence leaves an impression, a palpable hole.

Even though he is privy to exotic news in their routine life, Charles will never believe her report. Maybe he has the contract for the mail to Callville, St. Thomas, St. Joe, Fort Vegas (which is abandoned now), and on up to Pioche, Hiko, and Panaca. Maybe he has some wild stories to tell, lots of time to rehearse them—pounding over dry washes, gullies, and igneous rock that work overtime on Midnight's shoes. But he will never believe her when she tells him of the three who have visited in his absence: a stranger, a camel, an Indian taller than any man Sophia has ever seen. This sounds like one of the stories she likes to fabricate, a fantasy even.

"What can I say?" she says to Almira. "This is a day for the storybooks."

"You're right about that one," Almira says, giving Sophia a quick hug. "I guess I should get back home and try to figure out an evening meal. You need to be a magician for that one but we keep trying." Then she hesitates, hands on her hips, as if she has something she needs to tell her friend. But Sophia seems overwhelmed. "See you, friend," Almira says, then drops her arms to her sides, walks down the emptying road, and looks back over her shoulder before she shakes her head and bites her lip.

* * * * *

Sophia's husband Charles will be wary. He agrees with the Paiutes who say, "*Americats* vs. *Mormonees*," disliking anything to do with the military. He'll be suspicious of Geoffrey Scott before he knows anything about him.

On most days between mail runs, Charles tends to alfalfa and makes adjustments to the irrigation gate that keeps jamming. But today he's helping the brethren dig a ditch to carry water from the Muddy to St. Thomas—the river that's never much more than a stream and a muddy one at that—in a hopeless gully full of endless rocks: large, small, medium, endless, and he's arrived later than promised. Seth, the mail carrier from St. George who's bringing Charles' pouch of mail, hasn't shown yet, and this causes Charles' not so unfamiliar anger to simmer.

"Digging in gravel is a bad idea," he says to the others whose shovel blades are shocking the morning quiet. But no one listens, intent on making progress before the sun becomes unbearable. After a few minutes, he tries a second time. "Gravel loses water. Doesn't protect it like it should. We'll lose more than we'll keep."

"You were late, Charlie Hughes," Brother Haskell responds, his voice sharp as the blade of his shovel. "We already made the decision about the best way to do this."

Charles surveys the gullies creasing the rise and fall of the barren hills. "Not much that's good digging out here," he says, trying to keep irritation from taking over his body. "We should scout it out more. Find something better."

They all keep digging, everyone in the silence of their own sweat, too hot to say much. Charles pitches in, but later when his shovel's blade hits against an extra-large squarish rock and his frustration mounts, he leaves the tip of the shovel buried in the ground. He rests his arms on the top end and squares his shoulders.

"We're fools, putting our efforts to a thankless task." His voice rises. "Damn fools if you keep digging. You'd best listen when someone understands more than you do."

"Ain't nobody here needs your rattlesnake tongue," Brother Haskell says, digging out a rock among rocks and tossing it to the larger pile.

"Just who are you talking about?" Charles shouts, then pulls his shovel out of the sand and lifts it like a threat, almost like a spear to be thrown. Then he hesitates, remembering his temper and how everyone keeps telling him to keep it under wraps. "Count me out, Haskell. This is a fool's errand."

He doesn't wait for a response, puts his shovel on his shoulder, and struggles through the deep sand toward Midnight, his horse, the one he's tied to a bush. Hot sand trickles into the heel of his right boot. He stops to loosen the laces. Balancing on his left leg, he unties and removes the offending boot, then pours sand on one ear of a prickly-pear cactus.

"Take that," the words of Haskell still riding his mind and his tongue. "Stupid man doesn't understand I'm a man who accepts things. When the sun shines hot, I accept it. When the rain falls hard, I accept it. I take things as they come. Damn rights. People should listen to good sense. Who does Haskell think he is anyway?"

A large tumbleweed rolls across Charles' path. He kicks its stem with the toe of his boot, then sinks another three inches. A small landslide pours over the top of the leather and inside his stocking.

"Damn sand. DAMN sand." He stops to steady his butt on a stray boulder, unlaces both of his well-worn boots, then dumps the sand back on the ground where it belongs. Finally, he reaches Midnight, relieved to be done with sand that never stops pouring into everything. Taking the horse's mane in hand, he swings himself up and over, unties the reins, and turns toward home. "Gee-yup."

Before long, he sees the hovels of St. Thomas, some of them tents, many of them only half-homes rising out of the ground, the beginnings of something better when the cool of autumn returns. But late September's brought no change except the beginning of cooler nights maybe, and that's a maybe. He turns his head toward the chaotic landscape of steep, jagged mountains surrounding this hodgepodge Hades. A scout said St. Thomas was a better place to settle than Las Vegas, where a Mormon fort had been built, but Charles thinks either place is punishment for wrongs done somewhere along the line. One of the meanest tempers known to this earth's erupted beneath this sand and rock and vomited itself everywhere the eye can reach. "Meaner than I am," he mutters to himself and then scowls. "My temper's nothing compared to that one."

Charles sees his yard now, his place of rest, his shelter, his castle he wants to think sometimes, but the place he's built is an adobe concoction with an arrow weed roof: sun-dried sand and clay brick with straw mixed in to make everything stronger. Adobe, lumber, or brick, this is his home. Too much flooding in the first site they chose. Too much water and then no water.

"I'll never understand this place," he says to his horse and the desert. "Sophia better have something to eat."

"And that woman." He's gotten into the habit of talking to himself when no one is around. "I don't know what to do about her. She's promised to stay by my side, though this sure isn't the lakes she talks about in that poem she repeats when she thinks I'm not listening. She probably won't see that country again. Brother Brigham asked me to keep building the Kingdom. I told him I'd go where he pointed. I did. No hesitation on my part. I believe in Zion and in God's word, but all the same, I wonder if there's a God in St. Thomas. Unless God's the sun that pours over us every day, presses us flat like sludge, plays an 'I'm a lot bigger than you are' game with us. God showing us we aren't much. Me and the cacti." He smiles at the comparison. People have called him something like cactus before.

Lot 37, one of the vineyard lots. That's his. Built at least seven homes since meeting up with the Saints. A lot of homes, if he says so himself. He's been devoted, nothing else needs to be said about it. But he doesn't like people much. Thinks they're annoying fools. This two-and-a-half acres of land at the outer edge of what will soon be a town suits him just fine. He envisions Sophia tending grapes with unlimited water he'll get from somewhere, but for now, he sees wavy lines boiling the top of his willow roof. Something isn't right when a body can see heat.

He dismounts Midnight and ties him to the hitching rail he's built next to the road, next to a tall mesquite where the horse might find a drop of shade.

"Sophia?" he calls out.

No answer.

"Sophia?"

Still no answer. Funny. She's usually home. Usually comes out to greet him.

"Sophia? Where'd you take yourself?"

Charles' mind plays games before something that's not the truth talks back at him.

"Sophia?"

When she doesn't appear, his thoughts scramble. Maybe she's dragged off by the Indians who love her dark hair. Sophia's nowhere to be found except in Charles' imagination. He feels off-key. His nostrils widen. His boots sound heavy on the dirt as he heads for the door and calls her name for all in St. Thomas to hear: "Sophia? Sophia Hughes? Where are you, girl?"

There's nothing to be seen in the only two rooms where she could be. Nothing moving. He stands at the door. Hesitates. The sound of the cicadas beats through the heat of midday. The heat won't stop pouring into all of his folds, and Charles wants to unbutton his skin, take it off, turn it inside out, and throw it on the floor, and stomp on it. "This heat's meaner than a snake," he says to the walls.

"Sophia," he yells as loudly as he can until the 'phi-a' echoes: "Damn that woman," he mutters. "Damn her when she's supposed to be here. Where in tarnation is she?"

Suddenly Portia Kimball is in the yard, all the time putting her nose into everyone's business. Charles doesn't want to hear from her, but there she is, walking toward his door the same time as he's standing there. Too late to duck behind the canvas.

"Charles," Portia, font of all local information, speaks with authority. "Calm yourself down. Sophia has gone to borrow cinnamon from Nettie down the road. Dessert for you, lucky man. But you should see the camel. And an Indian taller than any man I ever seen."

"What're you talking about?" he says, trying not to be testy, then pays no attention to her answer. He doesn't want to hear that woman's mind at work, so steps back to pull the canvas closed. Separation. The brutal heat doubles and triples and decorates everything that woman hears and passes along. No one's story's safe with her.

He pulls the canvas closed, then, he can tell through the slits on the open sides of the canvas, she turns back toward her house.

"Thank God for small things," he says to the dust she's leaving behind. "Good riddance," he says, not caring if he's heard or not. Where'd Portia get her ideas about camels and Indians? Balderdash.

* * * * *

They both hear him calling: Geoffrey Scott who's returned from the river and now sits next to Abababa behind the house, his heels dug into the sand, his arms wrapped around his knees, and Sophia who's returned from Nettie's house carrying a teaspoon of borrowed cinnamon in a too-large bowl. "Charles," she whispers, hurrying faster toward her home, feeling worried by the timbre of his voice. She has not had time to assemble her surprise dessert, and he's worked up, which isn't news to her.

When she sees his horse tied to the rail, she stops to stroke the animal's wet neck, "Welcome home, Midnight." But then, suddenly, the horse's nostrils are widening, sniffing something alien, alarming. There's an abrupt revision in its eyes–rolling white, reeling in their sockets. Frozen for a moment, assessing, Midnight snaps to high alert and snorts deep from his lungs, his ribs expanding like bellows. He twists his neck and snaps his head skyward as if a string pulled him taut to the heavens. A thick rope of muscles bulges beneath his tangled mane. Then he turns in circles and snorts again. His hooves spark off the scattered rocks. Fear flares his nostrils pink and glossy, fills his chest, pricks his tail. Fear rather than blood courses through Midnight's veins.

"Charles," she shouts. "Your horse," she shouts louder. "Come out here right now."

In less than five seconds, his hat back on his head, Charles bolts from the inside of the house, runs to the railing, grabs the reins tied in a knot, and jams his foot into one stirrup. Charles on Midnight's back, the horse skittering from side to side.

"Crazy horse," he yells. "Settle down you damn fool."

Midnight bucks. Charles slips from one side of the saddle to the other, half on, half off. "This horse. Gone off its head. Sophia? What in the? What happened?" His voice is bounced into nonsense and hard to translate.

Charles flips one leg over the top and leaps from the frantic animal working itself into a white lather. Reins still in hand, he raises his arms. Makes himself large. Tries to take command. "Midnight. Whoa. Boy. Easy." The horse keeps bucking, opening and closing like a jackknife. It runs in a jagged circle, tethered to Charles who hangs onto the reins with every muscle he has. This drags him a few feet before he gets his footing again. Putting the precious bowl of cinnamon on the top doorstep, Sophia stands openmouthed, her hands against her cheeks.

Midnight bucks himself toward the back of the house, and thus Adababa becomes a greater part of the chaos, Geoffrey Scott standing by its side, its eyes half-hooded, a Prince of Araby who owns half the world and counts no one as his equal.

Charles Weston glares, his temper surfacing—his volcanic temper she hates to witness.

"Sophia. Son of a bitch," he shouts over the frenzy of Midnight's hooves still striking the ground, the horse dead set on bolting from Charles' hold. She runs toward him, but he holds out his hand to stay her where she is. "What's happened since I rode off this morning? What in hell's name?"

"I was out here, hanging my wash..."

Adababa is leaning forward onto its knees, rising, Geoffrey Scott trying to keep the camel seated so as not to further frighten the horse. But Adababa has its own mind and that would be that the horse is annoying the camel's sense of peace and quiet and interrupting a contemplative meal. The camel lets out a ram-like complaint when he finds his feet—his strange, two-toed feet with a padded heel, no shoes to protect them. Large feet on spindly legs. Knobby knees. A strange concoction.

When Adababa stands to full height, he stretches his neck to fetch another mouthful of thorny mesquite. Never having seen or smelled a creature like this before, Midnight spins crazy-wild berserk, catches Charles Weston off guard, knocks him down, yanks the reins from his hands. Fury. Horse on fire. In a flurry. Galloping down the road.

"What the hell was that?" Charles struggles to stand on the jagged road, then dusts himself off, his mouth wide open. Sophia knows better than to say anything. Not a word. She also knows he's due for a mail run tomorrow morning. While he was out digging ditches, a larger-than-usual bag was brought by Seth, the express rider from St. George. It is Charles' turn to disperse the letters, parcels, the news about the aftermath of the South being brought to its knees over secession and the developing slavery issues, according to Seth that is. No man should be another man's slave, he'd added to his endless chatter.

Charles slaps his hat on his hip, glowers at everything, his stare white-hot, his eyes ready to snap into pieces. He is annoyed beyond anything

Sophia has seen before. She can see the bald spot at the back of his head, the white skin exposed to this sun that boils and bakes and fries everything in sight. His beard is streaked with more-than-the-usual gray and filled with dust, and at this moment he looks like the devil personified.

He shifts the weight of his feet to find a reliable stance on the mud-dried road, 'road' being a poor term for the rutted, greasy caliche affair that has dried into stiff peaks and valleys. "Damned road. Damned horse," he's saying. "This day needs to be stuffed up someone's arse." He attempts balance on the uneven road that needs to be graded as soon as someone can pay that kind of attention or find that kind of machinery, full of impossible ruts that break wagon wheels, hopefully not his horse's legs.

When the dust settles enough to see clearly, Sophia sees Clete in the distance—a man who lives down the road—jumping on his horse and galloping after Midnight. Dead run. She watches him throw a lasso over the frantic horse's neck until they both disappear in their own blinding cloud of dust. "Oh, Charles," she says, wanting to put her arms around him. "How lucky is that?" she says instead.

"Never in my whole life." He can't stop shaking his head. "Midnight never runs like that. Never, and I'll get that son of a bitch who caused this trouble." He walks to the side of the yard, then shakes his head in disbelief. "Is that a camel in our backyard?" he asks. "Where'd it come from? It doesn't belong here. Belongs to the A-rabs."

The ball of fury is growing, not a surprise from the man who uses anger to deal with most anything out of his expected order. Sure, he delivers mail long distances, digs irrigation ditches endlessly, channels water for crops that aren't meant to be here—neat rows of alfalfa, lucerne, wheat hopefully next season, let alone cotton Brother Brigham wants for the home industry project. He's even been on a mission for the church. To England, though he never crossed paths with Sophia there. But he's full of rage that frightens Sophia, who backs away from him, out of the way of his twitching arm and his balled-up fists. Where had this anger come from?

The stranger and the camel have done nothing wrong except arrive here. Is it she herself, his youngest wife, too frail, too fragile, his delicate flower (he often calls her), whose first child has died already? A tiny girl not able to withstand bad water and choking dust? Not adding to Charles Weston's progeny? And now, his horse…

CHAPTER THREE

THE UNEASINESS

One fist pressed hard against his hips, Charles's squinting through the distance at the small pack of horses gathered by Clete's fence, sorting through the hindquarters, looking for Midnight with the braided tail even though it's probably unbraided by now in all the commotion. Something Sophia did last night, heaven forbid her girlishness. He laughed then, but, his actual opinion: who'd do that to a man and his horse? He starts up again to Clete's house, listening to his heart beating, suspecting it's overly loud. A hot breeze picks up as he stumbles over the ruts and surveys the few homes folks have built—low, squat, shabby willow affairs. No lumber anywhere.

Why did they name this place *Saint* Thomas? he wonders. He exhales frustration into the boiling air being stirred up by a pesky wind. He'd pound it cool with his fists if he could. 1-2-3. The word "saint" means perfection. Thomas Smith is a mere man. True, he was called by Brigham to lead in building an outpost for Zion. God bless him, his good intentions, his work. But couldn't the deciders have named the place something else? The town isn't much better than a hellhole.

"What's a stranger with a camel doing here anyway?" he bursts out loud, attempting to balance his feet on the uneven surface of the road, then remembering he doesn't want his neighbors overhearing. This is Mormon country. Pure in heart and all that. Connected to Callville where the Saints'll bring converts around South America and up the Colorado. Hundreds of converts. Eager for God and the Kingdom. Supplies, too. St. Thomas'll be a watering hole, though who in hell's name ever decided there's water for anything in this flash-flood-and-dry-up heaven? The cotton plants need more water than we'll ever see. Even the sturdiest fruit trees are spindly, leggy things.

Midnight bristles when Charles pulls on his halter and arches his leg over his back to mount him. The man knows his horse, calming it with a hand on its jaw. “Just ignore that camel,” he says, then spits a wad into the dusty corral.

The day is hotter than a tent fire, the road uneven and potholed as they make their way back home. The wind’s picking up. Getting close to gale speed.

“What do you think about them tilting mountains and flaming sandstone?” Charles asks, though the only reply is the sound of Midnight’s feet breaking rhythm as he negotiates the ruts. “Cock-eyed, I’d say. Sounds like you need new shoes, friend.”

The horse remains disinterested.

“Sophia calls this territory a wild menagerie. ‘The rocks are like weeds,’ she says. ‘Crowding in anywhere they can.’ At night when I turn over, I hear her whisper she can’t relax for all the bickering among the rocks. We chuckle over that, though I’m not sure how serious she’s being. My little wife with the imagination. I’ve got to say I’m feeling like a crowded rock about now. Not a good day.”

As they cover ground, the pesky wind blowing harder with every step, Midnight regains his personality—his horseness, some friskiness, his former state of being. Charles takes some pleasure in riding the Midnight he’s used to.

“You remember what Marshall said this morning, Midnight? He said Brigham Young, who called us here from a pulpit, no less, never set foot in this place. Not once. That’s what Marshall said, me trotting to the side while your hooves raised dust and blurred the rims and fellies. He said President Young never would have called us here if he’d spent one half-second in these parts. I pity Gil for his lack of faith. I do. ‘I’m pulling out,’ he told me. ‘Nobody’s meant for this place. And, according to Almira here,’ he also told me, ‘your Sophia is delicate these days, especially since she lost her baby. With all due respect, Almira asks you to look after her with a tender heart.’

“‘And don’t expect her to be something she isn’t,’ Almira had peeked around Gil’s shoulder and chimed in with her opinion.

“Brother Gilbroid Marshall. Riding on the seat of a packed wagon, wife by his side, three children tucked under the canvas. A table and a few chairs. A trunk. A cupboard poking out. Reaching his hand out to shake mine while his wife nattered her opinions. Who is Almira to tell me to look after my wife anyway when she’s hightailing it out of here?”

Charles is a physically strong man even though he’s older, a hearty man who can work nonstop from sunrise to sunset, never tiring, a man with a powerful chin and a definite purpose. Hearty stock from New England and England before that, though he has a streak of meanness that can burn like boiling water. A slight coil of disgust worms through his body when he sees his wife waiting. Disgust at his weakness for the woman whose very shape can stir his loins. Disgust at this frivolous female, doll-like against the backdrop of sand, cactus, greasewood, and gray brittlebush.

"The woman doesn't belong here, Midnight," he says, flipping his horse's mane to one side, combing it with his fingers, something Sophia might do. He laughs to himself though it is brittle laughter. "Her nature doesn't match up. Not like Mary Anne, and, I need to say, I'm glad she and I married before I ever met up with Mormons. Too bad she's getting old. Sick half the time. Hope she's doing okay up in Willard with Harriet. Damn, I miss that house. The orchards. The seasons even."

What flashes through his mind but does not stay long enough for formulation is maybe that's the reason he feels angry at most everything. People are always telling him to calm down. Even Sophia calls him an angry, unpredictable man. But she doesn't understand how Mary Anne watched over him and the family before God told him to take more wives. And here he is. Three wives. Living in St. Thomas, which isn't where he wants to be. Not if he's honest with himself. There's that second wife, Harriet, with a solid will and a steady head on her shoulders, though she's better than good at raising an argument and being bold with her opinions. It's best she's back in Willard watching over Mary Anne even though he's promised her she could come to the Muddy after shelter's ready. A man shouldn't have this many complications.

"And there she is," he calls out when he and Midnight are almost home. "I'll be. Sophia Poultney Hughes. A basket on her hip."

Her youthfulness pulls his whiskers. He feels himself turning to undifferentiated liquid around her. She isn't fully formed, he reminds himself. Too accustomed to finery in England, to the gracious things people above her station did. She even dreams fancy—silken hats, gentlemen with brass-headed canes and pocket watches. That's plain vanity. Malarkey even. But still.

After Charles fences Midnight in the corral, he notices Sophia's holding the clothespin in her hand—the one he carved for her on a whim one night, the bearded husband. It's one of the clothespin figurines he'd whittled, happy with a knife in hand. And here she stands, holding the clothespin firmly, her fingers wrapped around it, caressing it. As much as he'd rather not, he also notices the stranger and camel at the back. What're they doing in my yard anyway?

But he smiles—a brief pause from his overbearing self which is a burden at times, he admits. Something about clothespins and camels causes a slight gentling in his mood, the one that's been growing worse all morning. He removes his hat with a gallant sweep of his arms.

"Afternoon, Ma'am," he says, swishing his hat playfully, bowing to her, noticing her wide face and high cheekbones beneath the part in the middle of her hair, the impeccably straight line from crown to forehead.

She stands on her tiptoes and raises her face to him. He bends to receive a welcome-home kiss. "Glad you are home, Charles," she whispers in his ear. "Much has been happening in your absence."

"You could say that," he says. He surveys his property, his castle keep, that's what it is, and sees something foreign in his yard, something out of place, something he'd like to root out. "By the way," he' says, ignoring the camel and stranger for a minute, "I better tell you I saw Brother Gil and Almira on my way home. Pulling out."

Her face changes, her mouth curves toward the dusty ground. A pout even. "Tell me it isn't true. Please. Almira is my friend. And she didn't even say good-bye?"

"Big hurry. Couldn't get out of here fast enough."

"She should have said good-bye, Charles," Sophia says, more hurt on her face. "She was my best friend."

"Don't get all worked up about it. People are going crazy. Losing their minds. That's what's happening. She'll miss you, you know that."

"But… She was…" She purses her lips, and Charles watches her swallowing. "How could Almira leave me?" she says again. If Charles looked and listened more closely, he would see that her face is saying that her friend is her only tie to sanity, let alone levity. He would see a devastation—something Sophia can't put into words. But he chooses to inhale a larger-than-usual breath of air that pinches his nose in the overwhelming heat. He's got to take charge of this mess, all made worse by the wind. This blasted sun.

"Will you be all right, Charles?" Sophia asks, stepping back, not allowing anymore of her feelings to show. "I know this must be upsetting—another family moving out and then Midnight's panic."

What he wants to say and doesn't is, what in tarnation is going on here? What's a camel doing in the Mojave Desert? In our yard? Who do you think you are to be talking to some stranger as if you knew him? Making trouble. Making tongues wag.

But his temper. Yes, that. She says it frightens her and makes her tremble where he can't see. She says she feels like a young child in line to be lashed. Almira has warned him, too.

"Sophia," he calls out in a voice he measures with as much judiciousness as he can muster.

Sophia slips her hands inside the pockets of her apron. Charles sees a fist against the fabric. She must still be holding the clothespin. "Quite a surprise to see him spook like that," she continues, "just like it was quite a surprise for me when that camel and stranger showed up." Keeping one hand balled, she pulls the other one out of its pocket and touches his arm to reassure him. She's the good wife once again, he hopes, no sign of upset left.

Nevertheless, he wishes his horse were next to him. Even if the animal's only a few steps away in the corral, he feels buck naked at the moment, unsure what to do, not privy to Sophia's thoughts. Then he hears Geoffrey Scott's voice. "Now don't wander off," the stranger is saying, then leaving his animal to chew on whatever it can find, the sound like tiny bones being crushed. The wind has picked up even more and is strong and hot out of canyons. The sand is slowing his steps, but Geoffrey Scott is walking toward him, holding the brim of his cap tight in the stiff wind. He pulls on the bill , a gesture that looks like an apology of sorts.

"Sorry about your horse, sir," the stranger says when he is in close enough range to be heard. "Seen this before, wish I could say otherwise. The look and smell of camels sometimes panics horses. But your mount will settle down. Geoffrey Scott here." He holds out his hand.

"I hope this doesn't happen again," Charles says, irritated, pulling on his gray-brown beard that he longs to scratch but supposes he should shake hands. Dignity. Authority. He should show this young upstart a thing or two. He finally takes a passing hold of the man's hand then yanks the brim of his hat down around his face until the crown hugs his skull.

"Charles Hughes is the name." His voice is harsh, not unlike the wind. "You something to do with the government?" His eyes are small beads, wary.

"Been making my way north up the Colorado from Fort Mojave though I'm not military, I'll tell you. About ninety miles."

"Below Hardy's Landing, I believe," Charles says with a certain air of authority, a mailman, after all, more acquainted with activity along the river than most. He folds his arms and stands with his feet apart. Resolute.

Geoffrey Scott's face becomes a question mark, maybe asking whether Charles is attempting to best him, but then, almost second thought, he raises his eyebrows and twists his mouth in resignation. "Yes, sir. Pretty treacherous going in spots, though we mostly used the Old Spanish Trail. Camel's feet like sand, you know. The moon's bright enough for night travel."

Charles is looking like he doesn't believe a word the stranger says, though he's smiling a deceptive smile while stroking his beard.

Geoffrey Scott scratches his cheek, not knowing what else he might say.

"And I thought it was hot here." Sophia smiles, entering the conversation and patting Charles on the back. Her husband maintains his stubborn stance, however, and she draws back, accepting his mood for parley. She shades her eyes from the overhead sun. The 360-degree orb is everywhere, filling the ocean-blue sky with its insufferable light. The wind tilts the bushes and plays havoc with the careful arrangement of her hair. She walks to the back of the house where she can wait. The camel is demolishing a creosote bush, circling its lower jaw.

Geoffrey Scott re-buttons the middle button on his shirt, the hole too loose for keeping it in check. "The trip hasn't been easy, but, by the way, Charles, maybe you know about this."

Who's he to call me by my first name? Charles thinks, disgusted with the young man's brashness.

"Not far from here, maybe fifty miles, me and Adababa found stone-walled warehouses in the crook of the Colorado. Another river joins up there. That sound familiar?"

"The Virgin and the Colorado." Charles alters his stance by drawing his feet closer together. "You must have been down to Callville. I know that place. Those people. They've got wagons to take their freight overland into Utah Territory soon as the heat lifts."

"If you say so," Geoffrey Scott says, his eyebrows tenting in a doubtful expression. “But, sir, nobody’s there. Not a soul. Locked and chained. I even looked through bad glazing and dust on one of the few windows. Is this supposed to be a going concern?”

“Locked and chained?” Charles says, alarmed. Callville’s the commercial settlement he’s been relying on to put St. Thomas on the map and make it an important stopover for Zion. He paces in the sand. “Callville’s the furthest point up the Colorado where any steamship has stayed in one piece, but I haven’t heard a word about warehouses being abandoned or people in Callville pulling up stakes. You sure about this?”

“Sure as can be,” Geoffrey Scott says, no hesitation.

Charles darts hateful glances at the camel that’s run his horse off. And the young man. He doesn’t know enough about him though he sure seems interested in his wife. He better understand, and I mean right now, that nobody messes with my wife or my property. Nobody. “Somebody’s supposed to be there,” he says, irritation in his eyes. “They were there when I delivered mail a while back. Sure you looked around enough?”

“I’m sure, sir.”

“They weren’t ready to load last time I talked to anybody. Virgin Hill is one treacherous road. Never seems to arrive at a top. But they planned to take supplies and people into St. George as soon as the weather cooperates.”

“Callville looked abandoned to me, I’d have to say.”

Charles stares like a midnight owl, then launches into his bully-pulpit style, the wind providing a moaning background. “Government’s been sending all sorts of boats and surveyors up the Colorado. Long before we got here. Back in ’52 with the *Uncle Sam.* Again in ’57 and ’59, or so I’ve been told. I don’t trust the damn government. All the time peeking over your shoulder. And you seem to know too much for a regular citizen.”

“I’m my own man,” Geoffrey Scott rebuffs the implication. “Never wore a uniform in my life. Came West in ’57 with road builders—Lieutenant Beale’s survey party. Wasn’t much you could call a military before the Civil War anyway. I came from East Texas. Kansas before that.”

“You know Lieutenant Beale?” Charles is impressed for the first time. He’s heard of Beale, who’s performed admirable service when he opened up the country with a military road. A middle route. For the first time, he lowers the bar on his surly attitude. “There’s been reporting in the newspapers.”

"I helped explore that road from Albuquerque to Fort Mojave south of here," Geoffrey Scott says, pride in his service visible, though Charles notices he's checking Sophia to make sure she's hearing about his exploits even if the wind wants center stage. "Cut down a few bluffs to ease the wagons to water. Even dug a tunnel or two. But stories about steamships on the Colorado. Don't know about that. There's not a lot of smooth sailing water."

"In '57, the *Explorer* came up to Callville on the Colorado," Charles says, more than a little defensive while Geoffrey Scott unwittingly sidesteps toward the house, which would be a better place to finish this conversation. The wind's mean, bullish. But Charles turns his body outward, subtly keeping this stranger from the walls of his private space. They'll stay outside, no matter the weather. "An iron-hulled stern-wheeler with a howitzer on its bow, even. Built in Philadelphia. Reassembled by natives and Mexicans down in Yuma. But…" He lets his sentence drop, careful not to say how essential this place is to God and Brigham Young.

Geoffrey Scott hunches his arms, the wind whipping at his back. He adjusts his stance so he won't be blown away. He looks over his shoulder to check on Adababa.

"I've heard about you fellows coming into this territory. Trying to keep us under control." The harsh wind competing with his edge, Charles jams his elbows out to the sides like pesky wings. "You a spy?"

"Don't mix me with the military, sir," Geoffrey Scott insists again. "I told you once before. No desire to be part of that."

"So what are your plans now?" Sophia comes forward again, probably tiring of men and their troubling talk, Charles thinks. She reties the bonnet around her head that has been hanging from her neck. Everything is like a whip—the bushes, her hair, the sand flying with each gust.

"West's a territory for all Americans now, isn't it?" Geoffrey Scott says, still taking subtle sidesteps out of the wind.

Charles Weston Hughes holds up a finger. The Mormons were in this territory first, he wants to say, but then remembers the natives staring at him when he first rolled his wagon into this place. Their bare legs and arms. Their scanty clothing. Yet he's all too familiar with the government pretending to investigate transportation in the West while actually hoping to keep the Mormons and Indians in check.

"Yes, you could say that," he finally answers. "Depends who claims what first, I guess."

"That's the question," Geoffrey Scott says, looking straight down into the eyes of the four-inches-shorter-than-himself Charles Weston Hughes, who's trying to blink away the uncalled-for tears forming to protect his eyes. "Those Indians are being displaced. Scattered. Thousands of years they lived and farmed here. Nobody speaks up for them."

"Shame when people only want land for themselves," Charles says. How could that stranger consider the Indians worth consideration in the first place? Lazy. Living below the level of humanity. And, he obviously doesn't understand the Saints and their need to establish settlements where they won't be bothered. Places on the edge. Undesirable for most everyone else, except of course the Indians.

"You could say that about the Mormons." Geoffrey Scott touches the brim of his cap to show respect though Charles doesn't buy it. "But," he seems to be noticing Charles' response and backs away from his bold statement, "no doubt I'd say, the Mojaves would have been wiser to allow passage across the Colorado in the first place. Less trouble maybe. I see the Paiutes have let you come in here. I don't see any war paint."

"Camel's got its nose in the tent...."

Both men smile, though it's obvious their smiles hide a host of opinions.

As if on cue, Adababa leans forward on its knees and rises to its full height, mashing the branches in its mouth, turning them into something else entirely. It saunters closer to the men, unmindful of the blowing wind. When the camel arrives at his side, Geoffrey Scott strokes its neck. "*Attah Allah*. My Adababa. My partner."

"Animal's got a strong smell," Charles pinches his nostrils to stem the scent of the camel's aroma that seems to be covering everything—his lot, his house, himself.

"I'll give him a bath when I can. But did you know Adababa here can carry up to a thousand pounds loaded properly?"

Sophia claps her hands together beneath her chin, as if she can't hide her pleasure that this conversation has changed direction.

"Adababa, huh?" Charles asks. "And what sort of business might you be wanting to do with that weird mount?"

"I fix things. About everything, in fact," Geoffrey Scott says. "I also heard tell of a salt mine around these parts. Saw a chunk of salt as big as my fist." He holds up a closed hand and shakes it. "Adababa's good transportation."

"There's a salt mine," Charles says carefully, debating whether or not to say anything but then deciding this boy is a fixer, which is always handy even though he doesn't cotton to the outlandish opinions about the Indians. Or the Mormons. He's not sure he trusts him, but then the young man can't see the whole picture bookended by pre- and post-mortality lives. Charles assesses the person standing in front of him, almost buried in a covering of sand—a beige ghost dressed in brown dust and taking on more. He doesn't like him staring after his wife, but he's young. Got a head on his shoulders otherwise. Smart with the animal. And he probably won't be around for long. This man with a ridiculous camel can't do much damage to the Mormons.

"We mine the salt when we need it," he says while the wind keeps interfering, putting on one mighty afternoon show. "The salt mine's just there, not something somebody needs to own. We share everything between us around here. Check it out. You could stay down at the Marshalls' tonight. They left the doors open, but they're not made of much more than cloth."

But his mind's still on Callville. Not too long ago, he rode Midnight south to deliver mail there. Built on a skillet, not really a place for settlement. Or long life either. Maybe the Colorado wasn't much for navigation after all, no matter how much everyone wanted a piece of the action. "Back to those warehouses," he says. "I was just down there. Probably traveled the same road you came on."

"Before I left Fort Mojave, I heard officers talking about sending a garrison to what you say is Callville, though they called it something else. 'Need to protect government interests on the river,' they said."

"The Army's talking about moving in?" Charles says suddenly, alarmed about the cargo stored there, waiting to be delivered to St. George where supplies are in big demand. "I better ride down there. Soon." What he doesn't say is he needs to know more about this garrison. About military plans. "Meantime, it's only right to ask you for dinner. What'd you say your name was?"

"Geoffrey Scott. I use both names."

"And the queen of the house... What does she say?" Charles asks, watching carefully how his wife, thinking she's pretending not to listen to every word spoken, will react to the question.

"A stranger is always welcome," she answers with a carefully measured amount of eagerness, in Charles' assessment. "As my mother used to say, 'There's always room for one more.'"

"Then, consider yourself invited," Charles Weston says, standing straighter. "Tonight. I want to hear more about government interests, that is if you know more."

"Allow me to offer the services of Adababa here," Geoffrey Scott says, "if you need to transport supplies from Callville."

"Thanks, but no thanks. Might unsettle the horses too much. You stay in Marshalls' house. Stay's long as you need. Nobody's there. For now, I've got to get new shoes on my horse."

When Charles leads Midnight back to the road, he decides the young man seems decent enough though he better keep his distance from Sophia. The boy was someone he'd like to ask more questions. News travels with questions asked, he knows, and he's always looking for news from the outside. Thank the Lord, Geoffrey Scott's leading his ride–that camel that makes him look like a midget–to Marshalls' abandoned house. Leaving his wife to her chores.

He mounts, then turns to look after Sophia who's walking up their steps. Scant supplies for dinner, he knows, but most of the time she knows how to create fine things, even though she talks too much about that rainy landscape and her family in front of their fire, sometimes about that shop where she sewed satins and felted crowns and decorated them with feathers of birds. Ribbons. Bows. Culture, she says. The finer things of life. That's what counts for her. Vanity. Arrogance, maybe. But give her credit. She heard the word of the Lord. She came to Zion. And she'll soon be with child again. His child. He'll see to that. And this child will live a long life. When he thinks of her, he feels a weakness in his resolve to have everything ordered and well-planned. He pulls on the halter to let Midnight know he better behave from now on. No more panicking.

* * * * *

Geoffrey Scott's walking toward the house he's been pointed to. He's heard about Mormons but has never met one before. And now, there's two plus all the others in this motley town. And they're probably polygamists, though he can't see any bevy of lascivious wives hanging around, waiting for their man to satisfy their longings. Geoffrey Scott wants to know more about both Charles and Sophia. Why they're building a town in the middle of nowhere. That Charles is hard to decipher, he thinks. Seems open to the news, but there's something hard-edged about him, that Charles. Moody. Dark. He hopes he doesn't have to spend much time with him.

Leading Adababa to the Marshalls' deserted house, the wind pushing at his back enough that he holds onto the top of his hat, he can't believe he's in a town full of Mormons. Who would have dreamt that one? Odd brew, he'd have to say. But that Sophia is one beauty. Itty-bitty thing, but beautiful with that dark hair and slow smile. Somebody like that in a town that'll soon be blown out by the wind? Who would have suspected? And she speaks with an English accent, something he's not heard much before. More than anything, he wants her to speak more to him. He loves that accent. That way of sounding like she has an insider's edge on things. She doesn't belong here, that's for sure.

"An honest-to-goodness woman, Adababa," he says to his camel. "A real woman. What do you think?"

The camel sways down the road, a rhythm to his feet that seems comfortable in the sand that alternates from yellow to red. Adababa fits well into these surroundings—not much in the way of trees, or green, for that matter. Lots of sand. Gullies. Tumbleweeds. Water having its way whenever it's around, which doesn't look like much of the time, but he can see signs of former flooding—washouts, water going nowhere fast then disappearing as if there were an invisible hole. Wonder when rain happens?

Geoffrey Scott looks back over his shoulder and sees that Charles is still out in the yard, having a conversation with his horse, both of their hair blowing sideways in the wind: Charles' beard; Midnight's tail. Wonder what he's saying about now? How'd Sophia end up with an old man like that? He's got white hair, for hell's sake, and a beard full of streaky gray. Crotchety, self-important, even looks like he could be mean. I'd say she's a blossom and he's a rancid piece of lard. He laughs to himself. Lard. In this heat. Wouldn't last long. Wonder what their story's all about, Baba? But I guess you're not saying much about now, are you?

Geoffrey Scott nears the empty Marshall house, which doesn't have a corral. No place for his ride. But there's something that could be used for one next door, a fence around an empty yard. Apart from the house. No horses, no livestock. What dumb luck! Maybe he can strike a deal with the home owner, find a place to keep Adababa fenced in when he needs to be. There's a man outside. Hoeing. Looks friendly enough.

"Hello, sir." Geoffrey Scott raises his fingertips to the brim of his hat.

"Hello to you, too, stranger. Haven't seen you around here before." He rests his chin on the back of his hands and leans on his hoe. "And I never did see one of those animals either. How'd you come to be with one of those? Better question is how'd a camel come to be with you?"

"Funny guy. Name's Geoffrey Scott. This here's Adababa. Used to work for the military that brought him from the Middle East. Trainer and all. Helped explore The Great Wagon Road through country where there's not much water. We just arrived from Fort Mojave, though you should know I'm no soldier. Just wondering if there's any chance I can keep my animal in your corral? Looks like it's empty about now."

"Name's Allred. Glenn Allred. Nice to see someone new." He holds out his hand for a shake. "And a camel. Good Lord, I'm looking at a real, live camel." He took off his straw hat, held it tight against his chest while the brim flapped in the whipping wind, and wiped the back of his other hand across his sweating forehead. "I'm expecting two horses in a few weeks. Being brought by my brother from the north of Utah Territory. But you can use my corral until then. I can't see that's a problem."

"Thanks, Glenn. I'll return the favor before long. Maybe a slab of salt, depends on my luck."

"I can always use salt, that's for sure."

"But stay out of this wind for now so you don't blow away." He turned toward his camel. "Hey, Baba. There's a corral for you. And even a few bushes. What could be better?"

Adababa follows obediently into the fenced-in corral, seemingly curious to figure out his new surroundings. He pulls a few leaves off a stray branch hanging over the fence and seems content. Geoffrey Scott takes the pack off his shoulders, straightens up, pinches his backbones together, then walks back to Marshalls' house, tired, ready to lie down and point his toes straight up at the sky, bed or not. Gotta wake up in time for dinner, but there's time for a nap.

* * * * *

Looking across the tops of the two-by-fours laid across the long pegs secured in the wall, her cupboards, Sophia is not sure she can find anything worth fixing for tonight's supper. Charles can be picky and not too quiet about it, she knows all too well. She can use the parched corn and the jerky for stew. She still has some white beans in the limp burlap bag. Maybe dumplings, though dumplings made from mesquite flour can barely pass for dumplings. Oh, for some wheat, she wishes, but buck up, Sophia. You can use the precious cherries preserved in sugar, the ones in the crockery wrapped in wet burlap and kept in a dark hole to protect them from the heat. Cherries with cinnamon. Yes. That's what she'll fix for dessert. A special treat for everyone.

Charles brought that fruit from Santa Clara on one of his mail runs, close to overripe when he handed them to her, too full of themselves and their juice. She prepared them over the fire, boiling the sugar syrup, heating the cherries just enough to keep them from disintegrating. But she thinks twice about using them now. Something promising needs to stay in their larders. Something special for the most difficult days, though maybe good things need to be used for occasions such as this one.

She pulls the crockery from the hole, unwraps the bowl, and muses over the preserved cherries meant for her and Charles. And Sarah Ann. Would her baby have liked them as much as Sophia does? Would they have to be mashed even more? Sometimes she can hear her baby's bleating. And feel the way the little one snuggled close when she nursed and suckled her mother's plentiful milk. But stop. Now. It's best to think of cherries: luxurious red inside the crock. Should she use them for supper? This stranger is probably not used to feasts now, is he?

Wouldn't her prudish brother be envious of her now? she thinks, setting the cherries on the makeshift cupboard, deciding to use them. A stranger appearing out of the desert rocks like a genie? A camel in the West, in nature, not at a zoo in Doncaster? A native taller than anyone she'd ever seen before? He did not know that Brigham Young showed an interest in these Lamanites, the ones written about in the Book of Mormon. But he probably never saw one this big. She'd met Paiutes before, that's one thing. They came to the door from time to time, asking for food. She always gave them something, even if just a crust of bread. But they aren't to be trusted, Charles says. "Always hungry." She's heard other stories of Utes raiding tribal villages. How could one Indian pit himself against another?

She's glad, come to think about it, that Charles did not see Kwanyumai. Glad he was not here to know an Indian arrived when Geoffrey Scott did, even if that Indian went off in another direction. But Charles' invitation to a stranger surprises her. Sometimes he is generous to a fault. Her husband has stretched his hospitality this time, inviting someone who has nothing to do with their community. Did they even have an extra chair for him to sit in, let alone enough to eat?

And while she shapes the dumplings out of the mesquite flour, heaven forbid, the memory of James Milhaus crosses her mind once again. James, the trickster, the man she first loved. If only he could see her now—living in the most formidable surroundings of prickly hills covered with foot-cutting stones that will sooner or later be carried away by flash floods. Straining silt from the drinking water that keeps a red tint no matter how many times it is run through the cheesecloth.

She dropped the name Milhaus in Salt Lake City when James of the brown eyes, smooth talk, and complicated mind left her to fend for herself. The man who knew how to make her skin feel softer than the light of the moon, the one who had stroked her as if he wanted to know the map of her soul. He perceived who she was and what she was about.

He is a scoundrel, she reminds herself. Through and through. A Pisces with a flopping tail. He left without saying good-bye, without telling her he was leaving. She wiped her hands on her apron and found two candles for evening light. How can she even think of a man who abandoned her when they came so far to possess truth? Who had the gall to leave Utah Territory after they had walked for at least a thousand miles? And, besides all of that, James' tongue was something she had wished to hide. An embarrassment. The way he swore about no lubricant for the handcart's wheels, even when the men in the company killed a buffalo, the animal too old and tough, barely enough grease left to lubricate anything. But they'd found enough. Why was it that her faith grew with such things and her former husband's shrank to nothing?

The depth of his disillusionment must have been deeper than anything she could have known—this husband who had no patience with their transit in cattle cars, endless walking behind handcarts, and mostly with the mix of converts from Britain and Wales, especially the Welsh speakers. "Rabble," he'd called them in one of his extreme moods. If he could use that term for them, could she herself be far behind? She had no station. She knew that. No claim to anything except her devotion to what she believed and her ability to make a fine hat. And he had so little faith, even when she reminded him of their blessings. Luckily, there had been Franklin Giles on the trek—the blind fiddler who encouraged her to sing at nights after they had trekked all day, that is, before his family died. He, himself, had decided to die, but then she had buoyed him up, reminding him: "Don't forget our songs and our hope in Zion." And Franklin lived after all. He believed. He did. And she sang to herself while she kneaded the dough:

> I go where no tyrants dare come.
> Where oppressors would tremble to tread,
> Where the honest in heart find a home,
> Where the blessings of heaven are shed. . . .
> It is Faith, 'tis not fancy, that paints
> The vision of bliss that I see;
> I go to the home of the Saints—
> To Zion, the land of the Free.

"Good-bye, James," she says as she arranges dishes on the table, dishes for eating the evening meal: three plates, three cups, three knives, and three forks. "You are not allowed in my mind!" she says out loud and firmly.

But there's nothing else to do while she prepares supper. The house is lonely, the jerry-rigged one Charles built for them until he could get lumber for something sturdy. The cradle is empty. Charles is gone too much.

She stayed in Salt Lake, she did. Not much to her name, though James had left her with half of what he had. "Half of not much," she says to the empty room and the table she is setting.

But how could he possibly have left her after their promises to each other? She and James had earned something together, but he had the audacity to leave her, all because "he'd heard enough of this wild talk about Zion. Bunch of crazies!" he'd said. He left her with enough for three month's rent, not much at all. And then there was Almira. How could she have left without saying good-bye? Without as much as a wave in her direction or a last word? What kind of friend was that?

"Enough of both of them. Desist." The sound echoes in her ears.

Time to check on the camel, who is still sitting in her yard. She peeks out the door. The animal sits like a statue, its front feet hobbled. She secretly suspects the camel of mystical properties. The way it eats thorns with such ease. The way it might devour its own hobbles if she doesn't watch carefully.

"*Attah Allah*," she calls out to the camel, repeating the name Geoffrey Scott has used, telling her it means "gift of God." "*Attah Allah*," she says again to this camel that seems more like an illusion than reality. But the animal doesn't turn his head or blink his luxurious lashes. It is deaf to her attempts at conversation. Unbothered. Content with little or no shade. It must weary the camel to look down at the pettiness of all other creatures, humans included. Standing above the fray of the insufferable world. The King of Something.

A smile creeps across her face when she turns back to the kitchen and her supper preparations. How odd. How utterly unreal to have a camel in the backyard. Adababa, no less. It is better to think about a camel than the oppressive heat. That is like wishing for no wind or for coolness when there is no such thing in the desert, except maybe in January and maybe at night. Occasionally. A few cold days.

Maybe she should go next door and barter for one of Portia's chickens. Promise to make a simple hat with the remaining few yards of felt left in her trunk. Portia would be improved with one of Sophia's hats—a good trade. Maybe she can find one of the eggs Portia's hen sometimes lays at random, the ones that boil hard in the hot sand before anyone can crack them open to liquid yolk and white. Deviled eggs. Oh, the thought. Chopped eggs for a salad, if only there were some greens. No, Sophia. Stop wishing for what you don't have. Jerky will do. Soften it over the fire. With the parched corn and dried tomatoes, some white beans.

She measures out a scant cup of beans and covers them with the only decent water she has from the springs. She must tell Charles that the water is running low.

* * * * *

"It happened like this," Charles says to Geoffrey Scott, who has told him all he knows about the garrison, finished his meal, folded his napkin on his lap, and sits upright against his chair as a guest at a table should do.

"I left Midnight to graze on an island formed in the middle of the Muddy. Late March last year. 'You won't believe how lush the place is,' one of the men told me. Anyway," he continues, Geoffrey Scott not looking in

Sophia's direction, Charles notices before he speaks again. The stranger looks like he's listening to his story. Attentive. Smart boy. "I ford Midnight across the river to join with the rest of the livestock from St. Thomas and St. Joe. I can see why everybody's making big talk about this place. Thick grass for a change. Cows and horses eating until only their nightmares hint of scarcity.

"'Enjoy,' I tell Midnight. 'This may be the best eating you've had since we came south. But don't get lazy on me. I'm counting on you.'"

His story builds, but Geoffrey Scott leans back and is now resting his hands behind his head, looking as if he might close his eyes given the chance. Charles needs a captive audience, though. He's determined to keep him awake.

As if he's tuned to Charles' thoughts, Geoffrey Scott sits up when Sophia brings a dish to the table. But Charles notices the contents. They look a lot like the cherries he brought from Santa Clara. But those were meant to be personal, he thinks. Between him and her. Why's she making this dinner into such a big deal? Showing off, maybe?

"Why are you bringing those cherries out, Sophia," he says sharply before he thinks about who's listening, what he's saying, and how he's saying it. He's lit a match near dry kindling.

"I wanted a dessert suitable for a guest." Sophia hesitates next to the table, the ceramic dish and the towel looking small in her hands. She doesn't place her offering on the table where it belongs, confused by this sudden flare up.

"That's not something you should have done." Charles' voice is strong. It points invisible arrows at Sophia. "You know that."

"Please, Charles. Not now. We have a guest. We'll talk about this later."

"No one's telling me what time is suitable." The nerve of the woman, he thinks. She's his wife. She should know better.

"This is what I've done, Charles. For all of us," she pleads. "Let's have dessert."

He opens his mouth, then stops cold. Almira's words flash through his mind. He's expressed his temper again, he realizes. Funny thing, the way it pops out when he's least expecting it. And now he's let it out for everyone to see. Even that Geoffrey Scott has seen it. He pulls on his collar, manufactures a cough, and tries to reassemble his dignity. But how could she do this? She's acting like this stranger is some kind of special guest. Using OUR cherries.

Geoffrey Scott folds his arms across his chest and says, "You were telling us about the island. About the horses feasting there."

"Excuse me," Charles says, clearing his throat, leaning his weight on the arms of his chair, readjusting his seat. "Where was I now?"

Sophia sets the dish down on the iron trivet and spoons the dessert into three bowls, making sure the servings are absolutely equal.

"Oh, yes," Charles says, though there's still tension in the room as he starts again. "I was scheduled to go out on a mail run, so, next morning, after I say good-bye to Sophia here," he clears his throat again, "I return to my horse, my pants clinging to my legs from wading across that river. When Midnight and I walk to the edge of the island, ready to cross back, I remember thinking about how big that herd is. Progress's being made, I couldn't help but think. St. Thomas and St. Joe might make it onto the map.

"The next night comes and I'm building a campfire on the trail towards Panaca. At that same time, Tom tells me the Paiutes, you won't believe this, built a bridge to the island. On its quiet side. Nobody watching. By the light of the stars that they must've thought were clapping for them, they led the horses and cattle away, the same ones that had happy eating in that swampy place. Tall, abundant switch grass. Rare food for these animals."

The room has calmed. Charles is caught up in his story again, even though a bowl full of cherry cobbler has been set before each person at the table. He picks up his spoon but talks rather than eats.

"Thomas Day can't find his horse. He can't find nary a four-legged creature. Nothing. Nada. Nowhere, except for the cow pies in which old Tom steps when he isn't looking."

Charles is the only one who laughs at his joke. He uncrosses his legs, then leans on the table, two elbows. And pauses. Sophia has heard the story, he knows, but seems to be listening to every word. He's quite the storyteller, he assures himself.

"And the rest of the story?" Geoffrey Scott says.

"'Horses are gone,' old Tom yells when he reaches the mainland. 'Cattle, too. We've gotta find them. There's something wasn't there yesterday. A bridge out back.'

"Men from St. Thomas and St. Joe ran in from the fields, from the gullies where they're trying to keep sand out of ravines. They rounded up the few horses left in town and gave them to the hardest riders, who took off in a big hurry. But the tracks grew thin by the time our men reached the California crossing. Nothing in that direction. No sign of the cattle. Not one horse."

"Nothing found?" Geoffrey Scott asks.

"Nothing except for charred bones and carcasses. Tom Day's telling me this when I return to St. Thomas three days later, and I realize me and Midnight barely escaped.

"'They took all the livestock grazing on that island,' he says. 'Almost wiped us out. Our horses and cattle. They ate everything. Carcasses by the side of the road. Our mules. Our animals. The Paiutes.'

"Me, I'm a man of few words. I knew what it'd be to lose my horse, my livelihood, and my responsibility to this community. I bring letters and packages from the life we lived before this one. You can bet I held tight to the reins of Midnight listening to Tom Day carry on.

"'I lost a span of mules,' he said. 'Paid $500 clean, and they're gone. All of 'em. Kaput.

'You're one lucky son of a gun because you took Midnight away before it happened. You and your mail.'

"'Damn Indians,' I said to him, my upset growing, thinking Midnight could be a heap of bones. Cannibalized. The thought makes me sicker than my stomach ever gets.

"They been making trouble ever since we got here," Charles continues, barely taking a breath between sentences. "Make no effort to learn English. They grunt. Like animals. How in the hell did they make a bridge without anyone in St. Joseph knowing about it?"

"They're smart," Geoffrey Scott finally interrupts the soliloquy to make his observations. "They keep a better eye on us than we do on them, that's for sure."

"Could be," Charles says, though he's barely listening to anyone else's words. "I talked to the chief, but he speaks no-school English. Indians don't care, even if Brigham told us to feed them. They're not interested in hearing the Gospel, who's kidding who? But they're always hungry."

"That's a bit on the bleak side, Charles," Geoffrey Scott says, folding his napkin into fourths and placing it on the table, not mentioning his partner, Kwanyumai, and the fact that the Indian is staying at the Paiute village with the ones who eat animals, no less.

"I best be going. Thanks for the dinner, Sophia. And those delicious cherries. Mighty appreciated by a wanderer like myself. And thanks for the story, Charles, tough one though it is." He tops himself with the bleached military cap and straightens its brim. "Pretty savage to hear about your livestock. Hard pill to swallow, though I'm glad you and your horse are okay."

He walks to the canvas door and pulls it aside. "Off to the salt mines, as they say. Tomorrow." And he's gone.

After a short silence, Charles stares at Sophia with hard eyes. "I can't believe you did what you did. Those cherries." He keeps from shouting at her, though she's cowering—perfect posture for a scolding. Perfect for shouting as loud as he needs to. "Ungrateful woman!" he says in a shrill voice. "Who do you think you are? Making dessert for a perfect stranger with OUR cherries. You want to make an impression, do you? I've a mind to…"

He stops talking, realizing he's said enough, stomps out the doorway, and heads toward the corral.

CHAPTER FOUR

THE BEGINNINGS

ELEVEN YEARS EARLIER IN OSAWATOMIE, KANSAS—1856

The apron she wore that day was colored green and tied with a grosgrain ribbon. Drying one hand on her apron as the horsemen thundered into the yard, she must have lifted the other hand to tell them to wait. "Please," he heard her shout as loud as he'd ever heard her. The next word was timed to come out of her mouth as the bullet sank into her chest. Synchronicity.

Geoffrey Scott. Seventeen. Rushing from the back of the house, running to the window to see his mother fall, catching sight of one of the horsemen sheathing his rifle, turning his horse, and riding away. The boy frozen, stunned by the scene in front of his eyes. He hadn't been there to protect her on the front porch in her green apron. It was too late to stop her likely words that must have been. She had taught him that no man is subhuman, that misdirected, evil way of thinking that no God would ever sanction—no God no matter whose he is, though Geoffrey was too late to hear the prelude to her death. He only saw his mother crumble and the blossom of red cradling his mother's head, sticks covered at one end in cloth, soaked in oil, lit with fire, and tossed toward the roof. The sound of horse's hooves fading away.

His father had been in town that morning. Came back right after the three men rode away, soon enough to see his wife lying there, his son kneeling over her, the roof of the house burning. He dismounted in a flurry and ran for the porch. "Where were you, for hell's sake?"

"In the back. Didn't see them coming."

"You blind? Deaf, too? You couldn't hear the sound of horses? Whole world of silence out here and you couldn't hear that?"

"Not soon enough."

"Why weren't you there, son? What did I tell you this morning?"

"I..."

"You what?"

"I was...you know." He hung his head in shame. "In the privy."

"You were what?" His father put his head in one hand and the other hand on his thigh, too refined to ask him why he was doing anything other than standing at the ready with his rifle. Too restrained to swipe at his son with the back of his hand, to punish him with the force of this grief.

"Get up, son. The roof's on fire. We'll take care of her as soon as we save the house."

Geoffrey's legs had no strength in them. That strength had left when he knelt by the side of his still mother. So quiet. So unresponsive.

"Help me," his father shouted, running for the water trough.

* * * * *

He had been turned out. Nowhere to go. No one to answer to. His father refusing to leave the burned-out Kansas homestead Geoffrey had farmed at his side.

On the third day after the shooting, his father tossed off reckless words, angry at anything that moved and some things that didn't. "Find your own life. No need for you here in Kansas. Nothing good here. Nothing."

But Geoffrey didn't go far. At first. He stayed close to home with a friend in town, not inclined to take his father's words at face value, thinking his foul mood would pass. But two days later, when he rode his horse back to the farm that was mostly ash and ruins, his father appeared in the blackened and still-standing door frame with a rifle cradled in his arms. "Get. I told you once, and this is the last time. Kansas is poison. I don't want no son of mine anywhere near here. AND DON'T THINK for one minute I'll change my mind."

Sure that his father was only caught in the snare of grief, Geoffrey stayed on for a few days more and occupied himself in the evenings by talking with townspeople and passers through. Everyone, it seemed, was mired in the topic of whether it was right to own a man or not. But another subject was taking hold. Besides the talk of slavery, there was an itching in everyone's feet and bold words in their mouths about heading out West. "Riches. Land left blank and wide open since the Mexican-American War. Miles for the taking with a mere snap of the fingers."

Geoffrey was more than a little uneasy with talk of war and victor's spoils. The Mexicans may have been cheated by a land-grabbing administration or by their incompetent military personnel for all he knew. He'd seen what happened when men were blinded by a cause—men on both sides of the border of Kansas and Missouri. Raiders in both directions. Retaliation. Eye for an eye. No matter who was in the way. He'd seen the results of his mother catching a bullet in the chest. Taken by a pro-slavery man, probably soused. Because she didn't believe in keeping anyone in chains and had spoken out about it. Now his father had gone off his head, inconsolable, and too stubborn to leave something he thought he still owned, even though that something was charcoal and ash, mostly burned to the ground.

"I'll tell you to get yourself gone again, so help me God," Elias Scott swore loudly on both days he told his son to leave the farm and Kansas, the words feeling as though they had been hurled against Geoffrey's backside, words that caused water to shine in his eyes, something he'd never let his father see. "Go on now, boy. Get yourself out of here."

Geoffrey, who mistrusted answers found at the end of a rifle, had no choice but to leave.

* * * * *

When he rode away from Kansas in that late spring of '56, he made a vow: he would not be angry at the man. He knew his father better than the man knew himself. At least he fancied that he did. Elias Scott was a good human being, if a little on the crazy side anymore. But Geoffrey had failed to protect Elias' woman—his own mother—let alone their home. She never understood the fury of men feeling entitled to put other men into bondage. To treat them as two-thirds human. She had no belief in such things. Furthermore, she knew too little of the Kansas Jayhawkers who caused equal amounts of trouble in Missouri. Her mind could not conceive of retribution, revenge, and retaliation on her side of the equation, though it existed. She only knew what felt wrong to her. But he knew the wrong that had happened to her, his mother—a bull's-eye shot by a Border Ruffian, a pro-slavery man. Geoffrey had failed his parents.

As he raised Kansas dust for what might be the last time, his mother was alive in his head. He wished he could feel one of her kisses on his cheek and a hug like she always had for him. She'd been humane, fair, so gentle in the way she thought. He wanted to put his hands on her shoulders and tell her he'd be back soon. He'd be gone only a few minutes, he'd tell her, until he'd return to help with the farm. "I know you'll never forgive me, Mother, but I would have held you, I would have, if I'd been there. I was so close to being there. And Papa, you probably won't ever understand or forgive me, but I'd give anything—an arm or a leg even—to have a different outcome. I'm sorry, I am, though I know talk is cheap."

With those thoughts circling in his mind, he promised himself he'd never fail the Scott name again. He'd make that name sing, shimmer, glow even. Well, maybe that was overdoing a good thing, he decided. But to everyone he met along the well-chewed-up track, he introduced himself: "Geoffrey Scott is the name. Not one or the other. Both."

He wandered across Oklahoma territory, down Texas. He met up with homesteaders, itinerant preachers, westbound pioneers heading for Oregon, California, and Utah Territory— something those Mormons emigrants called Zion. Joining their ranks from time to time, he heard more talk about gold and silver. Most interesting to him, however, was the talk of miles of land up for grabs. Opportunity. Why not, now that the land was laying its chest bare to comers?

On the horse he'd used for plowing too many fields to remember, the one given to him when he was a young boy, he headed deeper into East Texas. On the way, he heard rumors about alternative passages around the formidable Rockies. Heard tell about a Canadian explorer by the name of F. X. Aubry, purportedly a too-sensitive, pint-sized kind of guy who took a large herd of sheep across the Colorado River north of the Mojave villages, only to be knifed later while defending his honor against wicked satire in the newspapers. Notes and maps had been found in Aubry's possessions, making the route along the 35th parallel not only probable, but definitely possible. This middle route sounded smart to Geoffrey Scott. The only other year-round passage to the West lay in the desert through El Paso and Fort Yuma, where Apaches could skin five cats with one shot of an arrow, leave dead victims to dry out on sand, and put the sweet bejesus scare into any and everybody.

But he heard an even stranger tale from one dusty soldier on an even dustier horse in front of a general store in a no-name town in East Texas. "Camels," I tell you. "Honest-to-goodness camels. I seen 'em myself over at Indianola. Senator Jeff Davis, that's who wanted camels, though other people talked him into it, I'll bet. Talked those government boys into buying up camels in the Araby. Had 'em shipped to the coast of Texas where I saw 'em being unloaded. Now some of 'em are corralled at Camp Verde out of San Antonio. Honest to goodness camels. Thirty-six of them. More coming. Seen 'em myself. People been flocking to the fort to see the circus. The soldiers, if you can call 'em that—what a sorry excuse for a military, this bunch of immigrants being told what to do by highfalutin officers from Norwich and West Point—tell them this ain't no circus. Mum's the word when anyone asks why the camels are in Texas. Lips are sealed, though that's a joke, mind you. Between you and me, I think they want to build a road to Caly-fornia."

That was the direction Geoffrey Scott turned his horse: north and west of San Antonio. Nothing to lose and no place to go but somewhere else, Geoffrey Scott arrived at Camp Verde, an army installation surrounded by a haphazardly built fence and a couple of casual guards at the gate. With his bedroll and blanket, he camped in between a few ramshackle buildings somebody was brash enough to call a town, complete with a rickety hotel to use for bathing when necessary. He talked to anybody who was willing: hotel guests and desk clerks talking about the Panic of 1857 and how that had unearthed so many bodies looking for work. A man from Germany who'd heard about the treasure chest of the West and didn't want to miss out. Trappers. Barkeeps. An old-salt cowboy almost buried in a white beard fanning across the width of his chest and talking about gold "just lyin' on the ground for the pluckin'." An almost-pretty woman who seemed lonely like he was, one who talked late into the night before they found comfort in each other.

The farm boy from Kansas mixed with these captains of adventure and also rode to the fort every day to ask about work. "I'm good with my hands," he explained to anyone who would listen. "And, I got a head for figuring things out...." While waiting for work, he was urged by ragtag soldiers to "Join up and serve your country." But he had no ambitions for the military, no desire to cultivate a warrior mentality or drink to excess like these soldiers did. He wanted to survive and find out about the camels. Bottom line.

Only two weeks after arriving, Geoffrey Scott had acquired a reputation as a handyman—wagon wheels, horseshoes, canvas wagon tops, saddles, bridles, harnesses, anything anybody needed. He could come and go easily to and from the fort and soon found himself there much of the time. When he saw a glimpse of the camels corralled in an out-of-the-way corner of the fort, he was told by a soldier not to head in that direction. "Camels are off limits. Too many gawkers." He did, however, while hanging out around the fort, overhear a snatch of conversation among some senior officers. "Lieutenant Beale'll be scouting a route from Albuquerque to California. Government's looking for a safe passage for the rush West." Other than that, nobody was saying much.

ELEVEN YEARS EARLIER IN DONCASTER, ENGLAND—1856

Sophia leaned against the wooden headboard, her legs tucked beneath the familiar quilt. The flame of the candle on her bed stand cast playful shadows across the quilt and the pages spread open on her lap. Yes, it had been her mother who had taught her to take the tiniest of stitches into the top layer of this counterpane, through the feather filling to the bottom, and back up again with a barely discernible flick of the needle. Dear Mother.

Tick, tick. The clock in the hall. The sounds of floorboards creaking—the house complaining of its arthritic pains or maybe of its having to support these inhabitants who required constant comfort from its halls, stairs, bannisters, and doors?

Her eyelids drooped without her permission, blocking what little light she had. The invitation of Nepenthe. She urged herself to stay awake. She had just skimmed over some important lines in the book her father had wrapped and tied into a packet for her twelfth birthday. Just before he departed for other worlds five years ago. How he loved words, schoolmaster he had been. Wordsworth's in particular.

She imagined the lines of the poem calling: "Sophia. Wake up. Take care." She forced her eyes artificially wide, then read the words her father had once recited, her lips moving silently:

> And I have felt
> A presence that disturbs me with the joy
> Of elevated thoughts; a sense sublime
> Of something far more deeply interfused,
> Whose dwelling is the light of setting suns,
> And the round ocean, and the living air,
> And the blue sky, and in the mind of man,
> A motion and a spirit, that impels
> All thinking things, all objects of all thought,
> And rolls through all things.

"A presence." Those two words wakened her. What was this presence that interfused the sublime with the natural world? "Interfused." What was it that compelled her to squint in the candlelight and reread the poet's words written a few miles above Tintern Abbey on the banks of the River Wye? Maybe it was the memory of her father's low baritone voice reading those words—a lullaby she had not heard in far too long. Maybe it was the hope that she could see out onto the other side of her ceiling.

Who am I? she wondered. Sophia Jane Poultney? A daughter? A milliner's apprentice soon to receive appellation of hatmaker? A shop girl? An artist or a poetess in embryo? And who is it that keeps asking these questions?

Enough wondering, she told herself, the seventeen-year-old girl who loved asking questions more than answering them. "A basket of questions," her father had once said of her.

Her seventeenth birthday. In May, and now it was October. Her situation was good enough, she mused, her eyelids growing heavy again. She did have a gift with a needle and thread and possessed an inherent sense of style and beauty. She was a dutiful daughter, contributing to the welfare of her family. But the same shop day after day? Toiling with a needle for hours upon hours? Waiting on those grand people with their carriages, drivers, and footmen? No one taking notice of her genuinely ivory complexion or her inquisitive mind, except to ask about this type of feather or that color of satin? No one to invite her from her narrow row house, tall and thin, a place where rooms were squeezed between thin walls and hips brushed against other hips when passing in the hall?

Is that what it is all about—waiting for a gallant man to recognize her beauty and intellect radiating from beneath the bonnets and hats she made so artistically? Not just a man, but one with enough substance to escort her to a better life? But most of those only knew how to look across their own dull horizons, unable to consider anything that existed above or below that plane of vision. Silly men in their top hats. Silly world of people and their places in the order of things they themselves had authored. Ceilings above which those below could not rise. What about a "motion and spirit that impels *all* thinking things, *all* objects of *all* thought?"

If she could only take a few days for herself, take the train to the ruins of Tintern Abbey. Wales. To the remnants left behind by the Cistercians who wished to lead a simple, austere, ascetic life to correct the abuses heaped on by those who sought luxury and power. She would climb the hills above the ruins to see what Wordsworth saw. To look on nature and hear the "still, sad music of humanity…of ample power to chasten and subdue," free from all thoughts of who belongs where and who is best or better than another.

The candle dripped to a dangerously low height, the base of the candleholder soon to overflow its pool of hot wax. It was time for her to stop her constant chattering. She was due at the shop by eight in the morning and needed the clearest of vision for assembling the hat that awaited her, the one needing to be ready by late afternoon for the Countess of Wheatley Hall. Cupping her hand behind the candle, she blew out the flame. She nestled into her covers, into the night hours watching over her until she awoke to a new day.

* * * * *

Much building activity was underway along her morning route to the Market Place and the shop. She turned onto Grey Friars' Road, then walked briskly at the edge of the curving lane around the building site of St. George's Minster, where men scurried and climbed ladders to secure the roof before winter snow flew. A sharp wind blew leaves from the tops of trees and scattered this flurry of reds, oranges, and faded-to-yellow greens. With her gloved hands, she rewrapped her scarf more tightly around her neck. Past High Fisher Gate. Toward the Market Place and the lane where the shop's bell rang noisily when she entered, the same as it always did.

"Good morning, ladies," she announced, full of the energy of brisk air.

Mary, the shopkeeper, rushed out of the workroom, even before Sophia removed her coat. Breathless, as always. "Lady Wheatley is concerned. An occasion, you know. She will be here at half past three to claim her hat."

"I am fully aware," Sophia said, tucking her scarf into the sleeve of her coat for safekeeping. This job had been given to Sophia upon the recommendation of Lady Hickleton, her word of praise passed to Lady Wheatley's ear. It was no small thing that she had requested Sophia's services.

When the Lady of Wheatley Hall had come into the shop a few weeks earlier to ask for her, Sophia was elated. She knew she could fabricate what Lady Wheatley envisioned, even expand on it. And she knew well enough why her customers mentioned her name to others. A hat would just be a hat to sit atop one's head if she did not fully concentrate on her cutting and stiffening, and she knew to be an overseer of the highest order to keep the hat from being average and spiritless. A hatmaker needed to put her best effort into every joining and not just chat away mindlessly while she sewed. A hat was a birth: Sophia, the mother of hats, such odd-shaped infants. A hat needed her labor pains, her full attention, and her tenderness. She understood how the felting and the grades of hair were dependent on someone knowing how to give it solid shape and often reminded herself of the mummies in Peru—their hair lasting longer than death, even longer than 2,500 years. Hair was the one element least liable to change. That was her secret. As simple as that. And thus she lengthened the list of satisfied customers each week.

The entire morning, she hunched over the easier part of the hat—the blue satin gathered into a crown—and dedicated herself to sewing the brim in such a way that the joining appeared seamless. Ah, Sophia's tiny stitches served her well.

"Would you like to go to the corner with me?" Georgie, one of the shop girls, as close as any of them to being Sophia's friend, interrupted her concentration. "It is nearly noontime." The two of them often shared their midday repast on the bench beneath the plane tree Sophia loved, the one with the ball-like, hairy fruit clusters that sometimes shed a fine brown fuzz. It was Sophia's favorite tree in all of Doncaster, complete with large, leathery brown leaves that could be snapped in two when they fell in the autumn.

"I both *want* and *need* to go with you," Sophia said. "The shop is especially stuffy today, but this hat needs to be ready at half past three. Maybe I can sit on the bench with you until a quarter past, but I cannot stay."

Their intended corner, which Sophia's tree sheltered, occupied a place in a park across the street from The Market, the gathering place that had outlived the Romans, the Scandinavian invaders, the many plagues and disastrous fires, and even the Church of St. Mary Magdalene, which had been demolished when Sophia was three years old. The memory of St. Mary Magdalene's demise lay hazy in her mind, but she remembered the sea of bits and pieces lying on the ground and her father letting her pick through the rubble to find a treasure. But The Market had remained, and people gathered there daily—locals looking for the catch of the day or the freshest lettuce, travelers on their way to London or Edinburgh, north or south, sojourners from neighboring counties.

"A comely American has been speaking on the corner," Georgie said, then giggled as they darted between carriages to cross the road and a sudden wind blew their hair into tangles. They both captured their curls by tying scarves beneath their chins. "Americans speak so strangely, but this man's appearance is worthy."

While everyone's feet shuffled noisily through the brittle brown leaves beginning to crumble powder-like beneath boots and shoes, Sophia observed the man who seemed close to thirty years of age. A maroon cravat at his throat. Dark, wavy, strong hair. Tall. Earnest. Intriguing, though his face showed scarring from a previous skin condition. He tugged on his well-worn jacket, frayed on the sleeves, and pulled it close around him. His physique implied certainty. Solidity. And he was standing beneath *Sophia's* tree, its ancient branches spreading over the crowd and the speaker, in the place where Sophia sometimes sat holding the tree's stiff, short-haired pods in her hands and picking them apart: "He loves me, he loves me not"—though that "he" had yet to appear in her life. He seemed less objectionable than some of the others who preached at the corner—wild-eyed men ranting and raving about repentance and the Second Coming and The Last Days, would-be-elocutionists lecturing on Dr. Arnott's views on carbon dioxide and distributing pamphlets, the gypsies with their unkempt hair, woolen capes, and exotic beads with tarot cards laid in various patterns on unfolded blankets.

Holding one arm up high to attract attention and reading from a Bible to the sparse crowd, he suddenly pointed his index finger with certitude. "And whatsoever ye shall ask in my name, that will I do," he spoke loudly, "that the Father may be glorified in the Son. If ye ask anything in my name, I will do it." Her father had read those same words to her from St. John, but she and Georgie had other matters at hand.

They found a bench beneath Sophia's tree, unwrapped their bread and cheese, and chatted about the increasing orders and deadlines in the shop. But Sophia found herself wanting to look more directly at the speaker and assess what he was all about. But responsibility seized the day. The blue satin hat. She must not disappoint Lady Wheatley.

At half past three precisely, Lady Wheatley fought against the door to shut it against the blustery wind. Sophia was ready. She counted to five, breathed deeply, then rose from her chair and emerged from the workroom to present the new hat. Lady Wheatley raised her eyebrows in surprise, then smiled generously, took the hat as if it were a new toy, placed it atop her head, and assessed its worth in the shop's mirror. Her smile was that of a young girl free of any title or pretense, enjoying her reflection. "Oh my," she said, turning to the other side. All of the workers in the shop had stopped their tasks to peer in at this occasion, but when Lady Wheatley turned from the looking glass, the shop's hum resumed. She clicked open a small beaded handbag that hung from her arm, reached inside, crossed her lips with one finger to indicate a secret, and pressed a significant coin into Sophia's hand, a pence even. Sophia's weekly wages did not amount to a pence, and, beneath her somber mask of deference, her insides danced. Her stars were shifting. The sky even. The constellations. How lovely it would be to buy a new frock, but she knew the coin belonged in the long stocking in her bureau drawer, an addition to her fate rather than a subtraction.

* * * * *

All of this was nothing she could have imagined when curiosity drew her to the crowd gathered around another preacher from America on a street corner in Doncaster. On that crisp autumn evening she'd gone to the apothecary for her mother, whose chest was congested and whose anxiety was increasing by the minute.

In the midst of a low-lying cloud that had hovered over Doncaster all day long, Sophia returned to the corner. The crowd was haphazard, different from the previous week's gathering. More scattered. Aimless even.

"Welcome, welcome," the preacher began. "How fortunate we are to be together in contrast to this dismal weather. May the Spirit of Jesus Christ, our Savior, be with me this night and with you, that your ears might hear and your eyes might see." He spoke of Zion, now located in the American West in something called Utah Territory. "The gathering place," he said. "For the pure in heart—those who can accept God into their lives without being blinded by the illusions of men's sophistry and rhetoric that attempt to explain away all belief in a divine creator."

This was the man she had wanted to hear again, the one now standing above the crowd on whatever pedestal impelled him to such heights. He held a leather book in his hand, pointing to it, and telling everyone that it was a second witness for Christ who taught us, above all, to love one another.

"It is simple," he said, his voice now almost a whisper, one hand accentuating the rhythm of his speech. "Come unto God's dwelling place and let your heart be filled with the spirit of compassion. Allow God to work through you and guide you at every step. Surrender your will, and do not confuse this with your intelligence. Your will would act independently of all creation and careen through life in oblivion. Your will considers nothing but itself. But we are not alone. We have a head—God the Father and his Son, the redeemer, the embodiment of God on this earth. We have the original gospel of Jesus Christ."

Maybe it was the man's surety, his conviction that he could answer anyone's questions about life and its meaning. Maybe it was the deep roots of his belief in Heaven and God, but Sophia liked the God he described—one with body, parts, and passion. One who would listen to prayers. To this man, God was a confidante, a friend, the source of unconditional love rather than a cloud of ether. Sometimes when she was alone at night, waiting for sleep to come, she longed for such a God. A presence that would disturb her with joy and more joy. A presence who would answer her prayers and love her forever and without condition.

After the crowd dissolved and departed to various homes and taverns, she approached him while he folded his stepladder cautiously, careful not to catch a finger in the hinges. His pedestal had been the rung of a ladder, no less. Her heart surprised her, the way it knocked against her chest. She hoped he could not hear its loud beat as she drew closer, unsure of what she wanted to say.

"How," she finally said, "is there such mysterious quiet on your face? Why am I drawn to your confidence when I already have a church and minister that sustain me?" Her heart doubly pounded when she asked these questions because something had spoken to her, possibly, as Wordsworth had written, "the motion and spirit rolling through all things."

"Christ said 'Come follow me,'" the man said. "I represent The Church of Jesus Christ of Latter-day Saints, reestablished by the martyred prophet, Joseph Smith, God's own church restored. Here on this earth. At this time. I am Elder Adam Wright. And you are?" He reached out to shake her hand.

"Sophia Poultney, sir," she said cautiously, placing her hand in his. "Pleased to make your acquaintance." When she curtsied, she dipped her head, careful that her hat's feather did not poke his eye.

"The question at the very bottom of everything I've been saying to you," he spoke as if it were a matter of life and death that she receive his message, "is whether you're willing to leave what you know to follow his footsteps, the most sublime experience known to humankind?"

His intensity both appealed to and repulsed her. How could anyone believe in leaving what you know? She wished she could fold herself up, tighten the strings around her, and close the discussion. She felt heat intensifying around her neck.

"I do not intend to be bold with you or take advantage, please believe me," the man said, his presence large next to her diminutive stature, except that the blue feather was level with his eyes. "I am here to serve God, not myself or my humanness. I have a wife, a family, and God to whom I am loyal. But my soul is bathed in flames. You can see this in my eyes."

"It is true," she said, remembering to breathe in the presence of something quite powerful, something she had not experienced before–such a direct look into the eyes of a man who loved God. A mixture of alarm and excitement, a sharp contrast of feelings over this unusual intimacy, gathered at the base of Sophia's throat until she forcefully swallowed it. The salt and the sugar. The bitter and the sweet.

"I thank you for your time, sir," she said, being it was improper for her to be out on the streets past this time, possibly giving the wrong impression of herself or her intentions.

"May the spirit of Christ be with you," he said, lifting his ladder to carry it away on his shoulder. "May you understand God's will for you."

"God's will," she repeated to herself, hurrying through the frigid insides of the cloud that still hovered over the town. But suddenly, an apparition emerged out of the mist–a man in a bowler hat and a black wool coat. He walked toward her. She recognized him as one who had been listening to the preacher. His well-made hat and long black woolen coat made her surmise he was a man of service in a grand household. She held her breath, but he simply walked past her, no threat, no encounter, though she did take a quick assessment of his head. It reminded her of a bust of a Greek scholar, one she had seen at the British Museum when her father had taken her to London years ago. On impulse, she turned and looked back over her shoulder and was surprised to see the man looking back at her. He smiled at having been caught. He touched the brim of his hat, then resumed his walking.

She hurried to Grey Friars' Road, turned to the left, then the right, happy to see the lamplighter and his ladder, his comforting presence brightening the gloom, especially with the cemetery close by her home. Walking quickly toward Saint Sepulchre Gate, she felt grateful the mist had thinned enough to reveal pale stars. The speaker's face that night had been a fierce, yet beautiful fire. And the man in the bowler hat...she knew him somehow. Something familiar about him.

* * * * *

Her small steamer trunk was nothing compared to the lavish luggage of the first-class passengers on the ship. But she had made an exquisite hat to wear on board—broad-brimmed, autumn leaf brown to match her eyes, a velvet ribbon cut and twisted into an exquisite floret. One that would serve her well in the new country, both for appearance and business' sake. She had scraped together enough to pay for the train to Liverpool, for steerage on the *S. Curling*, and hopefully enough surplus to pay for the wagons going west. Her hatmaking had been good to her, and she packed some of the trade's essentials should she wish to open a business in Zion.

Sophia would be leaving her family behind but had prayed as she sat alone beneath the plane tree. She now felt certain of God's assurance: her mother would be in good hands and the family could care for itself. Julia and Malcolm earned decent wages. Elizabeth had grown past a desire for or hope of suitors, a sweet if not outwardly attractive woman due to an overly pointed, pinched nose, elongated chin, and eyes appearing as close together as strung beads. She had grown comfortable with mothering the rest of the family and caring for their needs. And she understood Sophia.

Because most every member of the family, except Elizabeth, had been vocal against her leaving, Sophia had not told them about Mr. Milhaus. Her own life lay open before her now, not anyone else's. Hers. She wanted freedom from the title of "shop girl," from the shoulds and the oughts of English society, and the class requirements with which she was supposed to comply. And her siblings, in truth, weren't concerned in the same way.

"Stubborn Sophia," her older sister Julia said, filling the front door to say good-bye, the others standing beside her, all of them refusing to accompany her to a bleak and unworthy end or even to the railroad station or the dock in Liverpool. "You are bored with your life," her brother James had said more than once.

"That is what Sophia always does," she heard them muttering before they turned back to their various duties. "She makes up her mind, no matter what she is giving up or what is waiting for her. Everyone else must stand by and watch her strong head leading her in the wrong direction." Except that Elizabeth lingered in the doorway. Her narrow eyes spoke for her, as if complicit with the journey on which Sophia was about to embark. Interpreted, Sophia found them to say, "Go in peace, Sophia. May we meet again. I know your heart." A message which Sophia kept with her for the many miles she was about to travel.

As she rode on the back of a neighbor's cart to the train station, she imagined that once she made up her mind, she was much like a staunch boulder in a mountain stream that could change the water's course and not be dislodged before or after the water tumbled indiscriminately to a distant ocean. She had made up her mind to join with the Saints, to dedicate her life to something larger than herself and her hats, even though she dearly loved her hats and carried her needles, pins, marking pencils, and a supply of buckram and satin in her trunk.

James, she thought as the cart's wheels negotiated the cobblestones. She had not yet decided about James who had booked passage on the same ship. They had talked about their adventure in enthusiastic terms, and they would be meeting at the train station. But he was still a thought rumbling through the back of her mind. A slight thread of possibility. Mention of a man would create suspicion not only at home but in her own mind. It would muddy the waters of her very definite conversion.

* * * * *

For two weeks they strolled together on the lower deck of the *S. Curling*, water, water, everywhere around them. The Atlantic Ocean. They conversed about much, then stood silently watching the heaving of the ocean's breast, its depth not to be fathomed. After dark, they stood at the rail under a canopy of dense stars, free at last from the constant cover of clouds over the British Isles, though their voyage had its share of stormy weather. They talked. They stood close. They spoke of God and what that word meant to them. On occasion they touched fingertips but then drew their hands back to themselves, their touch a trespass of rules they both respected and observed. They spoke of caps, bowlers, and hats in general, and the lives they left behind. Then one night, James grasped her hand. He held it. He lifted it slightly and looked closely at her eyes. Sophia made no attempt to free herself from the hold.

When the first day of May drew to a close and the sun sat like a ball on the ocean's surface, soon to drop from view, the captain of the ship pronounced them husband and wife. As simple as that. Beneath the brim of her autumn-leaf-colored hat, they kissed each other properly at first. Sophia could feel the waves rocking the ship, steadily, easily, confirming the choice they had made. Then James removed the hats from both of their heads and kissed her again, this time with greater conviction. She peeked over his shoulder at the twinkle of the early stars. Her eyes shimmered. A new life. A companion.

They walked hand in hand to the ship's railing. Pausing. Kissing as if it had never happened before. Standing shoulder to shoulder. Breaking apart. Sophia threw imaginary rose petals to the wake of the ship. She threw kisses back to England and her family. James laughed. They both laughed, then kissed again, their arms and bodies beginning to tangle, quietly at first. In the darkening dusk, they stepped down and down the stairs to one floor above steerage. Walked through a thin corridor leading to a tiny room that seemed as large as the sky they had left behind, they reached out to touch each other's formerly hidden self.

"The soul of an artist," Sophia whispered when he first touched her on that night. A man, her husband, was reaching and touching her. For the first time. His two fingers worked the top button of her blouse, the one with layers of fine lace at the throat. He slid it through the buttonhole, no awkwardness, and Sophia felt the first loosening of her clothes. Then the second button, the second of ten, no less. The round buttons resembled pearls, though they were but a fabrication of the treasure of the oyster.

She had dreamed of this moment–what it would be like for a man to undress her and peel away the layers–the blouse, the petticoats, the chemise, the corset that made her waist so alluring, so petite, a circumference around which the fingertips of two hands could touch each other. She watched him unlacing the laces and unhooking the hooks and wondered at his familiarity with this maze of fabricated confections. He caught her looking at him and smiled a somewhat devilish smile, or so it seemed in the dim light of the lantern.

"At last, Sophia. We can be one together."

She heard his words and felt her mind go sailing on them. "Mine, mine," she said to herself, her cheeks reddening at the thought of belonging to someone. And suddenly she felt herself unbound, free of constraints.

James was unlocking all of the closets in which she had been hiding–the petticoats, the yards of fabric, the manners, the timidity.

His fingers made her skin feel like petals of flowers when they traced her body, not in a hurry, as if it were important for him to know the map of her before crossing boundaries. She marveled at his sensitivity, at the ease with which he knew her. He whispered next to her cheek, "Sweet Sophia." His gestures spoke to her soul. He was a gentleman. He knew how to receive who she was and what she was about. He respected what she was about to give him.

"Your skin is soft as a pink cloud at sunset."

"And you know the chemistry of a pink cloud?" she teased.

"I am enjoying being a chemist, learning the properties of such a creation."

Sophia laughed a throaty laugh, one that sounded less than proper when she heard it out loud. She was being taken into this web, this unmasking, and caught herself in the middle of surrender. Part of her mind was asking if this was a good thing, this relaxing of her boundaries. Even though she wanted to give herself completely to the moment, she could not help but wonder if it was the nature of the man to pursue until capture, then turn to other pursuits?

He stroked the side of her face, as if to contain her thoughts, stop them from running amok.

"My dear, Sophia," he said, his lips covering her mouth. "My wife." And he held the curve of her shoulders in his hands and pulled her against his body, disregarding the pile of clothes tossed onto the floor. The man. The woman. The moment when all was as it was meant to be. The urgency. The coupling. The tension. The pinnacle. The calm. All to the accompaniment of the creaking ship and the constant waves pushing against its sides.

* * * * *

For a while, the tiny state room on the *S. Curling* held the sky, the moon, the stars, and the sun in its cubic space. For a while, Sophia and James wished to be entangled forever and ever and never break apart or take a breath without the other. For a while, they believed in God's path leading them to the pure in heart and to the kingdom of God on earth. Sophia believed this to be their destiny but did not pay sufficient attention to a certain restlessness rising in her beloved.

After three weeks in their own private universe, James and Sophia ensconced in his stateroom, more private than steerage, both knew the voyage would be at an end in eight more days. Both had begun to feel the confines of a ship on a vast sea and the cramped tightness of their space. The presence of the real pressed against them: the feel of the waves pushing the boat relentlessly, the ship subject to squalls and thunder and lightning, a vessel that felt like a cork bobbing on a never-ending sea. On the few calm mornings when they walked together on the ocean-sloshed lower deck among the steerage passengers, they listened to the mix of accents, brogues, and the coarse, rough talk being exchanged. They became aware that life waited at the door to their stateroom, knocking, expecting an answer, knocking again.

"What are we doing with these people?" James said one morning when he returned from an earlier-than-usual morning stroll on the deck. "A very common lot," he said, unwrapping the striped scarf from around his neck while Sophia brushed her luxurious hair. "Factory workers. Peasants from the land. Rabble. Plain and simple."

"Rabble?" Sophia said, twisting her dark hair to the top of her head and fastening it with her precious tortoise-shell comb, a parting gift from Elizabeth. "A strong word, dear James."

"We understand the finer things of life, you and me. But these people. This.... What have we gotten ourselves into?"

Sophia closed her ears to his voice. If he could use the words "common and rabble" for those who had purchased passage in steerage, as she herself had done, could she be far behind? His minuscule stateroom was only one staircase above steerage, not so far removed or grand. "Common" was a word with a particular sting. She had been called common before, having no particular station since her father died so suddenly, leaving his family to make do with whatever means they could find—her mother sending her off to apprentice with a milliner, her sister Julia to a seamstress, her brother to a law firm. She had no claim to anything except her devotion to what she believed and her ability to make a fine hat. But then, she asked herself, feeling somewhat adamant, what station did James have except having been in service at a grand house?

"While you slept this morning, I spoke with a Welshman who said he had converted to Mormonism," James said, exchanging places with Sophia to remove his coat. "A fine excuse to take a voyage across the sea, in my opinion. He could barely speak the King's English, wore a shapeless round hat and an ill-fitting waistcoat missing two buttons, and then he says he knows God's will for him. How can he know anything if he cannot speak the language?"

"But James. Are not all men created equal in God's eyes? Part of His creation?"

"You are an idealist, my dear. Wanting a world full of good intentions and better acts. People will do what they have to do. Survival, it is called."

"Is that the case for you as well?" she asked, her eyes narrowing.

"Everyone has to survive. Do you think otherwise?"

What had he done to survive? she wondered. What had she done? Learned to make hats? Left her home in Doncaster? Had her marriage to Mr. Milhaus been an act of love or had it been borne from the lowest common denominator known as survival? Survival of the fittest? Survival of the species? Survival sounded so bereft of anything lovely, though maybe, come to think of it, adaptation was necessary to deal with changing environments. Why did any of those situations have to be called survival rather than destiny? She believed in the Kingdom of God. She loved to create beauty with her needle and thread. She loved James, even though she had known him for only two months' time. She paused, wishing to push aside the nagging suspicion that his easy familiarity with her body had been shaped by experience. Had he known another as intimately as he had known her? The question, this butterfly flitted quickly across the meadow of her mind, alighting nowhere. She pressed it to the back of her thoughts, out of circulation.

"And what have you done to survive?" she asked.

"Ah, that is a sticky wicket, indeed. I am not all of a perfection as you would have me be. I am a man. A natural man. An enemy to God, so they say. That is all, as much as I would like to believe in my goodness as you do."

"Cannot a natural man be changed by following God's will? By striving to do good works?"

"I want to believe, but as the *S. Curling* has been rough in its passage to The New World, I, too, feel the spikes and valleys of the passage of me, James Milhaus. I want to be worthy of your loyalty, but I have faltered. Love me for what I am, rather than what you wish me to be."

She nestled her head against the top of his shoulder and closed her mind. "You are tired of being at sea. Things will be better soon."

* * * * *

In the early morning on the deck of the *S. Curling*, Sophia penned a letter to Elizabeth. She sealed it and presented it to the purser before breakfast.

Dearest Elizabeth,

As I write, I can see you standing at the door—the elegant shape of your face and the way you care for others in your eyes. You have been with my thoughts since my leaving, most likely because you feel to be one with my heart. Thank you for that. I will say I am not discouraged, though I value the chance to speak to someone I trust.

I pray Mother is not a burden for you—I know she has little wish to seek improvement in her life. When Father died, it seemed she no longer had a wish to entertain herself except to cast her eye on parts of her body, always worried that one part or another was failing to serve her. I lament you being in her service, and yet, you have a most generous nature.

I wish you could find a suitable companion to love—someone who would cherish your high value. But the business of finding a companion is fraught with complexity, I fear. I should tell you I have married while en route to America. James Milhaus is his name—a fine fellow to look upon. Alas, I am not the only one who feels this way. Many of the unmarried women on board find a feast for their eyes, even those traveling with the group going to Zion. I have heard talk of polygamy from some of the Welch converts who speak English, though this may be wild rumor. It troubles me, though. The thought of sharing my beloved. That is not why I took vows with James. To give him away so quickly.

The restored Gospel of Jesus Christ has given me great sustenance, dear Elizabeth. I have found my purpose here.

The sea has been rough, though yesterday I saw the most gloriously red sunset. A sailor's delight, I am told. I will be glad when this journey ends at New Orleans. The New World. America. I cannot believe I am about to set foot on an entirely new continent. We will take a steamer up the Mississippi River (so many s's in that name) and go upriver to meet others traveling west with our company.

Please send me news of home when you can, and I trust you to keep my concerns in confidence, though you can tell the others I have married.

Yours,

Sophia Jane

CHAPTER FIVE

THE CAMELS

CAMP VERDE, TEXAS—1856

The officer Geoffrey Scott asked was fully dressed in the bottom half of his uniform only—long, loose, pressed woolen trousers, though he wore suspenders over long johns with an unbuttoned top. The sky clouded over. The morning was cool, for a change, though not cool enough. "You mean the Syrian?" the officer answered.

"I think that's right."

"He'd be the only Hadji around. Came with the first camels on the *Supply*. Somebody had to handle the nasty beasts that make a stubborn Missouri mule seem like a lamb. Milquetoast, anyway."

"Have you seen much of them?"

"Maybe too much. You should'a been here a couple of weeks ago. Two ungelded males in rut. Mean as sin. Bit anything in close proximity, and, I tell you, watch out. They'll spit if you don't watch out. Hadji keeps them harnessed up to protect himself, even. The biggest one mounted the female sitting on the ground, four legs folded beneath her, submissive as a slave. Sat on his haunches like a dog. Never saw anything like it. But say, boy. You a civilian? What do you want with a Mohametan anyway? One of those Oriental infidels, you know. First one I ever knowed about in the U.S. of A."

"I repair harnesses, bridles, and stirrup straps," Geoffrey Scott said, keeping his face impenetrable. This man knew nothing about camels and Hadji. "Help keep the fort in repair. Honest work from a Kansas man. I like animals and want to meet up with a camel. That's all."

"Those smelly beasts?" The officer screwed up his face, distaste in every crevice. "Hadji Ali worships them. You'd think they were brothers. Sleeps with them. Smells like one of them."

"Why camels in the first place? The military seems better suited to horses and mules, I'd think."

"You're right about that," the officer said. "But the politicians. You know them. They're debating several routes to California. 47th. 38th. 35th parallels. Anything south of the 38th is pretty barren territory, but that's what Beale plans to survey: a possible route from Fort Defiance to the Colorado River on the border of California. They need a passage that keeps clear of the Rockies, snow, and the scalp-happy Apaches near Tucson. The Mormons, too—those fools for blind authority. Secretary of War Davis got on the bandwagon a few years back. Proposed camels to help open the road. Says they can carry loads up to 1200 pounds, two or three times what a mule can carry. Can go six or seven days without water. But horses, mules, and horsemen don't cotton to them. Warts on a stick, you ask me. A bad idea."

"When is this road building supposed to start?" Geoffrey Scott asked, making sudden calculations. This was the work he'd been hoping for—a chance to go West. With the camels, no less. But he hid his eagerness with a mud-flat expression. "Any need for road builders? Civilians?"

"Survey party going out next month or so. Congress wants the road built soon, so much hollerin' from emigrants. But it's crazy to go when summer heat'd just as soon kill a body. No doubt about that. Military's busy building forts and defending the settlers from the Indians. And each other, I should add. Around September Beale'll need a work party, probably some civilians as there ain't that much military to go around. Lieutenant Beale. A Navy man, I should mention. A lieutenant in the Army now. Figure that. No wonder he likes camels. Been at sea too long." He laughed a wheezy baritone laugh deep from his chest then coughed, even sputtered.

"Thank you, sir. Much appreciated."

The officer pointed to a low shed in the far corner of the fort, still coughing, some dust stirred up in his lungs. "Hi Jolly, everyone calls him."

Geoffrey Scott walked at a fast clip past the soldiers who sat around tables made from barrels, playing checkers, one game of chess. Drinking coffee. Smoking. Pulling at their suspenders. He dipped his head in greeting to the men he recognized but was more interested in uncharted territory. Maybe he'd get to ride on the top of a camel's hump, how fine would that be?

Reaching the shed, Geoffrey Scott bent through the low door and peered into what looked like a dark cave. "Hadji?" he called. He saw a slight movement, an indistinct pattern of black and white checks catching whatever light was in the room. Hadji's scarf? He smelled the dense smell of herd animals, though he could hear nothing shuffling its feet. As his eyes adjusted to the light, he squeezed them tight to make out what was happening: a human figure rising from the ground, pushing himself from prostrate to an upright kneeling position, bending to roll something that looked like a small rug, standing until his head was close to the low-lying ceiling, all of this in barely discernible light. Then this what-seemed-to-be-Hadji sat in a low chair against an oversize pillow. A moment of indecision for Geoffrey Scott. Had he been too intrusive? Was this the man he spoke with the day before?

"Green boy." The voice sounded friendly enough, though distant.

"You said to come back today. Sorry if I'm inopportune."

"Today," Hadji said, though he made no move to get up from his chair and greet Geoffrey Scott.

"The camels?" Geoffrey Scott said, backing out the door and waiting, debating whether he should stand there any longer after too much time seemed to be passing. But finally Hadji appeared, shading his eyes against the sun that hit him full in the face. He rewrapped the scarf around his neck and the top of his head. "Come. Stay close."

The young man followed Hadji through the gate. Into the corral. He held his breath, unsure of what a camel might do, being privy to their reputation for nasty tempers and how some horses panicked when they inhabited the same vicinity. A few camels were bunched in one half of the yard, some large in girth, some smaller and more nimble. Others sat on the ground, their legs folded beneath them, chewing, constantly chewing. Calm. Disinterested in much else for the moment. Hadji stopped in front of a large camel about seven and a half to eight feet tall, measuring about ten feet long, and weighing about two thousand pounds by Geoffrey Scott's reckoning. A woven harness secured its head, fine dusky-brown hair covered its long throat, and a color closer to a reddish ash curled up from its humped back.

"I call this one Adab Abib," Hadji said, adjusting the harness on the camel's head, caressing its neck as he did and pressing his cheek next to the camel's. "He's the fastest camel. Can travel for many days." He pointed to the lip that was split on the camel's face. "Made so camel can strip branches. Happy with leaves."

"He's seen places I can only imagine." Geoffrey Scott envisioned the continuous hills of sand he'd only read about. Dune after dune. Hill after hill stretched beyond any line of sight. An ocean of sand with no borders, no horizons.

"Okay if I call him Adababa? My mother read me about Ali Baba. That'll be something I can remember." Impulsively, Geoffrey Scott reached up to stroke the camel's face.

"No," Hadji said loudly, blocking Geoffrey Scott's arm with his own and giving the boy a warning look. "You wait. The camel must trust you."

"I wasn't thinking. Sorry." He regretted the impulse and hoped Hadji wouldn't ban him from the camels.

"You sailed across the ocean with all of these?" he began in an unsure voice of compromise. "How did you manage that?"

Hadji waited to answer, taking a long inhalation followed by a long exhalation, closing his eyes. "Many days. Water, water, much water. The camels complained but they are patient. Not like you."

Geoffrey Scott hoped his face wasn't red, embarrassed. "It's like I speak animal, sir. I know how to talk to them. They understand."

Hadji lifted his half-closed lids to take a second look at Geoffrey Scott. He seemed to be weighing what he saw. A young boy? A naive boy? Geoffrey Scott watched the foreigner stroke his chin with one hand, assessing the extent of the boy's innocence. Then Hadji spoke softly.

"When camels have troubles, I sing to them."

"Sing?"

"Ya sa'ad," Hadji sang suddenly, loudly, unapologetically, as if he had been silent long enough and had been asked for a command performance. "A-a-a-a-mah. A-a-a-a-a-a-a-a-a-a-a-a-mah." Geoffrey Scott listened to this with his mouth slightly open, surprised by what was happening in the middle of a corral at a military installation in Texas.

"Ya Sa-a-a-a'ad." Hadji's voice was high, alien, otherworldly as he continued singing without the words Geoffrey Scott was used to hearing. All in a mode unfamiliar to Geoffrey Scott's ears, each syllable embellished with a strange-sounding melody that twined as a morning glory around a stem. Nothing like Stephen Foster, he laughed to himself. Every camel in the corral turned its head toward Hadji. Some started to rise from their seat on the ground, responding to the pied piper calling them to run across the deserts of their memory. Then he stopped singing and snapped his fingers. The camels settled back onto their hind legs, folding them beneath their substantial bodies. This included Adababa. A corral full of seated, submissive animals.

Now that they were all settled on the ground, Geoffrey Scott could get a better read on their single and some double humps, their knobby knees more like deformities than something natural to the animal. Callouses probably. Their profiles exuded a sense of peerage, as if they knew innately that they were superior to other animals. Nature had inscribed this expression on their faces.

"Come," Hadji said, gesturing to Geoffrey Scott to follow him to a far corner of the corral where a very young camel sat, covered with a large canvas tarp, fastened to the ground with heavy stones. "These stones teach the camel to carry much. Every day I add more weight. Little food and water for the baby. I teach him to survive."

"How long does the calf stay like this?" Geoffrey Scott asked, tucking his arms against his body, all the time thinking this method of animal rearing seemed barbaric. He'd broken horses before, but he'd never do something similar to a colt. Made them wear saddles. Ridden them hard. But this was different. The young camel seemed docile, patient even. Maybe bred to be a beast of burden, but a different kind of animal, definitely.

"Maybe fifteen days he stays like this. Learns to obey, to serve master."

"When do you put him to work?" Geoffrey Scott pantomimed a load on his back.

"He must grow to four years." Hadji reached down and stroked the camel's neck and tweaked one of its furry ears. "This will be good camel. Mr. Beale will be pleased."

"You know Lieutenant Beale?" Geoffrey Scott immediately tempered his enthusiasm and told himself to calm down. All in good time. For everything there is a season. Be patient.

"Good man. Yes. Respects *Attah Allah*. Teaches other men to show respect. But not many convinced."

"When is he coming here again?"

"I wait for him. He wants camels for building road. He wants to cross a desert. This is test for my camels."

"Will you teach me how to ride one?" And immediately Geoffrey Scott wondered if he had spoken too quickly.

"That is a big ask. I see if they like you. Do not hurry them in this."

"What kind of a saddle do you use?"

"Special saddle. Not for horses. Two Turks came across ocean. Build saddles. They know how to load camels. We don't need someone…"

"I can help you." Geoffrey Scott interrupted Hadji Ali, all while trying not to show his excitement. His pulse raced. "I learn fast." But then he realized he had interrupted Hadji. Once again. He was sorry but Hadji would soon understand. He would.

"Camels must be loaded in right way. Soldiers have no ears to listen about this."

"I can help you," Geoffrey Scott said again, this time waiting for Hadji's sentence to end.

"We will see." Again he looked off in the distance, as if his present, past, and future were out there waiting for him. Desert eyes, Geoffrey Scott concluded. Alert to wind and sand and shadows against the glaring sun.

* * * * *

Paying attention to every rumor and whisper regarding the departure of the camel company, Geoffrey Scott moved his camping spot from the side of the barely-there hotel to just outside Camp Verde's gates. He settled down in spare dirt and stayed put. He, his horse, his saddle blanket, and a bundle of necessities became a common sight to those coming and going. Here he would keep in touch with any changes, knowing to listen to the wind as well as to words. No one seemed especially well informed, subject to rumor that blew in and out like dust.

During the days, he performed odd jobs inside the camp and unwittingly became a familiar face. But his main preoccupation was not with the soldiers who didn't attract his curiosity. On the other hand, the men from the Middle East did. They spoke their own language and moved like liquid. Like well-warmed oil. Between jobs, he looked toward the camel corral and caught glimpses of Hadji tending the animals. Harnessing one. Then another. Loading one more rock each day to the calf's covering, the poor calf subjected to unbelievable weight on its back. Sometimes Geoffrey Scott found an obscure place near the fence, a rough-hewn bench beneath an eave, close to the camel corral. Here he could get a more intimate look but stay far enough away so Hadji Ali did not see him hovering.

One especially hot midday, while he ate the precious orange he had exchanged for beads with an Indian who was learning the slippery art of the trade, he sat on his favorite bench and watched two of the foreign handlers—Turks, Hadji called them. They kept to themselves. Seemingly mindless of the heat, they chopped down and split out small trees, whittled two-foot-long pieces of wood into something he couldn't describe: Lazy vees? Crescent swords? Boomerang shapes? Where he'd seen a boomerang before, Geoffrey Scott couldn't remember, but he recognized the bent-wing shape someone had once tossed through the air of his childhood, maybe back in Osawatomie or Boston before that. The Turks cut these in two pieces, stripped down one half of one side, and fit the pieces together, upside down. They repeated this. Two wishbones. The top of each about one foot tall.

After the pieces had been glued together, one of the Turks walked away, carrying two wishbones through the dust at Camp Verde, one in each hand. The other stayed behind, sewing pieces of canvas with long needles. Geoffrey Scott watched with his mouth open wider than he would have liked, the hot desert air drying his tongue. The man's hands were graceful, lithe, nimble, even. Then, he stuffed blue stem grass into the three separate pockets he had made with his stitching. Everything seemed somewhat inexplicable to Geoffrey Scott.

But the abolitionist's son from Kansas had other things awaiting his attention. After being asked to straighten a horseshoe, he finished eating his orange—peeling and dividing the segments into single pieces and taking bites carefully so as not to spray himself with the juice—left the seated Turk to his sewing, and took the bent horseshoe to the blacksmith's.

But today was his Middle East day, no matter his intentions. At the blacksmith's, the disappeared Turk was trying to explain, mostly with his hands. He needed the smithy to bend pipe and make a curve in the four pieces of half-inch pipe he'd brought into the shop. With arms shaped like the hull of a boat, the Turk demonstrated. "Camel's body," he kept saying, gesturing how the pipes must curve around the sides of a camel's hump. Then he took two pipes, made an X with them, and showed how they could be made into a crosspiece to hold the frame together. How they could be fastened with nuts and bolts to each side of the wishbones. Geoffrey

Scott wanted to step in and provide English answers about how the pipe shouldn't rub or irritate the animal, but he, realizing his shortage of knowledge about this particular subject, hoped the blacksmith understood.

The next day, after he put the straightened horseshoe back on the horse's hoof and received payment for his work, Geoffrey Scott (with a pocketful of cash—he liked when his pocket was full) received his understanding. Sitting in the shadows where he usually sat, always to the left of center stage, he saw a strange contraption being loaded onto the camel's back—something that looked like a saddle but sure as hell wasn't the kind he'd seen before. The wishbones. There they were. And the curving pipe that cleared both sides of the camel. All connected. Awkward but effective. For some godforsaken reason, he found himself wishing he could make this kind of saddle, not the kind for horses that required pieces of leather and a certain kind of skill. Horses' saddles were varied, even artistic, he knew that. They demanded expertise. But somehow, the camel's saddle seemed more enticing even if it was awkward.

* * * * *

The brutal sun had boiled the horizon long enough for the day when Geoffrey Scott consented to a game of checkers with a soldier who'd been as friendly as any: Davis Sheffield from Massachusetts. One of the places his parents had once lived. The rest of the soldiers were from somewhere in Europe or from the South—those speaking slow, drawn-out words like "d-a-w-g-s." The winning of Mexican territory had opened up vast stretches of land with endless possibilities. An expedition was about to happen. Men of all kinds would be joining.

"Bodies are needed to fill a work party," Davis said, quickly jumping one of Geoffrey Scott's double-deckers and depositing his friend's black king in the pile of useless-to-Geoffrey-Scott checkers. "Expedition is looking for willing civilians. I know you have no taste for the military, odd duck you are." He smiled, the left side of his smile higher than the right. "You've told me enough about that. And the way you sleep outside the fort so everyone will know you aren't a soldier."

"I can sign up now?" Geoffrey Scott said, the notion of winning at checkers now a thing of the past. Davis jumped another of his men and left three black singles on the board.

"Quartermaster." Davis pointed to a hastily built building across the road, the place that served as an office for Camp Verde. "Catch him tomorrow. Better stay in this game for now." Even though the office was closed for the day and even though he could wait, the game had already been lost to other schemes in Geoffrey Scott's head.

The next morning, he was the first man to sign his name on the hand-drawn line across a thick piece of paper, though he wondered how he'd explain to the quartermaster that rifle or none, he had no plans to use one. He'd seen enough bloodshed for seven lifetimes. People needed their blood, which was not as cheap as a rifle treated them. Once again, his mother was in his head. "They wouldn't hurt anybody if only they understood. Walk in another person's shoes," he heard her whispering. For sure he'd never tell the quartermaster his history—that he'd been teethed on a rifle, was a crack shot, actually, and that he hated what guns could do, let alone to his mother.

"You'll be leaving in three days," the quartermaster told him in the dark of the office, only one window allowing random motes of sun to float through the air. "Next Monday morning. A group of men from here'll meet up in San Antonio with Lieutenant Beale's survey party. You have your own horse? And a rifle?"

"Horse, I have. But what if I don't carry a rifle?"

The questioner paused in disbelief. A cloud over the sun perhaps.

"You funny in the head or something? I should send you out the door right now. You'd be a fool to go without one, don't you think? Comanches, maybe Apaches, before you know it. You're no frontiersman without a rifle."

"How can I get one?" he relented, promising the ghost of his mother, silently, of course, that this rifle would never be used.

"From me, of course." The quartermaster picked up a rifle from behind the counter, the barrel about 24 inches long. "This here's a lever-action repeating rifle. A Henry. Lever'll pull out a spent shell and, on the upstroke, insert a new bullet. There's fifteen .44-caliber bullets in the loading tube. Rimfire. Pretty impressive, I'd say. You'll need a scabbard, which I can issue right now, but make sure the whole thing's not rubbing a raw spot on your mount. You can adjust the latigos through the rings on your saddle. Y'all have a military escort for a few miles but'll have to fend for yourselves most the time. Everyone's rushing to California, and the Army's not ready for that. Needs to be bigger, and they're sending a third of what they do have to fight the Mormons needs be." He aimed the rifle at the small window and mock-shot. "Make sure you can reach your gun while you're riding."

And thus, Geoffrey Scott was armed, even though he had no intentions.

As the work party readied to leave on that following Monday morning, he, packed and anxious to leave, sheathed his rifle in the new leather scabbard he'd attached to his saddle and reminded himself it would stay that way. Waiting for the expedition to leave, he returned to his private corner to watch the Turks securing saddles to two camels sitting on the ground. Awkward contraptions for the one-humped backs—a tall saddle horn in the front and an even taller backrest. The animals accepted the load with no complaint, however, unbothered by the process. Then the men caressed their heads and fuzzy ears. Like brothers. Best friends. Affection with these detached and so-called unfeeling creatures who nuzzled them back. The Turks then sat astride and urged the camels to a standing position, back feet taking the weight first, then the balance transferred to the front legs. It all looked so easy.

Those men knew their animals. Knew who they were. Knew how to treat them to get what they needed. Mutual admiration. Geoffrey Scott, sitting on the bench and watching, biding what time was left, knew he, too, had a feel for animals. Whatever kind. He knew how to anticipate them. To feel what they wanted. For now, however, he knew to be an observer.

* * * * *

Strung out in a line, forty men and their horses stood ready at Camp Verde, prepared to leave the low-flung fort in the dust of Texas. An officer with no epaulets but a crisp hat and oiled shoes, starched shirt and pants, sat astride Seid, the only white camel—a sword in a sheath and rifle in a scabbard close by. A sense of adventure ratcheted high. Most everyone talked about what they'd encounter, though none, except for two West Texas boys, had gone in that direction before. The voices carried hints of Germany, England, Arkansas, Tennessee, and other diverse places in the young United States, Lieutenant Beale's among them. "We'll be meeting up with some of my friends from the North," he told the men before they started. "In San Antonio. After they join us, our expedition begins in earnest." Even the horses sensed the excitement, though they were not quite accustomed to the camels or this direction.

Some of the men said they felt free for the first time. Some wanted to see the scalp of an Indian hanging from their belts. Some rode in silence, inhaling the leather smell of harnesses and bridles, listening to the rhythmic squeak of saddles and stirrups. Three other camels were being ridden by two Turks and Hadji Ali, large bells hung around their necks while the rest carried supplies. Altogether, the camels were a curiosity to anyone who saw the party parading past. Pointed fingers and surprise in people's eyes.

"These camels're a waste of money and effort." A Texan by the name of Hoyne rode to the side of Geoffrey Scott, muttering an oft-repeated opinion.

"Camels're smelly." Hoyne chewed tobacco in one side of his cheek, a large bump swelling his face lopsided. Black juice rimmed his lips. "Just plain irritatin'. Whose idea was they, anyhow? Not worth the time and trouble." He spoke the gospel according to owners of horses and mules but Geoffrey Scott knew the man didn't know how to load, pack, or saddle the camels to keep their complaints in check or their backs from filling with sores.

Geoffrey Scott slowed, hoping Hoyne would ride ahead and join up with his pal, McFeeley, where the two could spout their distaste for camels together. Which he did, even if he was impatient to get wherever they were going. Then Scott found himself next to Ebenezer, the servant Lieutenant Beale had brought. A slave on the expedition. One of the men his mother had died for. What would she say about that, and why was there a slave here in the first place? He'd heard his share of talk from her—a woman who hadn't believed in the institution or the idea. Neither did he, truth be told, though this was the first time he'd been face to face with a man related to someone who'd been, if he hadn't been himself, in iron manacles and chains. He could almost hear them clanking—ghost sounds that haunted his mind. Ebenezer was quiet—a man with little to show on the outside. The two men tipped their hats to each other, exchanged greetings and good days, then rode on without speaking, the only sound the creaking of leather.

He couldn't help wondering what Ebenezer did when the day closed up and service was expected. Was he a phantom that turned invisible at night, no longer part of the expedition, only a shadowy appendage? Ironically, around the campfire at night, Beale would talk big about all men being free, but then refer to Ebenezer as "His Man" and have him making preparations behind a tent flap. Something Geoffrey Scott couldn't iron out in his head. But then, the Lieutenant was respectful to most everybody, he had to admit, especially to the foreigners from the Middle East. And he'd heard that Beale would give Ebenezer his freedom when the expedition was completed. No small matter, he guessed, but still.

Respect. Maybe it was something he needed to think about. Maybe he needed to show more of it to Hadji Ali, who was a person, a man with his own habits. What could he do or say that would let Hadji know he was respected? Everything had been about him taming one of Hadji's camels, but what about Hadji himself? Then his attention drifted back to Ebenezer riding by his side. This half-man, three-quarters of a man, whatever people called him, though Geoffrey Scott suspected he was like most everyone else except for skin color and thickness of words he didn't always understand. But nothing more was said between them. Both men settled into the rhythm of the road—the hooves, the wheels, their destination.

In San Antonio, after the gathering of Beale's friends from Pennsylvania and a first encampment for the night in West Texas, they were on their way again. Excitement high. Frisky horses. Animated men. Lively talk. Camels, Turks, and Syrians bringing up the rear, and Geoffrey Scott wishing he knew what they were saying, what they thought about all of this. He was a man who was listening to a language he didn't understand. But who were the speakers? Who was he? What mattered to him? Camels and adventure, yes, but there was more to the matter of who he was. He was both a child and a man. He'd been taught by his mother and yet told to leave by his father. What did he add up to? What did he need? These questions were a jumble in his head.

When Lieutenant Beale finally barked out orders to set up camp for the next night, Geoffrey Scott looked around, searching for Hadji Ali, but the man was nowhere in sight. Sometimes he seemed more a sorcerer than a human. A conjurer. A slippery piece of silk cloth. He was rarely visible, and tonight he was off with the other Arabs who kept to themselves. Off limits.

Stretching out beneath his blanket with his hands pillowing his head, Geoffrey Scott listened instead to rumors of the night, the talk around the campfire. The flasks. The cigars. The drifting smoke. Words about niggers who best keep their place, especially Ebenezer, Mr. Beale's man—don't let him forget he's worth less than one of those camels who smell. After the embers of the fire died down, Geoffrey Scott lay awake for an hour, wondering about his purpose in this increasingly complex expedition.

He stared at the cloudy sky that covered the moon, aware he didn't belong to the group of friends and officers who'd joined this expedition.

Ranks. Stations. Money. He didn't belong with any of that. And yet he wasn't just one of "the men" either, the unrecognized, the cogs of the wheel who watered the animals and corralled them at night. He wasn't Ebenezer. He wasn't Hadji Ali. He was Geoffrey Scott who could fix things, dig trenches, and pound posts. Nevertheless, he still answered to those above him—to Beale most of all. Tomorrow night, Beale would probably be sleeping in the comfort of a featherbed in the best house in the closest town, anywhere besides next to the road builders. He'd take Ebenezer to help him dress, undress, to provide him with water, with coffee or tea. "My man," he'd say. "My beckoning call," and he'd snap his fingers. Geoffrey Scott closed his eyes to sort it all out, but it was more than his mind could pull into a piece. He turned to sleep instead.

When he awoke early the next morning, folding his hands behind his head again to survey the campground, he saw the camels but no sign of Hadji Ali. Most of the men were still rolled in blankets, their heads cocked backward, snoring with their mouths open. No tents. The open sky their roof. The morning smell of a motley group. Hoyne and McFeeley were the only ones awake at this hour, attempting to load the seated camels between sips of coffee. Half-assed. Half-interested. Sloppy. Incompetent with everything except their horses.

"Dumbasses. Uncooperative bastards," they grumbled out loud without remembering everyone else was still sleeping.

Suddenly, Geoffrey Scott jerked up when he heard the commotion. He rubbed his eyes, slapped his cheeks, and saw Adababa, the camel he'd been admiring, shaking its head as if to rid it of all attachments. Then he saw its neck elongate, its mouth opening, its teeth biting Hoyne's right hand. He knew how strong those jaws were, having fed Adababa an apple or two, and knew how hard those teeth could be.

"Stupid asshole," Hoyne yelled, rubbing his hand, then protecting it in the safety of his chest. "Did you see what this son of a bitch did?" he said to McFeeley who was backing away from the fray. "Did you see that?" Then he hit the side of Adababa's long nose. Cuffed the camel hard with the full of his hand. "Take that, you bastard."

In one swift move, the camel closed in on Hoyne, pushing him backward until he stumbled. Hoyne put out his arms to stop the animal who would not be stopped, then shouted "Git outta here." But the camel kept nosing him backwards, its neck much stronger than Hoyne would ever be, even with his fists clenched ready to hit the animal again. He was powerless against the strength of an angry camel who'd decided on someone it didn't like.

Geoffrey Scott scrambled off his bedroll, waved both arms in an attempt to alter the charged equation, and ran toward Hoyne and Adababa. "Leave him be. You're hurting him."

"Get your ass out of my business. This camel here bit me. My fingers."

"I'm just telling you…"

Adababa swung its powerful neck close to the top of Hoyne's head, pushing him further backwards and menacing even Geoffrey Scott. His words, "Adababa. Stop," had no effect on the animal's intentions–not interested in anything spewed from the lips of a human.

"Baba," Geoffrey Scott begged. "Come on now."

With another sweep of the camel's neck, this time across his shadow but whisper-close to his chest, Hoyne lost his footing and fell onto his butt, his hands protecting his turtle-like head shrunk back into his body. "Somebody help me. Somebody."

Hadji Ali, dressed in a long tunic and a checkered scarf wrapped around his head, appeared out of nowhere. "Away," he bellowed to the two men. "Leave camel." Then he shouted: "Adab Abib. *Khallas. Khallas.*" Reluctantly, Adababa turned his head to consider his master's voice, Hadji Ali, then backed away while Adababa's entire body swayed with simmering dignity. "*Hadi! Hadi!*" His eyes cut into Hoyne's, almost like a knife into cold butter, and Hoyne crawled away, raising dust with his dragging knees.

"I tried," Geoffrey Scott explained, though didn't get much further with his comments.

"Silence."

Hadji Ali led Adababa away and was moot about Hoyne's hand and the camel's response. He paid no mind to Geoffrey Scott inserting himself. No notice whatsoever from this Syrian–no eyes or ears for anything but his task. The camels were his. He knew what they needed. Everyone else leave them alone. And, after Geoffrey Scott witnessed the full scale of a camel's temperament, he decided maybe everybody should let Hadji Ali have them all to himself.

CHAPTER SIX

THE EXPEDITION

1857

In less than two weeks, the whole expedition seemed off-kilter and out of sorts.

On July third, beneath an overcast sky with clouds redoubling, Geoffrey Scott watched Hadji Ali—grumpy and testy—load the camels by himself. The Turks had vanished after complaining to Beale about nonpayment for their services. He'd told them the expedition had cost more than his budget, but that he'd make it up to them when he could. Disinterested in this proposal, the Turks rode away on the two mules Beale gave them for payment. Irascible Hadji Ali was alone now, but whatever his temperament, the camels cooperated and showed affection after they were loaded. As much as Geoffrey Scott wanted to understand the man and his camels, he was always rebuffed. The Syrian had decided that no one cared about his animals as much as he did and that no one could ever learn all of the subtle intricacies. Hadji and his father had a few similarities, Geoffrey Scott decided: they thought they knew everything. No room for anyone else in their worlds.

Nevertheless, on this morning, the boy from Kansas wondered big-time why he'd left home. Except he'd been told to get out. He mustn't forget that fact. His father had said to let fate teach him what he needed to know. Crazy. Bitter man who spouted what felt like hate to his only son. He couldn't help but think about those words. "Make your own way, you sissy," though it stung to remember those last two words. He rarely let them cross his mind, but he was no sissy. Look how far he'd come from Kansas. His father was full of bullshit. Blind man, that's what he was. If only he'd open his eyes and see his son who was now a man, well almost, but when did a man become a man anyway? Getting Hadji's attention was thus complicated.

That afternoon, when the expedition reached Devil's River, surrounded on both sides by high mountains, the rains came. Water overflowed the banks. Men and animals sloshed through mud everywhere. Slipping. Sliding. Everyone tried to keep their horses, mules, and camels from getting swamped. There was no place to secure a tent. No place to sleep. Some climbed the edges of the canyons and found overhangs with ground dry enough to roll out blankets for the night. After coaxing two mules through a watery slime, Geoffrey Scott managed to sleep for a few hours on a ledge where rattlesnakes and gila monsters basked in the sun on warm days. But he felt numb when he woke. His legs. His arms. Even one side of his face. Maybe because he'd slept on stone. He turned his head, and there was Hadji Ali not far from him, curled in a striped blanket. This sight took the numbness away. Maybe the Syrian wanted someone to be his friend now? Or maybe, don't get excited, he just wanted the driest spot to sleep? But who cares anyway, Geoffrey Scott said to himself and curled tight on his other side to coax a few more hours out of this Sunday, their country's birthday. When buglers finally woke the entire camp playing "Hail, Columbia," "Star-Spangled Banner," and "Columbia, the Gem of the Ocean," no one moved. Exhausted. No sign of life until eleven o'clock.

Going through the gloomy Dead Man's Pass that afternoon, the entire party rode uneasy through the deluge of water. They knew five men had been mutilated and separated into pieces by Indians not so long before. Then, with no warning, no small thanks to an almost nonexistent road and water that ran everywhere, the tongue of the lead wagon split. Broke in two. Geoffrey Scott, riding next to that wagon, felt lucky to be so close by. Maybe fate was speaking its mind. "Sissy, my ass," he said and leapt off his horse. With the help of Hoyne and McFeeley locating the tools and nails, he pried the tongue apart with a crowbar and reinforced it with another length of wood. A hammer. A spike. Then, the fine particulars. He knew well what to do, but when he was near finishing, another team attempted to pass on the outside. Not enough room for two wagons on this road.

"Don't come through here," Geoffrey Scott yelled, hastily removing a nail from his mouth.

"Stay back," Hoyne shouted even more loudly, jumping into the wagon's pathway and waving his arms.

"Coming through. Move out of the way." Friends of Beale's from Pennsylvania rode in the wagon with Ebenezer on the back, gate and legs dangling, the only one alert to the warning.

"Wait," Geoffrey Scott yelled louder. "Maybe ten minutes at the most."

"Who do ya think ya are?" McFeeley joined in the shouting and the waving of arms. "Back off."

"We can make it," the driver yelled back, whipping the horses, and surging ahead. "It'll be okay." The wagon swung around to pass, Hoyne and McFeeley making themselves skinny, but then the two lead horses slipped in the caliche. Lopsided, one wheel spun. Two wheels spun. No traction. The wagon tipped to one side. Then all four horses were entangled with earth. Stalled. Swamped. Scrambling to rise. Ebenezer jumped from the back of the wagon, helping the discombobulated passengers to safety and then unharnessing the confused horses. But the world had turned sideways. Scrambled. Loose. Unpredictable pandemonium. The passengers collected what they could from their bags, which had been thrown every which way. "Lousy rain," they shouted, not knowing how else to express their fright. "Driver should have known better." The freed horses skittered sideways, then backwards, scared, then ran whichever way they could, leaving the wagon on its side, its wheels still spinning. Hoyne and McFeeley, who sometimes seemed like Siamese twins, ran after them to right the wrong, but everything was confusion.

By himself, as everyone else had left for higher ground, Ebenezer lifted a corner of the wagon, straining with every muscle, but the weight pushed down against his shoulders and sank him deeper into the sea of earth. Geoffrey Scott picked through the caliche to keep from sliding and joined Ebenezer to right the wagon. But the ground was too wet, too slippery, and neither man could get a foothold long enough to lift the wagon back onto its wheels.

"Have to wait till this ground's more dry," Ebenezer panted, barely able to take the next breath. He stood tall, arched his shoulders back to see if they still worked, and stretched his head to right his neck. Face shining with rain, he wiped oil and grit from his hands and grinned at Geoffrey Scott. The grin was no ordinary smile, however, but rather a comment on the fact that nobody else was interested in anything but their own well-being.

The silent partners wiped their hands on their soaked pants and looked for a place where they could find protection from the elements, where the rain that kept insisting on returning wouldn't drown them.

Thus, the company was stopped again, this time behind two inoperative wagons at the base of large, unforgiving, perpendicular mountains on a steep road. Vulnerable to attack. Men being hacked apart by Indians was the foremost thought in everyone's mind, though fortunately, after passing the night with two sentries on watch, the beleaguered party rolled forward. Animals dug out of mud. Wagons repaired. They crossed Devil's River for the second time, and then crossed it ten times more in eleven miles. Beale's men, their wagons, horses, and the camels forded the river, belly-deep for the horses and mules, thigh-deep for the camels.

* * * * *

By the time they reached New Mexico Territory, both Beale's friends and the road builders were less willing to comply with orders to make camp, much less to chisel arroyos or build temporary bridges. A diminishing number, maybe twenty-five, could be counted on while others turned to whiskey and peevish complaining. All of New Mexico seemed a process of hard driving on a river bottom full of sand. Even the animals who'd given their best all the way from San Antonio were showing fatigue. They needed more rest. And water.

"Maybe if we lighten the load," Beale said to Geoffrey Scott, a windstorm playing havoc with tent flaps and more sand than air to breathe. He covered his face with a scarf. Geoffrey Scott pulled up the collar of his shirt. "The camels are doing all right, but the rest of the animals are tired. I can count on you as much as anybody. Take a few men. Find some water, then lighten the load."

When the wind settled down the next day and some water had been found in a side canyon, McFeeley and Hoyne plus Ebenezer joined Geoffrey Scott in hoisting the "Little Giant" corn mill onto a wagon and carrying it to the local priest and his broken-down chapel in a town south of Albuquerque. After a jolting ride, the foursome found the priest—a heavyset man dressed in soiled robes, the loss of teeth affecting his speech and his smile.

"Mill's too heavy and cumbersome for the wagons," Geoffrey Scott explained to the priest. "Might be something you could use."

"I need corn ground fine enough to make cornbread. That is...," he curved his lips around his lack of teeth, "what I need."

"This is the best corn mill you'll ever find," McFeeley told the priest, though no one else uttered a word until Hoyne joined him like a glad-hander medicine man. "Just what you need. It grinds faster than lightning strikes."

"I need 'fine,'" said the priest with conviction. "Cornbread. That's what...I need to make. That's what my congregation wants and needs."

For all of the hype expended, the mill would not grind fine. "I try every setting," the Padre said. "Thank you, but this is not...," again he hid his lack of teeth, "what I need."

"Best mill ever made," McFeeley said, pushing the sale against odds. "You'll be sorry."

But the priest knew his mind.

"You're a smart man," Geoffrey Scott whispered and Ebenezer nodded his head in agreement. Both thought McFeeley and Hoyne were out of range.

"This is cruel country," the priest whispered back. "If a man ever did know anything he would soon forget it here." He made the sign of the cross and lifted his arms skyward.

With Ebenezer shouldering the majority of the weight, bull strong, the four men carried "Little Giant" back to the wagon, Hoyne and McFeeley mumbling about ingrates, about lost opportunities, how people like Geoffrey Scott ought to keep their mouths shut, and how they shouldn't have been asked to do this job.

"You should be carrying this whole thing," Hoyne said to Ebenezer when the mill was being hoisted onto the wagon. "You're the nigger around here. Why's this our job?"

"That's enough outta you, Hoyne," Geoffrey Scott said, grunting from the weight of the mill, his words barely recognizable.

Hoyne raised his eyebrows before the four men gave the last push to the heavy mill. Upright in the wagon now. "Uppity, aren't we? Listen to the man who thinks he's the leader around here. Thinks he knows stuff."

"Stop grumbling." Geoffrey Scott was bent over with his hands spread, wrists out, on his tired, almost shaking, legs. He inhaled three deep breaths to regain a balance in his lungs. "Let's get back."

The ride back was slow and jarring from the ruts in the almost-no-road. No one said much, everyone on the edge of irritation, lost in their own thoughts of possible retorts, but the wagon returned to Albuquerque where the mill was finally sold. The weight of the expedition, however, still needed to be lightened. Ebenezer, cautious, but warming to the Kansan with ideas about a manservant's place in the order of things, joined Geoffrey Scott to help dispose of photographic apparatus and geological specimens from Texas. But water. That was another story. It was becoming a scarce commodity. Harder to find with each roll of the wheel into the unknown territory.

* * * * *

Near Santa Fe, the sand became the texture of salt and pepper—especially small grains whipping the bare skin and the pant legs when the wind blew. Everyone needed an escape from the wide-open, windswept land. They needed to leave the expedition for a night. Go to a bar and attend a Fandango come hell or high water. "Women, women. We need whiskey and women."

Beale reluctantly gave his permission, though advised the men not to rile up the locals. Geoffrey Scott told McFeeley and Hoyne he'd join up for the ride into town though they weren't his idea of the best time. A woman. He hadn't been with one for a long time. That one near Camp Verde came to mind but it didn't matter where these girls he might meet would be from. Anything to escape the sand. Even the expedition, though he was still hoping for an in with Hadji Ali, who was always disinterested in anything besides the way he himself did things.

Hoyne and McFeeley had already broken into a slow gallop toward Santa Fe when Geoffrey Scott, after mounting his horse to follow them, saw Ebenezer sitting in front of Lieutenant Beale's tent on a camp stool. Hands on his knees. Lips tight in a straight line.

The man must be hungry for something himself, Geoffrey Scott thought, opening his mouth to speak an invitation. He needed to dance. Drink. A woman probably. But then he stopped himself. More than likely Ebenezer wouldn't be welcomed by the women in town though maybe they didn't care. Maybe it was only people like Hoyne and McFeeley who gave a damn. To them, Ebenezer was Beale's manservant, Beale's beckoned call. The one who was now looking up at the sky as if something important were happening there, not paying any mind to the boy from Kansas.

Geoffrey Scott waved a hand. No response. He wondered if Ebenezer had decided purposely to play blind. He lifted the reins, buried his heels into the horse's sides, and raced after Hoyne and McFeeley, already a good pace ahead of him. But then he couldn't keep from wondering about Hadji Ali. Hanging out with camels had to be lonely sometimes. Would he have liked to be included? Not that he'd invite him, probably for the same reasons he wondered about Ebenezer, but what was Hadji Ali like? Who was he? Probably off with his prayer rug somewhere. Nowhere in sight. As usual. Probably not.

* * * * *

Over the top of his whiskey glass, Geoffrey Scott examined the row of señoritas through the waves of cigarette smoke. The way they crossed their legs while their fans caught corners of stale air. He picked out one with the right kind of eyes—soulful, dancing, deep where Geoffrey Scott could lose himself. Her skin reflected the light from candles and seemed smooth like shiny satin, though he wished he could think of another way to describe her subcutaneous layer. He laughed at his mental gymnastics, but she seemed a miracle, he'd have to say. Maybe she'd dance with him. She smiled in his direction, and he thought about walking over to her side of the room but then someone else eased up to her side and laid claim.

The saloon was full of brown skin, their shadows playing on the far wall. He watched three men playing billiards—two of them thin as beanpoles and one with a stomach that poured over his belt—their newfangled cue sticks reflecting like lances on the wall. These men weren't so different from Hadji Ali or Ebenezer. Brown-skinned. Two arms and legs. Heads. Geoffrey Scott was mesmerized by the reflections on their faces. Otherworldly almost. Most of the people in the world woke up every morning with darker skin than he had, that is if his mother had told him right. He was glad his white chest was covered with a shirt. It felt dead-fish-like and colorless compared to this. He longed for some of the vividness he could see—the whirling, the glinting teeth, scandalous jewels, floating scarves. But then McFeeley, thoroughly soused, pulled out his gun.

"See this," he yelled with a heavy tongue, acting like a boy with a present everyone needed to see. He waved the weapon like a flag.

"Ye better watch out," he said to all of the men suffering from cabin fever and anybody else who was listening. "I'm a good shot. I kin hit anything I aims at."

"When you can see straight," said Hoyne, not quite as inebriated as his friend. The room was dark, no illumination except for candles and rows of eyes. Geoffrey Scott scooted his chair back to the wall. He only wanted to find a woman who would stroke his pale chest and tell him he was a man among men. Trust McFeeley to cause trouble.

"I see straight," McFeeley shouted back at Hoyne. "Straight as a arrow, mind you." He lowered the barrel and squeezed the trigger on his gun, heedless of whatever direction the ammunition would take.

The sound of a gunshot still ringing through the room, Hoyne held up his hand, his bloody fingers. "Damn you, McFeeley. Damn you to hell. You blew me to bits. Me. Yer friend." He winced. He cursed again. He tried to wiggle his fingers with no response.

"I'll shoot ye again if ya don't shut ye'er mouth," McFeeley said. "Damn everybody. Forgettin' I'm a man who knows guns. The trigger. The barrel. Last chance, Hoyne." He lifted the gun again, pointed it at his friend, then stopped to wave it over his head in a drunken figure eight. "You don't watch yer mouth, I'll send you to eternal wanderin'."

"You damn fool." Hoyne took a quick swig of his shot to ease the pain, then moved in close to McFeeley, catching his arm when he looped the gun over his head. "Look at my hand, you bastard. Same hand the camel bit." With his good hand, he knocked the pistol from McFeeley. It spun in the air, then on the floor, its barrel catching candlelight, silent sparks, the noise of metal spinning on wood causing everyone to stop breathing. The gun lay near Geoffrey Scott's foot, close enough for him to stop it with his toes. Then he covered the weapon with the sole of his boot.

The sight of flowing blood slowed McFeeley, though the drunken obscenities continued, sloppy, unreasonable. Red on the floor. Red on the table and chair.

Geoffrey Scott bent over as if to retrieve a handkerchief, picked up the pistol, and stuffed it in the soil of a potted plant. Then he swiped his hands together, traces of dirt dropping to the floor, and stood up as fast as he could. "Does anyone know how to stop this blood?" he said to the room, everyone inept at best, no one seeming to care or too paralyzed to do anything.

"Let me see what I can do," Jim Ballard finally said, one of the road builders, drunk himself and a person who had no doctoring skills anybody knew anything about. He held his hands high in the air, a truce, and walked through the smoky saloon. "Hold your fire." He picked up Hoyne's bloody hand with theatrical care. Held it delicately. "Looks like the shot hit the bones. First and second fingers. Lucky for you, Hoyne, it wasn't your heart or vitals. Wait a minute." Then he proceeded to wrap the hand in a towel retrieved from a puddle of gin. "Git back to camp. Find someone who knows how to fix this. Git. Now."

Like a shot from McFeeley's gun, Hoyne ran out to his horse, mounted it, and raced back toward camp holding his injured hand wrapped in a towel next to his stomach. When the dust from his departure settled, McFeeley wandered out into the night, looking for his friend, bleating his name. "Hoyne. Where is you? Hoyne." A lost lamb wandering through a dark town with no street lamps, all by his lonesome, no shepherd in sight.

"Enough of this Fandango," the rest of the men from the expedition mumbled wistfully, checking out the girls one last time, waving good-bye, one hand raised, a palm extended. In single file, on their horses that still hadn't been watered, they went back to the sand, to the camp, to the drudgery without the luxury of the senoritas. At least they had something to talk about besides the growing scarcity of water.

As he rode alone, not wanting to get back to camp too soon, Geoffrey Scott was glad Ebenezer or Hadji Ali hadn't been in the line of fire. After what he'd seen tonight, he didn't even want them cast in their usual roles. But, damn it all, he cursed, kicking his horse in the sides, he needed Hadji Ali to need his help once in a while. And Elias Scott. He mangled Geoffrey Scott's thoughts. Played havoc. Was there any way he could please that man? Return to his good graces if he had any left? But all this thinking was ridiculous. Shove it up something big somewhere. He corralled his horse and found his bedroll.

And, to everyone's relief, Hoyne and McFeeley were released from service the next day.

* * * * *

When he wasn't busy improving an embankment with his shovel, Geoffrey Scott, from a distance, took notice of Beale turning the soil, looking for evidence of a population once inhabiting the region. Of people. Who farmed. Who ate. Who loved. Who birthed. Who dreamed. This man of reason and composure had seen much of the world, but watching his interest in the unsurveyed, the unknown, and the unexpected said more to Geoffrey Scott than Beale's propensity to spend too much time with his friends and notable celebrities of each town. Geoffrey Scott watched the lieutenant handle Seid and was continually surprised at his affection for the animal. He also felt that Beale, though no words of recognition were spoken to him personally—the novitiate and the common road builder—thought the

Kansan was one who shared his vision of what camels could be to Western expansion.

One day Geoffrey Scott, pausing from his task of chopping down a tree obstructing the wagons, looked across the lumpy hills and saw the lieutenant unearthing a piece of clay pipe.

"An ancient irrigation system," Geoffrey Scott heard him say to no one in particular. "By God, that's what this is."

The find seemed a feast in many ways, mostly because Beale, for the first time, became an obvious participant in this place, this expedition. Geoffrey Scott found a new pastime when he wasn't sawing, tunneling, and trying to learn more about camels. He kept an eye on Mr. Beale.

That night, on a hill overlooking camp, the light in Mr. Beale's tent shone much later than usual. Maybe he was writing in his journal or maybe wondering about Hoyne and McFeeley and where they'd gone, those loose cannons. After unrolling his sleeping bag close to where the camels reclined, Geoffrey Scott found no solace in the night. He'd bunked on the ground close to Hadji Ali, a nightly happening now even though no words were exchanged, but tonight he was drawn to the light shining at the top of the hill: Beale's tent aglow with two glass lanterns hanging at each end, two human shapes inside the canvas. A shadow paced in Beale's tent between the kerosene lanterns, its profile changing size with proximity to the light. Sometimes one shadow gestured large, two arms raised, hands threatening. Then the other shadow answered in kind. An argument, an irritation, seemed to be growing larger with each word. This couldn't be the fastidious Beale, the promoter of camels, the leader of the expedition. Or Ebenezer, always careful and furthermore trained to be subservient and cooperative. But then Ebenezer came stumbling out of the tent, mumbling loose words. "Freedom's for all men at all times," Scott heard him shout back to Beale. "Not somethin' for one man to give another." Then he yelled loud enough to wake the dead. "I am a man," and disappeared into a shadowed grove of pinyon. Then beyond the trees. "I am a man," he shouted from a greater distance, singling out his horse, which had been corralled with the others. Beale had promised him he'd be a free man at the end of the expedition, no longer a slave to anyone or anything. Safe. But, as he walked into the night, Eb must have looked up at the moon and the stars roaming the sky and wondered why any man had the power to decide another man's direction. Geoffrey Scott heard the clip of hooves. The sound echoing, then disappearing. The silence. A hollow cave. A new moon shining which meant no moon at all.

He watched the shadow of Mr. Beale sitting down at his desk, putting two hands on his forehead, one fist clamped and shaking. Beale lifting a pen, its quills large in shadow. Geoffrey Scott searched the camp to see if anyone else was witness to this. No one. If he could say anything about this, it'd be that Beale was being forsaken.

But then he saw a movement in the tent that caused him to sit up, to pull on his boots. To run. He must stop what was about to happen. The shadow of a gun was being raised inside the tent. Scott stumbled, then ran faster toward the tent. But suddenly, rather than pointing the pistol at his own head, as Scott had feared would happen, Beale crashed outside and fired his pistol at the starry sky with no moon.

"Indians, Indians!" he yelled. "The damn rascals, give 'em hell, boys." All chaos broke loose. The dazed men summoned from their sleep charged with half-cocked rifles. Ran every which way, some toward Lieutenant Beale, some toward the empty hills, all alert to a raid. Beale jumped on the closest horse that reared back, frightened with the half-awake men shooting their guns in every direction. Then, with Beale clinging to the saddle and trying to catch the dangling reins, the horse spooked and ran faster than the wind. He only had the mane to hold.

Geoffrey Scott pulled on his pants and slipped his suspenders over his shoulders. Somebody needed to follow Beale, and hopefully the man's horse was headed for the canyon Scott knew. And hopefully, his own horse could run fast enough. On this crazy night, all the time slapping his horse's neck to increase its speed, he wondered if Beale had gone insane. But suddenly, he watched the lieutenant sinking to the ground, his horse's legs buckling in sand. The horse struggled to its feet, kicking forward and back. It shook its head, its mane flying, and tried to break away once again but became tangled in the rope tied to Beale's saddle. And Beale himself was injured—laying on the ground, bruised and damaged though, luckily, the rope tied to his saddle had entangled his horse's legs and stopped it from running anywhere. He'd hurt his back. Maybe his lungs. His pride, most certainly, even though it seemed not to matter. Beale was drunk.

Geoffrey Scott pulled on his reins, keeping his horse out of sight, knowing it best to stay hidden. Help would not be something the lieutenant would want. He backed into the cleft of two man-sized boulders and watched Beale grab his horse's leg, pull himself toward the saddle, and mount, all in what-seemed-to-be great pain. This time, on a much slower-moving horse who'd itself been injured in the irrational encounter with Beale's anger, the lieutenant stumbled back into camp. Scott followed close behind to guard against further mishap, then noticed Hadji Ali watching from a distance as well, the man hidden in a darker part of night. Both knew that Beale didn't know he'd been watched.

"Find water," Beale croaked to the men who'd stopped firing their guns, awaiting the return of their leader whom some thought had been captured. He held his side where ribs had broken. "Very soon. We're close to having none." He disappeared into the privacy of his tent and tied his door shut.

There were no Indians to be seen, and now, there was little water. A decision about continuing had to be made soon.

* * * * *

When the banks of creeks needed a pick-axe and shovel, Tad Williams worked shoulder to shoulder with Geoffrey Scott. He'd been born in Missouri, ordinarily a red flag because it was a slave state, but Tad was one of the few Union sympathizers—a different star in the cosmos. Not all men from Missouri hated everyone in Kansas. The next afternoon, work done for the day, he strolled outside of camp into the hills, wandering and then examining what might have been a mortar for crushing seeds once upon a time. He needed to find the pestle. Resting his rifle against a boulder, he searched while an Indian shimmied up to the boulder, lifted Williams' gun high in the air, and grunted. Williams turned and saw three Indians, one of them unbelievably tall waving his rifle overhead in a victory sweep, the other two with arrows pointed at his chest. The one holding the rifle jerked his head to the side to indicate Williams better leave. He dropped the ancient mortar and ran.

"I saw an Indian," he shouted to Geoffrey Scott, who was whittling at the edge of camp, surrounded by ribbons and curls of wood, an open knife in one hand. Williams was breathing hard. Almost a ghost with big breath. "Three of them. Picked up my gun." He pointed, though there was nothing in sight.

"Best tell Lieutenant Beale," Geoffrey Scott said, wondering if Williams had lost his wits, but hastily stood anyway, letting the whittling in his lap fall to the ground, running with Williams. "If they're there, he'll want to catch those thieves, sure thing." The two of them ran, then barged into Beale's tent.

"Indians. Thieves. My gun," Williams said between gulps for more air. "Set it right baside me, but they took it when I weren't looking."

Beale sat up, wan, pale, still in his bed recuperating.

"We can't stand for thievery," he said, though the men barely heard him, the lieutenant almost drowning in the gathered top of his white nightgown, the one that might envelope him if he lost anymore weight. He half sat up. Rested on one elbow to favor the other arm in a sling, then fell back onto his bed, too ill to issue a command. No further direction pending, the two men rushed out and mounted their horses to follow a jagged trail, but then there was nothing. The footprints Williams had made faded into sagebrush. Nothing but sand, maybe sand that had changed position. Other footprints had dissolved.

"Tracks've gone to heaven," Williams said, his face a white sheet of surprise. "But something was here. Somebody. I swear."

"What should we do when nobody's here?" Geoffrey Scott said. "Can't follow a ghost."

"I want my rifle back." As Tad spoke, his eyes searched the rocks. "They were here. Three of them. Yelping. Pointing arrows at me. They'd have killed me if I'd've stayed."

"Over there," Geoffrey Scott suddenly yelled. "About three hundred yards ahead of you."

One man dipped and hid. A head. An arm. A leg.

"Your gun," Tad demanded, though Geoffrey Scott'd promised himself he'd never use one again. Maybe he should shoot at the natives who'd taken Tad's rifle, which was a cardinal sin, a big sin, but the men were trying to kill them. The savages, but then he stopped himself. No man's a savage, just an unlucky bastard. That's what his mother would've said except she'd have used another word besides "bastard." The sun sank just at that moment, the sky turning red, orange, purple, then yellow, and, out of nowhere flew an arrow that zinged close to Williams' ear.

"Duck," Geoffrey Scott yelled, and grabbed his gun from its scabbard. He could shoot into the air. Shoot to the side of the men. Anything but kill them, even though they were trying to end both Williams and himself in this Wild West where the wiliest man wins.

The men kicked their horses and galloped toward the bush where the Indians hid, Geoffrey Scott shooting his Henry into the air—the first time he'd used it. Finally, two Indians emerged with their hands in the air, the third one disappeared into the trees or the sky or wherever. They secured a native boy about fifteen-years-old and a man of about forty-five or fifty dressed in little clothing. Tied them in a rope. Took them into camp. Set them in front of a fire close to Beale's tent because the night was cooling.

"Don't hurt them," Beale commanded weakly, drawn out of his tent by the noise and commotion, still dressed in his cotton nightgown. "They're innocent. They understand nothing of why we're here."

They understand plenty, Geoffrey Scott didn't say out loud. They knew what they wanted.

"But where's my gun?" Williams said, holding his horse by the reins and waiting for his rifle to drop from the heavens, it seemed. Whole. Intact. Beale was back, outside his tent now. Anything could happen.

"They obviously don't have it," Beale said, sinking onto a canvas stool, the one in which Ebenezer usually sat. "Where's Ebenezer? He can find something to give the Indians. Ebenezer," he yelled as if Ebenezer would appear out of thin air, even though he'd seen nothing of his man during the morning hours. "Where is that man?"

Ebenezer didn't appear. Nor, thought Geoffrey Scott, would he, but he kept his knowledge of Ebenezer's departure to himself.

"I wish Ebenezer were here," Beale said, a slight whine in his voice. "I promised his freedom as soon as I could deliver it. He said my words were 'insincere, my white man's words soothing to his own ears but unable to fix a thing.' Hell, he's a free man. I bought him and he's got his freedom when this expedition's over. I need him now."

Geoffrey Scott still said nothing, thinking there was always another corner to round before one reached a destination, wondering where Ebenezer was by now, if he had made it back to Fort Defiance or gone on to Albuquerque.

"Maybe he's busy relieving himself by the creek," Beale continued, up again and pacing when he should have been in his bed. "Getting a big head, that Ebenezer. Promise a man some liberty, and he gets a big head about it. He's still my man, he better remember that." Then he turned his attention back to the Indians, now appeased by a leg of lamb torn from the whole animal turning on a green stick rotisserie. Juice dripping from their cheeks and chins. Shining in the firelight. "Maybe these two can lead us to some water."

"Water more important than my gun?" Williams asked, incredulous, though sniffing the aroma and ready to cut a piece of lamb off for himself.

"It's scarcer than we ever imagined," Beale said under his breath, though, from the looks of him, he should be back in his bed rather than making decisions of any kind. "Water is what we need," he muttered. "Or we don't finish this expedition. And we need a guide to the Colorado." He kept his upright stance by holding to a tent support and pulled a blanket around his shoulders, the edge of cold having grown especially sharp on this late autumn night.

"Water," he said again, and then repeated the word to the two Indians. Finally, he resorted to dialects, even different languages, reengaging his skills he once developed as head of Bureau of Indian Affairs in California. No response. No recognition. "Please. Help us. Water," he said, turning again to native-speak and sign language. Then he tried charades, holding a cup next to his mouth, throwing his head back to swallow. Though it seemed that nothing had passed the wide gap between them, the old man pointed in a northwest direction. "'Aha. Hakuduuch. Iyuuk." He cupped his hands as if to drink from them, and Beale knew he'd understood. He'd help them because they'd fed him. They'd find water. They weren't far from the Colorado River.

* * * * *

Believing that the elderly native would lead them where they needed to go, Beale, strong enough to move forward the next morning, prepared the camp to disband and the expedition to leave. But not before an exceptionally tall, though ailing Indian walked into camp with a rifle over his shoulder. The man made a long speech in his native tongue, though anyone could tell Beale might faint anytime soon if he didn't hurry with the talking. Beale accepted the rifle, Williams' rifle, maybe being returned because of a code of ethics he didn't understand, maybe because he'd developed a keen observation of gesture. After he finished his speech, the stranger looked even thinner and hungrier and tried to hide his shaking.

"Give the man some of that lamb on the spit," Beale told the cook.

A foot taller than the other captives, the Indian sat near the fire, shivering, wearing no leggings or anything else around his body except a short forepiece of rabbit skin. Beale, one arm in a sling, suddenly reenergized, rustled through his belongings with his good arm and found a serape—a present when he was a houseguest in Santa Fe, a brightly colored one with the flag of Mexico woven into it. He wrapped it around the man's shoulders, but it was insufficient. The man was a giant, cracking the bones of sheep and sucking on them. And shaking.

Geoffrey Scott, suddenly deciding that the shaking would be a humiliation for anybody, moved to his pack for one of his blankets.

"Here," he said to the giant, almost looking up at him even though he stood and the Indian sat. The man was that big. "Here. Maybe it'll help."

The Indian grabbed the larger blanket and wrapped himself tightly. And kept shaking.

"Maybe you got the ague? I can get medicine."

The Indian had no answer, though probably didn't understand one word. He sat by the fire trembling, reduced in his power, reduced in his stature.

Geoffrey Scott walked uphill to the medic's tent to get quinine, then, as he returned with a bottle in hand, saw Hadji Ali watching from the morning shadows, keeping to himself as usual. "You are good man," Ali called softly to him. "You help the sick man." He dipped his head, acknowledging the young man in a way he'd never done before.

"You'd do the same," Geoffrey Scott said and made his way back down the hill. Elated. His heart beating faster than before. His whole body filled with yes.

He wanted to talk, to shout a thousand words maybe, if only to the dry air around him. "Hadji trusts me. Finally. Hadji Ali, old Stone Face. And that Indian is some specimen," he said, feeling the freedom of saying whatever came to mind, immune to the boundaries of language. "He's the most amazing man I ever set eyes on." He smiled at what he'd said while stumbling over rocks to descend the hill.

"Kwanyumai," the Indian whispered when he drank, as instructed, from the half-filled bottle, though Geoffrey Scott had no way of knowing this was his name or that it meant "Warrior" in the Mojave language.

"Kwanyumai," Geoffrey Scott said, liking the word on his tongue.

"Kwanyumai." The Indian pointed to himself.

Before the sun rose, before anyone else was awake, the bronze man slipped out of camp into the hills. Geoffrey Scott, waking to find the fire cold and the man gone, concluded the medicine must have been effective. That the man could be a giant again. Massive among men. Kwanyumai. He liked that word, whatever it meant. Maybe the man's name. Maybe his condition.

For the first time in ten days, Beale was well enough to proceed. The sound of men packing their horses crowded the air, tents were folded, and gear rearranged. Teeth were brushed for the first time in days. Morning mouth spit in the sand. Bladders emptied. Eating dishes washed in a cold pail of water. The expedition followed their guide down a steep terrain that led them to a spring and then, further down, to the Colorado River. The end was in sight for the first time.

* * * * *

Then there was the river. A sight for sore eyes, for the pack animals, and for the men who had been parched for much of the expedition. Water. A good bit of it.

Adababa hadn't seen many rivers in its life. It had splashed through some on its trip across the American West, maybe even buried in water up to its thighs, but this particular river was swift, maybe too swift for the four legs of a pack animal, Ababa's legs to be exact. Beale valued the camels, of course, but when they were led to the edge of the river and expected to swim, the roll of the dice seemed too dangerous to Adababa, who pawed at the water's edge, reluctant to step further. Balky. A camel stopped in its tracks, unbending, unyielding, except that Seid, the leader of the string and urged by Beale, pulled the rest of the pack behind itself as it forged ahead into the water. Adababa, second in line, felt the jerk on its neck, into the deep, the unknown. Into a substance it would rather avoid given a choice.

Unlike the horses, who'd been across more rivers and were thus expected to be more savvy about water and its crossing, the camels were connected by a rope to keep from losing any of the herd. The camels were thus led into the Colorado, less swift at this point of crossing—a bend in the river—but swift nonetheless. Beale had done his homework and knew the animals could swim if they had to, but everyone in the expedition held his breath when the first camels went deeper into the water, complaining all the way.

Luckily, they seemed to understand the nature of water, natively intelligent about the way across, staying to the right of a boil in the current, slowly approaching the distant shore that seemed too far away for a swim by anybody. Men had gone ahead in rubber rafts to help if their help was needed and the rest waited with their horses on the Arizona Territory side of the river, but all of them were temporarily rooted to the place where they stood, speechless at the surprise of the camels' progress.

"Well, I'll be..." Geoffrey Scott said, watching his prized animals work their way to his side of the river which he'd already crossed. "Them consarned camels are coming across. Damn camels," he said out loud, laughing, even crowing, almost flapping his elbows with excitement. "Look at Adababa swim. I'll be..."

Before they hitched a ride across on the remaining rubber rafts, the last cavalrymen slapped their horses on the rumps to get them into the water with strong undercurrents. The animals plunged, seemingly willing to try whatever their masters asked. But after they had been swimming for a few minutes, two of them hit a whirlpool, the boil that swirled them away from a direct line across. Two horses struggled—neck-deep in the water, holding their heads high and battling for a straight path to the other shore. Fighting against the current, their eyes wild with yellow fear, their legs unable to help them, they seemed like balsa toys bobbing. Slick bodies. Soaked manes. Breakneck water pulling them first one way, then another, then sideways, every which way but where they were supposed to be.

"Hey," Geoffrey Scott shouted. "Get your lassos, and bring them horses in. Stop the river if you have to. Keep it from swallowing everything that gets in its way."

Sheer bedlam. Men running. Men shouting. Ropes flying.

Some of the men ran along the shore to keep pace with the floating horses, yelling after them and shouting where to swim if they only could, but the current was faster than anyone could run or the horses could overcome. The river was a big one. Stronger than the lassos and the attempts to bring the horses back. Soon, the two animals were floaters in the water, mere specks troubling its shining face.

When Seid, Adababa, and the rest of the camels and horses climbed out of the water at the California shore, they shook themselves—relieved to have reached dry land again and be free of the treacherous current. But the crossing, as hopeful as it had been—the end of a successful but complex expedition—was now a loss. Two horses. Lost. Swamped. Drowned.

Downstream from the expedition, the Mojaves paddled their canoes to the eddy where the overcome animals had reached their end, overjoyed at the gift of horse meat—a meal for several days and nights.

CHAPTER SEVEN

THE LONELINESS

ST. THOMAS—NOVEMBER 1869

The horse vanished in the dust, Charles on its back—the man who asked her last night why she was serving such slop for dinner. Good riddance. He knows better than anyone there's little that is palatable in this godforsaken place. He knows better. She shakes her head, still in disbelief, thinking she might sew his lips together so he can never spout off again.

Even the sky is dusty today. Again. Ropes of dust blowing through the air, until she shouts: "Aeolus. You're a monster," then hopes no one hears her. This wind is disturbing any peace of mind she hopes to have. She wishes she could bid it adieu forever as she sits on the sandstone slabs that serve as their doorstep. She wipes her hands on her apron and feels the dust caking her face, its grittiness clogging her pores. Her complexion has suffered in this climate, and it is a wonder her skin looks halfway decent and isn't crowded with unsightly eruptions. A wonder the silty water can clean anything.

"Morning, Sister Hughes," says a passing citizen of this crazy place—Thomas Day. Sophia imagines him scrambling to make do without his horses. She still can't believe he could only find their carcasses. A bad omen for anyone around here. "Nice to see you out," he says, "even though the wind ain't so neighborly today."

"Good morning to you." She cocks her hand in a half-wave and tucks her hair back into its bun with the other hand.

"Where's that husband of yours?"

"Off on a mail run. Always on a mail run, you know that."

"Tell him I need to ask him a question when he gets a chance."

"Will do," she says, watching him until he fades in the distance, looking like the wind is pushing him down the road. Not many people are out today.

Her hands and fingers rub her thighs back and forth as if she were shining them. He is like a pesky insect, that Charles. Maybe he is a stalwart in the building of the kingdom. Maybe he is committed to Joseph Smith and Brigham Young. To the whole endeavor. Yet he is angry and almost all the time ready for a fight. Slop, indeed. What a crass word when she is trying her best to make something palatable out of nothing. Nothing! Who in the heavens is he to be so bitter? At me? At the world? And he's ridden off again. Always to something more important than home and tending his garden. Good-bye Charles who will never understand how much effort others make to satisfy you. See you in a few days, you tempest in a ladle or a teapot or whatever. And that might be too soon.

Their home, comfortable as she has tried to make it, and she has tried, will never be as important to Charles as the Gospel and the powerful men who are making it happen. Charles wants to be part of that, she thinks, as she traces a stick figure in the red sand with the sheared branch of a willow: a man on a horse surrounded by flames. Then she watches a horned toad making its way across their yard. Stopping. Starting. Head up, left and right, looking for anything that might interfere with its path across the sand. Or food. Or just exploring. Anything is possible. Her eyes follow its darting to the roots of some switchgrass.

Charles wants to be respected and revered, one of the faithful, even one of the leaders, if he had his way. But no one asks him to lead, not really. Almira was privy to that sort of information, being Gilbroid Marshall was secretary in the priesthood. Charles' name came up for a leadership position, she had told Sophia in confidence, and the men in charge moved their fingers down the list, past his name. Charles Weston Hughes doesn't have an easy way with anyone. People would just as soon walk around him and not engage. How could she have been so gullible? Probably because she didn't know him all that well when she decided life in Zion would be better with a companion or that she needed to be married and have children to serve God.

He showed his nasty fire again before he left this morning. "You need to be committed to life here in St. Thomas." He even shouted. "Stop thinking about yourself and how pretty you are. You're vain and vain. A cracked looking glass is the best thing that's happened around here. Without it you can't spend so much time on yourself." He shouted even louder. "We're essential to this cause, and don't you forget it. We'll make that steamship service happen but you need to step up. Put your hand in." He spread his five fingers wide as he spoke and paced the floor as if there were something he and he alone was concerned about. She watched him wearing the packed dirt floor solid. Then he lowered his voice and said, almost sympathetically, though she didn't know what he really thought in their nightmarish last hour together, "Things might have been different for you if Sarah Ann had lived."

They'd looked at each other with sharp eyes, eyes with so many stories to tell, some of them spoken, some of them not, and she was glad he had other children, even if by another wife. She feels his burning words, even now. God knows, she did everything she knew to keep their little one alive. Maybe she should become pregnant again. But she is in no mood to be touched in any way.

She wishes Almira were still down the road. They could talk about this, even laugh, and then the sting of Charles' words would feel less harsh. Oh, Almira. Why did you have to leave? Why are you gone?

You need to get busy, she reminds herself as she pours a cup of water from the brown ceramic bottle she has made, fashioned with her own hands, and brought to the doorstep with her. She sits down, sips the water, clear as it is, but today she feels abandoned. The stone is hard against her bottom. Even Almira has abandoned her. Her best friend! This place has nothing to offer and nowhere to go. Keep busy. The only answer. Make sure you go to a meeting .There's always one you can count on. Relentlessly happening. But thank goodness someone has them, she corrects herself, ashamed of her thoughts. She's being ungrateful again. She does enjoy meeting with the sisters in Relief Society and is glad the organization has been reinstituted. She is even glad she's been asked to chair the making of a few quilts for the needy. Even the Paiutes. Idle hands equal the devil's workshop.

She should get ready, straighten up, and be on time for this morning's meeting. Show she is a supporter of this community. But what a choice someone made without thinking much about what it meant to build a town here. This desert is too stingy. Too hot and uninhabitable for the most part, even though the sunsets are the most beautiful she's ever seen, she has to say. Last night strings of dark clouds slashed across the red sky like strokes from a pen. A quill pen even. She envisioned a feathery plume spreading out over an eternal hand. Quiet. Everything calm at that bewitching hour. Everything preparing for rest. The effect almost like someone's pulling a silk sheet over her body before she sleeps.

But another gathering? She sighs. Yes. She should go. They'll be discussing how to deal with mosquitoes that have been rampant this year. She must keep a smiling face for everyone in St. Thomas, regardless of the unpredictable Muddy, the seasonal Virgin, and Charles. Regardless of the silty water that poisoned Sarah Ann. Thank the heavens above, her husband keeps the two of them supplied with pure water from the spring. Sophia will not drink another drop from those rivers. Not a drop.

She slaps a mosquito on her arm. These irritating insects swarm when the river is low. Like now. Malaria. Dysentery. What next? God forgive her, but this is a harsh place, a harder place than she has ever been before.

Maybe if she becomes pregnant again, then her life will have a purpose. She will please Charles. She will please herself. A woman who is fertile, who is a conduit for spirits from the preexistence. A family. We will build a family, we will. Charles and I. She swallows the lump in her throat. Then she thinks of her family in England. Her sister, Elizabeth. If only she were here with her. But she, Sophia, is here now. In St. Thomas. She has made her choice. She will serve the Lord and those who desire the same thing. She will keep busy with her hands, with those fingers that understand how to make beauty from not much at all, at least when she has some ingredients to work with.

Slop, she thinks again, unable to keep the word from her mind. How could he say such a thing? He was a hornet. A horsefly. But she will serve others and think of them before thinking of herself. That is what she will do. She looks at her hands and turns them over. Strong hands. Graceful even though they are callused and not soft anymore. Ugly even. But graceful. You can do good. Yes, you can, Sophia. God knows we can all use a little help. Up from this slab of sandstone. Up. Serve. Do your part.

She stands to make a few last-minute adjustments to her hair before leaving for the meeting. Almost in passing, she looks down the road toward the Marshall house, the house where Almira used to live—God be with her wherever she's gone, the house where the stranger and his camel stay when they're not mining salt to take north. And while she is gazing, against all probability, Geoffrey Scott rides toward her on his camel, cakes of salt tied to its sides with some net-like contraption. He waves, smiles, and Sophia hopes he did not see her looking in his direction. Despite herself, she feels a flutter in her chest when she watches the man and his outlandish camel sauntering down the road, their unusual profile, a disruption to the constant horizon she witnesses daily.

"I hope people are being nice to him," she says to herself after they pass, then ducks into her house and sees that she needs to reestablish order after she returns from the meeting. That is what she will do. Bring order. Be repaired in spirit when Charles returns.

* * * * *

Charles has brought three letters—his personal permission to make this trip to Callville. Nobody knows he's headed south, especially Sophia, who would say he's obsessed. "Stop with this bee in your bonnet!" But he's determined to know the next move. He's listened to lots of talk about how Callville will be the essential settlement connecting Utah Territory to the Pacific. Brigham Young's brilliant idea—a Prophet whose ideas come from God so they should be brilliant. No doubt. Steamships on the Colorado. Goods from the rest of the world, all stored in Callville until the wagons can take them over Virgin Hill to the rest of Utah Territory. This means a bright future for Charles W. Hughes. He'll be part of something great, something that'll make people notice. He's been there to make clockwork out of chaos. An even greater Kingdom. He's part of all this. He is. Charles Weston Hughes. A man who knows what's happening with the Mormons and the world. Not everybody can say that.

He's heard about that big war in the East—how Jefferson Davis left the War Department and joined up with the boys who didn't agree with the North. He's heard about John Brown and how he got hung trying to gather Negroes to make a stand. He's heard how those Southerners are sore about losing. He hears lots of things on his mail runs—the silver hopes in Panaca, the uselessness of a fort at Vegas Meadows. Too dry. Too isolated, though some day, Charles will bet, someone will settle that place and make it fertile as St. Thomas, which isn't saying much, he laughs to himself.

The snake is coiled before Charles sees it. Ready to strike because it's heard hooves. Coiled like a rope, wound, its head swaying, its tongue forked and searching the air for what's disturbed its sense of well-being.

"Whoa," Charles says and jerks his horse to sidestep the threat. But Midnight's eyes are wild, its nostrils wide in anticipation of how the coil might react. The horse skitters. Dances. Wants to stomp on the diamond-back and smash the creature to bits. Dig at it with its hooves.

"No, Midnight." Charles pulls the reins to the severe right to escape the slithering diamonds that can ripple over every change of terrain. Midnight resists with every muscle.

"Damn horse," Charles says, slapping Midnight on its neck with the reins, pulling on its mane, jerking the tack to keep the horse from the snake. The horse moves sideways, then back, closer to harm's way. It skitters again. But Charles pulls the reins so hard that the horse finally responds to the pain, even if its feet seem like a runaway carousel, round and about, and every which way but away.

"Leave that snake be."

Luckily, Charles manuevers Midnight far enough away to elude the snake's lunge toward them. They gallop around the creosote, the low-lying cacti, and the up-and-down hills. They gallop toward Callville with only three letters in the mail packet, not enough for a delivery, but they'll do for now.

"This is the place that'll put us on the map if you can stay away from those snakes, Midnight. The place that'll bring in cotton, converts, and the Colorado River will be one busy place, filled with those many Saints coming to Zion. God's plan."

But when they arrive at the collection of warehouses, no one seems to be anywhere. Nobody's loading supplies onto wagons. Gone. Vanished. The place is a ghost town.

"Where'd everybody go, Midnight? What the…?"

He sees the evacuated office, one built by Charles' brothers in the Gospel, a place that should be busy with ledgers, pen, and ink, recording invoices of passengers or of cargo. Then Charles takes notice of the horses in the corral–sleek, all a deep brown, some of them mules. Appreciates their lines. Their dependability. But when he sees a wind-bitten Stars and Stripes flying from a skinny, short post, he realizes this must be the military he dislikes, even hates, being they're so sure they're right about Utah and the people trying to make a life here. The military full of no accounts who have no idea about building something based on God's laws.

Just then, a soldier appears in suspenders and no shirt, his pantlegs rolled up. He ducks out from under the eaves and scratches his head. Simple enough gesture. "Wonderin' what's going on. Thought I heard something. What you doing here?"

"I'm a mail rider. Delivering to the people who're supposed to be here."

"Hear tell them Mormons took off for Utah Territory. Folded up shop, no more steamboats coming through. Water too temperamental most the year, maybe most the time."

"So they up and left?"

"Up and left, that's right. About three weeks ago. Had to get back to their women." He laughs a laugh laced with inuendo, and yet Charles ignores him. He's still curious.

"But what about this port?"

"Pretty marooned, I'd say. Who wants to be here anyway? Stuck in the middle of nowhere? We're part of a detachment from Fort Mojave. Waiting for our order to change location which I hope gets here pronto."

"I thought this was going to be a place where boats would come with supplies, maybe even more people, in good-water time."

"Who's kidding who? This is a hellhole. Anyone who tells you otherwise is off his head. Military won't be here much longer. And the railroad's coming. That'll change everything. I'd say forget trying to figure when this river'll cooperate."

* * * * *

Sophia is sweeping their always-full-of-sand house. Sand works its way into every crevice of their home in this no-account desert. Scant relief from nothing. No water. No streams. Not really what anyone would call a home. She has written her sister, Elizabeth, that she watches scorpions for her viewing entertainment.

With a hefty swoosh and a "good riddance," she sweeps sand out the door for the third time this afternoon, remembering herself as the "wee might of a woman," standing up and having her say at the meeting about mosquitoes. To think she had something to say about mosquitoes! Charles had called her a "wee might" when they were walking toward the Endowment House in Salt Lake City to be married. She laughs about being in such a small body but with such a convincing voice. She can make herself known if needs be.

But then she hears someone passing on the road in front, peers out the doorway, then waves at Geoffrey Scott and his camel, twice in one day, no less. Heading out with Kwami riding behind him. When she sees the Indian, she can't help but remember the solemn Moquis, the ones she had seen in Salt Lake City. Dignified Indians, an enigma of a culture alien to her own. Not dark like most Indians she had seen. They had blue eyes and blond hair, but they were Indians, no doubt. This one does not seem to know that everybody closes their doors when they see him coming. She swallows at the thought of how big Kwami stands.

"Hallo there," she calls as they ride past, somewhat curious that the man from Kansas is staying put in St. Thomas for now. Who would have figured that? Staying in a Mormon settlement with a camel? An unlikely contrast in anyone's book.

"Good day," he calls out, tipping his hat, then disappearing into the sand dunes like a mirage—something she had never seen before she lived in the desert. She continues sweeping the sand that sits on every windowsill, every flat place. She will never get it all outside but has promised and re-promised herself to do well by Charles. He does not usually call her efforts "slop." She needs to be fair even though he can be the devil himself at times. She is his wife, after all. Maybe not the only one, but the only one for a few months or years, though the idea of years was most likely more than a body could take. Her body, anyway. Too much time in this desert where everything can feel harsh and unfriendly. But she will do her best.

"Charles," the officiator at the Endowment House said while she stood quietly beside him that day almost two years back. "This is the woman you've chosen. Your third wife. You must love her equally and admonish the others to love her equally well." And he looked straight into Charles' eyes, no flinching. "Equally. That is your challenge. Are you capable of this?"

Charles nodded, solemnly, believably.

"Sophia Jane Poultney," he turned to her. "You must love Charles and support him in building the Kingdom of God. Since his time in Farr West, he's been a builder for Zion and is a humble man who doesn't speak of himself and his accomplishments. I hope you know he cared for the Prophet's horses in Ohio, Missouri, and Nauvoo. Joseph Smith himself.

"He would have been in the first wagon train for Zion if Brother Brigham hadn't asked him to stay behind and build the flour mill at Winter Quarters. Two prophets of God trusted this man. Your husband's a stalwart. Be his helpmeet and a succor to his other wives. But don't forget. God is the One you must love first. The rest will be given to you."

Sophia knelt at an altar with Charles kneeling on the other side, face-to-face. Sophia felt shy, even girlish—little knowing she would be exposed to a sizable temper and desert sand by the bucketsful. This man's face had elegant lines, even if age and weather had done its work on his eyes and mouth. His hair was white as an albatross except for a few dark streaks, his eyes chestnut brown, the color of his favorite horse, Midnight. His nose was straight as a plumb line and his beard was cleanly washed, not some straggly piece of growth twisted with dust and bits of tumbleweeds.

Yet, tipping her head upward to kiss him for the first time, she wondered at her judgment. *Who is this man? I know so little about him.*

She'd buried her nose in the small bouquet of sweet peas the landlady at the boardinghouse had given her for her wedding day. Sweet peas. The smell of high summer. Fragrant. A promise of the good life. A promise of hope and beauty. Once again as she looked unashamedly back into his face, she realized she had no knowledge of the man across from her. No inkling of what mattered to him other than the church. And the word "survival" came to mind. Maybe it was only in her desire for protection and belonging that she had some understanding of traits that drew her to him, but he was a man who lived by the word he gave. That much she knew. She also suspected he had high expectations of those with whom he labored: his horses, his wives, the brethren, his and Mary Anne's children. No shirkers or slackers allowed. Understood.

She'd found a good man, or he had found her when she sat alone in church trying to forget Mr. Milhaus and recommit herself to her reasons for leaving her home and family across the Atlantic. God would listen to her prayers, she told herself that fateful evening she attended sacrament meeting with her landlady. God was waiting for her knock. He would answer.

She wore a close-fitting dress that afternoon, one showing her small waist to advantage, one of four dresses she'd brought in her trunk with the leather hinges—the wooden trunk with the difficult lock and key that challenged her skill with each opening. She sat next to Sister Lucy Pulsipher,

her landlady who had three young children, a woman whose husband had been called away on a mission to tell people to harken unto Zion. Now. Not later. Sophia volunteered to hold the youngest of Lucy's children on her lap and found surprising comfort in its squirming body and sudden utterances coming at the most inappropriate times. "That's mine," the toddler shouted to his sister during the quiet of the sacrament. Sophia bit her lips to keep from laughing.

Sophia turned to the people behind her to express a silent apology for the child's behavior and that was when she first saw Charles sitting across the aisle with Mary Anne on one side and Harriet on the other, though she didn't know any of them or their names at the time. She dropped her eyes, gestured 'he can't help himself' to complete her apology for the baby's outcry, then turned back to the child. But as she sat there, she could feel the power of eyes focused on her back, cross-examining her, the new young woman in the congregation helping Sister Pulsipher with her famous-for-being-unruly children. He must have noticed the hat on her head, narrowing his eyes at the paradox of the fancy hat and her sensible handling of children. He probably noticed her hands, how they moved, slender fingers on hands that weren't too small or overstrong. Hands supple as branches of a willow tree. Curious at the way she tipped her head, by the way she held that child tight to her bosom, kissing him on the top of his head.

The magnet of God must have pulled at Charles that day to remind him of his responsibility to build the Kingdom with more wives who must learn to be selfless and generous through living the Principle. When she turned to see whose eyes were burning the back of her neck, she once again noticed the older man sitting between two women, one of them as old as he was, the other in between the gap of Sophia's age and his. She knew he wanted her. Just like that, she knew he had chosen her to be his wife—a mother to his children, an assistant to the two wives who sat by his side, a lover even, though she wondered at all of that. She was not sure about the idea of multiple wives, even though that principle was spoken of as a law of God.

Maybe his choice was about responsibility. Duty to the Kingdom and posterity. But maybe—with this Sophia yielded to her own need for reassurance after heartbreak, her need to feel pride in her youth, her vanity even—he was beguiled by her full pink cheeks, her luxuriously dark eyelashes made even darker with secret touches, maybe even her hat. Maybe his manliness noticed Sophia. The younger wife on his left, though not so young as herself, seemed stable, sure, yet a bit blockish. His aging wife on the right showed signs of midlife immunity to the pleasures of desire. Sophia noticed the turned-down corners of the older woman's mouth, an agitation, maybe fearing her husband would be called by the Prophet to do something that would take him away from her again. Prescience. One glance.

The night before they were to be sealed in the Endowment House, Charles told her how he'd watched her that Sunday afternoon and how he'd known she was the right choice. The night before they married, he took her hands in his for the first time and marveled at their fineness and allowed himself to indulge in the sight and feel of those hands in his, hands he could love and cherish. He would do well by her, he told her after he'd kissed her fingertips. Charles had been smitten then, subject to that sharp bite in the loins, even to his sympathies. He was capable of many words the night before their marriage, not many of which she'd heard repeated since. How she loved words, poetic, resonant words, that bled into her senses as if they were a trill on the pianoforte, a rising from pianissimo to forte.

So it was that Sophia put her hand in Charles' hand that day in the Endowment House, rose from her knees as he rose from his, and trusted she was being led by God's wisdom as well as his mercy. She smoothed her dress and refastened a button that had slipped sideways in its buttonhole. She pulled her shoulders back. She was doing God's work. That is why she had come to Zion. She put her hand inside Charles' and together they walked out of the marriage room, Sophia, a tender flower, next to a man with white hair and a slight stoop to his shoulders that had carried much weight.

"Could I buy you a meal on this special day?" he asked, tucking her arm into his.

"Of course," she answered, surprised he would be so lavish when he preached frugality, of necessity, so often.

"I am pleased," he said in a softer voice than usual.

Sophia smiled up at him, and they took leave of those who had witnessed their union and offered practical words of advice about loving each other equally. Harriet and Mary Anne had stayed at home with the children that day; who knows what they were feeling when they were not so sure about sharing their husband with someone of whom they knew so little, someone younger than they, someone much nearer the bloom of the rose.

"We will have a son," Charles prophesied or so it seemed, except why was he mentioning only one son? Sophia hoped to fill their home with many noble children. She pictured herself with a number of teasing, playing young ones who loved her stories and her pies, her pasties, all of those things she herself treasured.

"And should we call this son after you?" Sophia asked him when he made his announcement. She touched his elbow and lifted her teasing eyes with a veiled flirtatiousness. She knew how to take a man's heart. Now if she could keep it. Small and vulnerable, she was willing to do what needed to be done to stay on her journey away from home.

But, Sophia Jane Poultney Milhaus Hughes. Oh my. So many names. She folded her hands and rested them and her chin on the end of the broomstick, knowing the sand would always need to be swept away. Could any of them describe who and what she was becoming in this godforsaken place, truly a godforsaken place and not just a phrase? Was this truly the path God had chosen for her?

Though there was an unspoken understanding that practicality and necessity were the mothers of their coupling, Charles did seem to watch over her well enough. He wasn't a romantic as James had been and came down on the proprietary side more often than anything related to love as Sophia understood it. He was not as suave or well-spoken, even a bit rough at the edges, and Sophia did love the speech of a well-read man, a philosopher even, a teacher, someone who had thought about the world and its meaning. Someone like her father. But Charles had a temper. A bad one that sometimes got out of hand. "Nonetheless," she scolded herself. "I've promised my loyalty to Charles for time and all eternity. I'll support this man in building the Kingdom of God. Nothing will come before that promise."

But then, she takes a firm grip on the broom to chase sand. The house must be addressed from stem to stern before Charles returns tomorrow. But does she love him? Can she hold him in her arms and stroke his hair when he returns? She isn't sure. She is not in love with his temper, that's certain. Her brief marriage to James Milhaus quashed the idea of a one-and-only. That daydream is a wish, a fantasy. After almost two years of marriage to the stern Charles Weston and the death of her fragile three-month old baby, Sarah Ann, she has come to understand this. And maybe she knows more about herself than she once did.

She rehearses her good points: she is tidy, no doubt about that, and can find itinerant sand on every ledge of the house. She provides a homey atmosphere for her husband—beauty in a barren land. And she can usually make a good meal from nothing, or almost nothing, though sometimes that's impossible. Slop, indeed. But forget that word. It is time. She needs to remember to be grateful—she has been given much: shelter, protection, a companion, though she has to admit to herself, the companionship is something more hoped for than real.

To the sound of a broom swishing like a clock's pendulum, she decides she is definitely stubborn. That makes her strong. Maybe Sarah Ann hadn't lasted very long, and what baby would in this dust and alkali and water? Maybe the child was the only smart one of this family, leaving this existence before life could meddle in worse ways with her. She and Charles had been fools to bring a new baby into being on the Muddy, fools thinking they could do anything they set out to do.

Char-les. Char-les. The broom has its rhythm. Work, work, work, is all he knows. Work for the Kingdom. Work for God. But he can be harsh to those who step over the line of order he has established. He has no sympathy for anyone not living his code and much impatience for those not fulfilling God's expectations. Whether they are God's or Charles' alone, she is not entirely sure. Sometimes he equates the two, putting God in his human mouth, God wanting something that Charles, the man, wants.

On the other hand, she has seen tenderness, especially when he calms a horse. Good with animals. He is. This particular aspect of her husband turns her sympathies back to him when she feels disgruntled. The thought gives her pause now. Though there is no guarantee, she should be safe with this man most of the time, she hopes.

She has an eye for beauty, she does, though the dress she wears is growing limper and paler with each washing. How did she end up here in Utah or Arizona Territory, whatever it is supposed to be, in a dress that has lost its crispness? No starch in her larder. How has she come to be here, though she knows this is a better choice than pining after Mr. Milhaus.

CHAPTER EIGHT

THE CAMEL CHARGE

BISHOP'S RANCH, SOUTHERN CALIFORNIA—1859

"Maybe you help with camels," Hadji Ali told Geoffrey Scott. "Lieutenant Beale is gone. Maybe you can help, but only when I say so."

"I know things," Geoffrey Scott told him, both hands in the pockets of his overalls, his attitude as laid back and casual as he could muster. He knew not to show his cards to Hadji. "Remember you said that. Keep your word."

"You help with camels if I say so. They need a careful hand."

Geoffrey Scott held up one hand, front, then switched it to back. "Careful as you'll find," he said, smiling his I-gotcha smile. Big on his face. But Hadji pretended to be busy elsewhere.

Thus, the dance continued between the two men—Geoffrey Scott anxious to be sanctioned by the Syrian and to be part of the camel experiment, Hadji Ali maintaining his status as knower and keeper of all things camel. With Beale out of the picture, however, the animals were more accessible. Hadji had been given an assignment to test these camels, their limits, and their endurance, and needed others to assist. Therefore, he did not have complete control over the camels for the first time.

In between odd jobs of milking the few cows, the female camels, and digging postholes, Geoffrey Scott sat on the north fence at Bishop's place, much as he had on the corral fence at Camp Verde, a stalk of dried grass in his mouth, the stiff breeze continually socking its fists at the ranch, the wind in this place never ceasing. The camels, however, didn't seem to notice, immune to blowing dust. Strangely docile animals, probably because of Hadji's training in the beginning: heavy rocks on canvas, days on end. But, Geoffrey Scott figured the camels knew how to put on a good show of not caring, savvy beasts that they were. He watched how they settled on their haunches and chewed thorns as if they'd been given the finest food, but he also saw them bite. They were temperamental. They had their biases about people they disliked. He'd heard stories how they could push a man against a wall and make him fall, Hoyne for one. Helpless. Then they'd sit on him to show who was boss. Or try to smash him to smithereens.

Bottom line, he wanted more than anything to ride a camel, especially Adababa. Beale's white camel, Seid, who was no albino but unusually light-colored, was the tallest and the biggest, but that animal was off limits to anyone except Beale and his closest friends. Geoffrey Scott resolved not to show his desire, in any way, to Hadji Ali, the man who knew gamesmanship, the dark-skinned man who still, in private, wore his long robes, though he was developing a penchant for overalls. He was trying to be an American, but most everybody else knew him, except Geoffrey Scott, as a Mexican. A foreigner always at the edge of what mattered, except he was captain of the camels. No one had any say about those animals unless approved by Hadji Ali.

When a man tried to ride the camels for one of the experiments, Hadji Ali folded his arms and leaned back to analyze them through narrowed eyes. The Syrian could be cruel, his mirth well hidden from those who belittled Arabs and their deserts or anyone who was ill-served enough to be born there. Geoffrey Scott knew Hadji laughed at the "blind dog" who was attempting to ride and shaking his head at his ignorance, his lack of wisdom about the great value of *Attah Allah*, his horsemen's approach to anything with four legs.

When Geoffrey Scott watched this experiment on the very camel he hoped to ride, he tamped his laughter because this man had more guts than he did about getting on a camel's back. Adababa was the perfect name for that particular camel. The rider bumping along, ba ba ba, until he was thrown into the sand. Something crazy and affectionate about the name Adababa.

But first he had to outsmart Hadji Ali to make sure he wouldn't laugh at him. He would know as much as he could. During the day, while everyone awaited word from Lieutenant Beale, scheduled to return to the Colorado River and California any day now, Geoffrey Scott became a familiar sight on the fence until even Hadji Ali held up his hand in greeting when Geoffrey Scott climbed into place during slow times, sometimes staring into space, sometimes puzzling over the animals, but always aware of the

Syrian's moves with the camels. During the night he dreamt of the desert passing swiftly beneath him. The sand far below. The Joshuas spotting the landscape, arms up as they surrendered to his vast knowledge and riderly abilities. The cacti, the shrubs, like a sandstorm, everything whirling. Only he and Adababa remained a stark outline in the sky, in the blue that was the most amazing blue ever known. Blue, stark blue, nothing hinting of another color. His learning, however, was more the stuff of dreams than experiential. This fact both soothed and irritated him.

"When can I ride?" he finally asked Hadji Ali one morning, casually, almost as if a breeze were blowing and he was commenting on its insignificance.

Hadji Ali raised his eyebrows in surprise. "You want to ride camel? You think you can stay on camel?"

"I have a feeling I better learn how to ride. Something's coming. Feel it in my bones."

"Bones?" Hadji stared at him relentlessly, almost stared a hole through him then rolled his eyes. Geoffrey Scott felt the intensity of that stare, a magnifying glass capturing sunlight, hard to bear, but he felt a greater resolve than he'd had before.

"I've been watching the camels. Understand them better than you think. Give me a chance."

"I don't let many men ride my animals."

"I respect your camels. I respect what they can do. I won't disappoint you, I promise."

"If you promise to know this is camel, not horse. If you promise to know you are riding wind to stars." Hadji Ali laughed out loud as he walked toward Adababa.

At that moment, Geoffrey Scott suspected Hadji knew how he'd been pining to ride this particular camel, that he'd been waiting for this moment to let his pent-up energy loose on this prince of the desert, this long-legged master of sand and travel, this magic carpet. Hadji Ali laughed when he put the reins over Adababa's head and handed them to Geoffrey Scott. "You think you can ride? That we will see."

When Geoffrey Scott found himself atop Adababa, sitting tall on the animal's back, reins in hand, feeling every muscle of the animal beneath him, feeling the animal's desire to run, he remembered what it was to be an excellent horseman. Yet, beneath him was a camel with its own gait, not a horse. He must remember to respond to its camel-ness most of all, its nuances, its flanks, its withers or whatever they were. Remembering those things, he and Adababa flew over the desert, much like in his dreams, and he felt the joy of hot sands and treeless terrain.

"Adababa," he yelled when he was out of Hadji Ali's hearing. "Adababa." He felt like a wild man, a free man, someone who never lived behind fences or walls. Master of the desert. Fleet-footed wonder. "Run, Adababa. Run." Then, all too soon, he was back to Hadji Ali, the man who watched without laughing, the man who knew when he saw someone who comprehended *Attah Allah*.

* * * * *

The word came. Finally.

Beale, making his way back across the 35th parallel toward the West, this time with a group of surveyors, sent a message via a rogue mail carrier whose horse swam across the swift current of the Colorado River to get to Bishop:

> "Supposed to be at the ranch in April but am still in Arizona Territory. Running dangerously short of supplies. Military escort is nowhere in sight, and Mojaves don't want anyone near their river. Too many white people flooding through. The expedition's in a bad way. Getting desperate. Counting on you. Don't want to starve or fail when we're so near."

After reading this message, Stephen Bishop convinced Hadji Ali and the adventurers hanging around the ranch taking any part-time work they could, that Beale needed help. Immediately. Even before immediately. Bishop chose twenty camels, including Adababa—ten of them for their swiftness, ten for packing supplies, and told Geoffrey Scott he needed him to ride with the expedition that had suddenly become more important than anything else. After all, Geoffrey Scott had built a reputation. Maybe he was a ranch hand, but Bishop asked for help more times than not. And he had ingratiated himself with Hadji Ali, the two of them having an understanding of sorts. Somehow, Bishop was privy to this information.

Against his will, Geoffrey Scott found himself in a fantastical web. He'd built roads in godforsaken places and dug loose sand that slid back down to where it was dug. On grades too impossible for roads. He'd labored to create surfaces for wagons and their supplies. He'd hung around the military and heard their talk about "slaves, savages, and Mormons." Now Stephen Bishop had ten pack camels and ten riding camels heading back to the same godforsaken territory. "We need you," he'd said to Geoffrey Scott and Hadji Ali. "Someone who has a feel for what these animals are all about."

Late in March, Bishop's team readied itself to leave the ranch near Los Angeles. Forty men and twenty camels. Six wagons. Six horses, oxen, a few pack and riding mules strung behind.

"Before we leave, I need each of you to get a feel for these camels," Stephen told the men, though he didn't say much about other plans. "You may need to do some hard riding."

The camels were taller than palm trees, it seemed, when each of the young men stood by their sides for the first time, trying to figure out how to mount them. Stephen Bishop, riding Seid, Beale's favorite, demonstrated. "Here's how to make the camel kneel. You'll have to fasten a supply saddle on this unwieldy body. Then spread your legs, jump on its back, and hold on for dear life. Wrap one leg around the horn and cross that foot with the other to lock a seat. A camel isn't a horse. It doesn't move like a horse."

A few of the boys mounted the camel without listening to Stephen's postscript about the animal's unusual gait. More than one found himself in soft sand, brushing red dirt from his collar, his hat, his britches. The good humor ran high while riders flew through the air, salt and peppering the landscape. Besting a camel was another matter besides being a good horseman. Some took this seriously. Some did not. Finally, with more practice than they would have wanted had they asked, the riders were able to keep their seat.

When it came his turn, Geoffrey Scott waved at Hadji Ali, and the Syrian held one thumb up. "You ride," he cupped his hands around his mouth and then clapped them together. "You ride fast like before."

Geoffrey Scott found a comfortable place on the camel's hump and hooked one foot to the other. The animal leaned forward onto its knees, slowly rocking to its feet, and Geoffrey Scott knew what to expect. So much power in the camel's chest, its mammoth torso, its gigantic heart ticking somewhere inside. Geoffrey flicked his wrist gently, the riding crop tickling one side of the camel, and just like that, he was flying again.

"Adababa," he yelled, remembering the freedom he'd felt when shouting the animal's name, feeling the surge of power, the joy of being alive and traveling like a man wrapped in scarves on a desert covered with the shapes of waves, the sun a brass horn. He was aware of Hadji Ali watching him and exulted in the glory of knowing what a camel could be.

After those who were horsemen became acclimated to the camels, they returned to the comfort of their own horses, some on mules, then embarked for their destination: Beaver Lake, not far from the Colorado River. Pah-Ute Creek. Good spirits ruled the day until they saw the pictographs. Bishop dismounted to interpret what the signs meant, then told the men to find warmth from their clothes, blankets, even their animals. Anything besides fire that night at Beaver Lake.

A sliver of moon shone dimly—a fragile crescent—and the circle of men huddled in their blankets to keep warm in the high desert cold. Hadji Ali made sure the camels were hobbled in a makeshift corral while the others tethered their horses and mules. Wrapped in blankets of every kind, hats pulled around their ears, the men sat quietly, sensing something big was about to happen.

They had seen the pictographs just before sunset. The Xs. The warnings to stay away. Not to cross. They could feel a rupture in the air. A strong message from the Indians who were letting them know they were not welcome. No jokes tonight. No loud laughter.

* * * * *

The sunset had been nothing dramatic on this, one of those soft evenings when the sun dropped quietly into the folds of mountains. High, dry clouds. No colors. No fanfare. Everything still except for a few birds dashing across the sky. Profiles of flight. Geoffrey Scott sat on a boulder, wrapped in the blanket he'd brought from Kansas. Nights were cold in early spring.

The contours of the desert floor slanted away from him, up, down, in and out of shadow. The configurations of Orion and Cassiopeia pressed into the dark background. He bunched the corners of his blanket and pulled it tightly around him, glad for the cold on his cheeks and ears. Glad to be part of this vastness that spoke with no words, this large world of the Mojave Desert. He breathed in the silence but was still perplexed. Tomorrow's expedition, a confrontation with the Indians, bothered him. Guns again. Rifles. Not his style to kill anybody.

Then he tuned into the familiar sounds of camp—the men preparing for the night, talking quietly, their words rising out of the stillness like smoke, then thinning into the night air. He knew they cleaned their weapons and tended to ablutions, thanks to Pah-Ute Creek and its ample spring bubbling up from the base of black and reddish boulders, and he put the toe of his boot in the water. He could hear this miraculous spring now. He could hear the mules shifting from foot to foot, then the sounds of the camels settling in for the night, their loads removed. Food nearby. Enough water in their bellies. The idyllic calm of this evening bore no predictions about tomorrow and what might happen. But Geoffrey Scott knew a line had been drawn in the sand. Pictures. Warnings. He suspected no one would rest well on this night, though Hadji Ali could sleep through the whining of the loudest wind, that was for sure.

But then the clouds began to thicken, curd-like, and there was his mother in his mind, framed by a ring of blood. His beloved mother who did nothing to those ruffians. The one who stirred curds. "Cottage cheese," she had said when she skimmed the milk for curds, standing in the kitchen, the skimmer in hand. And then her face and skimmer turned into vapor, thick into thin. Gone. His mother gone before she had a chance to know what a good job he'd done helping build a road across the Southwest, graded edges of arroyos, using his hammer and saw to make bridges for emigrants, mail carriers, and soldiers. She would have pulled him to her side, put her arm around him, and told him he was a "right smart young 'un." She would've kissed his cheek. Her face would have glowed. But his father interrupted the reverie and spoke across the miles. "Go. Be a man," saying the words Geoffrey Scott had played over in his mind so many times, his father's sunken cheeks lingering on the "Go." "Deal with your own life. Go." His father slammed the door and would have kicked him in the butt if he'd waited any longer to leave.

"Hey Scott," someone shouted out in the night that was becoming fuller of noise and clouds by the minute. "Get yourself back here, wherever you are. Time to reconnoiter." He picked himself up, brushed sand off his *chaparreras*, and crammed his blanket into his arms.

Tomorrow. What would they do after the warnings in the sand? War clubs on both ends of the line. Portraits of a mass of Indians on one side of the line and twelve sickly white men with hats on the other. Blood-covered arrows stuck in their chests. Actual red paint.

Stephen Bishop seemed preoccupied, moody even, when Geoffrey Scott returned to the camp, the toes of his boots still wet from the edge of the spring. He sat next to Bishop, who leaned back on a small wooden frame serving as his chair and wondered if the man would be approachable.

"Any chance you can tell us what we're doing here with these camels?" he asked in a private way. "Rumors are everywhere."

Bishop paused. Worked his jaw, bones shifting to the left then right. "I guess you'll know soon enough," he whispered. "The Mojaves have had it with all of us disregarding the crops they've planted. You know that. They're set on keeping us from their sacred river, but Beale needs supplies big-time. Hasn't reached the Colorado yet, and he's plumb out of food."

"But the Indians seem friendly, especially when we feed them," Geoffrey Scott said, as if he could be helpful by repeating what Bishop already knew. He quieted himself.

"Military promised they'd be here." Bishop moving his jaw sideways again, wrapping his blanket tighter around his shoulders, "but no one's seen hide nor hair. You saw that line in the sand, those signs that say 'Stay where you are.' Folks are panicking after the big dip in abundance. The country's feeling the pull of the West and wide-open spaces opened up by the Mexican War. They think they have the chance to start over, maybe homesteading, maybe striking it rich with the gold and silver everybody's salivating about. People'll keep coming, no matter what they're looking for. Beale's only trying to make that easier. But he wouldn't want what we're about to do," Bishop sank back into his chair. "But damn it, I have to keep the promise I made him, even if it means fighting the Mojaves. Maybe we'll have to build a fort someday. Military's ready for that, but they're not here now, are they? Sunrise'll tell us what to do for sure."

* * * * *

The next morning, the men rode single file in a caravan, Stephen Bishop in the lead. But suddenly, he reined his horse, motioned for a halt, dismounted, and knelt before a second line in the sand: more pictographs from the Mojaves. Riding a camel this morning, Geoffrey Scott signaled to Adababa to stop and kneel, then dismounted to stand behind Bishop who was examining the symbols created with the point of a stick. He counted the cartoonish figures. "At least a hundred Indians in that picture," Scott said. "These boys mean business."

The other men dismounted and crowded in behind them. "More like turn back or die," the man behind his shoulder said, adjusting the bandana around his neck, sliding it to the right until the tie looped even with his chin.

This was a far cry from the first reception for Beale's expedition. Two years ago, when they'd arrived at the Colorado, the Mojaves brought pumpkins into camp, even watermelons and cantaloupes, their men devouring the produce before the trade was complete. And the Indians seemed happy to trade for men's old shirts and kerchiefs. Tobacco, too. They watched like children when Beale's men inflated a rubber raft and the horses, mules, and camels swam across beside the boat made of air. A party almost, though the Indians weren't disappointed when some horses and mules disappeared in the current, only to be netted further down the river and served for dinner. Now, they were unwelcome white men. Enemies.

He stared down at the second set of pictographs. What happened in two years' time, he wondered, trying to find his balance in the sand, his heels sinking. More settlers coming through with herds of cattle, he mused. Using scarce water on their way to California's gold. Eating ripe crops. He'd seen what they could do. He'd been there. He'd heard the rumors at the fort, no attention given to source or reliability: rumors about wagon trains being wiped out by Apaches; rumors of scalps being taken, and savage men deflowering women. More rumors of Mormons unsettling the natives by warning them about the "Americats" who would push the natives aside. No regard. Rumors about a wagon train from Arkansas being ambushed and massacred by Indians up in Utah territory in a place called Mountain Meadows. More talk about how the government was going to control these enemies of Americans, and how the military would strike back from every direction: East, West, even from the South with troops brought up the Colorado. They'd unseat the uppity Brigham Young from his position as governor, the man who thinks he's king. Trying to take over the West.

But whatever had happened in those past two years and whoever had caused a change in the Indians' attitude, Bishop's group of men were looking at a warning.

"We can't just ignore them," Geoffrey Scott said. "They're drawing lines. These boys are serious."

But in no uncertain terms, Bishop spoke out: "I've read Beale's missive. 'The expedition's in a bad way. Getting desperate. Counting on you.'

Beale's words." He deflected Geoffrey Scott's caution with a wave of his hand. "We need to try. All of us. Getting to Beale is our only purpose."

Thus, they erased both lines in the sand with the hooves of their mules, horses, and camels. Bishop would keep this appointment come hell or high water. He'd keep his word.

* * * * *

On their first attempt at crossing, the Mojaves were nowhere in sight. Believing they had been blessed by good luck, Bishop's men launched a rubber raft with a supply wagon secured to its side. "We're on our way," some of them shouted and waved at those still on shore. But then, when the raft headed its nose into the strong current, at least seven hundred warriors rose up on the horizon, out of the ether, it seemed. They had painted themselves in black and red stripes. Most were taller than the average man.

As Geoffrey Scott stood on shore, standing behind Adababa where he could see nothing but the boat and its supplies in their fledgling crossing, the painted men moved forward, seemingly passive but menacing and mute. With arrested solemnity on their faces, they watched the white men and the rubber contraption crossing their river. But then the raft approached the halfway point. As if orchestrated by their gods, the Mojaves lifted their bows in concert and shot long arrows into the raft's rubber sides, transforming it into a limp, wounded animal. The men, so enthusiastic about taking supplies to Beale and his men, turned the boat, hoping for enough air to return to shore, of mixed mind about getting any closer to Indians who aimed their bows at their corporeal bodies. But the Indians disappeared. Puzzled, the men of Bishops' party inflated another raft to try again. But when the raft reached mid-river again, the warriors appeared, their arrows flying until the raft became lifeless as before, but this time more convincingly. The men returned to shore, grateful to be alive, and Bishop's party, at a gallop and in a flurry, retreated to Pah-Ute Creek. There they would reassess the situation. The Indians sank back into the landscape, almost as if the horizon were water.

* * * * *

That night, watching Bishop toast his hands by the campfire on the west side of the river, Geoffrey Scott knew Lieutenant Beale and his expedition were in trouble. They needed supplies. But, according to the scout, they'd be facing Mojaves who'd amassed several tribes, triple their original size. Maybe more than a thousand Indians were gathered at the river awaiting them.

Staring into the flames and shifting to the left of the smoke, he faced another dilemma: he might have to kill an Indian, or at least that's what, in one of his bursts of conversation, Hadji Ali told him. "Kill or be killed." By a man decorated with feathers and painted to look fierce with red and black paint. But he didn't want to kill. Nothing. Nada. The main thing the Indians'd done wrong was to let their peaceful lives be interrupted. He wasn't born yesterday, and he heard his mother's convincing voice: "Every man wants the same thing." But he also knew they needed to cross the river.

Stephen Bishop assessed every man around the fire, figuring who would be open to the next move. "I think I've figured out a chance we can take. Nothing's for sure out here, but we've been using camels to carry supplies, right? Unloaded, some can run over forty miles an hour, faster than your horse anytime. And a camel's more startling. Element of surprise," he winked, full of his last-stand plan to get across the river. "Twenty camels should do it, plus some hard riding. We're going to need speed. Top speed. I'll need volunteers willing to raise their rifles. Some of you practiced riding before we left, but don't think you know a camel just because you've ridden a horse. World of difference."

Geoffrey Scott raised his hand. "I know camels." He stood up, his chest tilted high in his tattered clothes, comfortable with the manhood he'd grown into since leaving Kansas. Hadji Ali raised his hand and stood, too. Count him in. Gradually, the two were joined by eighteen others, most of whom had been thrown from the camels back at the ranch. Twenty men, prompted to join up, partly for honor, partly because Bishop promised money to those who would cross the Colorado with him. They could all use the money, and Geoffrey Scott, admittedly, had plans to return to Kansas when this encounter was behind him. Money would help. He needed to see his father again. Needed to know there was something between them.

"The rest of you," Bishop ordered the men still sitting, "unpack the loads we took from the camels' backs. Bury those supplies in the tules and also the ones in the wagons."

These men rose in the firelight—black shadows tossing the remaining coffee from their cups, tucking them back in their saddle bags, and proceeding to unload the supplies. A line of men, daubed yellow and black by the fire's shifting light, started in on the heavy loads in the wagons. Soon, the night was filled with the sound of shovels cutting into soft sand.

"Okay, men," Bishop said to those standing in a circle around the fire. "I've sent a messenger to Major Hoffman and heard back from him yesterday. They're on their way but he won't divide his troops or send half in a hurry. They won't make it in time. No help, basically." In unison, the men groaned. "The military never seems to be around when they're needed," Bishop continued. "But all of you are good with guns. Savvy frontiersmen. Sure, the Mojaves put up an impressive resistance, but we have our own resources. I believe we'll get through. But remember, we're not here to make war. Only to cross the river. No wounding unless absolutely necessary."

"Easy for you to say…" one of the men said, but, receiving an elbow in the ribs, didn't finish his cynical comment.

"I'll make this short, maybe not so sweet. Three of you—Boggs, Hale, Swinton—you'll stay here to guard the supplies. We'll give you ample ammunition. The half that's burying supplies will leave for the ranch tonight and take the empty wagons and extra animals back. The other twenty will stay. Understand? And whoever is staying, get some sleep. Lots to accomplish tomorrow."

"There's no way twenty of us can go up against a thousand Indians," one of the men said.

"But we've got camels and rifles," Bishop answered. "None of which the Indians have."

"How'll we ever get through a mass of angry Indians? All I kin say is it's Maker time tomorrow." There was murmuring in the circle. A passel of concern.

"I guess we'll know the answer soon enough. But understand this, men," Bishop said, standing his full six feet to make a lasting impression. "We have no truck with the Indians. The Mojaves've had enough of us coming through their land and disregarding what they've planted, giving them no respect. But, lots of Americans—fortune seekers and adventurers they may be—ramrod their way west at a fever-high pitch, demanding the government give them protection from the savages, or so they see them. Some folks abuse the privilege of crossing Indian land, and now, we all pay. The Mojaves'll protect their sacred river at all costs, but try not to hurt any of them. Beale would be outraged if we did. Shoot your guns in the air but don't shoot at anyone unless you absolutely have to."

"But a thousand Indians? Who are you kidding, Sam?"

"Quiet down," Bishop continued. "It's crazy, but I think my idea can work."

During the next fifteen minutes, Bishop unveiled his plan of attack and the formations they would use: four lines of five camels and riders each. "The Colorado narrows to three hundred yards. Swift water still, but the crossing is more palatable here. Take your guns, but I think the element of surprise will be in our favor."

Hadji, the guardian of the camels, stood in the background, away from the fire, smiling an Ali Baba smile. Geoffrey Scott saw it, privy to the growing comraderie between the two of them. Bishop had asked which camels were fastest. Then he'd told Hadji to handpick the animals and load them lightly with two hundred fifty pounds rather than the thousand they could carry. "Bishop knows camels," Hadji had said to Geoffrey Scott when they were preparing to leave the ranch. Now he was smiling a knowing smile and looking smug about the power of *Attah Allah* and what's more, Allah.

* * * * *

Adababa liked to run fast, no doubt about it, though its pace—demanded by its human owners more than its own impulses—was ordinarily slow and steady. But when Hadji Ali and Geoffrey Scott removed the load from its back in the remote corners of the Mojave Desert, both knew the camel wanted to run—his flesh free of the burden he usually carried, ready to change its slow and steady pace to the speed of the wind. No more methodical for him. No more plodding. But Adababa waited until he was told to do so—the way of an obedient camel.

The six wagons, six mules, and twenty men had rumbled back to Bishop's ranch in the dead of night, hoping they were out of the hearing of the Indians gathering on the banks of the Colorado some ten miles away. When the sun rose out of the East, the remainder of Bishop's men rode forward on the backs of camels, sitting high and grand, galloping Lords of the Desert. Geoffrey Scott stroked the cover of his Beecher's Bible brought from Kansas in his pack. "Watch over us, Mama," he felt like shouting out loud. Adababa followed close behind Stephen Bishop who rode Seid, leading the charge at forty miles per hour. The motley crew would catch the Mojaves by surprise, though most of the men in Stephen Bishop's band of twenty had visions swirling through their heads that they were goners, ready to be encased in coffins, mere men facing hundreds of war-painted Indians, stubborn, angry, bows raised, in no mood for negotiating.

Adababa ran at top speed, faster than Geoffrey Scott had imagined he could run, all demands about carrying supplies gone, a release into freedom, run, camel, run. Run your heart out, Adababa. Every muscle. Every leg moving at maximum speed and efficiency. Everything transformed into lightning across the sand, padded feet perfectly adapted to this grainy skin of desert. Soft, two-toed feet bounding across the kind of territory camels were born to inhabit. Something primitive about the way he ran. Something invigorating—thundering toward a wall of bows and arrows that wouldn't be able to hit their mark because the camels had sprouted wings and were flying toward confused men in loincloths. And Adababa would do whatever Geoffrey Scott asked of him because the Kansan recognized his magic, power, and strength.

Hadji Ali rode neck-and-neck with Geoffrey Scott, riding hard against the Mojaves and more warriors gathered from the Pah-Utes and Yumas, tribes that were sometimes friends with each other, most of the time not, warriors who had overlooked old animosities and stood united to protect the Mojave's land, their crops, and most of all their river, the one the white man wanted as their own. Scouts had been observing the movement of the small band of white men coming from the west as well as the military troops approaching from the south and were prepared to confront whoever arrived at the river first.

Not unlike a waterfall disrupting the surface of a waiting pond, the twenty men, their massive camels, and the Indians were suddenly face to face—hundreds of barely covered bodies versus the twenty men and their mounts, one side wanting to protect the land of the Mojaves who harvested the fertile land of the Colorado's alluvial soil: corn, pumpkins, and wheat. A thousand years of repetition. The other side wanting to cross the water.

The natives wore red and black paint and strips of leather across their loins. On their heads, they wore full war regalia with elemental feathers. Horrific, painted faces; charms chanted over by the holy men of medicine. With the help of the mighty *Mutavilya*, who had created the river with its plants and animals, they believed they could stop the white man from trampling their crops and their lands where they grazed their animals. Stop them from using their river that they had tamed for centuries though they did not want to kill either, both sides testing each other's resolve.

The tribes were prepared for everything except what they saw: twenty huge camels racing toward them faster than any animal they had ever seen run before. Camels. In the Southwest. In Arizona Territory. Close to California. Camels that ran swiftly, that didn't hesitate. Given their heads. Given the whip. Given everything a rider could give them to keep them moving toward the natives. A gamble by Stephen Bishop, who told his men that his plan may or may not work but that it was the only ploy he could think of in the need to cross the Colorado and get supplies to Lieutenant Beale. A high-stakes gamble.

A gamble by Geoffrey Scott, thundering toward the many natives lined up in row after row after row, riding on the magnificent Adababa, overcoming fear about what might happen, closing his eyes only in the beginning. Geoffrey Scott was a man who would fight when needed. Geoffrey Scott, a decisive man, one to be counted on, one to be on the forefront rather than hiding behind, something he had always feared—that he'd hidden behind his mother's skirts, that he'd been passive and uncommitted to the cause of free men, except for the feelings he'd had when she told stories. Yes, he'd been influenced by her devotions that had trickled down into his consciousness, but now he was gambling his own life in a ride toward the Indians on a colossal animal unseen by most men on this continent.

The Mojaves had seen camels and their clumsy hooves before, but only as pack animals. They'd never witnessed them unpacked and running at top speed, and they darted every which way. Riding into the heart of hundreds of angry men dressed in animal skins over their loins and bare chests painted red and black, Geoffrey Scott feared the blossom of blood. But the surprise of the camels' speed and the sound of rifles being shot into the air caused the warriors to scatter in confusion, their strength and their mass foundering in the middle.

But then, among the chaos of hundreds of natives retreating and yelling and the massive clouds of dust rising from the undeniably dry earth, Geoffrey Scott found himself and Adababa at the side of one very tall Mojave who was running and angry that he was compelled to do so. Suddenly, Geoffrey Scott knew he'd seen him before: somewhere, though he couldn't be sure. To be safe, he aimed his gun at the painted man, the gun which had been pointed in the air. The Mojave stopped suddenly and jerked back on his bow. Their eyes locked, and a door on time and animosity opened. This bold man made of stone, not moving to the right or the left, though threading his arrow into his bow while all of man stared back at him in the eyes of one, pulled his arm back as if to shoot. But then the Kansan, knowing how much could be taken with one squeeze of a trigger finger, lifted his rifle into the air. He was not at war with this man, whoever he was. In the blur of dust and confusion, the memories of these two men sharpened: the other side of the Colorado, blankets, serapes, the ague—one man shaking uncontrollably, the other man helping. Geoffrey Scott had offered warmth and food.

Just as Elias Scott had been fierce about protecting his homestead and his family, the Mojave was protecting the territory where people of his nation lived, farmed, gave life, and gave in to life. Was the meeting of the Border Ruffians, the Abolitionists, and the natives blocking the river at the crossroads of his mind when Geoffrey Scott lunged forward and away on his camel without taking a shot? The warrior eased the string on his bow, both understanding the history between themselves—the shaking and hungry warrior, now the proud Mojave whose trees had been cut by emigrants and whose crops had been trampled with wagon wheels; the young man, Geoffrey Scott, the abolitionist from Kansas whose mother had been killed because she cared about people she'd never met.

Adababa charged past Kwanyumai who stood stock still, amazement on his face, his bow slack. Geoffrey Scott saw flinty pride carved into the elemental man dressed in scanty clothes, a proud man armed with a shaft of arrows. He wanted to bow his head or salute or show some sign of respect, but instead lifted the tip of his rifle higher into the air. The Mojave hesitated, then ran from the path of the huge animals disrupting the plans of his tribe.

* * * * *

When the charge was over, Adababa slowed to a walk, arched its neck, and stretched to its ten feet of height. Doubly powerful now, his mettle proven. Then he pulled his head back and tucked his chin.

"It looks like that camel's laughing," Geoffrey Scott said to Hadji Ali, riding by his side and patting the camel's neck in appreciation. "It does. Saying 'who cares what those Indians think they can do to stop us.' Never saw anything like that before. Never seen anything like that, period. Did you see that?"

"*Attah Allah*," Hadji Ali said, one proud man. "Now people will understand about camels."

"You rode like a whirlwind, Hadji. Like you've fought battles before."

"I know what my animals can do, and maybe I've done things you'll never know. Maybe you have no idea who Hadji Ali is."

"Maybe," Geoffrey Scott said, still surprised at that much information. Hadji was a man who knew about camels and kept to himself, wasn't he? A Mohammetan? What else should he know? But the success of the charge was still talking to him. "So many of those Indians. The plan worked. It did. And nobody got killed."

"*Attah Allah* can be miracle. You see with your eyes."

"*Attah Allah* did good work, my friend." He paused and looked back at the water soon to be crossed to get supplies to Beale. "You trained them right, Hadji. Right? I know something good when I see it. And you're my friend. I guess now's as good a time as any to tell you that."

The Syrian jerked his camel's reins to the right and trotted to the water's edge, pretending he hadn't heard, maybe uncomfortable with sentiment or with Geoffrey Scott's unfamiliar use of English words that he'd been learning in his time alone.

Next to the river, where they would soon inflate the rafts and send them across with supplies for Beale, Geoffrey Scott lifted his shoulders in a shrug then settled them, thinking again about Hadji Ali and how little he knew about him. Hadji'd taught him about camels, but there was nothing new in his nonresponse. So what? he thought. The man's not interested. Even so, the Syrian was his friend, even if he didn't lay claim to the man from Kansas. But, for now, he had other things on his mind. Mainly the man who'd been ready to shoot his bow. The one who'd unnotched his arrow. Geoffrey Scott or Adababa could've been lying on the ground with feathers lodged in their lungs. He could've been dead by now.

He told Adababa to sit, dismounted, then joined the men to inflate the rafts.

CHAPTER NINE

AN EYE FOR AN EYE

KANSAS—1862

Geoffrey Scott. Twenty-two. Riding one horse for too many days. Leaving Sam Bishop's ranch in Southern California and leaving Adababa in care of Hadji Al; crossing the Colorado River on a ferry at Fort Mojave where camels had surprised the Indians. Floating across that water made him remember his encounter with Kwanyumai. The warrior. He now knew the meaning of that name. He'd met him again this time because the Mojave had gravitated to Fort Mojave to build walls and become an interpreter. Kwami learned English in between time. Surprisingly well-schooled. Strange bedfellows, but friends of sorts.

Riding across the scraggly yet always brutal desert, riding over the same Beale's Trail he helped build, he rode on to Ft. Defiance where he traded his horse for a rested one and where his worst fears were confirmed: the Civil War was as vicious as ever in Kansas and Missouri, the place where he'd once lived, the border close to where his father holed up, if he was still alive. Kansas Jayhawkers were exchanging tit for tat with the Missouri Ruffians and vice versa. Bad blood boiled, both sides running roughshod over the border to take revenge and plunder anything left standing, his father most likely in the middle of the heat. Cutting up toward Kansas on the Santa Fe Trail he followed the Cimarron Cutoff where he made good time. When he rested, he groomed his horse's sweaty hide with a silver-backed brush belonging to his mother's father. Watering. Combing its mane. Sleeping five hours at the most, throwing the saddle on his horse's back again, riding off in the early morning dark. He had to get to his father somehow. He needed to know there was still family between them even if the old coot had slipped a cog; curse the man for sending him away in the first place.

No mail had come. No pleas from his father, though there never had been much from him except for a couple of lines in a cursory note near one Christmastime: "Hope you're a man by now." When would the man ever utter a different sentiment? No word from anyone except for Civil War rumors everywhere. People singing "John Brown's body lies a-mouldering in the grave." The tune flying on the air. Birds knew about it. Passed it on. "He's gone to be a soldier in the army of the Lord!"

How could he help from being in the thick of things, bitter as he was? He'd known John Brown from church before the man's son was killed. Everybody in Osawatomie knew John Brown. But something was not right with his father. Geoffrey Scott could feel the ailing. Could feel it on the ranch in California. Maybe he never should have left him. Not for one day. But the old man kicked him off the homestead while fire was still smoldering, stick-like fingers of charred uprights standing, only three of them. His father demanded his son take leave days after burying his mother. Mother, Father, Son. No more.

How many times had that scene flashed through Geoffrey Scott's mind when hacking at a stubborn cottonwood to get wood to build a bridge? And now, while he galloped back toward Kansas and the old homestead, he kept seeing the image of his father with his hand raised, the wrinkled grief on the old man's face, the bending into resignation, the pushing against the pain in his abdomen with folded arms.

Geoffrey Scott had been a disappointment, no doubt. "Honor thy father and thy mother, that thy days may be long upon the earth," he'd been taught when his father was in his right mind. Something like that. But his mother never understood the fury of men who felt entitled to put other men into bondage and call them subhuman. She knew nothing of retribution, either. Nothing of the Jayhawkers' big troubles in Missouri's pro-slavery counties. She only knew what felt right and wrong to her.

When the horse and rider crossed the last ridge where he could see the old homestead rebuilt, he reined in. Was his father still there, ornery as ever? Would he want to see the prodigal son? The homestead was a simplified version of itself. Only half of what it had once been—a bird with one wing. A square of four walls. No extra rooms. The charred uprights had crumbled to ash a long time ago and new ones had been placed to build half a house.

A thin curlicue of smoke tangled out of the chimney. Geoffrey Scott suspected his father was still there, though it was possible a stranger sat inside tending a fire. It had been six years since he'd seen the feisty man who wouldn't take help from any living creature except his horse. Crusty old bird. He probably wouldn't welcome his son, even though his boy had helped build a road, an important one. He'd proven himself sturdy. Manly, his father might say.

Geoffrey Scott tied his horse to a post in the yard. The old barn had not been rebuilt. Four scraggly goats in the pasture. No cattle. No horses. Just goats and a large stretch of pasture with yellowed grass. Cautiously, he grabbed the stock of his new rifle in his right hand, approached the house, and crossed a newly built porch, which made him think some things were good. The first step creaked. Geoffrey Scott looked down at his dusty boots streaked with traces of grease and weeks of mud. He knocked on the door. Again. Then he turned the knob with care, no need to frighten anyone inside. A slim crack in the door. A peek inside before opening wider. A man. White hair separated into oily strands. Rocking. Head laid flat against the headrest. Shoes tapping on the floor in time to an unheard song.

"Close the door," his father said.

"Dad?" He left his rifle in its sheath near the door.

"Saw you riding up the back pasture. Can't mistake my son for one of those hellions from Missouri always ready to do major damage when nobody's looking and even when they are."

Geoffrey Scott removed his hat and walked slowly to the rocking chair, stood to its side.

"I got a few of your letters," his father said, his voice less strong than last time Geoffrey Scott heard it. "Sounds like you're a man of the big world now. All that wide-open West. Working with important men from the government."

"You got the letters, then. I wondered if they made it."

"Did."

"But I came this time instead of a letter. Paper doesn't mean that much."

"I haven't been looking after you now, have I? Is that your complaint?"

"No, sir. That's how you struck the bargain. Taught me to look after myself."

"I am tired, Geoffrey. Bone tired." The once-deep baritone voice that could sing out in church, as well as tell people the right thing to do, sounded hoarse. Raspy. Worn. His father half of himself, maybe less. "Went to a meeting last night," he continued, his words flat, no particular emphasis. "Osceola was bad enough but the pro-slavers are preparing an attack again, maybe Lawrence this time. I need to get ready." He pushed his hips back in the rocker and pushed on the arms of the chair to settle more upright. "Bloody, bloody Kansas." He paused. Sucked in a big breath. Let it out. Sat quiet. "They could win. Those men who treat other men like goats, worse than that."

Geoffrey moved toward a wooden bench across from the rocking chair. Sat on it. Stretched his feet out, then took his boots off. "Should have left these at the door for all the dust they've seen."

The loudest sound in the room was the runner on the rocker creaking back and forth on the wood floor. His father's words sat quiet inside himself, though Geoffrey Scott figured that wouldn't last long.

"I met some of those men at posts out West," he said to a man he wasn't sure was listening. "Fighting the same war out in Arizona Territory. Coming to blows with each other over Negroes and cotton. Rounding up the Indians like a flock of goats. Put them here. Put them there. Goats. Do not let these goats go anyplace except where we tell them."

"You rode a long way, son." His father never stopped rocking his chair. Slowly. Methodically. Rocking steady. "What do you want?"

"I thought of you while I was out there, all rolled up in a sleeping bag at night under stars and the changing moon, sometimes clouds. I couldn't stay away longer, no matter what you have to say about it."

"We supposed to embrace now?"

"You're a crusty fart, sir." Geoffrey Scott smiled big. "Where'd you get so out of patience with the world? With me? Your only son?"

"Your mother tempered me some." The corners of the old man's mouth curved up, barely noticeable, a twitch of a smile. "Six years gone now." He paused again, as if the effort of speaking was a task. Rocked a few times. Looked up at the ceiling, then sighed. "If she were here she'd hug you up one side and down the other. She loved you too much, she did. Smothered you. A quilt. She was a quilt to you."

"Why'd you make me leave?"

"So that's what you came home for. To ask that whiny question." He rocked. A wooden man in a wooden chair. Long silence. Creaking floor.

Runners pressing into the wood. Back and forth. Geoffrey Scott checked to see if a rut had been worn. How many days since he'd left had his father sat and rocked in this chair?

"I told you already," his father finally spoke up, but still without any variation in his voice. "You need to do for yourself somewhere besides next to an old man and a smothering woman. Too tight, our little threesome. Suffocating for a young man."

"But you're still here."

"That I am."

"I expect to stay until you come West with me. Been working a ranch in California. Taking care of camels, no less."

The rocking again. The passage of time. His father's foot lightly tapping the floor each time he rocked forward. Up. Down. Up. Down. "You told me about them in a letter." He bent his head back again, paused in his rocking, and rested his hands across his midsection. "What good are camels except to those A-rabs?" He coughed a deep cough, dredging up something deep inside. "No self-respecting horseman would switch to a camel."

"They can go without water for days. You never saw anything like it. They stink, sure. Some of them spit, but they carry hundreds of pounds if you pack them right."

"And what would an old man do out West?"

"Better than being caught in the crossfire of this war. People in Missouri have no mind to back off. Look at Osceola. The murder that doesn't stop. This is a big war, stretched way west of the Mississippi. I hear the Jayhawkers are doing damage, too. Bile and blood everywhere. You need to leave this place. Come with me."

"A young man's world. Not mine anymore."

"That's crazy talk."

"Need to carry your own weight, son. Don't need you to carry mine for me."

"You're stubborn, Father. Go somewhere else. To a place where you can live life instead of be at the mercy of angry men and your own thoughts."

"Those Missouri boys killed your mother, son. Why should I leave them be if they took away the woman who made my life worth it all? Why should I hightail it out of here and let my skinny butt get filled with cowards' buckshot?"

"There is more to being alive than obsessing about the past. Revenge never ends."

"Fancy talk coming from a boy who thinks he knows something. I can take out of here anytime I want."

"I talked to a lot of people. Seen a lot of places. Places you'd like. Places to start over."

"I'm not starting over. I have something I need to finish."

"Then I'll help you finish whatever that is," Geoffrey Scott said, listening to the words float out over the room as if he didn't say them, wondering why he wanted so much from this man who was old, possibly senile, and not the same one he remembered from his time as a boy. "Don't think you can send me off again."

"I don't need a gobsmack stuck to my side." He stopped again. Blinked a few slow blinks, his eyes washed out, their color pale and bleary. More wrinkles than Geoffrey Scott had seen when he first sat down on the bench. "Let me die in peace, not have to worry about you."

His father suddenly grabbed at his abdomen. His face crumpled in pain. Geoffrey Scott leaned forward to spring up, but then sat back. The old man had his dignity, and the facts of his father's longevity were suddenly clear. Geoffrey Scott had sensed this, known it out on Sam Bishop's ranch. He needed to say good-bye, welcome or not.

"You always seemed a tower to me," Geoffrey Scott said quietly. "You're a hard place I couldn't climb. A fortress. High walls."

"True enough."

"But you can't shut me out. I won't let you." Geoffrey Scott could feel some tears rising from his chest, but he knew this was no time for tears. No time was a good time for those when his father was in the room.

"Nobody said this life was easy."

"You're supposed to make it a better place for me. Isn't that what the word, father, is all about?"

"Being a 'father.' That word. Mawkish." He leaned back again and rocked. "Never should have been one."

"But you were. You are."

"Let the Ruffians come and get me, son. They've done their damage. I'm ready for mine. I'm ready for them. But see my musket over by the window? They won't have an easy time of it."

He coughed and doubled over again, mucous coming out of his nose, and his mouth. He raised a stained bandana to his lips.

"I'll be here with you," Geoffrey Scott said, still wondering why he was here in this room and yet determined to be here, wondering why it mattered that he and this man were linked in the great cosmos. "See this," Geoffrey Scott went back to the door where he'd left his rifle. "I'm your son. That's the end of the talk about that. I'll stand with you, Father. I brought something you might like to see. A repeater. A carbine. Lightweight. Short barrel. Traded for it at Fort Mojave. A friend spending his nights experimenting with getting more out of a rifle. He actually liked building guns more than shooting them. This here's one of his trials. Something he wants noticed by the military. Better than anything those Ruffians have."

"Let me see that thing," his father said, bending forward, putting weight on his feet for the first time, rising out of the curved seat of the rocker quicker than Geoffrey Scott imagined he could move. He held out his unsteady hands to take the rifle.

"Takes time to load but look at this. Seven shells." Geoffrey Scott spun the cartridge with his finger. It kept spinning. "Seven rounds. Nobody can load their rifle fast enough to shoot back."

"Damnedest thing I seen in a long time." His father reached out again, this time taking hold of the stock. Geoffrey still held tight to the gun. "You traded for this? What for?"

"Bag of oranges."

"A bag of oranges? I may have seen one or two of them in my lifetime."

"Packed them in from California. Oranges, lemons, surprising things you don't ever see in Kansas. Even in Massachusetts, rest its soul. Haven't seen that place in a long time." Geoffrey released his grip. His father took the rifle into his hands, stroked the barrel, and twirled the almost empty chamber with a finger gone arthritic.

"I brought a few for you, too. California is something you need to see, I swear. Why waste time? Pack up your things. Let's get out of here."

"This loaded?" he asked, twirling the chamber again.

"I heard some godawful stories about what's happening around here. My mind's still spinning about Osceola and how close they're coming."

"With something like this, the ones who came after your mother won't stand a chance."

"So it takes a rifle to get a ticket around here?"

"You and your gun is right." The man's bleary eyes brightened, almost as if the irises had cleared at the thought of such a weapon that could take care of any invaders once and for all. Almost as if he would run out the door, find his horse, saddle up, and head for the border, frail as he was. Geoffrey could see the fight still alive in him even though it was moldering like John Brown. The man must have spent every day since she died imagining his wife at the stove, preparing something hot, something he hadn't seen much of in the past years after the neighbors helped him rebuild. Hot food. A good back rub. Imagining how he found her when he'd come home that day.

The man kept rotating the chamber of the rifle, almost as if it had hypnotized him.

Geoffrey Scott saw the war in his father's eyes, the chance to have power once and for all, the chance to have the upper hand. His old man's eyes lit up at the thought of taking control. He reached for the rifle, though his father wouldn't loosen his grip.

"We could do some damage to those Ruffians," his father said, finally uncurling his fingers, yielding the gun to his son. "Keep them out of Kansas once and for all. Blow up that slave-loving Missouri."

Geoffrey took the carbine back to the only door and stuffed it into its casing. We. His father had said "we." That was the first time he ever heard that word from his father when he was talking to him. It had always been "your mother and me think you should do this or that," like Geoffrey was some kind of stranger. Was his father actually wanting him to stay?

"You can stay a few days," the old man said, responding to his son's thoughts. "We can slip over the border with this thing. You want to be my son? You come with me, boy. We'll do some damage to those hellions who don't care about a man's life. A woman's life either. Shot her for no good reason. A woman who never did any harm to man or child."

"Slow down, Father. Nobody's crossing the border. Causing trouble."

"I've already signed on."

"For what?"

"I'm one of those people you heard about. A Jayhawker. We're at war. Better get that straight in your head. You can lend me your rifle if you don't want to go."

"You're not going on any raid, Father. And not with my rifle. Think about what you taught me. You talked about equality but never about killing for it."

"Your mother did most of that talking. And sometimes a man changes his mind. Sometimes might makes right. War's been going on around here for too long now. If you're not in, you can be on your way." Then he half-smiled because he never fully smiled. A crooked smile, the left part of his face looking pleasant for a second. "But I'll be asking you to leave your carbine behind."

Then a cough erupted in the man. He grabbed his abdomen again and coughed a hurting cough coming from way deep inside of himself. Bent. A portrait of the breaking down of things. Coughing repeatedly.

"You're not well. Is the doc still in Osawatomie?"

"Hell, you know I don't need a doctor. I need your rifle."

"How about Lawrence? Good doctor there?"

"I do not need, I do not want a doctor. Hear me? I have my own reckoning with life. With death. It's not yours."

"If you go on a raid, you'll be falling off your horse. You're a sick man. Look at the tremble in your hand. Your gut's killing you."

"Come with me, son. It's time to let those damn slavers know they shouldn't have come to my farm."

Geoffrey Scott was torn down the middle. His father was wrapped into this mess. No getting him out except to listen to him. Ride with him to make sure he didn't do ultimate damage to himself. "I've left you be for too long. I'm here now. Here. Standing next to you. Understand? You and me."

"I liked your mother well enough," his father said slowly. He paused and took in big air before the next cough. "She begged for the likes of you."

"Me. Your family."

"Well then, ride with me tomorrow. Against them damn slavers."

"I don't believe in killing. Mother didn't approve of it either. Remember?"

The old man went into another fit of coughing.

"Sit down, Father. You sound like you're about to keel over."

"No more talking right now," the man said, sitting in the bent seat of the wooden rocker, settling his hips against the back rungs, still coughing.

Yet, he'd brought the rifle to Kansas. Traded for it. He, Geoffrey Scott, had acquired a gun. A repeating rifle. An experiment. Made it his own even though in his mind he was still a gun-fearing man who would preach against arms to anybody. A man who would only carry one for protection in the barren land where no human rode. He, Geoffrey Scott, possessed a repeating rifle, something he'd needed to own though he didn't believe in it, something he'd listened to in the silence of the desert, the sound of gunpowder exploding over and over, repeating its act seven times. Life was short. Who knew when it'd pass away from his body?

"Turning in for a while," he said to his father who'd sunk back into silence, coughing once in a while, his whole body reacting when he did. Tightened shoulders. Arms across his chest. "Hope you have two beds."

His father said nothing. He rocked. Back and forth. Geoffrey Scott saw a small narrow bed in a back corner, sat on it, laid down on it, drifted off to sleep.

* * * * *

Not something Geoffrey ever thought he would do, but there he was: riding a horse alongside his father, crossing the border, riding toward Missouri on the outskirts of towns: outlying farms, as their farm had been outlying, something away from the center, something for amateurs, for the halfhearted, the unbold. But this was war. All was fair in love and war, someone once said.

Six weeks after the attack on Osceola, they were riding into Missouri, challenging the aggressor and being the aggressor. His father, Elias Scott, carried Geoffrey Scott's only rifle, repeating the words, "Damn slavers. Missouri slavers" over and over, as though he needed the words to heighten his rage. He acted as if the carbine were his, ticktocking it over his head. Waving it in the air. Tucking it beneath his arm.

Geoffrey Scott wondered why he'd decided rifles were necessary in the first place. Maybe it was the West, he told himself. Being out in the open with no protection. A rifle under his arm, or at least one in its scabbard making him less vulnerable. Now his father was holding his rifle as if it had been his forever. Geoffrey Scott was surprised at the new life his father seemed to have with this carbine under his arm. New energy. New determination.

In this, his last raid, he told his son, he'd pack the repeating rifle. "Thanks, son," he also said. "This'll help me do what needs to be done," thus laying claim to his son for the first time since the shooting of his wife.

The two rode together and rode hard, harder than Geoffrey Scott had ever ridden. He witnessed the resolve on his father's face. The anger. The self-righteousness because someone had crossed the border and killed his wife. Why shouldn't a man cross back over the border and return the considerable pain? Geoffrey Scott was there. By his side. His son, though his father was sick both in the head and in his body.

Geoffrey Scott's emotions vacillated between retribution and the innocence of the people they were riding toward. Who knew what they thought about slavery and the war between the states everyone was talking about? They probably had their ideas but mainly wanted to live through the days without too much interruption. So why was he riding with his father? Why was he participating in something he didn't believe? Maybe he needed to do what his father asked because there wouldn't be many more times for that to happen? His father. He needed his father, this crazy man.

A homestead came into view. By itself, as Elias' home had been standing by itself in the countryside near Osawatomie. "This is where one of the Border Ruffians lives. Might even be one of the men still alive who killed your mother. Who knows for sure? Follow me."

But Geoffrey Scott didn't want to be part of this when everything seemed normal, the way it was supposed to be when war wasn't raging. While his father kept riding toward the house, he reined in his horse to stay behind and allow the people of this house to sleep. But then a man stumbled out the door rubbing his eyes, getting a read on the top of the sun coming over the horizon. He saw the two horsemen, one galloping toward him, a rifled aimed straight at him. "What?" he said, his face full of surprise. "What in the hell?" The gun blasted the man in his nightclothes. A man, a mere man who had been so alive, just waking from sleep, was now lying in his blood just as Geoffrey Scott's mother had lain still and stopped seeing the stars, the clouds, the moon, plus everything else.

The early morning sun rose higher over the tip of the hill and caused him to shade his eyes while the other hand held his horse at a standstill. Geoffrey Scott had watched his father take aim. Revenge mattered to him, but that Missouri man was lying still in the grass. Still as a doornail. A toppled mannequin from a store. After his father tucked the rifle in its scabbard, he read his father's face. He saw revenge and satisfaction there. An eye for an eye. A tooth for a tooth. All of that was written and not something

Geoffrey Scott wanted to see. He needed his father but not this man. What did it mean when the Missouri man, lying still as unused cotton balls in a glass jar, was no longer able to stand and drink a glass of water? What did it mean to the man with the rifle and to the man who watched his father's fingers squeeze the trigger? The full scope of the meaning?

Matchsticks peeked out of his father's pocket—the coated end of the match slathered in phosphorous sesquisulfide and gelatin hidden in the shirt pocket, the bottoms of matches, no tips visible, looking like wood chipped off larger blocks of wood.

"No more, Father. No more, please," Geoffrey Scott called out then kicked the sides of his horse, no more the observer. "You've done enough." And yet his father was bent on equality. Even though he rode as fast as he could to stop his father, he could see his father's hand reach for one of the matches and scrape it into life on the back of a rock he held, scrape it into flame, touch it to the dried grass, bend forward, off his knees and onto his feet, the grass accepting the flame, the flames dancing at first, then collecting more fire, then roaring and racing toward the house where the man laid still in his nightclothes.

His father's face. Full of lips, cheeks, eyebrows. His father's face. Full of hate. Full of satisfaction that he had made recompense for the mother long lying in her grave. Full of his hatred, his illness, his cough. Geoffrey Scott didn't want this from his own life. Things could be brought to resolution otherwise. Too much sorrow in this. Too much that couldn't be undone.

They crossed back over the border, his father riding fast to reach his rebuilt home—one room instead of three. Before he dismounted, he tossed the rifle to Geoffrey Scott who'd galloped close behind. He swung open the door. He sat in the rocking chair. He removed his socks. He took a deep breath and reached up with two hands toward his son before he slumped forward, peace on his face. He'd finished what he needed to do.

Geoffrey Scott watched all of this in wonder and horror. His father, still, in the rocking chair, slumped forward, his breath no longer moving the least part of him. A scarecrow in the rocking chair. His father. His heritage. Gone, and yet there was something left, some scrap of something for Geoffrey Scott to hold to. He'd been with his father. They'd ridden together, father and son, though Geoffrey Scott was both devastated and relieved to see the end of that man, to have that ride behind him.

CHAPTER TEN

THE COMPLICATION

ST. THOMAS–MARCH 1868

Geoffrey Scott stands at the glassless window of the house abandoned by Gilbroid Marshall. No doors. No windows and sand on the ledges, but a roof over his head. He looks out at the repetition of sand, hills, skinless mountains—the people who live here so small and insignificant in comparison to this place. Nobody belongs here. No-man's-land. But who is he now that his parents are gone away, somewhere, he doesn't know for sure. Heaven? Hell? Did they crumple up and blow away, or did they live on somewhere, maybe in the heart of a chrysanthemum or stinger of a bee?

He's biding his time in a blown-out house in St. Thomas. The Marshalls took everything back to civilization with them. Every pan. Every piece of clothing. Everything that made this place partly civil. He's a strange bird on a strange branch, he admits to himself, and no longer a baby bird, that's for sure. He's flown the nest. But he is no saint either and has no desire to become one, even though his neighbors have invited him to their meetings, to their Saturday night dances. He's heard too many tales about Mormons. Finding out what they believe is too radical for his taste. Sure, they're hard workers. Strong and good in their resolve to make something out of nothing. But they keep close to the vest. Thin-lipped. Busy like bees. It wouldn't hurt if they chewed the fat once in a while. Sat around and jawed about anything, not so stiff about their religion that they think's the only way to live.

But he's thinking of a plan. He walks out the doorless doorway into the sunshine and checks on Adababa in Allred's yard. Seems just fine. Allred's two horses haven't arrived as yet, lucky Geoffrey Scott, lucky Adababa. They've been carrying salt from the mines to various places—Pioche and

Panaca. Caliente. St. Joseph. Salt transported on Adababa, the sight of which makes him think of Hadji Ali. A friend. He'd trusted him. The man had even waited to leave for Mexico until Geoffrey Scott got back from Kansas.

"Everything's changed. Nobody cares," Hadji Ali'd told him, packing his belongings to leave Bishop's ranch once and for all. He'd been waiting for Geoffrey Scott's return to tell him no one wanted his camels anymore. That he was out of a job. "Terrible stories about my *attah allah*," he said. "I go to Mexico. Better there for me and my camels. You keep Adab Abib. Yours now."

He'd said good-bye, knowing they'd never meet again. With his hand patting Geoffrey Scott's chest, the Syrian had given him his blessing—Hadji Ali, a man with a code of honor not understood by much of anybody. A man among men who'd come close as he could to calling him a friend. Geoffrey Scott would miss the Syrian and his *Attah Allahs.* He'd miss anticipating Hadji's wishes and whether or not the man wanted him around or not. Now the Muslim was taking himself to Mexico where he could pass and where he'd find work doing something besides wait for a government to make up its mind. Most soldiers didn't want camels. Never did. Washed their hands of the whole experiment. The deciders-of-all-important-issues gave Hadji a string of the animals to take with him. Payment for his services. Thank goodness the Syrian never knew Geoffrey Scott took Adababa back to Fort Mojave, believing the animal to still be the property of the U.S. government. Guilty for doing that, he admitted to himself, but what the hell? Why shouldn't he return what wasn't his? But the few camels left behind were ignored at the fort. Not curried. Not tended to. Maybe not even fed on a regular basis. That troubled him, and here he was—with Adababa looking out between fence slats while he stood in the open doorway.

Granted, Adababa was not his animal exactly, but both of them are in St. Thomas. In Utah or Arizona Territory or the state of Nevada, who knows for sure? Doesn't matter to Adababa. He's prospecting for shrubbery anywhere he can find it. Acting as if there is no tomorrow. Breathing easy for a little while when he rests in that familiar sit camels have. Not that Adababa minds working. In fact, he's been trained to work. Life isn't a matter of love or luck or gifts to Adababa. It's a matter of being a good pack animal—lifting, carrying loads that'd break the back of a horse or a mule, going for days without complaining, without water, no less. Above all (and there are those who appreciate what their camel can do, who love and nestle close to its fuzzy head as Geoffrey Scott sometimes does), Adababa will do what he's been asked. He'll rise, he'll kneel, he'll sit, then carry more weight than most thought he could. Adababa's patient, long-suffering, irreplaceable, and Geoffrey Scott feels lucky to be its owner, though he's only half an owner he better not forget. With the way Kwami feels about ownership, though, he's not sure who owns what. There is no such concept in Kwami's world. Only necessity. Geoffrey Scott folds his arms, bends his head back to catch some sun on the open neck of his shirt, and assures himself he knows better than most what that camel needs.

Since their trip north, they've been to Santa Clara and St. George, up Virgin Hill, which scares everybody else. Trustworthy transportation, that Adababa. The camel is more suited to Virgin Hill than wagons will ever be. Steep slopes. Sheer cliffs. Horses aren't strong enough to hold a wagon pointing downhill, the brakes on the wagons are too weak. There is no harmony between wagons and primitive roads. But he has a secret weapon: Adababa. The bringer of salt. Anybody in this part of the country thinks of salt now, they think about Geoffrey Scott and Adababa. And Kwami, of course.

He's thought about starting a transport company—he and Kwami, who's happier in a village than in a house in a no-account place named St. Thomas. Mustn't forget him. The Mojave walks back and forth to the Paiute village every day but it's okay not to have him around at all times. He can be overwhelming. But Kwami's not with his people and their ways either. Will he or Kwami find what they want out here in the wide-open West with these Mormons? He's tiring of this town, and maybe he needs to set his sights on something harder to obtain than salt. That could be a woman. Maybe a son or daughter. Someone who'll benefit from his work—the salt, the trips carrying salt.

He looks in the direction of Sophia Hughes' house—one of the sturdier houses in St. Thomas, soon to be whitewashed, with a chimney built at both ends to give it the look of New England stability, or so he has heard. But does anyone really need a chimney in this heat? Maybe midwinter when the warmth leaves the surface of the ground or maybe when the ground glistens with crystals of frost. Winter is brief, though maybe there are still a few days when the chimney can send out an invitation to come join the warmth.

A woman. A child, maybe. 1-2-3. Man, woman, and child. Like the Godhead he once heard about in Sunday School when he was a boy. That's what it was for him then; that's what it is for him now: man, woman, and child. The Holy Ghost has to be a female. God needed a woman to have all these children. He feels a strange kind of yearning he's never felt before. Yes. A woman.

There are some in St. Thomas, but they all belong to someone. But could be that polygamy puts a light in there somewhere. Not all the wives seem happy. Some might be interested in an offer he might make. Kwami's found a Paiute woman: Abey, which means "leaf." Pretty name. The Indian's made himself a nest, but a hornet's nest maybe. Mojaves usually mix with their own. At least the man's found himself a companion for now, something more than he's done.

The Civil War's ended. So much change–territories of Kansas, Nebraska, Wyoming, Colorado. And now Utah Territory which has been shrunk from Brigham's ambitious plans. He's talked to surveyors who maintain St. Thomas is in the state of Nevada now. But those boys could be saying something convenient, whiffing the possibility of gold and silver.

He looks at his hands, his arms hanging out of his shirt. He needs to be less of a skeleton. Less bone. More meat. Amount to something. Again, he stares at Sophia Hughes' house, knowing she's there by herself, Charles gone again. He saw him ride off this morning. North again, though Geoffrey Scott wonders if Charles has ridden down to Callville like he said he needed to. No sane person would stay in that godforsaken place. And, it's not easy to get supplies to St. George. Virgin Hill or too many crossings of the Virgin. Cattle swallowed by quicksand. Diarrhea. Bad diet. Red sand in your water.

Maybe he could settle here, though that wasn't likely. He'd feel pulled by the Mormons, and that thought makes him crazy. No way he can spout those beliefs: Golden Bible, consecration of all earthly goods to each other, sacred underwear. Too illogical, except Sophia seems moved by them, by it, and calls the place Zion and tells him the word means "pure in heart." That religion is one strong web of contradictions, but a web for sure.

But maybe, just maybe, Sophia doesn't want to be a third wife. Maybe she'd consider something else. He's ready for a woman with bountiful hair, hips to hold–a place to plant a baby. Fingers. Fingernails. All of those things. They can be his if he'd just do something besides plod to the salt mine every day.

But to stop by Sophia's house? He doesn't know about that. Will she hide her long underwear again and pretend he doesn't see it? Will she see Geoffrey Scott for who and what he is—a simple man, but a good one? She seemed interested in the camel. Maybe she'd like to go for a ride. Maybe she'd say yes. They could go to the oasis out in the desert, way above the Muddy. Or to the red rocks. Or maybe she'd like to see the salt crystals he's gathered, especially the largest ones laying in a pile, waiting for him to transport them elsewhere.

* * * * *

Looking out the canvas door, she sees very few neighbors standing or working by the side of their shelters, their tents, their primitive houses. Very few are busy with hoes or rakes at this hour. No straw hats bobbing. Or skin reddening or blistering, for that matter. The sun glares overhead, close to noon and the hottest heat. The wind is starting up. So predictable.

Sophia takes a few steps outdoors where the sun beats like a drum on her hatless head. She feels like a stretch of dried animal skin, pulled across a bent piece of wood, rolled into a circle of sorts. Her hair blows one way, then another. Lifts up. Blows to the left. Strings itself across her mouth. Into her mouth. She laughs, though it is a bitter laugh no one else can hear or, better yet, comprehend. The sound is sharp-edged, though she avoids thinking about the miscarriage that happened last week. Charles or no one else will know. This is her secret.

She rolls a paper-thin, brittle leaf in her fingers until it crumbles. God forgot to finish this place. Water nowhere—only bits in muddy streams. Disappearing too quickly. This land is inhabited by something not part of human sensibility, a red demon who lives in the midst of fire and flame, though she stops herself. She does not believe in such fantasies. She is committed to The Gospel, to the building of Zion, to practicality.

But, as she plucks a few more shriveled leaves, she realizes she needs a friend, someone she can talk to, someone to soothe her thoughts. Where's Almira when she needs her? And she wants some pure, cold water. Maybe a storm will come and the meandering Muddy will swell. Red water will run swiftly through St. Thomas, cleansing it of sand, grit, and human waste. But she looks up, trying not to look too directly at the brilliant sun that diminishes anything that tries to establish dignity, and sees her failing crops. The ones that flourish at first— thirsty, seeking light, ready to bear their fruits. No matter how much she hopes or even waters with what little she has, the plants become parched and their leaves curl to brown. "I'm dying," she can hear them pleading. Maybe that's what they are telling her now if only she would listen.

She cannot still her mind. And Brigham Young, who knows so little about this place, wants us to grow cotton? Does he understand how much water cotton needs? Those plants need to bask, loll, even wallow in water. She's tried a few patches, but the green shoots soon have brittle leaves and runners and no sign of bolls. The cotton these plants produce is uninspired, no matter how hard she tries. Maybe she should make hats out of lizard skins, something to keep her hand in the trade. They can at least happen. She smiles when she thinks of everyone wearing lizard hats to church. The scaly skin on the crowns. Rattlesnake skins even.

She scans the road where many wheels and horse hooves have traveled. Ruts. Tracks. What might be out and about on such a grainy day as this one? Down the road at the Marshalls' shell of a house, she can see Geoffrey Scott saddling Adababa. Why is he leaving so late in the day? And who is he trying to be in this community of Mormons, people living under the covenant, God's kingdom, where any other endeavor seems worthless and nothing? She attends her meetings and listens for the Spirit to inhabit the tongue of the Saints, telling them all is well in Zion, that they need each other, that they will be blessed if only they have sufficient faith, that they need each other to make this settlement work. But sometimes she feels she can never be good enough to live this simple life. She misses her hats and the beauty she can create, even the splendor and all she cannot see as she looks around St. Thomas. The dirt road is squalor, maybe a hopeful, even faithful, squalor, as speakers say at her church meetings, but her husband is off again on a mail run. That makes the squalor more obvious. More real.

Maybe another pregnancy will make a difference. A living child for her and Charles, who might be less moody and petulant with an arrow in his quiver, so to speak. Despite the sun, the mud, and the quicksand and sickness unto death, she will believe and have faith in this child. She has come many miles. She accepted the doctrine in England, carried it with her across the plains, and has even accepted the notion of multiple wives, though she secretly wishes she could be loved for herself and not as a doctrine, a principal, or a piece in a larger puzzle. She is not sure Charles understands her desire to be first in a man's consideration nor would even respond if he did. All he knows is that everyone is part and parcel of God's plan. No one is special or deserving of notice when everyone works together to bring about God's will. She is a grain of sand, like that beneath her feet, the endless sand.

Geoffrey Scott is riding Adababa past her house, sitting tall inside a cage of a saddle on top of Adababa's hump—a strange-looking contraption that squeaks and moans as he pulls on the reins to stop and speak with her.

"Good day to you, Mrs. Hughes. A hot day, for sure. The wind's mustering its strength about now."

"Indeed." She folds her arms across her breasts thinking Geoffrey Scott might see a curve he could misinterpret as a sign for something he wants. Careless wishing, perhaps. Something she tamps down and away without appraising the rest of her body.

"Off to the salt mines. Again." Wind whips Adababa's tail. Its ears twitch, and Adababa stands patiently while they talk. Sophia wonders what it is to be a camel.

"You're a bit late now, I would say."

"Hot start when a body waits this long. But things to do. Adababa here doesn't mind the time of day. He's always ready to go. Kwami's got other things to attend to today."

"Sorry you have to go alone but wishing you a good journey."

"Is Charles around, by the way?" he asks, reining in Adababa who has decided it's time to move forward. "I wanted to discuss Callville and the men who are supposed to be there."

"He's on a mail run for a few days. Up north. By the way, he was surprised when you said no one was living at Callville."

"They all went back to civilization, is what I think," says Geoffrey Scott. "Decided they'd had enough of bringing goods up the unpredictable Colorado. Steep canyon walls. Rapids. The brutality of Virgin Hill after that."

"I wish the Muddy were a more robust river. A real river."

"Sure would be nice, but dream on. I best get going now. Salt to get to St. George after I retrieve what's been scooped out of the mine." The camel moves forward.

"Good travels to you," she calls after him. More longing fills her voice than she has intended. She will be alone with the empty cupboards and even more empty cradle.

"Right. But," he pulls on the rope that holds Adababa quiet for another minute. "You want to ride Adababa someday? I indulge the children around here, let them play cowboys and Indians on the camel's back or make wrap-around scarves out of kitchen towels and play A-R-A-B. A ride would be a break from this drudgery."

Sophia brightens at the thought of being perched so high off the ground. "Maybe on a calmer day than this one."

He laughs more recklessly than he usually laughs, the rocks echoing his sound as he disappears into the fury of the wind. Sophia pats the looseness of her hair that has blown every which way. The pins that hold her together are gradually getting lost, blowing away maybe, who knew where they went.

* * * * *

Two weeks later, Sophia is in the house alone, once again, with the constant reminders. The cradle. The letters A, B, and C cut from buckram and hung in the room. Sarah Ann went off to heaven one morning without saying a word, without a whisper. Just stone cold one morning after hours of fighting a temperature. Cold cloths on her forehead. On her neck. Stiff. Unyielding. Not like a baby at all. Sarah Ann. A doll with arms that could only be moved by lifting them. Not full of life as she had once been, asking for things in her own baby way with arms stretched out, cooing rather than speaking. Sarah Ann—a beautiful baby with Sophia's expressive eyes, even at three months. And now those eyes are closed. Never to open.

And Charles. Last night.

"This food isn't fit to eat," he'd said, in one of his surly moods again, but he didn't stop there. "I could call it something else if I had a mind to."

"Don't you dare say anything about my food. You've called it 'slop' before and better not say so again. When did you come by that horrid word anyway? And just what do you expect from nothing?" She had wiped the perspiration from her cheeks and checked the way it ran down in streaks. Both hands. The frustration. The total lack of ingredients. The awful water. A cracked looking glass on top of that, split right where her face should answer back to her, a fractured reflection that might be more truthful than anything else she knew these days.

"I expect more from you. You're a lousy wife. Y-O-U." His fists were stiffly jammed into his sides, and he bared his uneven bottom teeth—a jumbled fan of yellow fangs it had seemed to her just then. "And don't you tell me what to do or say." His face screwed with sudden rage, and he leaned over her as if she didn't have ears.

"But I'm doing my best, Charles. I've been doing my best ever since we got here."

"Not much is all I can say. I should have brought Harriet down here. She's got more pluck than you do. More spine. You expect the world to fall at your feet. Just because you're fetching. If only the world knew the truth."

"The truth about what?" Her temperature was rising, too. Her cheeks had turned a hot red.

"That you think you're too fine. That you're vain. That you know anything about anything." He towered over her, his fingers squeezing open and shut as if her neck were under consideration, frightening her to her toes with his fit of temper.

He'd made her cry. What else could she have done? She wishes she could pull those tears back inside where he couldn't have seen a trace. She was glad he was out of her sight. She'd been happy when she'd heard the last of Midnight's hooves at sunrise. Surly old fool, unpredictable, and always feeling righteous about something. The puffed-up pigeon of righteousness had spoken.

Instead of rerunning last night through her head or spending anymore time thinking about Charles, his foul mouth and moods, she decided to go outside to their garden. She'll find something to bottle. Enough of something. She'd rather be outside working in the yard with no fence, though there isn't much to harvest when she looks over her sorry plot. She turns back to survey her living quarters, soon to be finished—a house with two chimneys. Charles has promised. She should be proud but of what? That she'd married someone who brimmed over with his anger? But no thinking of Charles. Not now.

Right at this minute, in all of St. Thomas, there's only a handful of half-hearted, half-bricked buildings, an architectural jumble of land, angles at every direction, broad swaths of desert decorated by tumbleweeds. The hills undulate, chaotic, much as she feels chaotic, stirred up as she is. Distant gray waves undulate—the horizon of gauzy mountains, unreachable mountains. The desert is stingy. What an irony that she, who loves mountain rills, the chill of an evening, the sound of a stream moving fast over large rocks, and even the sound of a stray boulder crashing its way to the ocean, is living in the Muddy Mission, the farthest thing from green and plentiful she can imagine. What a place, except the Prophet has called them here and Charles has chosen her to come with him. An honor in the beginning, but basically an honor no sweeter than a sour pickle. How could she ever have perceived this as an honor? To be the third wife, one of three, and chosen to come to this hellish place with a demon husband? The other two wives are living by streams and green trees right now even though they have snow in the winter. At least they have a change of seasons to help them count their days. At least they do not have to abide Charles' temper.

She needs to pick the few green beans struggling to survive. Now. Her upset with Charles will settle. It has before. It will again. But she can't help but look beyond the settlement at the hills bleached with alkali. Red shows in bared patches of soil, like lonely promises with no one and nothing to fulfill them. Bursts of red—the sand turning pink and red rocks eroded into hoodoos as the hills rise. This world can be vibrant at times, more than she would have thought it could be. She and Charles had gone into those red rocks one day. But their ride on Midnight was barely a ride. They'd caught a quick glimpse and galloped back to another meeting. Sophia wants to go there again. Into the red rocks. Anywhere but this endless grid of creosote bushes and sand, this boring desert, and this unpredictable husband.

Today there is a meeting in the bowery to decide what needs to happen with the changes from Utah to Arizona Territory and how to fend off forays by officials from the newly made state of Nevada demanding taxes be paid post-haste. Where does St. Thomas belong anyway? Sophia is tired of the confusion and wants, just for today, to be by herself. To lift herself from the doldrums of being married to a man she probably doesn't love enough, though she tries to be what a wife needs to be. She does. She needs to let her thoughts rearrange themselves. She can ask the neighbors what's been discussed, though she will, for sure, hear from Charles that she is slacking her duties.

Kneeling in her garden to pick the few beans she can find, she hears the sound of hooves, a different sound from horse hooves, then notices Geoffrey Scott riding toward her house on his camel, looking toward the mountains, skyward, ascertaining the temperature, perhaps. Sophia wonders what he thinks about his tentative place among the Mormons. The way he's one of the only, if not the only, nonmembers or nonbelievers. Does he ever wish there could be more between him and her, though that is a vain thought that never should have crossed her mind. Perish the thought! But still, she wants more than is possible even though she is a married woman. Geoffrey Scott probably doesn't think of women. Too much road-building. Salt mining. Too much living with men around forts, men who have no life with a female to soften it.

"I thought you and Charles would be at the meeting," he starts out, reining Adababa in, stopping the camel in the middle of the road. Majestic. Its head and chest high. "Glenn tells me there's a meeting today about who St. Thomas belongs to. Don't you want to hear what they decide?"

"I don't feel like being in a meeting today," she answers, tossing her head and biting her lip so she won't reveal that she's feeling down, busying herself with her poor excuse for a garden because she has a poor excuse for a husband. "Charles has ridden north."

"I'm taking the day off," he tosses his head, too, almost an imitation of the way Sophia has tossed her head. She notices this innocent gesture.

"Good for you," she says, poking at the beans, the ones barely showing their faces. The heat is not to be faced.

"How about I take you for a ride?" he says, and she looks at him with surprise. His boldness is a new thing, though she does not recognize her own willingness to be asked.

"On the camel? Really? I've wanted to do that ever since I saw it walk into my yard. But," she quickly hesitates, "I should take care of my garden. I need to bottle the few beans I have before the heat shrivels them."

"Sure enough. Heat's a bear, for sure."

"I can't leave here," she says without conviction. "I have things to do." She tries her best to be busily engaged in the good cause of beans, tying one spindly branch to the string she has pulled through the slats.

"Things can always wait." Even though he is naturally shy, Geoffrey Scott seems different on this day, maybe tired of staying out of her and Charles' way. Maybe he has observed her husband taking her for granted. Maybe he's even heard him on one of his bad days. Charles can shout from behind his full beard, longer on two sides with a short middle. It's hard for Sophia to remember what she admires about her husband at this moment.

"It's a nice day," he insists. "You won't have many chances to ride a camel, and today you have no obligations. At least none that can't wait. Come with me."

"I suppose it wouldn't hurt to go for a short ride."

"We can go up toward the red rocks."

"I was just thinking about them. Charles has shown those rocks to me briefly."

"We'll take our time. How about that?"

Of course, she wants to ride with Geoffrey Scott. She is tired of being at home with everything and nothing to do. She has seen the exotic camel around the neighborhood, carrying bags of salt, always patient, always obedient. Geoffrey Scott seems at ease around the camel, as if he himself were an Arab.

"For a short time, maybe I can go. I do have those beans to preserve. But let me get us something to eat."

"We won't be that long. Not to worry about that."

Geoffrey Scott slaps a willow switch on Adababa's rump and commands the camel to sit, slides off its back, and helps Sophia put one leg over to straddle the camel. "I'll squeeze right behind you. Usually a rider sits behind the saddle and hangs onto my shirt, but you're so little." He laughs as he climbs behind Sophia. "I made this saddle to keep Adababa comfortable when he's carrying salt and supplies, something that won't cause blisters. Easy now," he says, patting the camel's rump. "Sorry I'm so close," he says. "But then I can hang tight to you. Make sure you don't fall." The camel rises up, and Sophia can feel the shifting of its weight as it finds its balance. She can also feel its power beneath her thighs. Something different from the horses she's ridden. And much taller.

"Here we go," he says proudly. She can feel him smiling as if he has swallowed the sun, pleased at being high above the desert, pleased period, she likes to think.

Sophia thinks of railroad trains in England. She has seen nothing of the kind in the West as yet, though she's heard talk of them coming. Soon. And now she feels as though she is riding the engine of a train, riding on top of the metal hull except a malleable one, more pliable than she would have supposed, an animal with parts and passion, of course. She feels the thrill of being so tall, of feeling the camel's pace, of knowing it can go faster and still faster. She stops caring about her beans. Geoffrey Scott and Sophia cover the sandy ground in lightning time and cross the places where flash floods have carved streambeds into the desert. They ride up the hill to where the sand turns salmon pink.

Sophia's pall lifts. She is a desert queen, riding a camel across sand and stubble, imagining she has been a ransomed princess locked in an adobe abode. She feels her hair blowing from beneath her sunbonnet. She is free, whatever that means. Free from what, she is not sure, but nevertheless, she is enchanted with the sensation of being on top of a camel, of having Geoffrey Scott hold so tightly to her, of inhaling the smell of his hair close behind her shoulder when she turns her head.

Red, red, giant land of red growing redder. Sage, creosote, and tumbleweed–all against rocky red. Mountains. Valleys. Slopes of dark pink sand encircled by red stone. Bizarre outcroppings. Red, arches, holes, sand, red. Strewn rocks, big and small. Individual rocks, some split, red towers of confused rock. Jumbled rock. Alkali. Up one big hill. Down another.

And they reach the place which Geoffrey Scott calls The Seven Sisters–heads, necks, profiles–taking precedence over the gray landscape behind them. Red pillars called hoodoos. "Erosion," he says to Sophia. "Red stones. Alone. Together. Apart. Close to one another." He pulls the camel's reins and brings them to a sudden stop. The camel kneels. The two dismount to examine the garden of red rock.

They stand. They stretch. They look at the red in silence. All around them.

"So much red," Sophia says, feeling like a small girl in a gigantic land. "So many strange shapes. They surprise you."

"They are amazing. That one looks like a cat sitting on its hind legs. Sort of."

She laughs as she once did when she was a girl. "And that one," she points. "It looks like a huge stack of hotcakes." And then there is an empty pause. She's not sure what to say next, but then decides to say what's on her mind: "Thank you for bringing me here. I needed a break from the demands of the garden and the house."

He's almost a head taller than the tiny Sophia. "Glad you can be out here, too. Something beautiful about this crazy land."

"Definitely." She turns around and gazes briefly into his eyes. "Sometimes I think the desert is the worst geography I've ever been introduced to, but when I see the sunsets and then these arrangements of stones, I know there's much that I don't know." She turns back, and yet he stays close.

"What do you think of the sunsets," she quizzes, "that can be red, then so orange, then purple even? They're like nothing I've ever seen before."

"They make me stare like someone from a foreign country." He laughs an edgy laugh but still doesn't move in any direction away from her.

"You foreigner, you." They both laugh, a bit nervous, but enjoying this moment and this bizarre settling of red rocks. Something must have erupted, throwing the rocks in the air to fall where they would. But some of the formations look as though a hand had built them that way. Building blocks bringing order to the chaos.

"Ever since I first saw you," he says quietly, then stops. It seems that he speaks more to the wind than to Sophia, though she finds herself waiting for the end of his sentence.

"What?" she asks, unconsciously holding her breath.

"I know I shouldn't..." He is standing in red sand, becoming something even more red, his face even. "It's...I can't...but you belong...except you're his third choice. Third choice is no choice...in my opinion." The words come out in a frenzy, almost as though they are spinning about with no place to settle. "I've acted as...I don't know you."

These words tumble out of Geoffrey Scott's mouth, almost haphazardly. Sophia is standing in front of him, turning her head to the side to hear what he says, enjoying this escape from Charles who can be so mean when she's done nothing to deserve it.

Geoffrey Scott is bolder than himself, probably because he has waited too long for this moment. "I think about you," he says, putting his hands on her shoulders, somewhat calmer than he's been, steadying her on the uneven ground and thus steadying himself. "You must be unhappy. Losing a child. Coming to this place that doesn't suit you. Waiting while Charles fulfills his word of God. Who am I, I ask. But I..."

Words fail Geoffrey Scott. Maybe he's rehearsed what he should say too many times, the things he'd say to Sophia. Everything shifts, and he's uncomfortable again—a fish out of water, a caught fish with a hook in its mouth.

She is not without pity. Or compassion. Or the desire to be loved. Here is a man offering her more than she has. And he has a camel that can last for days in the desert without water, the water they all need so badly. That animal says something about him though she's not sure what. She turns toward Geoffrey Scott and, in a sudden impetuous moment, kisses him. On the lips. Fully on the lips, unlike something she would usually do. She, suddenly, does not care about anything. About anyone. Only this moment in the red, the wild rocks, the jumble of emotion she feels inside of herself. She wants to be loved in the way she knows she can be. Maybe it was being married twice that makes her want to be with him as a married woman would be. Not as a lass. Or a girl. Or a young thing. She is a woman now. She wants to be seen differently, not as a drudge who sometimes makes "slop," not as a plow horse, not as an everyday servant of God who wears faded dresses and sunbonnets when a beautiful hat is so much more appealing.

Geoffrey Scott pulls the saddle blanket off the camel's back, spreads it out on the hot sand, pushes lace aside, unbuttons buttons, and unfastens hooks and eyes. And there, beneath it all, she waits for him, she wants him, she does not care about anything except the fact that she's with someone who wants her, who's alive to her flesh, malnourished as it is in this parched place.

CHAPTER ELEVEN

THE SEARCH PARTY

ST. THOMAS–1868

Though he doesn't wish to think of her, Sophia's all Geoffrey Scott can think of in his blown-out home that provides a roof over his head and nothing more. The house is eerily quiet, no more than four walls, no chairs, no place to sit except for a hastily built bench hammered together where he can pull on his boots. Only a bedroll on the floor and a few of his belongings spread out on the one countertop built by Marshall. Once a door, maybe. A house, not a home. Four walls, nothing more, nothing less. He's used to bareness but things have changed.

He thinks of the curve of her body against him on the camel's back, the way she opened up to him in the red rocks. A careless time for Sophia when nothing else mattered, but something had made her yield. He was dealing with a puzzle.

She'd sat small in front of him on the way back to St. Thomas, and she'd talked. She said she couldn't take back what had happened and didn't wish to, not really, but that it was a fluke. A fluke? What was a fluke? She'd said she was lonely, out of her head, maybe out of her mind, set apart somehow from the good things about Charles Weston Hughes, the order of their lives, the fact she was a wife, even a third one. She kept talking. She kept saying she was sorry she'd gone against her principles as if that were more important than what had gone on between them.

Except, as they rode, she turned her head as far as it would turn to the right. She looked around at his shoulder, then into his eyes. And there was feeling on her face. Much feeling. He even saw something that looked like a tear. Something her words weren't saying. But she kept her distance. Order. A sense of rightness as she spelled out what she thought she wanted from her life. But he sensed confusion, a sense of, he didn't know for sure, but she didn't seem happy where she was. And he knew their time together had been a miracle of sorts. That she was fond of him even. Somehow he knew that. That was what crowded his thoughts on the day Kwami comes to him.

The Mojave seems taller than usual, a shadow in Geoffrey Scott's doorway, great in height, his head brushing the frame. Bigger than the house, almost.

"Adababa," the Mojave says. "I want camel. Now."

Geoffrey Scott is not ready for Kwami's request. He is asking to take the camel, the one they have been using to collect salt, their lifeline.

"Our camel?"

"Camel. Yes. I need it now. Another tribe has come to the Paiute village. On horses. I think Utes, the only tribe with horses. They take Abey and her son while I hunt deer for our supper."

"Not the first I've heard of your woman, but you've never mentioned a son."

"Abey. Niyol. Taken away. On a horse."

"And you want Adababa?"

"I want to ride fast. To find woman and son. Find those Utes and their horses before something worse happens."

"Probably trading with the Spanish." Geoffrey Scott abruptly leaves his reverie about Sophia and Adababa.

"They have fast horses. We can catch with the camel."

Kwami points to Allred's corral where Adababa is staying. The camel's in sternal recumbency, his nonworking position, immune from trouble. Geoffrey Scott is paying a fee for him to stay in that protected place until Allred's horses arrive. Any day now. But he stops paying attention to anything but the man in his doorway. Kwami is massive. His outline steals light from the sun behind his back. His body is strong like a large cat, and his face is clouded with an anger Geoffrey Scott has never seen before.

"We'll find your woman and boy," he says. "Let me tend to a few items. A few. I promise."

A pile of salt is gathered in Marshalls' abandoned backyard–large chunks of pure salt hacked from the walls of the salt mountain. He doesn't know his neighbors well enough to ask to borrow a tarp, but maybe he can bother Allred. He's friendly enough. Agreeable, even when Geoffrey Scott said there'd be no meetings for him. No baptizing. No clan or tribe for him. St. Thomas is not a place he means to stay, he knows that. Even with his hankerings for Sophia. Even with his occupation at the salt mines. Still, he needs to borrow a tarp to protect the salt he'll soon take north to sell for a good price.

"Come," Kwami is insisting. "Hurry."

Hurry, he says. Kwami's serious. Go. Now. Help him find Abey and Niyol. But why is he doing this, he asks himself as he packs a few items of food that they'll need before too long. Has he said he'd go because he believes in friends and he doesn't have any? Kwami is one of his few friends these days. Why or how he isn't sure though they are comfortable around each other. Or is he viscerally against the idea of slavery? People buying and selling? Indians kidnapping other Indians to sell them to somebody who'll use them for servants, all in exchange for goods and acquisitions? He mulls the answers to these questions as he rolls his bedroll and ties it with a soiled rope. What can he do but help Kwami?

Then he knocks on Allred's door, returns to the pile with a canvas tarp in hand, covers the salt, and puts rocks on its corners to keep it in place. He carries the jerry-rigged saddle that rests in the corral's corner and fastens it to Adababa, makes sure it sits in the right way.

"You are too tall to fit inside this saddle," he tells Kwami. "You'll burst the beams," though Geoffrey Scott wonders if Kwami has any idea what a beam might be. "Ride on the hindquarters," he says, pointing to the camel's backside. "Hold onto my back. Or to the frame."

After the men are mounted on the camel, they leave St. Thomas for the Paiute village. They'll follow tracks. Horses are rare in this country of root diggers, and nobody in this tribe has one.

* * * * *

Sophia is two months pregnant. She is relieved when her menses cease even though her wishes of a better place have not been fulfilled. She is not barren any longer. The swelling, though small and almost insignificant, feels good. She is with child and at the beginning of a strong pregnancy, a sure one. She knows it is good. Secure even. She pats her stomach and looks out the door at the Marshall place down the way.

Deep in her heart, her mind, her conscience, she suspects this child belongs to her time alone with Geoffrey Scott. Maybe. She is not sure but she won't create any suspicions. Nothing. One baby planted, ready to grow, ready to be part of this earth and its doings. She is happy to be with child, though she cannot rest easy about who the father is.

When he is at home for a few days, half-dressed and ready for bed, she tells Charles. "This place, this St. Thomas by the Muddy, will be a good place." Charles is elated. "One child at a time. Our faith is rewarding us, Sophia. A child. You with child. There is harmony somewhere out there." He is uncharacteristically giddy, maybe because he is still virile at his age and everyone will know it. He is beside himself, enlarging the Kingdom even while he is burdened with the fact that Callville has become extinct, a lifeless settlement with only flat buildings serving as warehouses, a few military men assigned to stay behind, and none of his brethren to receive the goods. He was still a man who'd work with no questions, a man who'd do what he said he'd do. He'd help St. Thomas be a way station anyway, a piece of the living channel toward a more effective Zion. It was a place where the drivers and their strings could find respite. Even some food and water and some dancing and merriment. St. Thomas. Still a cog in the road. A link in the chain.

"A baby seems unreal," she said. "Here in this place with no green except maybe those thin mesquite leaves that dare show their faces." She speaks the words, buttoning buttons, adjusting collars on their nightclothes. "But I'm thrilled, Charles. I am."

"Truly?"

"Truly. A baby. Another child."

"And when will he be born?"

"Sometime in December, who knows for sure?" though she suspects the exact day, the exact moment that this baby was an egg and that it joined with a sperm to become a child. Something she has wanted. Something she has needed. More than he knows, Geoffrey Scott has given her a gift, though that is making assumptions, isn't it now? He has gone away on Adababa. No message. No news. Gone away with nothing to say to her, though she did tell him she did not want to be alone with him ever again. He's taken her words seriously, hasn't he? And now he's gone away. No one has been at the Marshalls' house in several weeks. No lantern. No people. Not Adababa. She has secretly spied, hoping for some signs of life there.

"We'll have a party to make the announcement, maybe?" Charles says, still celebrating his manhood. An observer would assume that, rather than being dressed in nightclothes, he stands in the small back room in a tuxedo with a stiff, pointed collar. He is proud. His chest swells. Sophia smiles to herself and wonders at the man. He would soon be out the door on another mail run to Pioche, leaving her behind, standing in the doorway as she is now, always being left behind. And where is Geoffrey Scott? Why isn't he at the Marshalls'? What is it about her that she can be so easily forgotten, she thought as she almost sank into self-pity. But she is with child, after all. She will soon be a mother again. Sophia Jane Poultney Hughes, and, for a moment, she wonders if she should have kept the Milhaus in her long list of names. James was the man who taught her what it meant to be in love. But what about Geoffrey Scott? Maybe she should add the name Scott to her list of names. After all. But she was not sure of her feelings. Maybe he had no larger purpose in life, except he told her he would like to settle. Settle to what? she wondered and looked down the road again at the empty Marshall house.

* * * * *

They ride. For miles. For hours. For days. They lope together on Adababa, Kwami holding to Geoffrey Scott and the well-nailed saddle he's made, watching for the tracks that will take them to the captors. Up slopes. Across rivers. Careful to track through coarse sand dampened by rains. Along the base of slanted terrain, along a path teetering on the slope of tall mountains. One camel following three horses: one horse with two people riding—Abey and one of the men. Another with two people riding also, but on this horse Niyol and the other man. The tracks tell the tale, Kwami says. The second animal's tracks don't dig as deep. And a third horse carrying supplies creates the lightest tracks of all. The kidnappers are planning a quick raid by the look of it. Three horses. Headed east now. Across the top of the Great Canyon to where, Geoffrey Scott and Kwami were not sure. Probably headed for Ute country. Which nation can travel so quickly while the rest of the tribes are bound to their two feet?

As they ride across land that repeats itself and bores Geoffrey Scott, he can't help letting his mind run to the Confederate and Union armies. He thinks of Jefferson Davis who defected to the Confederates. The war was behind them now but was still troubling, no matter who'd won. Brother against brother. Cousin against cousin. Ebenezer leaving Beale's expedition on the run, hopefully somewhere in the West where feelings about black men didn't run so high. The splitting of the United States, the young country that needs divine help to pull itself back together. Lincoln. Shot in the head. Where was the fairness? And why was he riding a camel in no-man's-land with a Mojave Indian hanging onto him? What a strange life he'd carved out for himself, no small thanks to his crazy father who he'd never see again. He hoped his anger, or maybe his disbelief, was at rest, behind him now, though why had he just sat there watching his father shoot that rifle? Why did he watch him kill someone because that man lived in Missouri? Even if the fool was a Border Ruffian? Why didn't he interfere or wash his hands clean once and for all, a question he couldn't answer then or now. It isn't the time to revisit that one, is it? His father was his father, a proud man who'd lost his head when his wife got shot. His father.

He turned his thoughts to something easier to think about. Jefferson Davis was all for the purchase of more camels, but his opinion had lost muster—a large stone in a small shoe, some said. Before the war, Congress recommended a thousand more camels be brought to the United States, especially after Beale conducted his successful experiment. But after Davis defected, the coffers of the United States government dried up. Maybe it boiled down to a deep mistrust of Davis, despite the animals' admirable performance. No money for another new expedition or for more trials. Besides, railroad tracks were being laid, developers not skipping a beat, making the West accessible for anyone who wanted a new life.

To add oil to the embers in his mind, some ranchers were using camels for target practice. That rumor is a hard one for Geoffrey Scott to hear. And what about Camelopardalis—the constellation in the large space between Ursa Major and Minor? But Adababa doesn't exist as a free and independent animal, one able to roll through the sky as a constellation seems to do. Adababa is an even-toed ungulate within the genus *Camelus* providing transportation for a Mojave and a Kansan. Who can say otherwise? The animal is enslaved. A beast of burden, and Geoffrey Scott isn't sure that's a good idea—to enslave anyone or anything. Adababa is a land ship that can travel as far in one day as a horse can in nine or ten. He is wool, milk, and meat to many men, and now he is a compliant servant to Geoffrey Scott and Kwami—a flesh-and-blood animal beneath them, used to sand, though Geoffrey Scott is unsure whether or not Adababa's feet will survive the rocks more numerous every day as they head higher into the mountains. Or that his stomach will survive the sage—one bush that's not high on the menu.

Sometimes Kwami walks to lighten the load. Sometimes he changes places. Adababa can handle most rocks with his versatile footpads though some of the sharpest ones might cut his feet. Both men hope the animal's feet won't bleed deep between its two toes—the blood working its way into the crevices and chewing up the surface of the leather.

They head east, following tracks. Geoffrey Scott hopes the Indian horses will bolt when they see the camels—the power of surprise, the power of the camel's strangeness. *Hza tayibana wafaqak allah.* For good luck, Geoffrey Scott says to himself. Then he repeats it out loud, one of the Arabic phrases he's learned from Hadji Ali. "*Hza tayibana wafaqak allah.* We've come this far, Kwami. Here's to finding your woman."

"What are you saying?" Kwami asks.

Geoffrey Scott puts his hands together in a praying position and leans his head forward.

"You are a strange man," the Mojave says.

"I'm with you, aren't I? That makes me very strange." He laughs, though Kwami cannot quite figure the joke.

"It is good," Kwami says nevertheless. "Good you are strange."

They still have tracks to follow. And the horses, though not in the distance as far as they once were, are ahead of them. Unseen as yet.

* * * * *

When he rides Midnight to the post office to pick up the bag of mail for delivery, he tips his hat to the new postmaster who sits outside on a barrel reading a month-old newspaper.

"Need my mail bag. Gotta go north."

"Sure, though I have to shuffle through a few things to get it." He folds the newspaper, rises, and walks around the back of the building.

Charles feels more a part of the village than he has for a long time. Recently, it seemed he and Sophia had kept to themselves because of their troubles with Sarah Ann. And, of course, he was out on his horse delivering mail much of the time except for Sundays, when they worshipped with their neighbors, took the sacrament, and recommitted to Christ. But now, Sophia will soon have another baby. He's maintained his vigor. For all to see. Charles. A man with three wives. A passel of children and soon to have more. And don't forget Sarah Anne. Ten children and he's not far from sixty years of age. He's contributed to the body of Saints. A son, yes it will be a son. An important part of this community, a St. Thomas man, a stalwart.

He steps inside the post office—an adobe affair with added logs and chinked mud. He waits for the postmaster to come out of the shadows. After some searching, he'll hand him the satchel of scarred and road-weary leather that Charles'll carry north. He and Midnight. As he waits in the darkened interior, he feels pleased that there will be another child in this settlement. His child.

But his baby girl had taken her last nip of humanity here. St. Thomas can be a nasty place, maybe the hardest place ever, but Charles will never say that out loud even if it's fact. The settlement sits in a land of limestone, sandstone, ungodly pillars of eroded stone, and rocks the likes of which he's never seen before. It's built in a land of lava flows, volcanoes, salt, silica, razorback ridges, a land that confuses Charles, even though he's delivered to Panaca and Pioche hundreds of times. It is like one large repetition of something that's not pretty. Predictable bushes. An occasional giant Joshua. Once in a while, skirts of dark debris. *Bajada*—the tilt toward the sky. Nothing flat or stable. A place where men don't belong. Or women. A land that should stay what it is with no interference from humans.

"This place doesn't give back much," he mumbles to himself. "St. Thomas doesn't work in anybody's favor, however you slice it. But I'll be a father. Soon. That makes things better."

While he waits for the postmaster and the pouch pocked by blowing sand and torrential rain—a pouch used by someone before him, someone who tossed up his hands and said forget it, or maybe someone on the receiving end of an arrow—he thinks about his report to the town officials about Callville being abandoned. And military men moving in. "It's a Mormon settlement," he'd told them. "We built it. Nobody should interfere."

"The port of Callville seems doomed," they decided after they pulled on their matted beards, not quite knowing what else to do with the news he'd brought. "Most of the year, water's difficult. Dangerous even. No-man's-land," they'd said when they decided the meeting was over.

He whispers to himself while he waits in the post office, tapping his foot. Impatient and growing more so even though the day had started out to be a fine one. The men who make decisions about St. Thomas—the

St. Thomas wigs—they should have had a fiercer response. A bigger upset. Callville's been abandoned for hell's sake. And all they can do is say it's a No Man's Land? Maybe everyone's too hot. Can't care about anything when the thermometer tops 120 degrees. Heat's like a heavy blanket you've got to wear.

Just then, Richard Kesler walks into the post office.

"Every town has a few wigs," Charles wisecracks while he tamps his anger at what he considers the crazy response from the town commissioners, Kesler being one of them. "And here's one of them."

"Hey, Charles. How goes your day?"

"Fine enough," though he wants to tell Richard to think again about his casual remarks about Callville. The man doesn't know squat about the overall plan, and he is an idiot not to get it that Brigham Young has big plans for their town.

"I've been thinking about your report at the town meeting," Kesler says, having no suspicions that Charles is an about-to-be-lit plug of dynamite. "I'm not surprised about Callville. Hotter than Hades. Drier than it is here if that's possible. How can anybody be expected to maintain a warehouse in that hellhole?"

"But it's supposed to be part of a big chain of immigration," Charles says, still surprised at Kesler's negativity about Callville. He wants to do something to wake him up, maybe butt his head into this idiot's chest. "A new route for supplies. A master plan."

"Bad idea to begin with, you know that," Kesler says. He puts his empty bag made from flour-sack dish towels on the counter. "Steamboats up the Colorado. Who ever heard of such a thing when you're battling just to grow something to eat? Nothing should try to go upstream. Too many rapids. Smithereens is what you'll get."

"Those rapids are pretty serious most of the time." Charles tries to shape his next words carefully. He already has enough people who aren't fond of him in this town, and he doesn't want to be too prickly about this matter, even though most of the commissioners don't know squat. "But then there are those days. . . ."

"But those days are rare. Rare as a full meal around here."

"Brigham Young ordained it." Charles can hear his voice rising and feels his temper getting higher like a thermometer about to burst its tube.

"The Deseret Mercantile Association hired Anson Call to build it—the warehouses, the whole thing."

"Brigham tries a lot of things. He isn't afraid to experiment, though I think if he'd taken a look firsthand, he'd never sent anybody here."

"Brigham speaks for the Lord," Charles insists, still trying to keep his voice calm and his temper reined in. "You don't understand, not one whit." His volatility is rising close to his mouth where he could shout at this imbecile.

"He's human." Richard turns to receive his two letters from the postmaster, who's frustrated in his search for Charles' leather mailbag, then stuffs them into his cloth sack. "See you later, Charles. And congratulations. You're going to be a father afore too long." For a moment there's the light of sunshine, then the door closes again, leaving no illumination for the small room except for dust-covered windows at the back.

How did Kesler hear about the baby? Charles sputters to himself. Sophia has months to go. And that Kesler knows next to nothing about Callville.

Those behind Charles are curious, unable to keep from listening. They've come to build the Muddy Mission because Brigham asked them to come. They are strangers to dissension, or at least their doubts never reach their tongues. They believe.

"Good morning, Emma," Charles says to the first woman in line, turning his back to the counter, folding his arms trying to calm himself, and biding his time while the postmaster shuffles through rope-bound boxes and bags, back to looking for his pouch. "How are your bees?"

"Bees seem happy enough. Made some honey, for sure, though not as much as we'd hoped. But there's smoke comin' out of your ears, Charles. What's up?"

"Oh, nothing." He swallows hard, though if he had his way he'd be shouting at Emma and telling her what wimps the town leadership is. Hell's bells, the idiots, not caring enough about Brigham's wishes."

"You don't look any too happy. Something to do with Brother Kesler?"

"You mind your own business."

That's why I'm here. My own business," Emma snaps. "Don't you tell me to mind my own business. That's what I do. I came in here to send a letter north. It's mail day, you know. And I'm hoping for some news from up near Salt Lake." Then she shuffles her feet and looks to both the right and left. "Settle down, Charles. What're you so upset about? And what's this about Callville being abandoned?" she adds in a whisper. She must have eavesdropped on the tail end of Kesler's remarks.

"No one was there when I went down last month," he answers in a trembling voice. He's vexed. Infuriated. Indignant. Close to raging. "Except a few military men."

"Aren't the steamships bringing in more converts? More supplies?"

"That's the idea."

"Maybe the ones who keep it going have gone somewhere cool for a few days. Maybe they'll be back."

"They better be."

Their exchange ceases when another resident cozies up directly behind them to wait in line for mail delivery, most likely wanting to hear the conversation.

"No matter what Richard Kesler says to me or Sophia, even to you, Emma," Charles is speaking as softly as he can, "continue to believe in Callville. It was Brigham Young's idea. He's our prophet. Kesler would say Brigham is anxious to populate everything to keep the land for God's kingdom. Influenced by reports, mere reports. But God moves his hands and the earth shakes. The word of God. These men at Callville have abandoned Brigham's idea. Pure disobedience."

Emma's attention trails off when she sees the postmaster coming back to the window though Charles continues muttering to himself, wanting to believe anything is possible when God ordains it.

"Found your pouch," the postmaster says, handing a half-filled, worn leather sack over the counter. "Mail for the outliers."

"Mail must go through," Charles stops mumbling and laughs as if there's not another thought in his head. "Rain, sleet, hail."

"Even if it sometimes takes months, right?" The postmaster holds some letters in his hand, and the anticipation is high that maybe there's a letter for each person waiting in line. "Trains are coming before long. Not yet, but soon. The news will be newer then."

"Trains. I can't imagine them running across this land," Emma says, speaking up from behind Charles, elbowing him aside. "Nature is too full of distemper."

"If only we could see what this land'll be after we've passed on. Or through." Charles tries to chuckle as he yields his place in line. He could laugh except he'd like to tear Kesler's head off. Dumb man. Thinks he's so smart. What a mouth on that man.

"If only," Emma says, stepping up to the counter and receiving the one precious letter she's been waiting for from the postmaster. She rips it open and steps to a dark corner of the small building to read, with eagerness, her letter from her aunt. News of Salt Lake City. News of the new fort at Ft. Douglas.

"Any news I need to hear?" Charles says, hesitating before he faces the heat and the day again, still trying to calm himself to go back to what needs to be done.

"Nothing you ain't heard before, except all of it's new to our ears. Right?" She reads to the end of the letter, then starts over again. "Just so I can pass on something, they're proceeding with the temple, but slowly. Craftsman. The right ones. They'll come, even if it takes an invitation from Brigham Young," she says.

"I hope I'm alive and standing for the dedication." Charles tips his hat and hopes smoke doesn't fill the air. Who is that Emma to tell him he has smoke coming out of his ears?

"I'll wish that for you," Emma says, tucking the letter into the pocket of her stained apron and heading for the door. "Good travels when you calm yourself down."

Damn that Emma for her snoopy ways. Damn her. Damn Kesler. Damn this whole town. But he'll do his job, and delivering mail is his job. It is what he's been employed to do. His part, even if he can't get it out of his mind that Callville is supposed to tie them to the Colorado, to the world, converts, and supplies.

* * * * *

The feeling of life inside her. Like a seed, a pomegranate, she thinks. Why pomegranate? she does not know. Maybe because of the woman in the myths. Persephone. That is who she remembers. She washes the dishes in the sink Charles has built for her out of mesquite wood. "But wood swells," she'd told him, though he said she needed something until he could find a better replacement.

The plates. The forks. She rinses them in a separate pan with silt in it. Maybe semi-clean was the order of the day. She daydreams, wondering what grows inside of her. A fruit. A seed. A potato. Her eyes twinkle. She knows it is a son, as Charles knows it is a son, but will he be hardworking like Charles, solid and bereft of airs? Or will he be simple, earnest, and straightforward like Geoffrey Scott? She smiles, her lips tight together.

She does not know what the child will give to the world, but she is nonetheless happy to be watching her small waist balloon with child. What a surprise not to fit in thin places anymore. Soon there will be small feet pushing against her stomach, pushing against the boundaries the baby must feel about now. Surely God devised this plan, this miracle of a child?

She finds the dish towel hanging on its peg, wipes the dishes dry, and thinks about the disappearance of Geoffrey Scott and Adababa. Even Kwami. One day they were gone in a puff of smoke it seems. Pulled out of a rabbit's hat and sent on their way. No word, though maybe, and she hopes this is not the case, he believed her when she said she would never see him alone again. She meant those words, and yet…

She stacks the plates in the cupboard built for dishes. She knows that their time, their few moments together in the red rocks, was one time only. One occasion. One slip in Sophia's dedication to doing right in the world. She is ashamed of herself, except she feels some strength in knowing what it is she wanted on that day, the freedom for which she longed, the interruption to the yoke of building the Kingdom of God every single day, even if it was a careless pause in her life with Charles. She hopes she will be forgiven because she believes in Christ's atonement. He understands. He knows she believes in the right, in truth.

But still and at the same time, whoever's son this is will be someone who makes Charles proud. Charles will never know there is a question. Two fathers. Not a bad idea, though she cautions herself about too many fathers spoiling the broth. The morning sun slants through the window, its rays almost touchable, the way they make a line that looks real. It reminds her of music this morning. She loves her alone time where she can feel an abandon, an acceptance of everything that is.

This child will be a model of perfection. Not spoiled, she is sure about that, but she needs to move quickly this morning. Time to stop daydreaming, fold the wet dish towel and fold it over its peg. She has promised to help with the quilt setup at Nettie's house—the coverlet that will keep Nettie and her new baby warm when the days grow short. The baby is due in three weeks, and this quilt will be ready. Maybe by next Monday. Winter could announce its wintriness any time now with cold wind and grey skies. It is coming though it's unlike any winter she's ever known. Sophia is glad she can prick the top side of the quilt with the point of a needle. She loves small stitches. She is the master, maybe the mistress, her laughter pierces the quiet of the room, of the small stitch. The sisters are always happy when she arrives to help, and she enjoys their smiles and supportive words that sound like truth to be sure.

Suddenly, she's filled with a longing to make a hat. To felt the hat and make it shrink in scalding water. To watch the hat grow tighter and smaller before it is given its final shape. When a hat is felted properly, it cannot be torn asunder. To others, that process is a mystery, but it is a mystery she understands. She wipes the remaining utensils with her flour-sack towel and then places the cracked mirror against the wall. She checks her hair. Her bun needs to be redone. The part is crooked. Her lips are chapped. She looks like a garbled stranger in the misshapen glass, but then, who has looked in that mirror with any satisfaction for a good long time now? Cracked in transit, that mirror is not a good place for looking one's best. But, she wonders, has she lost her desire to look her best? The thought is sobering, but she is not going to think in that way any longer. She is determined to be helpful, to contribute, to be a part of this settlement, part of all that means in this desert. She is with child. She is part of the gossip. Part of the concern. A going concern, she laughs again and contemplates the distorted smile she can see in the mirror.

Doing dishes and watching the sun's rays dance through the windowpane has made her quite giddy. She's going to have a baby. She dances as best she can, twirling in two circles before she finds her bonnet for the day. But birthing in St. Thomas, of all places...She should not raise this boy beneath such a strong-willed sun that almost blares like a trumpet when it enters the sky every morning. Would her son do well here, or should she ask Charles if she can go to his home north of Salt Lake City, to Willard, where he has built a house for his first wife, Mary Anne? But it is supposed to be a family home, not just meant for one wife. She's part of the family now, she needs to remember. Sophia can ask if she could trade places with Harriet, the wife who got left behind to care for Mary Anne. Though she has felt some pride at being the one chosen to come to St. Thomas, silly woman she has been, Harriet might have a better constitution for this desert and not such a deep yearning for something different. Being in St. Thomas would serve Harriet well. Serve her right, Sophia thinks, in a moment of which she is instantly not proud. She is not a petty woman and won't sink to that kind of thinking. But Harriet is so proud of her wifehood, her preeminence among women. Sophia is not fond of Harriet, needless to say, even though she likes Mary Anne well enough. But maybe the two wives can trade. Sophia can deliver her baby where the climate is more suitable to a small child bursting its boundaries into manhood.

This idea hatches in her mind and ferments and grows as she ties the strings on her sunbonnet and walks to Nettie's house, and yet, when she passes the Marshalls' empty house, she finds herself wondering about Geoffrey Scott. Maybe he is only a flash in her memory but thinking of him makes her wistful. A poignant wistfulness. He is young, alive, handsome, and determined to make something of his life. But she knows…what does she know? That their moment had grown out of sheer loneliness? Maybe, but, whatever the case, she had taken no vows with him. She has gone off with him when she should have stayed home and remained faithful to her vows. How can she be so heedless? But Charles, bless his soul, does not understand the subtleties of love, of caressing, of being tender and holding her in the night when the wind blows harsh. He barely knows how she loves to be touched. This is not something he has learned or been taught, but then, who should be his teacher? Sophia? Mary Anne? Harriet? It's ludicrous to be a third wife with so many possibilities.

Buttoning her cardigan because there is a cool breeze today and she must protect her baby, she suddenly knows, without a doubt, that she must return to Willard. The winter months are bearable in St. Thomas, but she would rather be in Willard when the baby is born: December. She won't be strong then. She might even be sick, considering the water they have to drink in St. Thomas. Charles will listen. He will have pity on her. "Yes," he will say, and he will be impressed that she should be thoughtful of Mary Anne, that someone will be in residence with her to help her through the hard times of her illness, her old age, maybe. And he would have Harriet to help him with matters in St. Thomas.

Does Sophia care what the others might think? Maybe, though people in this town have been helpful in unpredictable ways, respecting her need to grieve and knowing that Charles is gone so much of the time. Everyone knows that neither of them is afraid to work hard when they can and knows they are not frivolous. But sometimes Sophia wishes she and Charles were more frivolous, more sociable, more integral to the town, though she has made her own mark at quilting bees. She has made some friends there. Some good women, no doubt. She's been having some good conversations lately, especially with Nettie, though she still pines for a good tit-for-tat with Almira.

But, as she prepares for the quilting bee, adjusting her image in the cracked mirror, she can't help but wish the women would wear fancy hats once in a while. They would be so much more gracious than the droopy sunbonnets, the ones that hide their eyes and their faces. She wishes she could make a hat for every woman in the town, that their eyebrows and eyes would be magnified and peep out from beneath a beautiful hat of silks and satins and an organza bow. That they would remember how to be flirtatious, how to be a woman, how to live the female version of life. She imagines an Easter parade, where the women would be dressed impeccably, topped with one of her hats that makes each of their individual beauty shine, even glow. But most of them are working hard to last in this outpost, working with an eye single to the glory of God, and to making a mark on this wild place where everything could blow away, given enough time.

As she steps out the door, off the sandstone steps, and creates a puff of dust with the first footstep she takes, she accepts the fact that there is no demand for her hats, however beautiful they may be, but she still dreams about an entire array of women dressed extravagantly, posture perfect, walking down the streets of St. Thomas with pride in their appearance. Like in the big cities of the world. But, as she walks on the well-traveled though unpaved road to Nettie's house, she resolves to leave all of this thinking behind and to be of service to Nettie and the other women who love her small stitches, who raise their eyebrows with delight when she comes through the door. Sophia's touch on the coverlet. Her gift. That she promises herself she will do.

Until she is too cumbersome to do so, she will do her best in the next months to contribute. She will dance at the dances and give herself over to the hilarity of the evening, the forgetfulness she feels when she is part of the music and the fiddle pulls a taut string inside her. She will wear one of her hats to services, but the day will have to be a special day so she will not appear vain. Not that she isn't vain, she chuckles inside herself. How can she think otherwise? Why not be truthful, at least when it comes to her own truth? But vanity doesn't have to be a sore point with her, does it? It doesn't have to mean something empty or valueless. Some vanity is important in this dried-up world, at least some sense of pride in that which can take one's breath away, in that which is graceful and of excellent quality. She will remind the sisters that there is beauty in this world, even if there is so little to be seen in St. Thomas. She will recite Wordsworth while they are quilting together, reminding them of the cultured shores whence they all came. She will lend her hand. That is her task—to remind everyone of beauty.

She stumbles over the uneven ground of the rutted road and trips in a pothole bigger than most. She double vows to help the women remember. That will be what she is about for the months while the baby, her son, grows inside of her and is ready to make an appearance. And she will convince Charles to let her go to Willard for the birthing.

CHAPTER TWELVE

ANOTHER EYE FOR AN EYE

NORTH AND EAST OF ST. THOMAS

Geoffrey Scott recognizes the bleating sound. The complaining sound. He knows Adababa is saying he's not interested in continuing, period, but they have to keep going, period. Granted, there are too many rocks in the rock field they're passing through—boulder-like, sheer on the sides, slippery with dried red mud. There's the soft sand between rocks, soft from when the rain pounded its impressions in the dirt. Unpredictable. Geoffrey Scott suspects Adababa is unhappy not only with the profusion of rocks but with the wet ground and the sucking sound around his feet. He has to pull out of each step, and no creature should have to bear this kind of walking. He's always been obedient since he was born. He's cooperated, rarely saying much about what he's being asked to do. But maybe Adababa, the strong, needs a rest. Even camels need a rest once in a while.

Why should he carry two men on his back when one is indignity enough? Maybe the two men should find a horse that can carry one of them, at least. Then Adababa will not have to carry so much through these rocks. But trouble is, no matter how the problem is sliced, they have to keep going. They can't lose time if they're going to find those kidnappers who know how to raid corrals and have probably acquired guns along the way. Maybe they'd gotten the animals from the Spanish in the first place, but Geoffrey Scott suspects most of them belong to the Mormons who've built small settlements here and there. For a minute he considers where he might find a horse to borrow for who knows how long, but though he may be many things, he's not a horse thief. Therefore, Kwami and Geoffrey Scott, even though they take turns walking, keep riding Adababa—their sturdy transportation and their only way to follow the tracks that are taking them toward the Utah-Arizona Strip. Indian country.

"Abey could be sold for Spanish goods," Kwami says as Adababa picks his way through the rocks. "Niyol, too." Geoffrey Scott's given up trying to ascertain what the Indian thinks but is surprised to hear he knows as much as he does about this. Slavery is a real possibility.

"Most likely to those Catholics in New Mexico," he says back. "The ones who can justify their purchase. They'll swear their Christian homes are a big help to the Indians, complete with their crosses, milagros, and statues of Saints. Indians to serve the White Man is what that amounts to."

Kwami points to some tracks following the riverbed. "Follow there," he says. "Don't let camel stand when he drinks."

"Adababa might sink is what you're saying. Right?"

"Not a good place for standing."

They keep careful watch for the Utes, probably still wearing war paint on their cheeks. Carrying guns, no doubt. They ride through another canyon and head northeast where the tracks turn north of no-man's-land—the biggest of all canyons. There are a few settlers at Kanab, then at Pipe Springs, and Fredonia. They replenish their water from a rusty pipe at one ranch but stay out of sight as much as possible. They know they're an unlikely combination in the ponderosas.

"John Lee? See him?" Kwami asks as he hangs onto Geoffrey Scott's jacket, sitting on the downside of Adababa's back, riding through the trees and careful to avoid branches that might scrape his arms or gouge his legs.

"How do you know that name?" Geoffrey Scott has heard talk of John D. Lee, the man some are blaming for the Mormon Meadows Massacre that happened back in '57. He heard some of this from Sophia. How Kwami knows this name is beyond him.

"He blames Paiutes. Abey tells me."

"For that massacre? About ten years ago?"

"That one."

"I hear he was sent to Lonely Dell on the Colorado. Keeping out of sight. He's minding the ferry across a big horseshoe bend in the river. We might have to go that far, by the way. Depends where these tracks take us."

"Mormonees kill Americats at massacre. They were painted like savage Paiutes," Kwami says. "Bad medicine."

"I can't think of one who would do what you're talking about, though I gather they aren't all the same."

"Mormonees take land and water. Don't care about people before them."

"Don't hold too close to talk like that," Geoffrey Scott says, even though he's aware the Mormons have settled in places already inhabited by the natives. The subject is discomforting to him as well as to Kwami. "Loose talk will make you angry."

The conversation ends, both men turning to their own observations of what they are passing through, the sun past full over their heads. The sound of the camel's hooves picking his way across the rocks is all the two riders hear for a while. But Geoffrey Scott, distracted for a minute, is thinking white people have overdone their elitism in the West. Then he remembers to keep his mind on the pursuit at hand.

"East still?" he asks.

The Mojave looks at the hoofprints embedded in the ground between the scattering of rocks. He points to rugged country, to the East, which means miles and miles of vacant land, though it could also mean plentiful springs and easy hunting. At least this country seems plentiful compared to St. Thomas. Pine trees and needle-covered hills that cool off at night.

"Adababa's feet are hurting," Kwami says, the camel complaining again, tired of two men on its back, let alone having to swim in deep water when a river needs crossing. He was probably unhappy with the rocks sheathed off from cliffs, maybe during volcanic upheaval years or endless shifting of tectonic plates. Some of the sloughed-off boulders are small, some medallion-sized, some of them carriage-sized. Everywhere rocks, and one or two of them could even roll onto the riders and camel. It is difficult for Adababa to find his balance in this challenging terrain.

"You saying we should check Baba's feet?"

"Give him some rest. We will walk. Now."

"That'll slow us down," Geoffrey Scott warns.

"Now." There was no compromise in Kwami's word.

They dismount but the Mojave keeps watching for signs of the kidnappers. He has a practiced eye. He can see traces. "This way," he says as Adababa steps carefully over the strangely angled stones, shaking his fur and obviously relieved to be free of his burden. The rim of the sun touches the tops of the mountains. "*Muatagoci,*" Kwami says when the top of the moon appears on the horizon. "You ride now. I will walk."

"I can walk, too," Geoffrey Scott says, though Kwami motions his head for him to remount. "Okay. If you say so."

Geoffrey Scott straddles the camel again, then rocks to the sides. There is silence in the dusk, in the falling of day into night, in the appearance of the stars one by one it seems. He can hear a hoot owl somewhere in the distance, but then turns to wondering if he has any chance with Sophia. He can almost hear the tongue lashing she gave him after the Valley of Fire. A volley of words. Agony in those words, maybe. He can almost feel her soft skin when he thinks about her, the malleable expanse beneath the buttons and snaps. He's awkward with women, he reckons. Sophia is probably no exception. He's not been with the fairer sex for a long time, but he remembers her skin—the only skin he's touched that's been so yielding, almost begging for his fingers to travel in circles on its surface. She needed him to touch her even though he's been rolling across the prairies and the desert and was probably naive. He won't give up hope. He wants her warmth against his skin. This particular woman. Her breasts. Nothing else feels like a breast does. Pillow? Home?

"I feel free," she told him as they rode into the red valley. "This place reminds me of fire, a valley of fire, where the rocks quiver inside the earth before being spewed onto the flat ground. Beautiful chaos." He was enchanted by this talk. Curious. But afterward, when they rode back to St. Thomas, she changed her tone: "I don't want to care too much about anyone. The only way to survive is to be careless, not attached. Why care so much?"

"And there is no such thing as true love," she added as he rode behind her on Adababa, knowing nothing of the source of her words or why she would speak in that way. He leaned to one side to hear what she was saying, not always easy with the wind blowing her words in a different direction. "It is best to be indiscriminate about love and its trappings. I've come to believe that," she continued. "True love is only an idea we have both heard about. I don't wish to be ruled by anyone else's ideas or canons."

Those were the words she spoke as they rode. Yet she didn't live by them, Geoffrey Scott surmised. She was afraid of Charles, and she wouldn't face the fact that she was buying her religion lock, stock, and barrel, not all of which she agreed with. Despite all of those things, she still believed there was a God to make everything possible. Maybe a God that made her feel she must line up the toes of her shoes parallel to an immovable line, but God regardless. She was caught by her commitment, Geoffrey Scott decided. Ruled by shoulds and oughts. Maybe a different person from the one who rode into the red rock with him. Truer to what she was supposed to be rather than what she was. He should forget Sophia. Maybe she's a third wife, but she's a wife and is committed to her vows with Charlie Hughes. He'd best accept that fact even though she doesn't belong in St. Thomas or with Charles Hughes any more than a satin slipper is something a horse wears.

Then, suddenly aware of the pines, the smell, the silent Mojave walking behind him, Geoffrey Scott remembers he needs to pay attention. The evening tells him. The rising of *muatagoci* tells him. He must help Kwami find Abey and her child, his *Mamaci* and Niyol.

* * * * *

As he carries his saddlebags toward the house, Charles stops to watch Sophia, pausing in front of the pane of glass he's procured on one of his rides through the small settlements of Utah Territory. At the end of daylight, he stands in the shadow from the rooftop and an overhead cloud. The desert surrounds his home. Quiet at this hour. The crickets are beginning to sing, and he loves that sound. Rubbing their legs together, somebody told him, though he prefers to think they are singing. What else is hiding behind the scrawny bushes, he wonders, but his attention returns to the window. He watches as Sophia moves from corner to counter, lighting candles, and setting a dinner for his return.

As he watches her without her knowing he's watching, he isn't sure about this wife. She doesn't seem strong and robust like some of the other women in St. Thomas. She's beautiful, everybody says so. Fetching, one man said, though that statement feels hollow as he watches her prepare a meal for him—too domestic to think other thoughts. She pauses and raises her arms in an "I forgot that" gesture. Then she puts her knife on the counter and whirls, almost like a top. What is that about? He watches her dance, almost float, across the candlelit room, her stomach showing as she turns. His baby. Growing while she dances.

She was beyond his well of words, that was a sure thing. Maybe she was a piece of fine china, he thinks, as he rests the saddle against the house, stretches his spine, and rotates the bones of his shoulders, but whatever she is, he's proud of the fact she is with child. His child. Maybe he'll stop giving her trouble and stop being irritated at how she does things. He's hard on her, no doubt, and says things better left unsaid. But she should know that all he wants is to add extra hands to build temples, farms, hoe crops, build irrigation ditches, to take part with the Saints. He will be the father of his own world someday, and Sophia will be one of his wives. She can help him get there. Children on and on. Forever. Into eternity.

And St. Thomas, whatever he thinks about the place in his dark moods, is one of the settlements needing good hands, good people willing to give their all to make it work. He can do that on his way to running his own world. He knows he can, especially when he returns home after a long trip on Midnight, opens the door to his adobe house, and looks at the quiet movement in the room. Then he remembers he's a servant of God. That both he and Sophia are servants of God, even though they are mere mortals.

* * * * *

Sophia is scurrying to have a meal ready when Charles returns. She feels pale, even wan, but she'll not entertain her regrets. Those she keeps hidden away from onlookers, especially Charles, who should be back any time now though she did not know he was outside looking in. The past is the past and will remain there. She is not well tonight and has not been at her best since she and Charles arrived in St. Thomas. But she is determined to see this second pregnancy through to the end. She will be smarter than the fever, ague, the dysentery, the malaria, the mosquitoes. Determined. No one will stop her from having this baby and giving the life it deserves. If she had only been more careful, maybe given birth to Sarah Jane in a more favorable place...If only she had known what to do. And maybe this new, soon-to-be-born baby has been fathered by Charles. That is a possibility. Definitely. No one will ever know she was with Geoffrey Scott.

Scraping one lonely carrot and cutting as finely as she knows how, she repeats the words: "I want this baby no matter how ill I might be." This means much to Charles. She knows the promise of a child has added to his happiness, his temper, even. But, truth be told, she also wants this baby for herself, to prove she can nurse a child through any trouble and beyond. And at times, when she is incautious, she knows she wants this baby for Geoffrey Scott, though he'll never know that the possibility even exists. She will never let him know. That would be ludicrous to him—the fact that he has fathered a Mormon boy.

He is of no import in her life, not really, though when she is washing the dishes or smearing the counter with a dishcloth that will soon be rancid—not enough clear water to make the cloth fresh again—she thinks of that day in the valley that brings out the fire in her passions. She thinks of the time when she helped unbutton her worn dress and kisses the pad of that finger that made its way through the seamed buttonhole. She should be preparing dinner, but lays down her knife, closes her eyes, and spans her arms like an eagle in flight. She turns herself around, faster and faster, knowing she's not as small as she once was, but still dancing until everything whirls with her—her dress, her stays, her petticoats, even her underthings. All of her desire for beauty emerges into this one expression. She feels a cool breeze on her cheeks while the setting sun outside accentuates the calligraphy of clouds in the sky and turns them gold, then pink, then red, then blue, dark blue. She thinks of Geoffrey Scott—his strong back, the way he held onto her as they raced across the sand. Even though she knows she shouldn't, she feels him piercing her open, vulnerable, coming inside of her, and she knows that moment is part of her now. She puts her hand flat on her enlarged stomach. Words will never cross her tongue or her lips about red rocks. Or about Geoffrey Scott. She'll never betray this child.

But then, she finds a third candle and puts it on the trestle table. Three candles for Charles' return, two to brighten their meal together, one so both can see the things written on their faces. She is not a woman to lie or cheat. She is not, not, not of that nature. She has standards. That time with Geoffrey Scott was one moment in time which she will not think about anymore. It should never have happened. And yet, though she tells herself she must not think in this way, maybe it was destined to happen.

Everything is so big, and she is so small. But somehow, all of it is encapsulated in her being. She can feel God in her chest cavity and in her womb where life is unfolding. She understands something huge that cannot be put into words or cannot be felt, except momentarily, almost like the weather. The land around her is barren but can be so beautiful when the light is right, when the heat has abated, when the air is cool and breathable, like this night. And it does not matter whose baby is inside of her. It only matters that there is a baby being formed and that this baby will live and breathe and do good works.

She will make Charles happy, she will. She will shore up his feelings that what he is doing is right, correct, an acceptance of and obeisance to God. They will work together, servants of a larger cause. They will make a home, even several homes, and tonight, she will ask him if she can return to Willard and take care of Mary Ann. She can bide the remainder of her pregnancy there. The days and nights are cooler there. She can hear the breeze saying, "Yes, Yes."

* * * * *

"Welcome home," she says when Charles walks through the door and removes his tired hat. He has a sunburned face, a white line across his forehead, and a few sticks of kindling in his right arm. "I'm glad you have returned safely." She reaches up to put her arms around his neck and peck his lips. Then she rubs her neck. "It hurts my neck to stand on my toes and reach up like that."

"I'm home," he says, brushing her lips with a perfunctory kiss though his eyes survey the room while he does. He is a man with many things on his mind, always wanting to bring order to something.

"Lots of riding," she says, backing away, picking a stick of cat's claw from his jacket that has broken off and is clinging to the cloth.

"Sometimes more than Midnight wants. But he's used to the heat if I've enough water for him." He tosses what kindling he has on the stack of wood in the corner.

"I should have said something before you dropped that," she laughs. "Now I need you to hand it back. We could use a fire tonight."

"Sorry about that." His voice has no inflection, no passion. Only tiredness.

Why is he not more responsive? What can she say to Charles who is her husband and her protector though she never feels quite protected by him? Her voice is a beguiling one—something she knows about herself: the queen bee with seductive tones. With that voice, she can bend Charles' will and divert his attention, though he'll never let her know—that's something she understands. But what does it mean that they are together? That he comes home to her after being away for days? What do they have between them? He's built a house with walls for shelter, for that she should be grateful, but at the moment, she wants something more from him.

Charles reaches past the new layer of kindling and into the box of screwbean, mesquite, and cat's claw gathered on the bottomlands of the Muddy River, after the rush of flash-flood waters have receded, after the rivers dry to small streams. They'd scoured the bottomlands for this kindling together. Sophia was so tiny she could dance on quicksand, she remembers him saying. "You're almost as light as a mosquito, though I don't much like to think of mosquitoes and the malaria they bring to St. Thomas." He hands Sophia enough cat's claw to start a fire, then adds a handful of driftwood to keep it burning.

"We'll boil some water and add the potatoes," she says. "No meat tonight because the men could not go hunting. The Paiutes have been stirring up trouble."

"How much trouble?" Charles is alarmed. This is maybe the first time she's heard a worry about the homestead from him. Maybe he is feeling guilty for leaving her alone for such long stretches of time. Maybe he realizes he needs to protect his wife. She needs that from him though there is such a distance between them. A gap. A gully. How can she ever let such a man know she needs protection? That she misses him even though his anger repels her and makes her want to run away?

"Do we need to go to the fort?" he asks, new worry in his voice. An adobe fort is located west of the town. Built on a knoll, a small hill, a bump among bumps on the earth that gives the appearance of strength.

"I think we will be all right at home, for now, but there has been continuing difficulty with the Indians."

What she doesn't say is that Geoffrey Scott has talked about Mormons moving in and appropriating the land used by the Paiutes, the same way the military has done with the Mojaves to the South. How unconscionable that is, he said, but then, she thinks somewhat petulantly, Geoffrey Scott is refracting a salt mine that has been mined for hundreds of years by the Indians before the white men arrived in wagons, on horses and mules.

"You should know there was a raid on the Paiute village not far from here," she adds, sprinkling the boiling water with salt. "Some Indians on horses and with guns. They seized a woman and child. I think they were connected to the one who partners with Geoffrey Scott, though I don't think you ever met him. Rumor is that the two men have disappeared on the camel. You know. That animal that caused Midnight to rave out of his mind. I wonder where the Indians got the horses. There aren't many left since the raid on St. Joseph."

"A raid? Guns? When did this happen?" Charles seems as upset as Sophia has ever seen him. She's been worried, too, even though she heard the news a few weeks again and hasn't wanted to worry Charles who has so much else on his mind.

"A while ago. I should have told you before now but I didn't want to worry you. All of this makes me want to stitch quilts all night, even on the very elementary frames the women are using. We do need quilts. Granted, maybe there are only two seasons—hot and windy—but we need warmth for a January or February night. Not that they are much protection, but I do not want to think about anymore trouble."

"I don't like the Indians coming so near these settlements. Not one bit. Same as I don't like to re-dig the water canals that keep filling with sand when the wind blows."

"This is a hard place, Charles."

"Indeed."

She pauses, picks up the corner of her apron, and then lets it fall to rest in its natural folds. She wants to speak but turns toward the fire instead. She lifts the lid on the pan to see if the water is boiling yet.

"I think I should go back to Willard," she says, more to the wall than to Charles, who barely hears her words. But when he hears "Willard," he suddenly becomes all ears. "I could take care of Mary Anne while I wait for this baby," she talks continuously, even in a hurry, to avoid any interruption from him. "It is hard for me to stay here if I should say so. Maybe hard means one thing to you, another to me. But the Indians, the sand, the heat, the diseases. And the mosquitoes. There are too many of them. Can you not take me to Willard? To protect the baby? I know this child means much to you."

Sophia watches Charles' anger stirring like bubbles at the bottom of a pot. Who is she to ask those kinds of questions? He is the one who decides what is best for his family, and she had better remember that. Of course. Of all his wives, she's the most foreign to him but he still demands that she recognize him as the decider of these sorts of questions. He has the Kingdom of God to tend to, no less. Sophia watches him calming but decides he is a man who is up and down, in and out like an inflatable bag. Big with anger, and limp from spent anger. The man is trying to be reasonable but she has irritated a bone in his body. She watches him calculate.

How many months of her remaining pregnancy seemed to be the first question he considers. She can see him counting his fingers. The second notion is that Harriet might trade places with Sophia until the child has a good hold on life. "Maybe it won't hurt if I bring Harriet down here. You can even befriend Mary Anne. Take care of her. It's not good for her to be alone." Final consideration, though it is an unspoken one: if he takes Sophia back to Willard, then he won't be showing favoritism, which Harriet has accused him of doing. He's been commanded to love his wives equally. Granted, that has been hard for him. Maybe one of the hardest commandments.

After a lengthy pause, he reaches a conclusion. "I think the time away for you would be best for all of us. I don't want to lose the child to mosquitoes and lack of water. This is the right choice. After giving it some thought, I think it's a good idea. I'll bring down Harriet to help me while I continue building St. Thomas and delivering mail."

This he can do. He agrees. She closes her eyes and breathes deeply with satisfaction but mostly with relief. Yes, he'd do this for her and for the child they were bringing to this good earth. Yes. Yes. He'd said yes.

* * * * *

Adababa seems listless. His hump's withering, though Geoffrey Scott's unsure the animal's wanting for water. That could be a wrong assumption. He and Kwami have given the camel plenty to drink, he's sure, though he doesn't know everything. This trip has made him wary of what he does know, and it's true that Kwami anticipates what Baba needs before he does. Damn Indian thinks Baba and he are better friends than Geoffrey Scott will ever be. But no one can change an animal's preference, that's for sure. Animals like what they like. Maybe there is something spiritual or open-book between them, who knows?

The threesome has not reached the Colorado yet or at least the part of the winding river that is supposed to be northeast from St. Thomas. They should come to it anytime now, and a ferry would be a welcome sight. Fat chance of that. Adababa can swim across, that much he knows, though the river's swifter than anything Geoffrey Scott's ever seen. He isn't sure how much Kwami knows about swimming, though, truth is, he doesn't want to chance it either. The river's a monster—the only way he can describe it. But they're closing in on the kidnappers, and maybe Adababa will come across the Utes soon. That matters most.

As if thinking about it made it happen, Kwami sees a fresh track. "Soon," he says in almost a whisper, though his word is decisive.

Geoffrey Scott doesn't know how much the man understands, but Kwami's a smart one. Smarter than he is, at least in more things than he would have figured. But he takes favor with underdogs, the acorn not falling far from the tree, not far from his mother and her opinions. Again he asks himself why he's decided to come with Kwami, not something he is sure about. Riding a camel into the middle of nowhere? How smart is he?

Suddenly, in the fresh breath of morning, they hear a crack. It sounds like the breaking of a limb, and they both slide down the side of Adababa and tether the camel to wait behind pine trees growing thickly in these parts. Kwami holds his fingers to his lips.

A foot breaking a limb? A stray branch giving away the Utes who have Abey and Niyol? Geoffrey Scott hides behind a pine tree with wide skirts, a tree growing in that spot for many years, a tree that weeps sap, and Geoffrey Scott can smell the pine tar as his eyes survey everything around him. A strong, pungent smell.

Kwami hides himself behind one of those trees, his bow ready, an arrow notched into place. Carefully, Geoffrey Scott creeps back to where Adababa is tied and draws the repeating rifle out of its canvas bag, the gun his father used in Missouri, the rifle that has been pointed at a man now counted among the dead. It is a gun Geoffrey Scott never wanted to use. He dislikes the sound of the word even, but feels the curve of the trigger against his finger. Has he turned vicious on his journey across the Southwest, in his days away from his parents' farm in Kansas? Is he now a person who'd kill as soon as fight with his fists? He wonders, then catches sight of a Ute with his gun ready to fire, a gun aimed directly at him, though a tree blocks a straight path between them. The Ute surprises him with the confidence of his stance, and Geoffrey Scott flashes on a picture of his dead father and mother. Will he soon join them somewhere he cannot name? Will he bleed profusely or will the wound be tidy, neat, and clean, only a little blood dripping from the hole made by the bullet?

The native slides through the trees and branches. Glides like a feather floating before it finds a place to land. He maneuvers to a place where he can make a clean shot at Geoffrey Scott, his valor soon to be touted around a campfire and beneath the dome of his willow house. Then, a slicing sound of blunted feathers cutting through space. A strong sound. The Ute, finding a straight line between himself and Geoffrey Scott and about to squeeze the trigger of his gun, crumples. Falls. Tumbles. An arrow pierces his lungs.

Geoffrey Scott, in shock because a gun has been aimed at him at such point-blank range, looks over his shoulder where Kwami is preparing another arrow for his bow. Clean. Pure. Quiet. Efficient. A tower of a man standing straight, accurate with such primitive weapons.

Kwami puts his finger to his lips and notches another arrow. Standing on a slight rise behind a row of pines, another Ute is looking for his partner. His rifle hangs at his side until he sees a flash of Geoffrey Scott's hand. He lifts his rifle quickly, ready to take aim. Geoffrey Scott's scalp would add to the price of the woman and child. To the stories he can tell when he returns to his tribe.

Kwami's next arrow is precise. As if his knees failed him, another Ute falls to the ground. Geoffrey Scott looks down at the rifle he's carrying and is grateful for its silence. His eyes search the trees that now seem thinner, no shadows behind them. Sun shines at a slant, its rays filtering through the stand of pines, its lines almost straight until they are broken by an intruding branch. The landscape seems innocent. No Utes mar the scene. Yet, Kwami and Geoffrey Scott have figured three, not two. Something smells of another Ute full of the medicine that pushes young men to do what others will not.

Kwami pushes the branches aside with his arrow. His face is passive as he releases the next shot which slices the air and sinks into nothing at all. The movement of a leaf, perhaps. He threads his bow again. Geoffrey Scott and Kwami move slowly through the pines, slowly to the ridge of the hill. Suddenly, they see one more Ute pointing a gun at the woman's head.

Her hair has been pulled tight by a leather thong, and her reddened face has seen the backs of hands. Scarlet. Crimson. She looks up but seems to see nothing. Then she collapses over Niyol, both arms encircling him. The Ute is yelling in his language, maybe telling her to straighten up, but she stays like a tent over her young child, covering him with her arms and her shawl, anything to keep him whole. Her face is more proud than afraid of the gun and the man.

Kwami prepares to shoot but the Ute has seen him first. He's fast. The bullet from the Ute's gun hits Kwami in the bent arm meant to release the arrow, his fingers, forearm, whole arm turning numb, covered with blood. Filled with sudden anger, Geoffrey Scott raises his gun and finds the Ute in its sights. He pulls the trigger–something he's never wanted to pull, something so easy to do–to let a bullet fly. And he can't believe his eyes when he sees the last kidnapper fall to the ground. Dust soaring high and making a figure in the air. A waltzing wraith. Dust blows. Dust settles. There is no movement.

"Three," Kwami says. "No more."

The woman and child run to Kwanyumai, who stoops to take the boy in his unwounded arm, more demonstrative than Geoffrey Scott has ever seen. He seems joyous. He, Adababa, and Geoffrey Scott, have found Abey and her boy. *Mamaci* and Niyol with black hair and a dusty belly. Hungry. Thirsty. Naked. Dust on his back and his forehead. But Kwami needs to stay the blood from his arm which runs profusely in all directions. *Mamaci* offers her skirt, tears a piece from its circularity, and wraps his arm with a strip of cloth. When her task is accomplished and the blood has ceased running, she circles her hands with gratitude, cups her cheeks, and says words no one but her son understands.

Through it all, Adababa stands observant. Quiet. Still, though Geoffrey Scott suspects he's aware of the reunion and the staunching of blood and the dead men who don't move. This is an end of something. There is even a hint of peace on the camel's face, as if he knows a task has been accomplished and that he'll soon return to smoother roads where nothing will cut into his hooves. To a place where he can gallop and never stop. Maybe he feels some satisfaction that the kidnappers have been stopped cold. If only Geoffrey Scott could know what an animal thinks. Or not, though Kwami puts his arms around Adababa's neck and pats its coat as if the camel were his best friend.

CHAPTER THIRTEEN

BACK TO WILLARD

Whenever a day has blue skies, which seems to be the case most every day, and when her work at home is done, Sophia walks to the center of town where she can find people engaged in the same cause as she is. On this afternoon, she walks toward the quilting bee at Emma's house assessing the "eighty-five one-acre lots," the ones people drew for, paper slips in a bowl, ten to a block. The town should be, she figures in her head, nine-and-a-half or ten blocks if you count the two-and-a-half acres of garden lots and five-acre farm lots. She and Charles drew Lot 37, a garden lot, where they're supposed to be able to grow what they need plus, everyone hopes, much more. She is unsure of the divisions but then she feels a bump stretching to a point on her stomach. An arm or a leg. "My baby," she says as she ties the strings of her bonnet, straightens the seams of her skirt, and checks her bag to make sure she has brought enough cots to protect the tips of her fingers.

St. Thomas is growing. On the side away from Portia's house, people have moved in, and even the Marshalls' house might soon be claimed. There has been talk. Despite herself, she wonders where Geoffrey Scott has gone but today is not the day to think of him.

The fields outside town are almost green: tiny shoots of wheat growing out of paltry soil—strangers in a strange land—and she wonders what the wheat stalks think of being here in this place where it is unsafe for anything to grow very tall. The sun will shrink whatever tries to grow there. With flattened hands, she presses her bonnet close to the sides of her face. She'd best protect her fair skin complexion. Keep it white. The sun has its ways of browning or reddening skin if one doesn't take the greatest care.

There seem to be more tents than adobe homes, but the town is growing from sand and wind into something. According to Charles, St. Thomas is meant for a fate greater than an agrarian way station: trade, maybe even shipping when the season is right, a respite for weary travelers. With Callville gone, however, that cannot happen. She suspects he hasn't told her that he'd ridden down there to measure whether or not the place could be salvaged.

She climbs the hill where she can see the mouth of the mountain gorge on the southwest side of the Muddy. Because it is late spring, there is now an almost-big river—snow melt in the mountains, now running into the Virgin River—that joins the Muddy close to here. Sophia eyes the fort on this glorious morning when the wind is not blowing and the world feels ordered. Safe. Built to protect them against the unpredictable Paiutes, who mostly want food but who sometimes seem a threat, sometimes carrying a knife. For a moment, she is puzzled when she thinks of whose land this might be, though she would rather not think about something that reminds her of Geoffrey Scott and his abolitionist-thinking.

Before she can walk much further into the morning that, for a change, feels how a morning should feel, she needs to turn back. She will be sitting for hours at the edge of a quilt, watching it be turned as the quilters make progress, watching pieced fabric become something useful, and she needs to relieve herself. Everyone in St. Thomas has to relieve themselves or blow their noses or remove wax from their ears once in a while. She squeezes her eyes and screws her face in merriment at the thought of people and their private moments, though those are tasks for ordinary people, not for those who live in St. Thomas. She knows she is on the edge of being judgmental. Too bad Almira Marshall rode out of here with her family and never came back. She was exceptional. As I am exceptional—she laughs again. When she is in this kind of mood, she is above everything, not accountable for anything.

But Sophia catches herself before her thoughts run to something too large to keep under control. She knows her mind is busy at work, trying to make trouble on such a glorious day as this. But she'll have none of it. The ordinances of the body are the levelers. She is like others, even though she does not want to be. But she cannot help thinking that the people of St. Thomas, for the most part, seem coarse and have little eye for the beauty Sophia knows is in the world—the red of maples in the autumn, the rocks along the seashore, the measured boards on covered bridges. She is from England, and yet, she is also from Doncaster, an industrial city, the south of the north, which is clotted with factories, yes, of course. But there is rain in Doncaster. In England. Rain that refreshes and carries everything away. Rain that falls on everyone, she must remember.

She lumbers toward the center of St. Thomas, aware she is showing now, that her stomach cannot be hidden any longer, and that walking is getting to be a challenge for her. Dainty. Small steps, please. Closer to Emma's house, she can still see the river. She sees a hazy blue light above the water, almost a swirling of blue and gray, a mixture of something that seems more substantial than air. The light changes quickly as does the shape. Sometimes the surface of the river water sparkles, the yellow sunlight creating patches of light, and sometimes the river appears as a steely gray snake when the clouds pass overhead. But this afternoon, a hazy blue plays just above the water, making the Muddy seem bluer than brown. Sophia feels the urge toward a poem. She must memorialize this occasion with an ode to the Muddy, something like "Oh river of red and brown, nothing blue, oh, Mojave." She likes the Indian word "Mojave" better than its English translation of "Muddy." This sand moves from heel to toe in her petite shoes, even though they are still smaller than most of the women's footwear found in St. Thomas. Her footsteps fill her shoes with sand and, though she wishes this weren't the case, blackens the spaces between her toes.

All around her there are red rocks, table mesas, mountains resembling cardboard props for a stage. She feels small when she thinks of how far these mountains stretch away from her and how they seem to go on forever. At the edge of town, she can see a gully whose edges have been broken by flash floods—uneven, crumbly edges that could collapse while she watches them. The land sinks and falls in unexpected places. Even with the improvements the Saints have made, this land is still not a place for sane people to live, hard as they try. Wherever she steps, she feels the burn of sand beneath her soles, almost always hot like the surface of an iron placed on red coals to heat. These things will be something to talk about at the quilting bee.

"Good day," she says when she turns the corner toward Emma's passable home, though it is more like a hovel. But first she sees Martha Evans raking sand, trying to tame it maybe. Martha. She sometimes joins the quilters on Fridays, though her stitches are too big, thinks Sophia, who's aware of her precise stitches.

"Good afternoon," Martha says in return, standing upright with her rake, straightening her back. "Are you on your way to quilting? We need women good with the needle, such as yourself. I hope you're comin'."

"I am on my way with my needles and cots. Will you be there?"

"Soon's I finish this raking."

"How could anyone miss our quilting day?"

Martha laughs. "The quiltin' goes better when you come. Your stories, you know. Even your poems. The way you help us think about the word 'green.'"

As she moves along toward Emma's house, Sophia is happier than she has been in a long time. She has seen green this morning. At least an almost-green and full-bodied color. She believes in the miracle that the people of St. Thomas are performing. And she understands that everyone wants the same thing and must remember that. She is one of many pioneers, not the only one.

You have an urge to be superior, she whispers to herself. It rides your back. Your waste does smell, after all. A big grin spreads across her face, and she is laughing at herself. She throws her head back and smacks her forehead with the palm of her hand, entertaining herself this morning, no need for anyone to perform for her.

She passes more homes. She's almost there. Some men tend to their plots at this hour, some wave, working their hoes and rakes in the sand which they hope against hope will turn to fertile soil. Oh, to have a magic wand that one can wave over the top of St. Thomas and its soil. She felt as if she could cast an enchanted spell if she had one to use. It was one of those days.

"I hear you're with child," Emma Stout calls out when she sees Sophia approaching her house. "Like me." She stands in the garden plot close to her home, trying to clear a growing space for melons that she hopes to harvest this winter, trying to hurry before quilting begins. Sagebrush has been pulled out of the ground and is jumbled into an unsightly pile.

Emma speaks too loudly, Sophia thinks. Not much education but then, Sophia realizes she is judging again.

Emma wipes her hands on her midsection when she stands from a kneel, still supple enough not to lean on the wall of the adobe house. She absentmindedly pinches her middle where there is not much to pinch. She is very pregnant—her baby due one month before Sophia's.

"Nobody has enough to eat," Emma says, smiling through her crooked front teeth, "but congratulations on your baby all the same. Not much chance to survive around here for the little ones, but we're making progress. That's what we like. Progress. Maybe this one will be stronger than the dysentery or the ague. What's your prediction? A boy or a girl?"

"A boy, of course," Sophia smiles, almost mischievously, suddenly wanting to tell the story behind her smile though this story will never be recited in public. She will not advertise anything about her child-to-be nor acknowledge the fact that Geoffrey Scott and Adababa have disappeared from St. Thomas. She also will not tell anyone that Charles is taking her back to Willard in the early weeks of October—on the new Utah Road built with money from Utah Territory. She will be almost seven months along by then. That is their secret. Not to be shared. Traveling should be safe then, the extremes in temperature not as extreme. "A boy named for his father," Charles has said, "though we'll call him differently. Weston Charles instead of Charles Weston. Do you like it?" Yes, she likes the name. She likes the idea of another child about to be born, though she does not want to be labelled as someone who quits, who leaves, who deserts. But her exit will be part of a plan to save a life. Maybe her own, she muses.

"A baby in St. Thomas," Emma is saying. "Blessed be. Population up to 130. Almost a metropolis when you add your contribution."

The two women laugh together, happy to have something to laugh about, happy to be bursting with life.

"We'll get established one of these days," Sophia says, and she is relieved she's no longer bothered with thoughts of superiority. Those are not hers to have or to keep. "We'll have a library, a courtroom, a meeting room for our Relief Society."

Emma puts her arm around Sophia and squeezes her shoulder. "So good to have you here," she says as they enter through the low door. "This quilt'll keep me and the baby warm when I nurse it."

"You look close to birthing, if you don't mind my saying so."

"I wish it'd come early and still be healthy," Emma says. "I'm tired of carrying this bulge around. Let me check on the lemonade I made without lemons. How about pink water?" She coughs, almost as if she's swallowed four of them down her trachea. Then there is more coughing until she finally heaves a big sigh of relief. "Find a place you like to sit. You're the first one here."

Sophia sits and empties the contents of her bag. She pats her stomach, proud it is rounding and filling out, growing. Her child has become more important than anything to her. More important than her graceful hats even. Better than Charles returning from a mail run.

"For now, we'll use the bowery for school," Emma yells from the other room. "It's too hot to be inside anyway, at least most of the time."

Suddenly, Sophia clicks her heels together beneath the quilt and feels an unleashed joy in her feet. If only she could kick her leg high in the air. Lift the pinwheel blocks pieced together by Nettie and the stubborn C-clamps off the frame with her toe. Make a tent. An Arab tent. If only she could move to the music inside her. Dance. Move with the wind as she once did on Adababa's back. Sway to the rhythm of his hooves. Words are unimportant. Words need not be spoken. Maybe people would get along better if they kept their words inside and just let the world be abundant, plentiful, a place of richness and worth. If only she could keep this sense of abandon, this sense of all's-right-with-the-world. Maybe she will go to the dance this Saturday night. It doesn't matter if she dances with a woman or a child if Charles is not back yet. Dancing is what's important. Everyone dancing. Forget with who.

She threads her needle with heavy white thread, eases the cot over her pointer finger, and imagines herself hooking elbows with people whose cheeks are ruddy from the dancing, their hearts beating faster than they have for a long, long time. "Do sah do. Clap your hands, then take the little filly and swing her to the sky." Her feet want to move to the rhythm of the music she can hear in her head. They want to kick, whatever she can do to express the joy she is feeling for the life growing inside her. Her grieving for Sarah Anne is over, at least for this moment. It is time to move forward, though she'll never forget. Not ever, she promises, as Nettie hands her a glass of pink water and others arrive to help with the quilt.

* * * * *

They are almost to Willard: the wagon, Charles, Sophia and the baby inside her. They've survived the trip, the heat, the potholes, the hills, mesas, and mountains. Now, they are passing east of the Great Salt Lake, sun dappling the water as it sinks low and casts horizontal shadows. To the right, steep mountains rise behind homesteads, still covered with the green from spring and summer—trees, shrubs, and flowers competing for sunlight. The colors of the leaves are definitely changing: brown at the edges of the leaves, yellow, orange, but she still sees some green. Summer still wimpering.

"Glad we're almost there," he says, whipping the horse on its butt, coaxing it to hurry, probably because he wants to be there. Wants to be at the home he's built. With the other wives. His complete family.

"Mary Anne will be pleased to see you. And Harriet, too."

He smiles and nods his head, nothing more to add. A man of few words.

While the wagon wheels roll forward, she sees peach trees. A flock of them. In rows. An orchard.

"Baby Weston," she whispers to her stomach. "Peach trees. I'll give you a large peach when you have teeth. Next summer if we're still here." She pats her stomach, hoping the extra curve means he is raising his head, Weston Charles sitting up with anticipation of tasting a peach. "There aren't any blossoms," she keeps whispering. "Nothing to decorate the branches. They have fallen to the ground and broken into tiny petals that have disappeared with the wind and rain, but someone has forgotten one peach hanging there. I wish you could see it. Wizened, shriveled now, but it was once fresh.

"Are these your orchards, Charles? You never told me about peaches."

"Yes, Ma'am," he says, curling his shoulders together to ease them, hunching momentarily. "My back is about ready to be done with this ride. You ready to be there?"

"I've heard so much about Willard, but you never told me about the peach trees."

The wagon wheels negotiate the bumpy approach to the house while she thinks of peaches—almost red, but still orange in spots, juice dripping on her chin even, careful as she is to keep it contained by a napkin or a soft rag. But there is no juice. There are no light pink, red, or lavender blossoms. She can barely remember the color of a peach blossom. It is twilight, the end of the day. Tomorrow her mind will be clear. She loves peaches and hopes that her peach, when one is in her hand, is a soft one but not too soft. Covered with a pliable skin that gives way to her teeth just so. A mushy, grainy, or overripe peach is not what she wants. Too bad these trees are done for the year. Are there peach trees in her yard, or in Mary Anne's yard, maybe she should say, though Charles has married her, too? She has always thought of the home in Willard as her own, at least until now. This is her family, her Mormon family, isn't it, though she feels less than a part of anyone's family right now. More like a blister on someone's heel.

Evening is near. Temperatures are cooler. The sun is sinking at the edge of the lake, and indiscriminate breezes casually clip the trees of Willard. Wild hair. Sophia laughs but knows she is the only one who will think this funny—trees having hair. Charles gives her a sidewise glance with a look that says she has been seated too long on this tedious journey. They are weary of each other's company.

The horses strain to pull the weight up the final hill while the sky is filling with ever-more-menacing shapes, but even though the trees are bending east in a show of late-evening wind, Sophia barely notices its direction or whether it is cold or hot. She does not care if it is unkind to her hair and dress. She is in Willard. At last.

She has ridden on this hard seat for many miles. Too many miles, she would say if she had someone to whom she could tell the truth at this moment, though there is no one next to her but Charles. He has no ears for any words that have the slightest shade of discouragement, or imagination for that matter. He has little to say in response to anything other than practicality. She stretches her shoulders open, pushes her abdomen forward, adjusts the small of her back, and shifts her buttocks while Charles hunches over to avoid the direct hit of wind. Luckily, thank the stars, though they've crossed a few slow rivers, most of the time they've traveled on roads, real roads. When the route was smooth, she and Charles chatted about some things, mostly about their son and what might be in store for him when he grows tall and sprouts whiskers. And now they have almost arrived. At last. All of them will be together, three wives plus whatever children are at home. They'll have a few days together before Charles returns to St. Thomas with Harriet. That is the plan.

Sophia listens to the horses' hooves making their final ascent to the homestead and can see Harriet on the porch, shading her eyes, making sure it is Charles coming. Why does she allow the woman to inhabit her mind? In all the times they have met, Harriet has never recognized Sophia. Not really. She ignores her presence with a non-glance, trying to make Sophia invisible and thus nonexistent, or so it seems. There she sits on the porch, waiting for Charles to look at her, waiting for his eyes to light up. It would seem she is the only woman on the porch: Harriet's husband is back, the man she claims as hers, even if there is supposed to be equality for every wife. According to Harriet's expression, the reunion belongs to her even more than to Mary Anne, the one who's been with Charles through more trials than Harriet can ever imagine.

But whatever is happening on the porch, Sophia is happy to be in the north of Utah Territory. She is happy to be removed from the gypsum sediments, the tilt of the rarely horizontal land, the white-tailed ground squirrels, even. St. Thomas, St. Joseph, West Point, Callville, too, though that settlement has not lived up to its promise, begrudgingly becoming an extinct notion in Charles' mind. He so wanted it to be something more. Now he brings home reports of boundary discussions. God forbid, the latest talk is that St. Thomas is part of the newly minted state of Nevada. Sophia will keep telling people that she lives in Utah Territory, no matter what anyone says. People should understand that the word of God is the supreme law. Period.

But now, before she considers the women again, she notices the grass growing at the foundations of the brick house. Straggly but green. She counts three cows, two goats, and two horses in a nearby pasture. She arches her back and wishes she could touch the points of her scapulae. Her body does have a life other than what it has known within the square corners of this wagon seat. She needs to stand on firm ground. She needs to move. She has been sitting too long. But they are here now. They've arrived at a real home. A place with green shrubs and bending trees, and even weeds—spent dandelions scattered across the expanse of the front yard.

She rubs her arm with two fingers. The two women, the two other wives, are sitting on the porch. An exchange will soon be made. Harriet for Sophia. One for another. An even trade. She touches the hard skin of her calluses, the ones that have grown tough while she worked to make things grow and to make the kitchen clean and free of sand. She wants to hide both hands, but her skirt suddenly feels too skimpy. She turns them over. Cradles one in the other and observes the women rocking on the porch. Two more wives are alert to the wagon's arrival and preparing to stand.

The idea of plural wives still catches Sophia by surprise, though this will be the first time she will be living with another of the three. A surreal idea, born of some other planet, it would seem. But The Principle is what

God has commanded. The Prophet has promised the highest glory if she's faithful to the calling.

"Charles is home," says Harriet too loudly, up from her chair and caching her knitting in a bag. She is a blocky woman, her figure firm, round, and demanding. Sophia is glad that she and her shoulder are nestled next to Charles. She could be a showpiece—especially diminutive and innocent, maybe doll-like next to the man she's not sure she loves. But she's where Harriet is not. Yes.

"Charles is back." Harriet rushes down the stairs and runs toward the wagon and Charles, who is climbing down. She almost hollers, like someone who tends cattle or sheep in a lonely dell. To Sophia's ears, Harriet's voice is harsh and annoying. To her, Harriet is telling everyone she's not been remembered in the way she thinks she should have been.

"Charles." Mary Anne follows Harriet, not so quick to her feet as her sister wife, but she too is glad to see her husband. Maybe polygamy was a wild idea by Joseph Smith, Sophia thinks this woman must have reflected more than once. But then she reminds herself she is working her way toward salvation. This is not a time for doubt. Or parley.

Mary Anne holds to the high back of her hip, climbs down the stairs, and stands aside to receive Charles after he has hugged Harriet. They've been apart for a long time. After they embrace, so naturally it seems to Sophia, they chat, back to the important square of their life together—her health, their children who are growing into adults. Eight out of twelve babies have made it to adulthood, four still live under the same roof, her last child born in 1860: seven years old, Jonah Wright Hughes. These children are nowhere to be seen, though Sophia imagines they will cross paths before too much time has passed. She met some of them on the day she first saw Charles. After church. Before her marriage.

"I hope they've grown in intelligence," he says, scratching his beard and looking around the homestead. "Where are they about now?"

"Upper meadow. They'll be back before dark," Mary Anne says, hooking her arm into Charles'.

By herself for the moment, Harriet stretches up on her toes, then rocks back on her heels. She does this at least three times. All of these women have their claim on Charles, but Harriet seems more demanding. She obviously thinks of herself as the most important. Mary Anne loves her husband, Sophia can tell, but she seems wiser, more philosophical, more cautiously generous in her advanced years. The difference between the two women is marked.

Watching Charles and Mary Anne so comfortable with each other, Sophia suddenly feels a streak of competition herself and wants Charles to put his arm around her waist. Maybe she should stand closer. Even though she admits that she's happy there are now other wives to care for his needs, she's not even sure she wants to be with him. All said and done, she wants him to be more demonstrative toward her. To show the others that she counts. But remember, she reminds herself: this baby will be Charles' son forever. And there is Sarah Anne, not here now, but waiting for them in the eternities. Sophia belongs by his side no matter what. And she is here in Willard when the other choice is the desert with its tarantulas, snakes, and bushes, which don't give off the smell of lilacs and might never.

Mary Anne coughs. Her lungs are fragile, barely able to deal with the brittle rattle in her throat. She splays her hand across Charles' chest and rests her head on his shoulder. She is not healthy, Sophia realizes. She needs to consider the woman's health in any comparison she might make. Besides, this woman was the first. Even though she, Sophia, has married Charles by the ordinance of God, not of man, she must be compassionate, no matter what else she feels. And she must learn the perimeters of love—not an easy task when it comes to sharing. "Behold, mine house is a house of order, saith the Lord God, and not a house of confusion." This she believes even when it seems she shouldn't, even when the idea of polygamy seems ludicrous.

But Harriet. She's another matter. Sophia will not be sad when that woman disappears in the dust of the road. Is that woman more than Charles bargained for when he took a second wife?

Sophia takes a closer look at Mary Anne, who's now standing alone while Charles pulls bags from behind the front seat of the wagon. She catches a glimpse of the pensive side of Mary Anne. If her face is to be read correctly, it seems a partial mask. There's a politeness to her smile, an attempt to be receptive and open. Good manners, no doubt, but she seems distant, maybe aloof, and off in a place where she feels a world of hurt. One thing Sophia must remember, no matter what else, is that she has lost her own children. Her Sarah Annes. Mary Anne would have empathy because of this. That is a bond nothing else can sever. She might seem formal and even stiff, but Mary Anne may be a woman who understands. Sophia vows to break whatever barrier there might be between them.

Rather than congregating around Charles as he unpacks the wagon, much as she would like to display his stamp of approval, she straightens the seams of her stockings and fixes the twist of her skirt. Then she removes her hat to allow the perspiration to dry. Her matted hair blows, one strand this way, another standing straight and tall like a soldier with a fuzzy hat at Buckingham Palace—the kind she once saw on a trip with her father. She pulls it back into place. Quickly, she replaces the hat on her fast-becoming-unkempt head, reties the bow, and moves from the front of the wagon to the back. Unwittingly, she takes Charles' arm herself, catching him by surprise.

"Thank you, Charles. A safe journey we've made, and I thank you for your expert handling of the horse and wagon." She kisses his cheek, not sure if the kiss is for him or for the other two women to see. Everyone wants a piece of Charles, she realizes. In the future, she must be more careful not to hold onto him except for support, maybe balance. He is the husband of three. She is only the latest to come into the fold. This she knows as she witnesses his happiness at seeing Mary Anne. He's even greeted Harriet with enthusiasm.

"You go ahead," he says to her, tapping her lightly on the shoulder in the midst of the hubbub. He seems unusually happy. Not one sign of his usual broody temper. "I'll bring the heavy bags. Don't want you hurting yourself or that baby."

"Thank you, Charles." She picks up the carpetbag full of quilt swatches. She and Mary Anne will make a quilt together, that's the plan she devised back in St. Thomas.

This triumvirate of wives is now her lot in life. Her place is not at the front, nor is she the first in Charles' affections, she can tell now that she's here. But then she thinks about Charles' soft spot. He is usually seen as an advocate of work, work, work, most of the time, except he is different when he comes to her bed. Their bed. He is still a man, not only a lion of the Lord. Beneath the geometry, the figuring, and the math of this man, she knows he will always be bothered by her, by her delicacy. She knows that he holds her tight until sometimes she cannot breathe, hoping to catch her and keep her. She allows this for as long as she can before she pulls away to find a comfortable place on her other side to sleep. Probably neither of the other wives have this power.

Oh pride, there you are again, she sighs to herself as she climbs the steep stairs to the porch, bag in hand, and then to the front door painted dark blue. Navy blue. A blue door in Willard through which she walks while the other wives in the driveway touch Charles on the shoulders, on the back, on the arm, happy to see their man, to feel of his substance, his earthiness, his shoulders, his strong body.

You and your ugly thoughts, she thinks dimly of herself, settling her bag in the room to the right of the stairs, the room she has been told will be hers for as long as she needs. Always vain pride, isn't there?

CHAPTER FOURTEEN

BACK TO THE MOJAVE

They've taken the horses from the three Utes, the ones who lie dead near the Vermillion Cliffs. They've left them in a less-than-shallow grave covered with a few handfuls of dirt. A small gesture. The animals will find them before the night is over, whatever is left from the vultures—players in the cycle of life where everything takes care of the dead. There is an order here, in life, in death, except Geoffrey Scott is nagged by the thought that he and Kwami shouldn't've taken time to bury the three men. To have at least covered them completely, maybe dug out a half-hole with their hands.

Abey and Niyol ride two of the Indian ponies—their hindquarters reminding Geoffrey Scott of maps of a different world. Kwami sits the third horse, though the animal looks like it's straining with someone so huge on its back. Geoffrey Scott straddles Adababa, whose hooves have not fared well on this trip. Kwami thinks the return path will be smoother, but that Adababa will need a good rest when they get back to St. Thomas. Some days off. Some repair.

Everyone's quiet, releasing themselves to the cool air and the spread of stars overhead. Everyone's together once again. They can concentrate on something besides rescue. Maybe on the future. The four of them follow a worn path, something they've found now that they're not following tracks, something where the stones have been cleared away and bushes cut back. Indians? Pioneers? Gold seekers on the way to California? Geoffrey Scott wonders who and what business they were on and wonders how Adababa is faring. This trip's been hard on the camel. Not the right terrain for his two-toed hooves. One good thing though. He's complaining less, probably finding some comfort in the powdered dust.

The moonlight is strong, full and cold, on this October night. A frigid moon, forecasting the winter to come, causes Abey to pull the blanket tighter around her shoulders and Niyol to ask his mother for the skin of the coyote she carries in her bag.

"Please. Bag," she'd told the three Utes when they pointed their guns and told her to follow without uttering a further sound. "Please." They had not been in the mood to stand over her while she shoved a few things into this pouch, but she mashed things in a bag anyway. Rumpled. Wrinkled. The coyote skin—one necessity.

Four of them are riding quietly beneath the moon's full circle and its rings. Beneath the stars studding the black, the points of light on the concave bowl of heaven, they're finding their way back to the Paiute village and to St. Thomas.

What a night, Scott thinks to himself, the rhythmic sound of hooves accompanying his thoughts. Mission accomplished. Woman and son in tow. He wants to make a song as he rides, something simple he could sing to Sophia, the woman who occupies too many of his thoughts and who wouldn't be interested anyway. She'd been blunt, no question about that. She'd told him there's no future with her, with anything to do with her, but in some way, he didn't believe her. She'd taken part of his heart, she had, though that sounds too much like something his mother might say—the woman who spoke poetic English, maybe the only person he ever knew who did that except for Sophia. His mother recited poems and stories, even when he suckled at her breast, or at least that's what she'd told him. When he was older, when she watched over him squirming to find a comfortable place for sleeping, she kept reciting. A poem. A story. Her repertoire was broad. But then those thoughts carry Sophia back to the middle of his mind again. He pictures a crudely drawn heart broken in two pieces, the kind he drew for Valentine's Day when all the children at his one-room school were supposed to make something to commemorate the day. A pencil. A pair of scissors. An eraser. He reminds himself, however, that hearts are not shaped in such a childish way. Hearts are more complicated.

Things will be different now, Geoffrey Scott knows that. Kwami wants to ride south and return to his tribe. He's been away from his tribe for a long time. Maybe he'll take Abey and Niyol with him. Maybe not. She'll most likely stay with her tribe but Kwami needs to return, the feeling stronger in him every day. Geoffrey Scott can feel the pull. But how will he and Kwami divide Adababa? They can't cut him in half, one taking the front or back, the top or bottom, King Solomon saying he'll cut the baby in half, though he knows the real mother would have none of that. That'd make no sense. Geoffrey Scott wants to make a bigger concern of the salt mine but needs Kwami to help him dig out the precious salt, pick up the pieces, pack them on Adababa, and deliver it to its destination–north, south, wherever salt is needed.

He strokes the animal's neck, silky, softer than it appears. Camel hair, rugs, mats, coats. Scarves, even. He feels light-headed touching the camel's softness, his fingers buried in partially matted but seraphic wool. Is it really possible that both he and Kwami have access to a camel and is that even something anyone else could fathom–two "owners" of one camel, neither of them Arabs or Turks? Why should either of them insist on keeping Adababa anyway? Why doesn't Geoffrey Scott ask if he can ride behind Niyol and release the camel to the wilds? Just as he needs to release Sophia from his head.

Except Kwami wants Adababa to take him back to the place where the Indians are being corralled by the U.S. government. A reservation, they say. Boundaries. Even now, Navajos are walking toward Bosque Redondo, their hands tied, a long line of them headed to a reservation where they can be watched because Indians belong where they won't pose a threat to those crossing the territories to California. But of what use can the camel be to his tribe? Truthfully? Military men prefer horses and mules anyway and are serious about corralling the Mojaves, full of notions about where a Mojave should farm their crops and live their lives. They could give a fig about camels. So why does Kwami want Adababa?

Then Geoffrey Scott remembers the sound of the camel's hooves pounding the desert sand, flat and dusty as he rode into the middle of painted men. The natives had scattered like water in a drop from a cliff, dressed in so little, their manhood on display so unapologetically, so boldly, these specimens of manliness in chaos. Adababa must be one of the reminders of this confusion. Too quick of a surprise for anyone to take aim, the only option being to run out of the path of the thundering camels. No wonder Kwami wants to ride back to his people on Adababa. His victory would be the camel beneath him, the camel tamed and obedient. Kwami, the master.

But what about him? The camel appeared to Geoffrey Scott first that night, hadn't he?

* * * * *

They ride away from the house in Willard, the wagon bed loaded with a round of cheese, plant starts, saplings, a chest of drawers, flour, coffee, all of the things so hard to find in St. Thomas. Charles and Harriet are leaving Willard, a husband, a second wife, and their three-year-old son on a most picturesque day in Indian summer—warm enough to ride in shirtsleeves, gentle on the face, on the shoulders, even the back. A day made for good things to happen.

Life will be good, he promises himself and says that out loud to Harriet. "We'll have a good life. Some more children," he says, though he blushes inside when he thinks of Harriet and himself in bed together making children. He knows that is the commandment, and he'll follow the Lord's word, but he finds her the most difficult of the three wives. A bit clumsy, he thinks, not unlike a small bear. Fur on her arms, even. A snout? He snickers and rolls his eyes at the thought. He's overdone himself. She, on the other hand, beams as if she's thought of cohabitation many times before this one, the moment when they will lie together again and she can say she belongs to him and that he is truly her husband.

But his mind travels from that subject. He's built a comely homestead in Willard, the one he's leaving behind. It's one of the seven houses he's built since joining the church, this one the most sturdy, the most secure, the one that feels like home with its irrigation/running water burbling over the rocks in the ditch. It is the home to which he will return someday, to his Mary Anne and Sophia and their new child, all depending on what happens in St. Thomas.

There is progress in that desert, he needs to remember, slow as molasses on most days and full of the sand that gets in all and everything. But he'll serve in that arid place for as long as he can, Lord only knows why. He's getting up in age. He knows that. He feels the pains in his hips when he stands in the morning and when he puts the wrong kind of pressure on his left leg. But he hasn't said much to anybody. About his body and its restriction on his eternal soul. Damn skin and bones. He's determined, but there'll come a time when he'll have built enough and served enough. He doesn't know when that slowdown will come, but thinks about it at odd times like this one.

In between bits of conversation between him and Harriet, Charles thinks of Mary Anne, the Reliable. Then of Sophia and their baby that will be here soon. These are the two women he loves, he admits to himself, though he'll never understand the young filly who wants to make hats even when no one cares to wear them, or at least when there's no place to wear them. She might be too flighty for Charles, the stolid, sometimes dull postman, people have said of him when he's not in a temper. He's a hard worker but he's not dull. Just busy working on this and that.

Harriet sits proud on the wooden seat beside Charles, their son beside her nodding with drowsiness while Sophia and Mary Anne remain behind to tend to each other, the peach trees, the livestock, and the chickens. Pride courses through the woman as if it's her blood. Her face, if one looks close enough at the set of her lips and the high plumb line of her cheeks, tells the story. The other two wives are behind them, standing on the front porch waving good-bye. She's with Charles now.

"What do you need me to do in St. Thomas?" she asks before they've turned out of the long driveway, almost in a rush to endear herself to this husband whom she's seen so little of and with whom she's only been a few times in an intimate way—right after their marriage, it was. She has one child to show for it.

"There's lots to do there," he says, shaking the reins to get the horses to move faster, but they seem reluctant to leave, even as Charles wonders why he is leaving again and why he has this wife by his side.

"Procure water," he says after they make the decisive turn. "Find kindling. Fix meals. Tidy the house. Keeping the canals open and clear seems to be the biggest job. Work in the fields. Wheat, corn, sugarcane, cotton most of all. First class cotton lint, that's what Brigham wants. Cotton to make clothes, forget bringing it in from the South, all mixed up because of that crazy war. Not much cotton coming from that direction. Maybe you can spin flax on your spinning wheel. We have one or two of those plants at the homestead. I hope they're still alive. Everything seems to have a short life around there."

"I want to be a help to you. To St. Thomas. To anything that needs my help."

"You are a strong woman. No doubt. Good stock."

Harriet laughs and covers her mouth when she does. Her fingers are short, shorter than he likes, though he needs to find a few more things he likes about this woman. For both their sakes.

"St. Thomas," she says. "Will I get to meet Thomas Smythe, the man who took you all there?"

"He didn't take us there. We went together." Charles is unhappy she shows any interest in the man he knows but doesn't love. Tom has his own ideas about building a town that don't always agree with those Charles has. "Brigham Young asked him to be the leader, but he didn't take us there. You need to know that."

"But doesn't someone need to lead?"

"Leaders need followers, right? Depends on whether you want to lead or follow. Two sides of the same coin. But the name St. Thomas means someone was benighted, or whatever they were. Saint, I still can't get over that name."

"You don't sound happy about that." Harriet pats the top of his broad straw. If he wasn't wearing that hat, she'd probably caress his skull with the palm of her hand, hold the crown, stroke it, but it's good she's still hesitant about how much familiarity she should have with him. These things take time, and they have lots of that commodity in front of them.

"When we reach Salt Lake City, which we can do today since we have good road," Charles says, "we'll find a place for the night, maybe near the Beehive House. Can't believe Brigham has over forty wives. I do well to keep up with three."

How he ever takes care of them, Charles reflects when there's a pause in their conversation, only God knows. Then he looks over at Harriet, a flatline smirk on his lips. Her face seems made of pure sunlight at that moment, and he is pleased that tonight he'll be with someone as interested in him as anybody. And she'll be the bearer of many children, he can feel this in his bones. Even his loins, though he refuses to think much about that.

Most of the time, her square, broad, cumbersome body doesn't interest him as it should. But maybe this time, he'll impregnate Harriet again. They'll build the kingdom. That's his work. His plan for his wives, his children, and himself. He'll have his very own kingdom someday. He'll be like God with his own world, and maybe he and his wives will live on one of the moons of one of the planets. Zillions of planets and moons. Even comets, though he smiles and thinks it would be hard to live on a comet unless there were comets that stayed put. But whatever the details, there'll be enough room for everyone who's been faithful. They'll all have their own kingdom. That's what matters.

Mary Anne, he thinks reluctantly, is finished with her duties of bearing children, which means he won't be seeking out her bed as much as he once did. They've found a comfort together, which he still finds when he climbs under the covers next to her, her lying on her side, her lips kissing her pillow rather than himself as she departs for sleep. He is not immune to the allure of love, however, and now he has Sophia, beautiful being, the young one, and she is almost seven months along, which thought brings pleasure to the too-soon-on-the-road wagon ride he's undertaken in a hurry to return to his mail route.

She should be birthing by Christmas. He wishes he could be there, but she'll be with Mary Anne who knows the signs. She's been a midwife before. Been there twelve times herself. Lots of children he's helped bring to the world, if he counts the baby who died in St. Thomas. That baby needs to be counted. Fourteen, and now a fifteenth with Sophia, and maybe more with Harriet. A legion springing up around him. An impressive family. But he won't be at the birth of Sophia's baby. He'll be in St. Thomas, tending to the settlement, to the mail, and to Midnight, the one he's left behind to rest up, and to Harriet. That woman needs a husband, someone to look after her so she won't be by herself. That woman needs to belong somewhere, and Charles has as much to offer as any man. The right place for Harriet, ah yes, Harriet.

* * * * *

Not that he expected her to be home, but he's a man whose love begs a response from the beloved, at least hints to someone who's never been in love before. He's dreamed of Sophia riding far away from him on a ghost horse. Turning. Calling after him, and he's drowning, sinking into a too-deep pool of water of nothingness. They never touch hands. They never come together. He sinks. She calls his name into the emptiness.

Even though he's just come back to town, he rides Adababa past Sophia and Charles' home anyway. Just before sunset. He's advised Kwami to take Abey and Niyol to the Paiute camp. To watch over them and settle their fears. Tomorrow he and the Mojave will decide their next move.

Their customer base is broadening—at the salt mine itself, throughout Arizona and Utah Territory, even in Nevada, which is a very young state, maybe three years old by now, though most of the silver miners have moved elsewhere. But there are still people who need salt, still ranchers and farmers, the few miners who stayed behind. Geoffrey Scott grins to himself, thinking of the chunks of salt that've literally fallen into his hands with minor coaxing from his clawhammer, but he knows he doesn't belong in St. Thomas. Not really. And he doesn't belong with Sophia Hughes, though he longs for her eyes that dance a hundred dances when he walks toward her. Beautiful Sophia. She's been out of his sight for a long time now. And he's been tracking Utes for longer then he thought that'd take. Tomorrow, he'll be back to mining salt and tending to his own business. But maybe she's speaking the truth when she says they should never meet alone again. But she doesn't mean that, does she? Where is she?

"Evening," he says to Portia Kimball who's pouring muddy water on her few plants that look as if they have one, at the most two, more days of life. She's coaxing plants out of the ground after the most extreme heat of summer has passed, at least she must be hoping it's passed. October's supposed to be a cooler month, especially at night because the days sometime seem hotter than midsummer.

"I see you're out on a ride," she says. "Haven't seen you and your camel for a while. You been away?"

"Kwanyumai, my partner, you know him—the Indian who looks like a giant?"

She shakes her head yes, seeming anxious to hear what Geoffrey Scott might have to say. "He doesn't belong here, you know."

"He had business over in Arizona Territory," Geoffrey Scott ignores Portia's words. "I was with him. Me and Adababa here."

"You and that camel never seem to be parted, I'd say," Portia puts her watering can on the ground and wipes her hands on her skirt, faded from either too much sunlight or too many washings. She folds her arms across the tops of her breasts that are almost too ample for her chest.

"Funny a camel's your best friend," she says, the sun dipping low in the sky.

"I'd say that's funny. Especially when I like people as a general rule." Geoffrey Scott is turning into a profile, a cutout of black paper against a reddish sky. His face is on fire with the last red of the sunset. "I'm not so keen on people who'd lord it over others though," he adds. "The Utes kidnap women and children to sell or trade. Don't care a bit about anyone in particular. But you know that."

The sun sinks to two-thirds of itself behind the mountains that heave into the sky west of St. Thomas. The ridge runs like ruffles on the western sky in the half light, reminding Geoffrey Scott of a wave of water. He once saw the ocean when he was in California, once saw how the waves repeated themselves over and over, except they were never the same. The desert slowly turns a dark pinkish color—the sunset color. The land seems quieter with the last hesitation of light. The animals are quiet, the people inside are holding matches to candlewicks and eating what food they can find. Most of the residents of St. Thomas are probably preparing for the evening and the night before them.

"I wonder where the Hughes are tonight," he asks, a polite tone to his words, as if he were a complete stranger inquiring which way to turn. He's determined to keep Portia at bay, no questions asked, and he shifts weight on Adababa's back. "You have any idea?"

"Last I saw, they were riding in a wagon toward the North. They didn't say much to me, but they been gone about two weeks or more now. Must be needin' to replenish their supplies. That's one tough journey, and I'm not sure why Sophia would be riding in that direction, especially in her condition. Anywhere to the north of here ain't easy."

"Been gone about two weeks, you say?"

"At least. Maybe longer. Maybe she'll be back. Maybe she won't. I figure that Christmastime is her time—a good time."

Geoffrey Scott's confused by Portia's words about Christmas being a good time. Would she feel better by being away? The woman babbles, he thinks, his mind focused on where Sophia's gone, though he knows to maintain a dispassionate expression and act as though he and Adababa have more important things to do. "I wonder who's carrying the mail for Mr. Hughes?"

"Brother Hughes can take some time off, seems to me. Everybody'll get their mail. He's reliable, I'd say, though he has one quick temper. I sometimes hear him carryin' on."

Geoffrey Scott regards the home where Sophia washes clothes, cooks meals, and lives with a man she calls her husband. He wants to ask questions of this neighbor but he doesn't want to compromise Sophia. Not in any way. He'll be subtle, above all. Not give anything away for this woman to chew on or conjecture about. He and Sophia had been in a dream that day, lost in time and in each other. The air surrounding them was light blue with pink at the rim of the blue. Airy. Gauzy, even. That's how he remembers it. There was some kind of town meeting Sophia was supposed to attend that day, and maybe she should have gone. Maybe she should have said 'no' to Geoffrey Scott. 'No' to a ride on Adababa, though everyone wanted to ride on Adababa, Geoffrey Scott knew that.

He stroked the camel's neck once again and dug his fingers into its fur as he sat high above Portia. She was shading her eyes from the last brilliant rays of the sinking sun.

He and Sophia had ridden away, invisible to everyone except themselves, at least he likes to think this as he looks wistfully at Sophia's one window, the glass that has a feel of impermanence, some flaws in its glazing, in its formation. Crude maker of that pane of glass, even though it was possible to see through to the other side.

"Do you have any idea when they'll be back?" Geoffrey Scott asks, trying to be casual as he sits astride Adababa's one hump, one leg crossed over the other.

"No one said a thing to me," Portia says. "Maybe Sophia ain't coming back."

The words punch Geoffrey Scott in the stomach. Sophia. Not in St. Thomas? His reason for sticking around?

"She's been feeling poorly, far as I can tell. Sick in the mornings. Maybe she's not strong enough for the place."

"How do you know all of this?"

"I know things." The sun has surrendered to the mountains, and Portia becomes a shadow, a suggestion of a person. "Maybe she's pregnant, with all the sickness in the mornings. Too bad about the last one."

A baby? Sophia's going have a baby? He's unable to swallow his surprise. Good the evening light is indistinct. Sophia is a faithful wife, no doubt, willing to surrender to her husband whenever the act of love pleases him, maybe pleases both of them, for all he knows. And there's no way this could be his child, is there? That's a pretty far-fetched thought.

"I suspect around Christmastime," Portia says, wiping her hands again, brushing the dirt from the skirt of her dress, resetting the hairpins in her droopy bun before she turns toward her house for the night. "See you around."

With the sun disappeared and Geoffrey Scott turning Adababa toward home, the memory of Sophia's face gives him trouble in his innards, an abdominal pain slicing through his middle. He uncrosses his leg and shakes the reins. In this disappearing light, his imagination runs toward frightening shades of gray. A baby. Is she okay? Is that why she's away?

"Evening, ma'am." He puts two fingers on the rim of his hat as he rides Adababa back toward the Marshalls'. "Nice chatting with you," he calls over his shoulder. "You can tell Mr. and Mrs. Hughes I came by if you see them."

"Soon, I hope," says Portia, opening the only entry to her house, the one with the screen door, one of the few screen doors in St. Thomas.

CHAPTER FIFTEEN

LIGHT AND DARK

WILLARD, UTAH TERRITORY—CHRISTMAS 1868

Though she's had one baby—Sarah Anne—this second pregnancy seems a symbol of Sophia's current soul: it has its share of torture, of torn conceptions, even though she's accepted answers from above, from God, from The Prophet that she is doing the right thing. Even so, her condition sometimes terrifies her. It is a time filled with uncertainty. Her moods rise to an elevated state, then drop to sorrow, then turn back to middling normalcy. Ups and downs in Sophia. Extremes.

Again? she keeps saying to herself. It hurts to have a baby; it tears; it's agonizing for a body to squeeze another body from itself. She is not smart to take on the burden of birthing another child let alone caring for one. She is careless in this strange country where no one seems to care about what might happen, especially if she has difficulty, hopefully no more than a cut in her perineum to facilitate delivery. How foolish she has been to leave everything and everyone, her warm home in England, the eccentricities of her brother and two sisters, her mother. Strange as they are, they belong to her. Who will help her through this burden, this business of having another child who may or may not be the child of her husband? Each night in her bedclothes she swims the sheets in nightmarish terror. Three weeks. Then one week. Then any day. Any hour.

As Sophia struggles in these last moments before her delivery, Mary Anne bustles about, doing the washing, the dishes, and changing the beds, and saying such things as "Your skin has a greenish cast. There is fear in your eyes, Sophia. Please don't be afraid."

"God save the Queen," might be closer to what she's thinking, Sophia decides. Here she is, ready to deliver, a woman so much younger than Mary

Anne, a woman who's interrupted her life. In truth, Charles is probably the only man Mary Anne has ever loved. The only one who makes her heart beat fast. Sophia had seen that when they'd returned from St. Thomas before it was time for her delivery. Mary Anne's love, yes it must be love even though it must have changed through the years and become deeper and stranger, is still strong, even though she's an older woman now. Maybe not so desirable anymore. Not a bearer of children. Not a young mother who caresses and cradles babies, except for grandchildren, of course. She no longer has a womb where seeds grow and bear fruit. She is withering, Sophia thinks, though she stops short from thinking about those possibilities in her own future. There's concern on Mary Anne's face, that much she knows. They both are aware that life has its lessons to teach, that it can change expectations, even determinations. Life will be life, no matter. Sophia hopes against hope that Mary Anne will stay by her. She hopes that is true concern on the woman's face, though Sophia is unable to do anything other than trust. No one else stands by. That is the barest of truths. Mary Anne will help her, please, she hopes as she watches the first wife keeping the household fresh and ready for the new arrival.

When the pains tell her it is time, she lays back in a bed too big for her small but bloated body. Yet it provides comfort between pains. White sheets. Rumpled. Craters of cloth at every turn. Waves to drown in at times. Waves to swim through at others. Mary Anne brings bowls of hot water and fresh towels recently hung out on the line during the sunniest part of the December days. Then she sits by the bed and takes Sophia's hand into hers.

"We're in this together, are we not?" Sophia says to Mary Anne between labor pains, breathing with difficulty, yet happy to be alive after each pain that feels like she's at the end of everything reasonable.

"That we are," Mary Anne says, turning Sophia's hand over in her own, patting the back of her sister-wife's hand to reassure her. "No one totally understands the ways of the Lord. We obey and follow and become mothers to populate this earth. Make bodies. Teach. Be selfless. Give when we think we cannot."

"I have been selfish," Sophia says, her hair in a tangled mess, yet still holding Mary Anne's hand and squeezing the three tallest fingers. "I've thought I was a woman among women. I have wanted all the love for myself," she confesses, then stifles a sob. "I've been told I was vain but considered it envy. And here you are. You barely know me—a young upstart fresh from England—but you are helping me through this." Then she cries in earnest. Shining water stripes her cheeks. "You believe I matter. You believe that, thank God. But how can you when you have so many infirmities yourself? When you're making ends meet on your own, with Harriet, no less? She's more selfish than either of us put together."

"That's for someone else to decide, not us," Mary Anne pets Sophia's head, fanning both sides of her part, flattening her hair even more than it's already flattened. Sophia is perspiring. Working hard. Sweating in preparation for the next labor pain. "We are all sisters. Sisters in the Gospel, but sisters, no less. We must watch out for each other in both good and hard times."

"Thank you for taking me in," Sophia says after the next pain subsides. Her child will be here soon. "I will pass this goodness forward. Somewhere."

"That you will," Mary Anne says. And there is quiet until the next disturbance of air, until the baby crowns, then emerges.

* * * * *

Of course, the child is a boy. Everyone knew this baby would be a boy. And he is healthy, which is the best Christmas present Sophia could ask for. She helps tie red and green ribbons to the pine tree brought in from the hills, and, though she says nothing out loud, she ties one especially for Weston Charles and the baby's father, thinking of Geoffrey Scott as she does. Strong lungs. Robust heart. Strong cry. His legs are bowlegged as a baby's legs are usually bent—so much time spent huddled in the womb. His baby stomach protrudes. Sophia loves to rub this and his bellybutton after a bath, though she is careful of the place where Mary Anne used the scissors, the remnants of the umbilical.

Sophia cannot get enough of him. He is her baby. Her second chance. She will keep him forever. She smiles to herself as she puts one pin in her mouth and the other in the diaper. No matter how hard she tried not to think this, Wes reminds her of her day with Geoffrey Scott and Adababa, he does. In the red of the sand and the stone. The resemblance is strong, she knows. The build. The eyes that are turning green and the wiry torso and the extremities. He is shaped more after Geoffrey Scott's physique. Less stocky perhaps? The crooked smile. He is a lovechild, though Mary

Anne, Harriet, and Charles Weston need never know anything other than that he is another of Charles Weston's progeny. She will raise him to be a strong man who will bring much honor to her name. To Charles' name. Charles will be most pleased to hear of this birth, to know that this child lives and is healthy. Except, that reminds her, there is the matter of St. Thomas.

Should she take the baby back to be with her husband? Does she want to be with him and be the third wife with another wife in the same house? Most seasons, St. Thomas is discouraging. It is so bleak, empty, windy and subject to dust storms. Being in Willard with Mary Anne gives her a sense of normalcy—water, trees sprouting leaves when the time is right, bulbs planted for the springtime, irrigation ditches murmuring on the property, mountains that receive snow in the wintertime and send torrents of water to farms below in the springtime. In Willard, Sophia is once again living four seasons. The fertile. The dry times. And she is also, in theory, with her sister, Elizabeth, as Mary Anne and Elizabeth have much in common. Neither is overly attractive to the eye, but both have much substance beneath appearances. Both are kind women.

The letter she receives from Elizabeth, written before Weston Charles is born, speaks the truth of inevitability: "I wish you were here, dearest Sophia. Mother has come upon her last days. Her breathing is uneven and almost stops at times. I am amazed by the process, but I know you are where you need to be. Nevertheless, I miss you at this critical juncture. I hope your baby will be healthy like its mother. Please write when he or she is born."

Sophia buries her longing to see home one last time, quells its insistence, and maintains to Mary Anne that her mother's illness and approaching death is a matter of fate and that she will not return for the burial because of the fragile condition of the new child. Living is more important than dying, she says, though in private she wishes more than she wants to wish that she could travel back to say her last good-byes. That she could hold her mother who is wasting away and tell her thank you for her life. All of England fills her room at times—her sisters, her brother, her mother who has sacrificed more than she's been acknowledged for. All the candles, the dining table, and the warnings they'd given her when she didn't want to listen.

But now she has a son. Her baby. When all is said and done, maybe Elizabeth can come to Utah Territory. Maybe she can become a sister wife, though she's probably too old to have children. Polygamy is supposed to be inclusive, and she wants her sister included, the one who believes in Sophia's dreams as something more than impulse. Prescience. Spirituality. Foreknowledge. Those are words with which Elizabeth is familiar.

Sophia says prayers of gratitude in the morning and evening. The baby is healthy. She holds Weston next to her heart with firm and educated hands, knowing the two of them are bonded together in this and the next world. Fathers like Charles are too busy peopling the earth and the coming kingdoms. Mothers care more closely to the needs, to the hearts, though she knows she may be overly sentimental in her quiet hours.

ST. THOMAS

"You're pregnant?" Charles says to his second wife, Harriet, hanging his hat on the peg, thinking for a minute she must've become with child when they first breathed on each other in Willard.

"Dinner'll be ready shortly," she says with an unwipeable smirk on her face. "I put Jonah to bed early so we could have some time together."

He sinks into the ample rocking chair near the kitchen, the only chair in the room, actually. He leans his head against the back slat and takes a deep breath, glad his boots will soon be off.

This pregnancy seems soon, he thinks, almost as if there'd been someone hovering in the next room before he arrived in Willard. But he knows Harriet isn't one for flirtation or excess. She's dedicated. Look how she tends to Jonah. Maybe she's blocky, but she'll bring many arrows to his quiver, and he loves those words: arrows to the quiver. Children numerous as grains of sand. He's the father of all this. That'd be him.

"I'm here to give you lots of children and good meals," she says. "How's that?"

"Sounds good," Charles laughs. Harriet laughs, though the sound she makes is slightly off-key, making Charles think of something close to a donkey though he's not supposed to be thinking such things. She doesn't laugh often, he reminds himself. Let her laugh however she does. The homestead in St. Thomas feels like a home again, and winter is here—a time of relief from the pesky old sun. A puffy cloud had stood out of the blur of clouds today. A solo. A picture-perfect cloud.

"Maybe there'll be rain," Charles says. "Whatever that is."

Harriet turns toward the larder to find a finishing touch for their supper. Charles unties his boots and puts them together, toes pointing in the same direction, trying to find a definition he can use for Harriet. A steady wife, not given to flights of fantasy about beauty? Sensible? Right for St. Thomas? But then, he can't help himself. He's picturing Sophia in one of her fancy hats. Smiling, mostly to himself. He's glad she's with Mary Anne, and vice versa. And, to be fair, he's glad he's got Harriet battling the sandstorms of St. Thomas alongside him. Glad she's hardheaded and fertile. Perfect for building God's kingdom.

As he rocks against the plank flooring, Charles Weston Hughes surmises he just might be one of the valiant. Not to be boastful about himself, but maybe truthful. He puts God first and that would mean he listens to God's spokesman, Brigham Young. He'll do whatever that man asks. He also believes that, everything weighed into the mix, he's chosen three good wives, though some might not be as desirable as others. He winces when he thinks of Sophia again and the way she walks and talks. She knows men, she does, that they're fools for a sophisticated woman. She's got beauty and sophistication in spades. He almost becomes aroused thinking about her, but then brings himself back into the room.

"I'm disappointed Callville's folded," he says, turning slightly toward Harriet, folding his arms and stretching his legs out in front of him, wishing he had his hat to pull down over his eyes to get some sleep. "That means Brigham Young's plan for supplies and converts in from the Gulf of California's disappeared. Thin air. Almost as if he never talked about it."

"I wish I could see it someday," says Harriet, grating a carrot for a salad Charles likes, though no dressing today—no eggs for mayonnaise. No oil. "Maybe we can take Jonah there when he's old enough to ride by himself."

"Callville isn't much," he says. "The military's taken over now. They don't like the idea of Mormons owning much real estate along the river or getting too powerful. Some soldiers are still complaining Young wants a nation apart. If you ask me, I'd say it's a perfect plan tossed aside. Granted, the land isn't the most cooperative: desert, disruptive mountains, mesas, rocky slides, and hard rain that turns to flooding. But I still can't believe everybody just left Callville. Poof. Gone. Left those brick storehouses behind. Must have come through when I was on a mail run."

"That's a large puzzle," Harriet says. "But I think it's probably no longer important to Brother Brigham."

"What're you talking about?" Charles says, suddenly unhappy with what he's hearing, ready to pull hard on her arm and shake it good. Does she think she can speak for the Prophet rather than listen? Speaking like she knows what's on everyone's mind? Of course, Callville's important to Zion. St. Thomas, too.

"I can't figure the motives," Harriet chatters, unaware she's goading Charles' ire, putting the grated carrots in a brown bowl she's shaped herself and sprinkling the top with preserved raisins. "Wish I had some dressing for this."

"Word of the railroad, maybe," Charles mutters, unhappy with the conclusions of his second wife who suddenly seems like someone he doesn't know.

"Don't worry your mind," she says, scurrying around the kitchen. Like some mule-mouse, he laughs to himself. "We'll soon have another little one to brighten our days. And even though Callville no longer has anyone to receive letters or packages, you can still deliver mail up north. Your load is lightened. Like that." She snaps her fingers, and the sound snaps something in Charles.

Thinks she knows what's going on, does she? "You have your duties. I can look after my own," he says gruffly and leans his head back against the broad back of the rocker, closes his eyes and his ears. He won't be hearing anymore of her words tonight. He doesn't want to get more riled up than he already is.

"But," he adds, repenting slightly, lightening the tone of his voice and making an effort to sound pleasant, "we'll be parents again soon. Good for us." He'd best not alienate the woman who's so fertile, who's such a hard worker, who's his only companion in this godforsaken place.

* * * * *

Kwami stands in Geoffrey Scott's door. He's set his feet. Solid in the ground. Not unlike a centuries-old tree that can't be moved by wind or water. His arms are folded across his chest, and he exudes a power Geoffrey Scott hasn't seen in a long time, even in the plaid shirt too small for his biceps, even with the opening of that shirt stretched at the buttons. Behind the open door, a gauzy curtain of sky resembles udders of an overfull cow, giving no moisture to the ground but suspending it midair. Maybe rain. Maybe not. A dramatic background for a man with something on his mind.

"Time to return," Kwami says. "I will take Adababa. To *Pipa Aha Macav*, my people." His hands cramp into tight fists, expanding his shoulders more, making them even bigger for the powder-blue plaid shirt someone has tossed away in this village where there is so little to toss. In a box for the "Needy Indians." There is one tear in the shirttail, but the shirt covers his arms and chest. He rarely wears his animal skins anymore. Or bares his chest. Not in St. Thomas.

Geoffrey Scott's sitting at the built-in table, the only item of "furniture" left behind by the Marshalls. Its legs are wobbly because he can't find the time or the inclination to fix anything for himself. "The Americats," he muses out loud, not paying as much attention as he needs to the man standing in the doorway. "I like that expression. I'm writing my aunt about what we've been doing. She'll never believe I've been living with Mormons. Thinks they're a crazy cult in love with the idea of wives. She won't believe I've brushed with the military, either. Or with you." He taps the end of his pen, beating out the rhythm of a song he's carried with him over the years, humming its first line, "Swing Low, Sweet Chariot. Comin' for to carry me home."

"Sometimes I can't believe it myself," he says under his breath, but then he knows he better turn his full attention to the human pillar set like granite in his doorway. Kwami. The Mojave said it was time. What does he mean?

"Time?" Geoffrey Scott asks, hands on the table, pondering that four-letter word and the sketchy thought of losing his partner and camel. Is he talking about going away? That would mean he'd be by himself in an alien settlement with alien people. Is that what Kwami's saying?

He smacks down the pen and pushes the scrap of paper forward on the desk. "Maybe the government's backed off," he says as he stands, folds his arms, and speaks with a fake hope in his voice. "Maybe the military's leaving your people alone by now."

"The fight is still happening," Kwami says, his voice sure, even decisive, surprising Geoffrey Scott because the Indian usually speaks flat, basically no expression. "I hear about Fort Mojave." He hawks phlegm into the sand that's the floor. In the dry air, the wetness evaporates though a dark spot stays behind. "Built for Americats on Mojave land." Accenting every word he speaks, his eyebrows raised, and incomprehension on his face, he says, "You and me helped build it. You and me! We helped. Now Navajos are walking where they don't want. In long line. Bosque Redondo. My people are told to leave their homes. I hear things."

Geoffrey Scott puts the heel of one hand on his forehead, rests his elbow on his other hand, and bows his head, his mind heavy. The

Mormon pioneers, first of all, have been digging canals from St. Thomas to St. Joseph, using every drop of water they can, almost as if the water's theirs alone. He's seen that. And how can the military pen the natives who lived here before any American ever marched his butt in this direction? The world's crazy when white people have to go where they have to go and get what they want to get. But, truth is, he's considered joining the crazies out there. Leaving St. Thomas. Finding work more rewarding than selling crystals of salt. Leaving these Mormons to their doomed patch of ground.

"Geoffrey Scott?" Kwami says more strongly to the man from Kansas who whirls in his own thought, though he has no idea Scott's thinking about how he needs to move to greener pastures.

"Geoffrey Scott." Kwami claps his right hand on the left palm and repeats that irritating word. "Time. Do you hear me?"

"Okay, Kwami. Sorry," he says, dropping his hands to his sides and curling them. "Things on my mind. I'm not deaf to what you're saying. But look at yourself. You live with the Paiutes and have Abey. A place you call yours. Better than I'm doing. I'm just waiting here. We've mined salt and rescued your woman and her son. You, me, Adababa. Now you want to go home? With our camel? Baba is OUR camel, not yours to do with just because you have some notion."

Kwami stands solid with both feet still planted firmly. Intent. "*Mutavilya*, Creator of Big River, speaks to me and Adababa."

"Even if the military is rounding up the Mojaves, telling them where they can and cannot live?" He points his finger and shakes it. "You want to be part of that mess?"

"Time," Kwami says, the collar of his shirt unbuttoned because there's no way that collar will ever fit his neck. His shirt belonged to a smaller man, and he's long and large in every way—his arms, his legs, his torso. A colossus whose left arm is still healing from its wound. Sometimes he holds it for support but now he's rubbing the scar under the sleeve of his shirt. "Many of my tribe have decided to leave the land. I will tell them to stay where they are planted. Like corn. No white man should dictate. Baba knows it's time. He knows to show strength."

Suddenly, maybe for the first time, Geoffrey Scott realizes Kwami actually believes in *Mutavilya*, whatever the name. And in Adababa's and his connection to some immaterial world. The Indian actually believes the camel's his to take and furthermore, that Adababa's convinced he should go with him. The *Attah Allah* that stood on a hill beneath a starry sky, the incidental moon as an accent. In front of his eyes, Kwami's showing his stubborn side. His warrior side, maybe. He totally believes Adababa is a gift from the Great Creator. No one's going to change his mind. No matter that the camel appeared to Geoffrey Scott first though there shouldn't be a queue here. No first in line. Kwami knows what he knows. End of discussion.

Not a man given to violent thoughts, he nonetheless wants to do something to put some sense in him, maybe even punch Kwami in the face. He might have to knock him down. Who does he think he is? He considers his two fists and clenches them, but they are paltry compared to the size of the Indian filling the doorway. Almost twice his size. Nobody crosses Kwami when he's made up his mind. Nobody. But that Indian's doing something Geoffrey Scott can't abide. Adababa was his camel, wasn't he?

Geoffrey Scott quickly surveys the room, his anger flashing and rising as fast as lightning strikes. He wipes his palms on his overalls and rubs his knees. Who in the hell does Kwami think he is to up and take the camel they've been using to mine salt? Who in the hell is he to break up everything and head out of town? He's even willing for Kwami to go if he has to, not that Geoffrey Scott would like it, but the Indian can't be taking Adababa.

He sees his rifle lying on the floor, asleep in its scabbard, the one he'd used once in Arizona Territory. Necessity. He's a good shot when he needs to be. In a few seconds, he could reach the rifle. Kwami has no right to change things, and he, Geoffrey Scott, is the boss, end item. Isn't he? Kwami needs to respect that. Just a bend at the waist, then a swipe of one arm, one finger on the trigger. He could do that before Kwami understood what was happening. With that rifle, he could have his way. He could cradle that carbine, send a bullet into that Indian, watch him crumple, watch blood seep from the wound. Adababa should be with him. Nobody else. Time to demand what's his. Just like his father had done. Time to take charge, except he can't move. Something holds him in check. He's frozen as he watches Kwami exiting the doorway, heading out to the corral and Adababa. "I am *Pipa Aha Macav*," the Indian says loudly as he takes long steps in the sand, nothing stopping him. Almost like a locomotive heedless of the cars it's pulling. "I will follow the old ways, though I will speak to you in your language, Geoffrey Scott from Kansas, whatever Kansas is. I am traitor if I speak your language. My people need me and Adababa to know there is strength for them. This is not time for confusion. My people not like Navajos, walking in single line to their prison. They must stay where *Mutavilya* and *Mastamho* say."

"Maybe they can't see," Geoffrey Scott says, following Kwami to the corral, suddenly fearful of this man who's become a stranger, this man who now seems bigger than anything he's ever met.

"Their eyes cannot recognize hand of *Mutavilya* that creates what we need," he says. "Each of us. Land is a gift to Mojave. I must go."

And he turns back toward the gauzy sky, the clouds having changed from udders to puffy shapes of air. He opens the gate to the corral and commands Adababa to sink to the ground. The camel cooperates as if he's been expecting the order and even seems compliant as Kwami ties the halter around its neck and climbs on its back. When Kwami issues the order to stand, the camel puts weight on its front legs to rise. Kwami bends his leg around the horn and squirms to find the best position. He holds the reins that direct the camel's head, and the gate is soon behind them. He turns the animal to face the canyon country, and Geoffrey Scott can see plain as day that Kwami won't be contained by anything he says in protest or by a reservation whose boundaries are determined by people in the faraway capitol of Washington D.C. A reservation is made by white hands, not by the *Aha Macav*, as Kwami would say. The boundaries they've set are push-worthy.

"But Adababa was given to me," Geoffrey Scott calls out, taking enough steps to stay by Adababa's side, trying to keep the two from moving away. He holds up his hand to stop Kwami, though the Indian is impatient. "Just wait, will you?"

"Baba knows it is time. We go. Now."

"But…"

Geoffrey Scott's camel is about to vanish, the one given him by the night sky. Adababa and Kwami will soon be gone. They will become a fantastic dream–something no one could conjure if they thought about it forever. A camel and a Mojave Indian riding off together in the vast desert, the sun shining too hot as usual, the sky too blue, no clouds anywhere. He moves as close as he can to the camel and cups its face in his hands and nuzzles it as he's seen Hadji Ali do. He feels the shaggy hair next to his cheek, the heartbeat of this animal somewhere inside, its very soul perhaps, though he's not sure if camels have souls. He strokes Adababa's nose with the back of his hand, presses his own against the camel's long one, and then sings into its furry ear. "*Ya sa'ad*," whatever that means, he's not sure, but Hadji Ali sang that to soothe the camels. Then he grabs the hand of the Mojave, feels his fingers against the Indian's strong ones for a brief moment, anything to keep him. But, after that brief moment, Kwami pulls back his arm, rearranges his seat on the camel, lifts the reins, and cocks his other hand in a farewell salute—something he must have learned at Fort Mojave.

Geoffrey Scott is a friend losing two friends, his only friends except for maybe Sophia. For this he is feeling a pain he doesn't allow himself to feel on most days. Like a slit in his gut. Like a knife someone's using to clean out his insides. And then, the camel takes its first step away. Then the second.

Maybe, he debates. He could grab the reins to keep Adababa from moving further. But Kwami's in charge now.

Then they're out of reach. Geoffrey Scott watches the strange gait of the camel as it covers road. The large man sits around his hump, holding the reins, both moving away from him and leaving him behind. The Mojave's almost to Sophia's house where Charles and Harriet now live. Charles and Harriet. What a farce. Who's she? One of the wives probably. More anger rises in him until he feels full of rage. He feels the vast emptiness of the desert. The wide-open nothingness of where he stands. What's he doing here, and why's he watching everything he cares about ride away from him? It's time to get out of here. Time to look beyond this scrappy village and this scrappy existence.

After he watches Adababa and Kwami shrink into the horizon, he walks toward his excuse for a house. He's a ghost in St. Thomas, actually—a man who doesn't matter because he's not working for their Kingdom of God. He doesn't belong anywhere right now. The salt mining business's paltry, who's kidding who? He can use mule trains and packhorses to go elsewhere. He doesn't need a camel or a business partner. He can wait for Sophia forever but she'll only see an outsider. An intruder even. He's standing in a giant hole with no sides. No bottom. He needs to leave.

And yet, he stops and looks over his shoulder, feeling paralyzed as he sees the swirl of dust in the distance and watches how it hovers, then settles back to the ground. Dust that hides his camel now. The Mojave. Kwami. He can't pierce the scrim because everything's a blur—the shape of the camel and Indian riding the ground like one of the heat waves that make the horizon uneven.

He could have held a rifle in his hand. He could have put Kwami in its sights. Except he hates rifles. He hates anything that can change the equation so quickly without discussion. He knows this as sure as he knows the nights are getting cooler, thank the stars. He hates what guns can do, but more than that, he's speechless at the side of him who would even think of sighting a rifle. All of this over a camel, he had to say, though Adababa's not just any camel.

He slouches down on the three-board bench outside his house with no doors. "Damn," he says. "Damn it to hell." He bares his teeth. "Damn Indian taking my camel. Damn me for not having the balls to take him back." But he takes deep breaths, even if the air's hot and the heat pinches his nostrils almost closed. Breathe in as much as possible, he tells himself. Accept that there's a turn in the road. A change. Maybe Kwami's will's forcing him to head elsewhere. Maybe further west. To California, to the Gold Country—Americans, Europeans, let alone the Chinese and who knows who else. A land of opportunity. He'll amount to something one of these days. For his parents. God only knows what story they'd tell if they were still alive. For Sophia, who'll never know what he's all about or what matters to him. Except it would be nice if there were somebody who did.

The bond between Geoffrey Scott, Adababa, and Kwanyumai is broken. Yet it won't ever be broken, he decides. It's not a matter of losing his camel. It's a matter of letting another man do what needs to be done. That he needs to remember. Nevertheless, he leans against a wall of Marshalls' blown-out house, his barely-there house, and sits there, feeling a huge emptiness. He and Adababa belong together. Two fingers on a hand. He's feeling as if he's fallen into a deep, dark hole where he'll never see him again. And Kwami. The Mojave. What does it mean to be an Indian? To have a tribe? To be riding off to save your people, fat chance of that? He looks out in the desert to see if there's a camel or a Mojave on the line of the horizon, a moving profile, maybe tiny but still there, but all traces have vanished.

* * * * *

In a piece of sky above him, one cloud sits solid, as if to block his view of the heavens and their secrets. But in other places, huge puffs of clouds ride the blue expanse, sometimes majestic, sometimes thinning out. The fickle clouds keep rearranging themselves as Kwanyumai makes his way south and as jagged land rises up, then has cracks and fissures that he and his animal must watch. The cliffs offer the best route, the ones that line the river, though some of them drop below the water. Straight edges. Precipitous drops. He'll be careful.

Listening to the sound of Adababa's hooves against sand and rock, he offers his prayers, thanking the handiwork of *Mutavilya* and his parents who are long gone, the ones who died at the hand of another tribe when he was younger than a young man. Very young. He remembers some of the stories about them. Now he's riding toward his tribe that has always lived at the edge of the big river. Longer than his life and his parents' before them. Giants. No stranger to work. The military has rounded them up to plant them in little holes, little places. Too small for the people who are giants, who are made of his own blood and bones, born from the same clans–*Oach*, *Maja*, *Hipa*, *Masipa*. Intruders have bullied them with guns and fast horses, all because his people do not want strangers crossing their river or trampling and eating their crops. They only want to farm what's left when the river floods at high-water time, to follow the instructions of *Mastamho and Mutavilya*, the plan they were born into.

Touching the skin of his exposed arm where his sleeve is rolled up above the elbow–copper-colored and rippling with the same muscles as the men in his tribe–he slides down his fingers to touch other fingers and has a feeling that both hands can reach for whatever they need. *Mutavilya* is good. Many blessings have been given, though Adababa seems balky in this unpredictable terrain. Dotted with sage that's not good for him. Geoffrey Scott, his friend that he's left behind and who must understand the reason why, sings if Adababa is uncooperative. Maybe he should sing. When he hums a familiar song, one he learned as a child, it has a magic effect until they come to a sheer place with a narrow edge, some of which crumbles and falls to the water below. Rocks falling. Sand following them. A spray of the now-half-ledge in the air. But Adababa, with his four legs, has stepped nimbly beyond the ledge that's falling away. *Mastamho* and *Mutavilya*. They are watching over him and the camel.

He remembers the night when Baba appeared to him, offering a way apart from the white ones that swarmed like flies toward his people, the ones who wanted a bigger life for themselves in their little wagons supplied for their journey to gold and riches. He should never have left the fight to keep them from the river early on. He should have turned the riders back, he and the others, but then there were the camels. Something they'd never seen before, coming at them like spirit ghosts. Adababa even. But whatever the past has to say, he will help his people remember their strength. Baba will remind them what *Mutavilya* knows. Granted, the guns of the military are big. His people are confused, turned backwards even, but he has the camel beneath him. The animal that chews in circles—its lower jaw passing its front teeth at the top of the circle. He leans forward, reaches up, and pats him behind the ears as they trot at a gait that makes the native bounce. Kwanyumai digs his knees into the animal's sides, riding with this camel rather than against it, absorbing the uneven gait until he seems a rider who's known camels from the beginning of time.

It's still morning. Wind scuffles up strings of dust and removes the patterns on the sand, and he wonders where it comes from and why there is always wind. If he follows the cliffs, he should soon arrive at the Colorado—the river of his people. Like a glistening snake with sun shining on its back, winding through rocks and sheer walls. He wraps a cloth around the lower part of his face to protect it.

Maybe, especially if he encounters trouble, he should head for the secret places—the winding tunnels through the walls of the canyons. Of those places, he is quite sure, if he'll be still and allow himself to know which way is best. Trust the inner voice. It has been a long time since he picked his way through solid rock, but he knows there are those older-than-old places. Not often used. He is not so sure about Adababa, though he must take the animal to his people—a totem that will remind them of their power. Men among men. The camel will help them be strong, though sometimes one must wait for the right time. That is the message he must take to the tribe splitting apart like an overripe melon that cracks where it will. There's talk of two tribes now, a division of those *Mutavilya* has created as One. Some are staying near the river, and some are going where the military tells them to go. Kwanyumai must tell them not to divide. Adababa will help them understand this.

They continue south, traveling as familiars. Maybe they've known each other forever, even if he's let Geoffrey Scott take the lead in camel tending. His eyes narrow as he rides between sage bushes and tall creosote bushes and glances up at the wide blue sky, now without a cloud. Today is turning out to be a difficult day to ride. Full-out sunshine. Hot. Adababa is complaining—a goat-like bleat—something Kwanyumai only hears in Arizona Territory. He kicks it in the sides, thinking that will make it go faster, but Adababa has a mind of its own and a kick in the flanks is not in its repertoire of moves. He is picky. He bleats, bawls, and makes obstinate noise in the empty desert.

Regardless, the camel is for *Mutivalya*'s purpose. His people need this animal. For his people. Little matter that it is morning and that Kwanyumai is riding away from St. Thomas with a camel Geoffrey Scott insists belongs to both men, not one. He must stand firm against the Americats who need to hear his anger about his tribe's movement away from the river. They need to stop asking the Mojaves to "re-locate"—their word for their desire to grab the land. But maybe he should tell his people to allow the Americats to cross the water if they promise not to disturb tribal land. They could do this simple thing, work out a compromise, but both the men in uniform and his tribe need to understand that no one is leaving.

The Indian rides through canyons, fords what is left of the Muddy and the Virgin, often fool's mud at this time of year, winds his way to the tops of plateaus and then down again. He sleeps for a few hours that night and rides early in the day because the sun will be hot again. When he sees the flat buildings of Callville, he assumes no one is there and that the buildings are empty. The Mormonees he's heard about have given up, at least by way of water. He looks at the buildings and skirts around them on the complaining camel to get a view of what the builders had been trying to do. But he doesn't realize he is showing himself to military personnel. He doesn't know there is a small detachment waiting for something to occupy their time.

A garrison has been stationed at Callville to protect the warehouses and keep them available for military use if need be. The garrison is hungry to act because they have nothing to do in this country that is desolate, a no-account assignment. Nothing happens here. They've been abandoned. "The land should have been left to the devil," they say to each other when sitting around a campfire together on nights that are colder than they think they should be. "No one wants to take a steamship through Black Canyon. You should see it if you don't believe me. Tortuous rapids. Unsuspected rocks that'll slice your boat into pieces. Too many months when river travel's impossible."

The military know Kwanyumai is coming before he knows there are men waiting for him, though they are out of practice. But suddenly, men appear, seemingly out of nowhere, with guns aimed at him. He is on the wrong side of the triggers, the wrong side of something. The soldiers are scrambling, their suspenders undone, their pants being pulled on hastily, but in this chaos, they are aiming guns at him. Has he done something wrong?

Maybe he should speak to the soldiers in the English he has said he will unlearn and forget and that he will never let his people know he can speak, especially now that they hate both the language and the people who speak it. He is confused by the soldiers, but knows he must move out of harm's way quickly because guns have a power of their own. That he knows. But he is used to being a giant. He is used to men feeling fear when they see a larger-than-life man like himself. Something is wrong here.

The bullets come fast, but Kwami and Adababa are faster than their accuracy. The Mojave knows how to zigzag and move ahead of where the soldiers think he will be. But these are bullets. Hard. Fast. The Indian kicks Adababa in the ribs. "Move." It responds with a moan the likes of which Kwami has never heard before. Maybe it has been hit, though that fact doesn't figure into Kwami's thoughts.

Adababa is invincible. Adababa is beloved by *Mutivalya.* By Allah. The gods. Nothing can happen to make a difference in Adababa and its gift-of-Godness. But bullets can sink into flesh. Bullets can turn both men and animals into stone, into nothing, a hillock on the ground, a rug, a wrinkle on the earth. They can also hit Kwanyumai in the leg and make him forget his purpose, that he is a friend of Geoffrey Scott. He is not above bullets or out of their reach.

Kwanyumai moves fast away from bullets while Geoffrey Scott is still asleep in St. Thomas, planning to mine salt, and resigned to the fact of the three horses Kwami has left behind. The Mojave rides as fast as he has ever ridden, believing in Adababa's invincibility, the docile animal being stronger than a mountain cat.

Then he feels blood running down his leg. He has been hit—in the thigh. Or maybe in the calf, or maybe both. He's not sure. His leg aches. The entire length. Maybe the camel has been hit, too, to judge by its complaining. The Mojave can't see the camel's eyes, though the animal is still running, and the eyes tell the tale. Adababa stumbles, then rights himself, his pie-plate hooves finding their balance and Kwami sliding to the ground away from the bullets. He hides behind the camel to examine what has happened, but the soldiers are running toward them. They are coming with the long barrels of steel pointed at both of them, at Kwanyumai in particular.

The native grabs his beaded leather bag with his belongings, the one that has been sewn by Abey, the one he will always keep to remind him of her and her loyalty. He runs, though his leg has been blown into something other than itself. His thigh seems absent, and Adababa is bawling in a way that the Indian does not want to hear because he knows he can't help the camel. Not now.

The soldiers run past Adababa, familiar with its awkward feet, the slope of its back, and their conclusion regarding its general uselessness and its distinctive smell that makes them gag. They don't stop to see what has happened to the four-footed animal, nor do they care. They only want to find the giant. All Indians belong on a reservation, not wandering along the river. They do not belong here. Only where the military says they are supposed to be.

Kwanyumai half runs, limping, grimacing. Every step hurts, and the soldiers are gaining ground. But he runs anyway, afraid he might not outrun the soldiers. But then he sees it. He's not sure that it is what he thinks it is, and then he's sure. A modified cairn built of flat rocks. A sign. Something placed there by *Mutivalya*, who knew he was coming. Since time began, maybe. The rocks are prepared to receive him.

He turns into the cliff, into the honeycomb. He climbs. He scales the boulders and forgets he has a leg that is bleeding profusely. He lifts his weight. He pushes. He climbs until he arrives at a stopping point where he finds one of the secret places, one of the narrow passageways through the rock. Ever since he was a boy learning the land, he has been told of these hidden paths. His ancestors are with him.

He's suddenly glad Adababa is by the river and not with him. The climbing would have been impossible for someone fitted with four legs. The path is almost too narrow for Kwanyumai's huge physique. He takes small steps, sliding around the points of rock where someone, long ago, has chiseled a pathway. It is not an easy path and is sometimes shockingly spare, but gradually, he makes progress toward the cliff's upper regions, all the time leaving blood behind him.

The soldiers are looking for him. He can hear them below, their voices echoing and bouncing off rock, though he is confident they won't find the passage unless he's left too much blood. White men cannot see such things as secret passageways. *Mutavilya* has prepared a way for him and helped him find the secret passage, making him feel as if he has been there many times before. He knows the signs left by the wise ones. The subtle cairns. The petroglyphs pointing in a certain direction—the ones only he can read. The soldiers can't see past the blank wall that stops anyone who doesn't know how to find a path they had no idea was carved into the rock. The soldiers are frustrated. He can hear that in their voices that are echoing in the labyrinth.

"Damn Indian. He must be hiding around here someplace. Look at this blood. It's everywhere, but he's disappeared. You go to the right. I'll go left. You go where you can."

"Do you think he climbed up?"

"He's too hurt. Besides, the cliffs are steep here. He's hiding behind some rock."

"We'll find him. Damn Indian belongs on a reservation. Must have stolen that camel from the military. The only camels around here are property of the U. S. of A."

Kwami secures his good leg. The foothold will take him higher. Did *Mutavilya* know these travelers would dig up the Mojave's crops, trample their plowing, and create such disruption in their lives? Why has his tribe not been helped by The Great Spirit? He pulls himself to the next layer of land, the top of the secret place where he can run from these men who have no idea he's climbed away from them and their guns. Guns cannot go where gunmen cannot go. Because of this unacceptable-to-the-white-man factor, the native is a free man. He wants to mock them. To yell at them and tell them they do not belong in this place. He stands on the top of the cliff looking down at the soldiers trying to find him. He watches them looking behind rocks, guns at the ready, careful to stay where they can be defended. He is a free man, at least until the next time someone decides he is not where he is supposed to be. He better move fast. Keep going.

First, in the shelter of a closed arch of red sandstone, which will one day be an opening when wind has blown against it long enough and water has dripped over it the exact number of times, Kwami stops to bandage the wound in his leg. He tears into pieces the plaid shirt he has worn, the shirt given him by Geoffrey Scott, and winds it around his thigh and calf in a crazy pattern, one with no rhyme or reason. He finds a bullet hole in the thigh, but the bullet itself has burrowed too deep for him to pull it out. His whole leg feels as if it has been scourged by bullets. He looks again. There is another bullet in his calf, which he pulls out from its secured place with his thumb and finger. Pain sears his leg. He's been a human bull's-eye for the soldiers.

Wrapped in the plaid bandage, he makes his way carefully along the edge of the cliff again, still hurting, though getting away from the soldiers takes precedence over the pain. Even though he is above the soldiers and their guns, high on a cliff that they cannot or do not know how to climb, he is cautious. He looks back to see if he can catch sight of Adababa.

From one sliver of his vantage point, he can see the camel sitting on the ground, his front legs flat, his back legs tucked beneath his haunches. He is chewing. Kwami can see its jaw and its round movements, his lower jaw scribing circles. Maybe the animal doesn't care what's happening. Adababa looks calm enough, but Kwami is too far removed to know whether or not the camel will survive. The soldiers may decide they've had enough of camels for a lifetime. They might kick it or curse it. They might shoot the animal, for all he knows, and leave it to die in the desert. He can hear Adababa braying, bawling, and alternately sitting quietly and chewing whatever it is the camel chews. The two are now parted and useless to each other. Adababa could never make it through the secret passage. Of this Kwami is sure.

Thus he knows he must keep traveling to the south, even though he is now on two legs rather than four. He also knows he's losing blood that he needs to keep, but he also knows he will live.

* * * * *

A week later, Geoffrey Scott's riding solo on one of the three horses inherited from the Utes, deeded to him by Kwami who's taken Adababa and disappeared. Hidden by miles, everything always disappearing in dust, what's new? What in the hell was this all about? The camel appeared out of nowhere, outlined by the moon for emphasis, and changed his direction. Adababa'd showed up for him and changed his direction. That camel wasn't just a camel. Kwami knew that. He knew that.

Geoffrey Scott's moseying this morning, leading the other two horses on a string. He's got about three more miles to go to Salt Mountain, rumored to have a shimmering ledge of crystalline salt, a boost to his livelihood, if he can find it.

Forget Kwami. Forget Adababa, he decides, even though that's not an option, if he's honest with himself. He'll never stop with the affection for Adababa and the vision that night that gave him a new angle to life. New lenses. New binoculars, maybe, he laughs. Camel thinking, that's what he's doing. But then he wonders just how a camel thinks and then turns his own thoughts back to his task for the day.

He'll blast the tufa by himself and work the sides of the canyons. He can cut through to fifty or so feet to find outcrops of salt if it isn't laying open for the picking. He hopes it will be easy for him to pluck off the sides. Wouldn't that be a boon? The mine isn't far from sea level and is supposed to be better than the one Kwami showed him first.

The day's pleasant enough. Buttermilk clouds cover the sky, making a net that'd catch fish. Big ones. Sheets of clouds. Silent rows. Everything feels like spring the way the weather has settled today—slight chill in the morning but warm by nine. Rain should be close behind if the sky has anything to say about the weather, but it's been threatening for weeks. And rain might mean flash floods. Time to get out of St. Thomas—his second season here. Maybe he'll find a large salt crystal today, one large enough to carry in two hands, one that'll bring an outrageous price when he takes it north. A profitable sale, he's thinking, as he rides the horse inherited from the Ute who's no longer riding it, currying it, or needing it for much at all. Geoffrey Scott has no reason to stay behind in St. Thomas. Not any he can think of.

Sophia's gone. For months now. Nobody's told him what that's all about except for those hints from Portia. Charles's come back to town with another woman—someone he's overheard being introduced as the sourpuss' second wife. Sophia's the third. One-two-three. Ducks in a row. He laughs to himself. Polygamy. What could one man do with all that womanness? And how can any man treat all of his wives equally? He never could. He wouldn't want to try. The love of one woman is the best idea.

Neither Charles nor his second wife have spoken to Geoffrey Scott, though that shouldn't come as any surprise. Scott isn't Mormon and has no thought of becoming one of those overzealous, overly committed people who can't see beyond the beliefs they have. Maybe he lives on the outskirts of St. Thomas in a lopsided house built from adobe and topped with a blow-away tule roof. Maybe he has no desire to haul lumber from Sheep Mountain—150 miles away— to make himself a better something, a house that belongs to him alone. Probably he doesn't have a reason to mix with the locals except to doff his hat to the worker-bees coming and going from their fields. He's been polite, even considerate. Problem is, he doesn't mix in with the locals. He knows the unspoken rules and chooses not to abide by them. He's lived at the edge of the military for years, so maybe he'll always be on the edge of something. He steers the horses between a sad-looking giant Joshua and a healthy sage. The cactus needs water to beef it up. He hopes it will rain except he hopes he's not out in the path of one of those quick floods. Spurring his horse on, he rides across an arroyo, dips into a basin then up a hill. The business of being an outsider goes on forever, it seems. Maybe it's time to change that, to be part of something, if that's possible, even if he's used to being an outsider. A loner.

But maybe, just maybe, Charles knows what's happened between Sophia and him, though Geoffrey Scott has never understood how this polygamy thing works if someone asked him. Sophia who doesn't seem too much in love with Mr. Hughes. Who knows when and if she'll ever come back to St. Thomas, though. But he's fixated on the idea of blending into that "one" he's heard about in songs and loose talk, the one he's felt with her, if only for a few minutes. He's only been with a few women, but she's the best. He doesn't know why she's stayed away. For months now.

And Kwami's gone. Everyone's gone. Empty spot next to him, behind him, wherever Kwami used to ride or walk. The Mojave was heading south on Adababa, back to his home along the Colorado. Maybe they were already in the secret places Kwami'd told him about, but maybe the camel could get taught in a twist of the labyrinth.

Should he pack up his few belongings, leave his hollowed-out home, which is only a place to lay his head after all? Can he, Geoffrey Scott, be happy with the three horses Kwami left for him? Not a bad trade because the horses are strong and quick, except he keeps thinking about Adababa, *Attah Allah*.

He's approaching the salt mine. He's heard jokes about salt mines and people who waste their life in caverns, but salt is a need. Soon he'll be ready to take a batch north to Panaca. Reap his rewards. Next week. Maybe he'll leave then. Once and for all. Sophia doesn't love him, or at least that's probably the case. How could he want for her to give up everything for him? To ride away on Adababa, except the camel isn't around anymore? Gone and gone. But why should he stay and try to make something out of nothing, except she was somewhere. She responded to his fingers. He felt that. He wasn't born yesterday. The way he unbuttoned…

He turns his horse into the path made awhile back by a momentary raging river during a flash flood, now a flat and harmless riverbed with no water, and the horse leaves perfectly formed tracks in the soft sand. Tracks anyone could follow if anyone should choose to: Utes, Mormons, military men looking for minerals. But no one's following him today, and he doesn't care if he's persona non grata to anyone. He's philosophical today. A smile crosses his face.

The salt mine Geoffrey Scott rides toward is different from the one they've been mining, the one that's two miles west of the Rio Virgin on a beach of the Colorado. Natural to its surroundings—a well with a funnel about three hundred feet in diameter, water seventy feet below, saltier than the rock salt whence it came. This is the mine Kwami said was worked by Indians long before a white man ever walked on the same sand. He claimed it was "the oldest man-mined mine" in this entire country—the United States and its territories. Maybe that's Mojave talk, but maybe not.

No matter. Today, Geoffrey Scott's headed to Salt Mountain, a better proposal for salt crystals. There is no need for Kwami at this point, but has the Mojave betrayed him, taking the camel away, no longer a partner, no longer a salt miner? Or is he merely a man trying to survive, doing what he thinks is a necessity for him and his relatives? Geoffrey Scott wishes he had a better head for rights and wrongs.

Events of the past six months have made him pause in his certainty. Who made up that word "certainty" anyway? Or that idea? Maybe he's only a particle of sand who calls himself a human being. One among zillions. Millions anyway. Maybe human beings are not as big or important as they think. Maybe he's not so big in this universe as he likes to believe. Maybe. Maybe.

Today. What is important is today. He'll amass a load of salt. Pack it on the horse he's riding. Water the animal before trekking back to St. Thomas.

Next week he'll leave though he still hopes Sophia will appear somehow. He'll go north. Take his load to Panaca and Pioche, both infiltrated by miners. There's talk of gold bullion and silver in the quartz formations. He's wondered about it for himself. Nothing for him in Kansas anymore. But as his horses near Salt Mountain and Geoffrey Scott wraps his reins around his wrist in preparation for a dismount, his thoughts turn back to the woman who's disappeared.

Sophia'll return someday, he thinks, as he ties his horse to a Joshua—prickly, but the only place available. She loves him, he both hopes and believes, but he doesn't understand her notions about man's reason for being on this place called Earth. Maybe she's susceptible to beauty, something larger than either himself or her. But this insane belief in the unseen, a plan whereby people can be saved, is something he doesn't get. Saved for what? Maybe there's an Infinite out there somewhere. An Organizer. A Decider. It's not for him to say. But being saved? What for? At least his horse won't eat the tree he's tying it to. Adababa would. That camel loves to eat about anything. What a beast.

CHAPTER SIXTEEN

THE RETURN AND THE DEPARTURE

WILLARD—1869

She's nursing her son. This healthy child, thank the stars, thank God. He is blossoming in a safe place, and Mary Anne and Sophia have become allies: a friend in need is a friend indeed, a sister, almost. Mary Anne, who was a tender midwife for her son whom Sophia is going to keep and raise and teach. Her son.

But whose son is he? She closes her eyes and thinks back to the red rock in the valley that should be called fire. She replays, even relishes this memory, but does not want to admit she has fallen short of her vows. She's married to one man with three wives. Why should he be upset if she has one brief suitor? Having sex does not feel like sin unless one listens to the clamor in one's head about breaking vows. Is it a sin to love someone? To celebrate life itself?

She herself is a true believer in the Atonement of Jesus Christ and believes He will understand her heart and her intentions. But she has gone against the vows she made to Charles in the Endowment House. That is true, she needs to be honest. But she is confused. She has loved deeply, as deeply as one could love: James Milhaus, her first husband, even if he is the man who left her alone in Salt Lake City, even if he has proven himself to be worthless, all said and done. She signed papers. She is no longer a wife to him, but that's all a blur to her. Almost a lie except she loved him.

He believed in principles, definitely. His own, of course. As she nurses Weston Charles, the son she now loves more than she loves her own life, she remembers that day of his departure. She'll be with this baby at every curve in the road, she promises him with a kiss on the top of his head. Almost bald for now, but she understands how hair grows and that it will thicken.

"I can't stay," James had said to her. She didn't like the sound of his voice, even in memory. The day's sun was setting through the window, its fingers invading the cloth that looked like lace but was printed lace at the most in the room they had rented. She rolled toward the wall, looking at the imaginary cat in the water-stained wallpaper, looking as if it could yawn at any moment. Watermarks. Blurs. Her senses wanting to return to the quiet repose of nighttime.

"This place," he continued. "It is not what I thought it would be. It's too petty. Brigham Young, to be exact. He changes his mind to suit the occasion though he says he's a prophet. For instance," James's words spilled out of him, running every which way. Sophia willed herself to stay in the room and listen to this overflow. "He says he's not courting the Indians as allies and then boasts to the military that these Lamanites, as he's convinced they are, will side with the Mormons, side with the Lord. I've heard him say both things."

Sophia turned back toward him then, finally ready to deal with his words. "Brigham is a man, but he's also a mouthpiece for the Lord. Don't you believe he will give his all to make Zion a reality?"

"He's a man, that's for certain. A glazier. He has little education and, worst of all, he speaks from both sides of his mouth. And we're supposed to do his bidding?"

"We must do as he says," Sophia says out loud to Weston, who starts from his nursing, turns his head to one side, and squeezes his face red to cry, though not for long. He seals his lips back to her breast to suckle the abundant milk his mother has to offer. Milk runs down his cheek. Sophia wipes it with her finger then dries it on the bodice of her dress. Then she remembers James again. That night. Tucking the pillows behind her back and sitting up in bed, believing she could straighten his mind if only she could find the right words. "If we follow Brigham's lead, then everything will come together. We must believe that."

"But that is where we differ, my dear Sophia. You believe good things about Brigham, but I cannot. Not anymore. And what about the reformation—the weeding out of the 'half-believers,' Brigham calls them. I haven't been subjected to his henchmen yet, but when they come, do I lie and say I fully believe?"

"I can't believe you are talking like this," Sophia said, sitting even taller in her bed, her nightclothes crooked at the waist. "You'll be asked to leave, to join with the disenfranchised, wherever they end up."

"Nobody's getting out of here, believe me." James sat on the side of the bed, his feet flat on the rock-imbedded floor. "You have to get a pass signed from Brigham to move anywhere these days. He's closed the territory. And no one can move sideways lest he knows about it. Mark my words."

"But why don't you get out of your mind and get to work to make Zion happen? You know—God's chosen children who serve each other. You don't believe in that?"

"You are so stubborn, Sophia. You can't see anything beyond your nose. You follow those hopeful words as if Brigham is singing you a lullaby. You're gullible."

"Call me what you want," she had said before she sat up even taller, trying to gain the upper hand in the conversation, trying not to cry. "I believe in a goal. Sometimes Brigham is a man, I grant you that, but he is inspired. There are too many holes in the dike right now. How can he ever have enough fingers to stop them all? We need to help, not criticize our leader."

"You can keep after this illusion, if you wish." James now stood on one leg, stepping out of his worsted trousers that had been too hot for the day he'd just finished. "Me, I'm ready to leave. First chance I get, before I do something that will disgrace both of us."

"You would leave me behind?" she remembers disbelieving, the moment being a turning point for her. James was leaving her? And yet, after being startled by the conversation when she recalled it in the middle of that night, she knew she could not give up her belief to follow him. She had come too far and given up too much. Besides, he was gone when she woke. Disappeared. Good old James.

"I've come too far," she says to her baby, who has fallen to sleep, full of mother's milk, satisfied for the time being, and resting gently against her breast. Bliss. The sleep of babies.

She thinks of all the things she has done since James left her behind—hatmaking for the unappreciative, cleaning rooms, folding sheets, ironing for a pittance, trying to create a home and a garden in that thankless place, St. Thomas. And marrying Charles Weston Hughes. Was she a fool, or was she following something that was true to what she knew?

Sophia squeezes her breast which is still swollen with milk, rebuttons the buttons into their appropriate slit, and sits with Weston asleep on her legs, the beautiful baby that makes this world a better place. She respects the man to whom she is now married but does not love him. Nothing can change that, at least now that he's lost his temper so many times. She looks at the sleeping child on her folded knees. So peaceful. So heedless of any of this. Secretly, she is glad someone else besides Charles is his father, though she'll never know for sure even if she knows. She wonders about Geoffrey Scott and the passion they knew together, then smiles a bitter smile. Maybe she could have pursued what it would be to be with him if she were not married, but probably she and Geoffrey Scott are too differently paced—a horse and a camel, if you will—though she does not know how fast either of them can run, truth be known. They seem worlds apart and besides, her belief has gotten her through times and troubles when nothing else will suffice.

Maybe her true love will be her son—her beloved, sleeping, perfect son, though it is time for her to stop reviewing the past and help Mary Anne take the Christmas decorations down—the clay beads painted red, the pine boughs that have filled the house with the scent of the forest, the popcorn they grew in their field and popped in the kettle and strung on a waxed string to loop around the branches. Together, they have sung of the Christ Child's birth: "Silent Night, Holy Night"—a new song from Germany they sang during Christmas sacrament along with "The First Noel" and "While Shepherds Watched Their Flock." And now she and Mary Anne will untie the red and green ribbons on the pine tree. While they stretch, bend, sort, and box what needs to be boxed, she will think of Weston Charles and Jesus—one flesh wedded, goodness wedded, shafts of light blessing the earth.

SPRING 1869

Geoffrey Scott clicks his tongue. "Hyi," he says. "Move."

Leading a string of nine horses, not counting the one on which he rides, he lopes to the north of St. Thomas, toward Pioche and its settlers. He's been making good money with canvas and burlap bags of salt, and he likes the sound of horses moving, their feet scuffing the ground, hooves clattering over rocks—a musical sound. He's moving on. Sophia, Kwami, and Adababa. Memories. The past. Soon to be dust like everything else.

He trots. These beasts are a different ball of wax than Adababa. Horse flesh needs the right food and water. The right pace to last. Sophia, he then thinks against his will, a nettle in his thoughts, how could she buy into the business of polygamy, of being a third wife. Something can't be right for her to think that way, but so let it be. Her choice. He won't interfere. At first, he'd hoped she'd come back. But she hasn't. Too many months have gone by since he's seen her. Something about a new son has gone around the town, though Geoffrey Scott knows sparse details about that rumor, that news, whatever it is. He thinks of the empty cradle he once saw at Sophia's and Charles' home, but why should he waste his quiet time? Of course, they would have another child.

How can she care for a temperamental old man like Charlie Hughes? Geoffrey Scott can smell meanness, it's a fact, though he's seen some generosity in Charles. He needs to be fair. Regardless, he doesn't want to be on the receiving end of nasty when it turns nasty. No more St. Thomas for him. Time to pull out while the weather's agreeable. Before he needs to wear a collar up to keep out the wind that can be cold.

"Take what comes to you," he tells himself. This is what his mother taught him. He can see her in the kitchen, wiping her hands on a towel after working in the flour, white dust of flour rising in the air, white flour on her cheeks. She's telling him to be fair and go where you're called to go. That's what she did when she convinced her husband to move from Boston to Osawatomie, Kansas, God forbid that decision. New Englanders in the territories. New Englanders and their states' rights clashing with the pro-slavers, and their guns. Guns. His bugaboo. His enemy, though he's got his Henry shoved into the scabbard attached to his saddle. Security measure maybe.

"Ho," Geoffrey Scott yells out to the pack train that carries salt, this time for silver processing in the mines. Some of the horses are trying to pass the one in front of them, none of them as obedient as Adababa had been. The camel. The way it could go for days without water, no complaints. No replacement.

"Kwami is one smart Injun," he says out loud, maybe needing the sound of a voice, even his own. "Knows what he needs. But, all said and done, one camel isn't enough for all this packing. Be patient, little doggies. We're on to new things."

He agreed to Kwami's demand for Adababa, not that he could change the man's mind. He'd accepted the three horses and he can still hear Kwami's voice, his plaintive statement: "Time to take Adababa." That word 'time' mixes with his thoughts, and he wants to spit it out. He hates thinking about it. But Kwami was definite about what he needed. No equivocation. No indecision. No doubt. But he—Geoffrey Scott—who hated guns, had considered using a rifle. He shook his head, maybe to grant he was a man of many parts, many sides, maybe fooling himself with impulses other than what he thought he didn't have.

"Fairness," he says, not loud enough to startle the horses but enough to remind himself. "Be fair. Kwami needed the camel."

No animal belongs to any man, he thinks, same as no slave belongs to any man. Maybe animals don't mind helping, but there's no such thing as one thing owning another. That's what the Mojaves say. But Kwami was adamant about that camel at that hour, at that minute, and no one had the right to interfere. Geoffrey Scott, to his surprise, is glad for the three horses. He can carry more with a string that he's gradually expanded and still transport salt. But who is Kwami to make demands and take Adababa away? With no permission given by his partner?

"A man," he concludes out loud as he pulls the reins tighter and spurs his horse to a gallop. "Kwami is a man. One with rights. Part 'owner' of Adababa." He needs to put that behind him, look to the future, to what he might become.

With the money he's earned processing salt, he'll eventually put a mule train together to caravan north where silver is being dug. Nevada—Pioche, Elko—or California, even. He knows enough about mines. He can be of service to those who need packing. To those who need food, actually. Men have to eat. He'll be there. He'll take their traces of gold and silver for food. This he understands and wonders what Elias would have to say about his new plans. Elias, who buried his hate before he died but that hate was so deep it meant harm to somebody else. Permanent harm. He'll take a different direction. He'll be the best of his mother and father, take the best traits, become something to make them proud if only they were around as witnesses.

He reins his horse to the left to pass around the lead and head up the caravan. He'll survive without Sophia, too, the one he'd choose, given a choice. But now, he can stop trying to make a square peg fit a round hole.

He'll make good money and find something he's supposed to be doing. He'd prove himself to himself, if no one else, though maybe his parents were watching from some distant place he didn't know the name of, maybe from the sky above his head. Who knew these things? He'd find a decent woman though those were scarce, he'd have to say. Maybe there's one out there for him somewhere. Someone like his mother, bless her. For now, there's nothing to lose anymore. He's alone but that isn't so bad. He's riding north, smelling leather, listening to the creaking of saddles, being part and parcel of the rocking movement of his packhorses. People need what he has to give. He's found a future, even as he rides away from St. Thomas and the son he doesn't know belongs to him. Love is big, he's heard. More of it likely.

"Ho," he yells to the caravan, the horses in a line on the rocky path up the steep hill.

ST. THOMAS–1869

Willard, she repeats to herself as the wagon bumps along the road that is smoother than last time she traveled it but still full of ruts. I would rather have stayed in Willard but am now riding with Brother Daniel Huntsman who has come north to replenish his supplies. Weston Charles, who is almost a year old, is asleep in the back of the wagon. Dreaming of what, she has no idea. Do toddlers have dreams? Visions of heavenly mansions, she laughs to herself, entertaining herself. His dreams are probably concerned with cows and sheep. They'll both miss the mooing and baaing of the animals. Those sounds, not unlike the horses' hooves that are lulling her into a poetic rhapsody with their constant rhythm. For a few minutes, she is lost in a tumbling enigma of thoughts. She loves Jesus Christ, the savior of all humankind. She has accepted his Gospel after all and has traveled from England to embrace everything he has to teach and everything she can learn about living unselfishly, though sometimes that is a tall order. About embracing all as children of God. It's not time to renege. But, truth of it, she has some fears about Weston surviving the desert. It's not a place to become strong. Hardy. Or maybe even generous. Too much hiding away in the shade. But if she did not accept Charles' invitation to join him in St. Thomas, she would become irrelevant. And what place would there be for Weston Charles then? Where else would she go anyway? She could stay with Mary Anne but she would always be a third, probably insignificant, wife there, a paper doll waiting for a paper doll husband to take her hand, an addition to Charles' collection. She's heard Harriet is pregnant again, prolific with her ability to bear children. One after another. Maybe Charles prefers her now, or at least she thinks that is the case, but why should she care? The number of children—the stars in the sky, the sands on a beach he would call them—is what matters to Charles. He lives in clouds and is so upset with the world as it is.

"Did you see the color of those fields?" Daniel interrupts. "Gold this time of year."

"Autumn is my favorite season," she says. "You must like it, too."

"Sure thing," he says, though he doesn't say much else. No problem. She has plenty to think about.

Weston needs a father, even a harsh one. Charles, with all of his intemperance, is the proper father of her son. No more need to agonize over this fact. He is proud of this boy and has said so in letters he has written. Sophia wonders, though, about the child's resemblance to Geoffrey Scott. Will Charles suspect anything? Will he still be a good father and teach Weston to work hard and love the Lord? Or will he draw back and ignore the boy? She wants so much for her son. She wants him to be filled with the knowledge of something greater than himself: a compassionate God, one who loves all beings, and a world much larger than he can see with his finite eyes.

"Mary Anne…" she says to Daniel. "She's my sister wife, you know. Too bad she has stayed in Willard." But he is more intent on managing the horses on this road that can be precarious.

"Mary Anne seems like Elizabeth, my older sister," she continues, even though she realizes she's talking to herself, wanting to tell someone she has accepted Mary Anne as a sister wife, something that still surprises her. She's come to respect that woman who is like the good shepherd, "Love one another. Watch over my lambs." Maybe Mary Anne suffers with arthritis and the difficult pains in her abdomen but, whatever has happened, she and Mary Anne are friends. Maybe they sidestepped each other when they first met and pretended to comradery, but then things changed. They need each other to enter God's glory.

Sophia pats her breast pocket, knowing there is a letter from Elizabeth tucked close there. Then she puts her hand on her chest to calm her heart.

Elizabeth, her beloved sister, is actually considering whether or not she should come to Zion. Together, they could practice for The Great Perhaps, as Elizabeth calls it, though Sophia believes The Gospel is more than a perhaps. She will have to inform Elizabeth, if and when she arrives, of her opinion.

"Willard would be a good place for you," Sophia had written to her sister, "seeing that our mother has finally died, bless her soul for the silent sacrifice she made for all of us. How I wish I could have been there to put my arms around her frail shoulders and say my last farewell. I would wager she wished I hadn't left, but then I cannot let regret be the measure for my life. No doubt about it, I could not make the trip with a newly born child. Nor did I have money for passage but I'm sure you understand. Please take some flowers to her grave for me. Tell her I loved her even though she cannot hear anymore. I'm feeling some tears welling up inside, that I am. I'll stop for a minute to clear my eyes.

"Again, I wish I could have been there," she continued writing after wiping her eyes with her only linen handkerchief. "But, true to form, she left you enough money to make your way to the Promised Land. The railroad runs further than it has before. You can get to Zion much more easily than those of us who had to walk with handcarts or ride in wagons pulled by balky oxen who had to be fed and watered and controlled on steep hills. It's a terrifying sight to see one of them slip on an edge! There is no reason for you to keep house for Malcolm. He is engaged to someone who will soon be his wife and will probably take over as mistress soon. Time will tell that story! Julia has married and no longer lives at the home, so you don't need to be concerned about her."

"Can you make the trip?" Sophia asked in smallish handwriting, suddenly timid when she wrote that she wanted Elizabeth nearby. Was she forcing something not meant to be? Was she supposed to be with Charles and the other wives alone?

"You must come to Zion," she wrote more boldly. But then she added something she wonders about having said. "It is not always easy here. The people in Zion are taught to sacrifice for each other rather than for themselves, but, I confess, not everyone hears the same message. The Saints are trying to live as Jesus lived and are filled with the spirit of giving whatever the next person needs. It is an enlightened way. Of course, not everyone lives this perfectly. I would so love to have you join me in this Golden Rule that is alive and operative, though I hesitate to prejudice your decision with my enthusiasm. I only want you to come if you feel it right for you. We will see what happens in St. Thomas, but I think Willard would be best for you."

Thoughts of her letter keep her company while Daniel is preoccupied with guiding the animals who have been in the harness for a good long time. The ride to St. George is more pleasant than anticipated—the breeze of travel on her face, the sight of fallow fields at the sides of the road. Part of the effort to build up this desert. However, there are so many questions she would like answered, some of which she hesitates to ask.

Whatever she is thinking, Daniel speaks up. "The town is growing, though still struggling. Sometimes I'm not sure how long the Saints can last. A hard land. Alkali. Blowing sand. Indians more aggressive than ever. Wagons are pulling out faster than the rest of us would like. Some of those called to serve have decided they're better off elsewhere."

"Where are they going?" she asks, remembering her friend, Almira, whom she would love more than anything to see again. She'd been longing to see her and to laugh all her troubles away.

"Back to Utah Territory. Helping build a new settlement in Orderville. Still hot, but more promising. More water. You ready for the heat again?"

"Oh, yes. The heat. How can anyone forget those temperatures?"

"That water." He screws up his face and sticks out his tongue.

Sophia wonders why she is returning to the Muddy Mission with her child who has done so well in Willard. Why is she putting them both in jeopardy? Subjecting them both to dysentery and malaria and whatever else might overtake them? But in her prayers she's been told that she's making the right choice.

"I tried to create a garden in St. Thomas," she tells him, dutifully keeping her voice from cracking, checking on her sleeping child in the bed of the wagon—a blissful sight. "But it needed more water than I was able to procure. I only wanted a little corner with blossoms. A place where I could stand when the sun was setting, the sky and the cliffs lit up like fire. You know how pretty everything is toward sunset."

"Gardens are not meant to be in St. Thomas," Daniel says flatly. "Usually the leaves turn yellow and the produce shrivels. Or the Indians take the fattest squash or the largest ears of the few corns. Thieves take whatever they please."

"Whatever they need, perhaps?" Sophia asks. Geoffrey Scott is suddenly at the back of her mind, influencing her thinking that maybe the Mormons have taken more than their share of natural offerings.

"Too much trouble, all around. Showing up at the doors when the women are alone, acting like beggars, grinning their savage smiles when they have a knife tucked away in the smelly leather wrapped around their ankles."

"It is a problem, no doubt." But then Sophia changes the subject. "And how is Charles doing?"

"He's as ornery as ever, but he's prepared an addition for you and the boy, if I forgot to tell you. He's quite a builder, you know."

This is the first news of an addition, even though Charles has made a few hints, and Sophia has mixed feelings about that. She'd been hoping for a house of her own. Partly because she now would be living in such close proximity to Harriet, who has her own ideas, just as she, Sophia, has hers. But, having her own room—hopefully her own kitchen—is the next best thing. At least she won't have to wake to Harriet's snide comments every day and pretend to like her and her baby. She, Sophia, would be by herself a good deal of the time, just as she was before, just as she has always been. Faring with her needle and thread. Soon she will share her bed and her time with Charles, though that is not something she relishes. Thank goodness he has much else to accomplish.

Sophia and Harriet are supposed to be related. Sister wives. But Harriet is one woman who has no appeal for Sophia. None whatsoever. If beauty were important before, it is doubly important now, and Harriet is a bulky, balky, outspoken threat to the female species. Therefore, Sophia is glad to hear of an addition Charles has built for her and Weston Charles, even though she knows he will be mostly absent. He is a busy man. A postman. A builder for Zion. But she has her son. No one can take him away from her. Nor should they ever try.

"I wonder why I am returning," she says to Daniel who angles the horses to the right to circumnavigate a pothole. She sighs. "But Charles is there," she adds quickly, reassuring her traveling companion and herself. "I've promised to be a support to him."

"Good for you," Daniel says, lifting the reins to adjust them and keep the horses moving at a clip. "That's something we all need."

Why bother to talk to him? she thinks, then proceeds to delineate to herself her reasons for returning. (1) I believe the Gospel of Jesus Christ and its promises; (2) I believe in the prophet. (3) I made promises to the man who is my husband. Yet here she is with a son who favors Geoffrey Scott, more handsome than the craggy Charles. Weston is also a youngster with a sweet disposition, sweeter than Charles will ever be.

Despite her efforts not to, she wonders if Geoffrey Scott has returned to St. Thomas while she has been away. How can she ask Brother Huntsman without being obvious? Someday she hopes to see the man she rode with into the red rocks. Somewhere. Weston Charles' father, she smiles with barely a twitch in her lip. Maybe with the turn of an Ali-Baba key, he'll appear. Then she can show him his son, though he probably should never know. That wouldn't work, though suddenly she can't stop thinking of him and hopes he will be part of the scenery of St. Thomas, odd camel and giant Indian in tow.

The journey takes several days of coughable dust and shooting pains in Sophia's back when they hit deep ruts in the road. They stop for the night in Fillmore and Cedar City to water the horses and take rest at the neighborly home of a local Saint. Fresh bedding. A lively breakfast complete with news of the area. On their last morning of travel, as Brother Daniel urges the horses back on the road, Sophia tilts her head back to take in the huge sky, all of its blue blueness, its cloudlessness. As she examines the cracks in the tilting land that seem more diagonal than horizontal, she feels the heat of the early sun soaking into her skin. The jagged hills. The bounteous foliage on one side of the road, the spare spikes of tiny-leaved branches on the other. The red and orange hills. Unearthly. Everything about it has always felt lifeless before, but maybe she understands its personality for the first time. It is not an easy land nor is it meant to be. It rarely gives hints about itself, much as she's decided she needs to do. She is not easy to understand either. Life has changed the contours of her face and emotions. It has altered her sensibility and made her more sober and subtle, not unlike this land. There is something strangely appealing about the fact that the desert has wound, has twined, whatever it has done, a path into her finer feelings.

About midday Daniel brings the horses to a stop in front of an oddly built house, not one she recognizes at first. Then she realizes she is looking at the home in which she once lived, this home that has grown while she's been away. She and Weston will live in this strange-duck-of-a-home—hers,

Harriet's and Charles' and the three children of course. This will be the first time she has actually lived face-to-face with the coming and going of her husband to another's bed, and she's hoping Harriet will be different from what she remembers. Will she gladly share the house? Will there be any tenderness between them? Sophia's only brought a scant portion of her belongings to tuck in somewhere. That is all she needs, but she's wondering how things will be regardless.

She needs to be grateful to have a place to live at all and needs to remember the miles she came to be here. The addition has one window, she notices, but the glass looks better glazed than in the main house where, in the past, she could only see misshapen figures moving along the front of their home. Or misshapen bushes of one kind or another. Or rocks and cliffs blurred beyond recognition. She spent many hours making shapes from these blurs, one of her favorite pastimes. Pastiches of color. Pools. A mixture made into something recognizable. Ah, but that is thinking of the past, and the past has moved to the present.

She climbs down from the wagon, rouses her baby from his sleep, sets him against her hip, unloads her few belongings with Brother Daniel's help, and steps into this changed house for the first time, her son in her arms, a new world opening up to her.

"You are here," Harriet says, a red-faced, fussy baby resting on her hip, its jowly mouth sporting a long string of drool. "Welcome." There's an odd smile on Harriet's face, one Sophia can't help but feel has been arranged to appear welcoming, the eyes telling a different story from the smile. "You can put your things there." She jerks her head to the left. "Charles'll be back next week, but that new room's for you and your boy. No kitchen in there yet, but there are plans." A flat, unemotional greeting. Nothing Sophia can read as welcoming or tender.

She had pictured embracing Harriet, a sister wife after all is said and done. Making amends. Let's move forward, she planned to say, hoping to get started right with her and the new baby. But there has been no invitation between them. Instead of talking further to someone who doesn't seem in the mood for conversation, she walks into the new room, Weston Charles sitting on her hipbone, through a door that used to be a wall. Down two stairs. There is an honest-to-goodness wooden floor. Strips of yellow pine. A four-poster bed, though she's relieved Charles will not be back to share it just yet. He's probably flying across the desert with the mail, the eternal mail, that never stops coming or going. Back next week, Harriet has said.

She walks across the wooden planks laid together to make a floor, somewhat uneven, and presses on the mattress with the heel of her hand. It appears to be a firm one that has been brought to St. Thomas rather than inherited from someone leaving the old and limp behind. New enough to the touch. She climbs back up the two stairs and assesses the main house—the kitchen and living room, the other bedroom where Sophia used to sleep. Harriet is gone, probably to put the baby down. She stands in the room of many purposes—a kitchen, living, and dining room—and sees that the window has been changed to real glass. The outside now matches her notions of what a tree or a rock or a sandy hill is actually like in this geography.

Gratitude. She needs to remember. Wes is in her arms after all. That's what matters. And thank heavens she does not live in a tent or sleep on the ground. Creatures are still out there doing their part to frighten. If she bedded on the bare earth, she would be visited by scorpions, snakes, and tarantulas, bothered by their sleuthing during the quiet hours, and when she thinks of a scorpion taking a slow walk across her face, she shudders.

The way Harriet has greeted her leaves her wanting something. Maybe she should turn around immediately with a fresh horse and borrowed buggy and go north to Willard, to the water, the grass, the tall trees that give shade. To an upstairs and downstairs with a sister-wife she has learned to appreciate, not just to these three cramped rooms—two bedrooms, a combination of kitchen, living room, and entryway. How utterly bereft of anything soothing this place is. But for good or ill, she is here. She squeezes Wes' body close to her own and kisses his sandy hair that's finally growing in. The baby down is almost gone. She refreshes a pillow on the bed that exudes a large puff of dust but also encourages her because it has been placed there for her. Probably by Charles.

Before she can dwell further on her situation, there is clamor at the door. Friends, old friends, are knocking on and coming through the door. At least ten of them. Maybe more. People she has worshiped with at church, women she has quilted with, men carrying shovels in hand on their way home from keeping the irrigation ditches free of sand.

"Sophia," says Dancey Pulsipher, squeezing Sophia's arm with her right hand. "So glad you're back and look what you've brought." Dancey pats Weston's head, and he draws back into his mother's arms, shy and unfamiliar with so much that's new.

"He looks to be almost a year old, is that right?"

"Yes. A Christmas baby. One month shy of a year. Weston Charles, meet Dancey Pulsipher. A woman to be admired as well as respected."

"He's a beauty," Dancey says, blushing at the generosity of Sophia's words, then caressing the child's cheek that he doesn't want caressed. He buries his face between his mother's breasts. "You and Charles should be proud."

"That we are," says Sophia, determined to be Charles' loyal wife again, a partner who makes him proud. She has brought their son to St. Thomas who will give Charles pleasure. This is a good son, a truly good son. Harriet stands in the background, impatient, bouncing her red-faced baby by bending her knees up and down.

Looking at her seeming resentment, Sophia wonders why she's listened to Charles' entreaties to return to her "family" in St. Thomas. Her family is really Weston, her baby, her son, and maybe Mary Anne and Elizabeth. But for a few minutes, Sophia is surrounded by warm embraces and by the knowledge she has been missed in St. Thomas.

"We're elated to have you back, Sophia," says Mona Gibson. "We need your tiny stitches on our quilting days." She smiles big, a smile that would swallow any discouraged feeling or look, a smile that invites Sophia's smile in return. "And welcome to your son."

"His name is Weston Charles Hughes, Weston being Charles' middle name."

"Very good," says Mona, folding her arms in acceptance, looking the baby over as if to see everything has grown in the right place.

"I guess Charles is out on a mail run?" Tom Day interrupts, doffing his hat and shaking Sophia's hand, squeezing it almost too tight though she welcomes the gesture for some unknown reason. Anything to avoid thinking of this house that she is to share with Harriet. Or what it means that she has returned. "He should be back soon."

"One week," Sophia tells Tom. "That's what Harriet has told me. Harriet," she says to the woman almost plastered to the back wall and its shadows. "Come join us."

Harriet finally comes forward to shake Tom's hand. Hesitantly. One could say she was shy, or, Sophia thinks, one could say she was counting the hours until she would win the day and be the confirmed mistress of the house again.

"My wife will be pleased to hear you've come back," Tom says, giving little attention to the handshake with Harriet, genuinely glad to see his old friend, Sophia. Then he returns his hat to his head and bends through the door, being taller than the door frame. "A good day to both a you."

"Anything we can do to help, let us know," Mona says, turning to follow Tom out. "There's always work to be done, that you can count on. But there's always a place for you, you know that. We'll see you on Sunday."

"Thank you for stopping by," Sophia says as the last person closes the door to the new but old house. Those friends and their words have touched her emotions, and she takes a deep breath. "I thank all of you. It's good to feel welcome, believe me. Excellent." Closing the door, she bites her lip to keep from crying. Gratitude is the more important activity at the moment, and she must not forget these friends.

The people leave her, Weston, Harriet, young Jonah, and Harriet's fussy baby alone in the living room of the house that Charles built. Harriet eyes Wes, her lips a straight line, her eyebrows concentrated into a furrow. "You will have to excuse me," Sophia says when the silence between them is too thick. "I need a rest. The trip was lengthy."

"Of course," Harriet says after Sophia takes two steps down into the new room, her voice chilly with no warmth or acceptance in it.

Weston grabs her collar, pinches her cheeks, and says "Mommy, Mommy," over and over. "All right, little one." Then, over her shoulder, she tells Harriet. "I'll help with the supper. Maybe not tonight, but tomorrow."

"That'll be fine." But then Harriet adds, "That baby don't look much like his daddy," before she goes into her bedroom and closes the door to a silence bigger than Sophia can take at the moment. Her eyes fill with tears, brim over, then streak her cheeks. Why is she here? Who is Harriet to be her judge and her jury?

Seating her young child on the only chair, the rocking chair, Sophia folds a blanket into fourths, straightens it in a square on the floor, and puts the toddler on top of it for a first-time-in-days uninterrupted sleep. After a slew of kisses on his rubbery cheek, she watches him relax into slumber.

Wiping her tears with the back of her hand, she sets herself to the task of sorting out her belongings, putting personal things in the one and only dresser and the rest in a pile of boxes on the floor near the window.

She is, no doubt, on the tail end of wifery—a third wife—which means more glory to Charles and his progeny than to her, maybe. But Charles loves her, doesn't he? Look at what he's done to make things nice for her. She will give no thought to any other option. As for family, she is not sure who and what that is or where she belongs. Different people came to call when she arrived—Tom Day with three wives, Dancey, who's a plural wife. Polygamy is part of life here. Not lustful or vengeful, though this new and everlasting covenant, through which she is supposed to have exaltation, perplexes her—to have no end but to go from everlasting to everlasting. She thinks of Mary Anne, of whom she has grown fond, even attached to. The woman with all manner of bodily pain who stood by with pans of warm water and towels when Weston was born. She is an angel. A literal angel. For this wife, this friend, she is grateful. Mary Anne has been a gift. A blessing.

And, her sister, Elizabeth. Sophia has not told her about polygamy, even if Joseph Smith said this is the path to being crowned in heaven. Polygamy is the one thing that unsettles her and makes her uneasy. She wants to follow the Prophet's words—to abide by the fullness of the law—but this particular direction does not sit well. She has made her mistakes, God only knows, but this commandment seems arbitrary to her. Out of sync with so much else that's good. One of these days… Not until then, however. Not much seems to have changed while she has been gone, except for a few more homes. A few more experiments with wives. Additions. Subtractions. Maybe St. Thomas is not the best place for her, all said and done. But for now, she will give her marriage and this settlement the best she has. She will.

* * * * *

In the morning light, she can see that Charles has used some honest-to-goodness lumber for her walls and only door, probably brought it from the mountains near St. George. The room is fragrant, especially fragrant when the sun warms. She sniffs the newly sawn wood with its aroma of forest, birds, and squirrels. It must have been purchased in a land covered with trees, a place from her memories—green grass, brooks, mountains made of more than rock. How many miles must the mules and wagon have traveled to carry logs to Brother Simmons' sawmill north of St. Thomas? Two or three hundred? The mill that has come to fruition while she's been away? He probably planed Charles' logs into the boards that enclose her tiny room, though she must not call it "tiny" anymore. She must be grateful for every good thing that comes her way. Most important.

Weston is still sleeping, but maybe, quietly, she can find the last letter Charles wrote and read again how he'd remodeled the house, nailed boards to the skeleton of what it had been, and then, in the last line, promised to finish whatever was left to do. "Only minor details need be tended to now," she rereads after she finds the letter. She remembers. In the dim light, she sees where the structure is wanting for more wood and where there might be a kitchen, or at least a place to prepare food. Charles has used bricks strengthened with bits of straw—his stopgap measure for her arrival. Charles cares for her and her well-being, and this marriage, strange as it seems to her much of the time, is why she has returned. He will be home soon, and she hopes her son, their son, will be awake when he arrives. Charles can play with Weston and his ten fingers and toes while she makes their first meal together in a good long time.

But then, she looks at the door she has closed, the piece of wood that divides the women and gives them a sense of privacy. What about Harriet? There is only one kitchen. They will need to share. Work out a schedule. A routine. But Charles will love this baby, this son. Charles' eyes will be filled by his love for this child. That will be all that matters.

As the clock ticks further into the day, she is surprised by the change in her breathing when she thinks she hears Charles' horse in the yard. Or thinks she hears him coming through the door. Something is of value to her, she's not sure what. She and Charles came to the Muddy together to make a life here, though it is now complicated by the fact of Harriet, her baby, and her toddler. Two wives in the same house. How she wishes Sarah Ann were alive, a sister to Weston. They could be a stronger family if they were all together, though that is useless thinking.

To busy herself while Weston sleeps, she goes outside to plant a few starts of lilac bushes and three Dutch elms with the trowel she has brought from Willard. She rehearses what might help her be more loyal to Charles and St. Thomas. She can listen, she reminds herself. There are those who are more experienced who can teach her. Tell her. She is not unlike Alma's sons in the Book of Mormon, instructed to listen when their father was old and ready to die. Charles is more experienced. He has seen many things. She needs to humble herself and listen to his counsel. Listen and hearken. How archaic, she smiles, patting the soil to bury a bulb, almost laughing out loud when the word "hearken" occurs to her. But then she remembers she has much to learn. She promises herself she will cooperate.

With her bare hands, she drops bulbs into the three-inch holes she has dug, no gloves, dirt beneath her fingernails, some of them with roots and bits of dark soil clinging to them. She is planting them late, but today is mild and the sunshine is weak enough. Maybe they will blossom into the beauty she imagines each has. Then she notices Harriet peering out the window, looking as if she were measuring her sister wife's plot and making sure Sophia keeps to its boundaries. A bird of prey. Considering Harriet and making her part of her decision-making will be a challenge for Sophia.

Back in coolness of the house, after using the cracked pitcher to wash her hands free of the sandy dirt, Sophia closes the top drawer of the dresser Charles has built for her, replacing the pair of socks she has dried on the line. The drawer squeaks, fitting more closely than it should, a small error in calculation, perhaps, making it the only drawer that opens. But where is Charles? He should be back by now. He is a day later than forecast, and then she notices the pounding of her heart as the clock ticks midday into afternoon.

She both wants and does not want to see him. She is like the pendulum of a clock—back and forth in her affections—except she has decided this is her most fortuitous course of action—to re-blend her life with Charles, to fully accept polygamy, though it still feels alien to her desire to be special, even number one. He will probably come to the door dusty and ready for water and sleep, but then she stops to wonder for the first time. Will he brush Harriet aside and come to her first? She erases this impression from her palette of thoughts. In polygamy, all wives are equal, were they not? At least that is how it is supposed to work. A lack of selfishness. Enough love not to care about being a one and only. Rubbish, she can't help but think. What is wrong with being a one and only?

Maybe her husband is part of a new domestic scene, the one he has created with Harriet. What does she care? She coaches herself, battling her sense of entitlement. She will toss off the thought of Charles' allegiance. Give it a ride on a carousel on a horse painted red with jeweled ears. That is what she will do. If that is how things are, he and Harriet can have each other. Sophia can survive by herself. She has friends who have asked what they could do to help her and Weston. They seemed genuinely happy to see her, her son, her bag of thread, and swaths of material she carries wherever she goes. Maybe Charles has two wives living together now, but, at least, these friends will do what they can to ease the pain of adjustment. Most know the difficulties of being anything other than a first wife. Yet how unnatural to allow one woman to make the important decisions for all, especially when one of the wives has been away as Sophia has, especially when proud Harriet knows nothing except her own province. Harriet does not care for Mary Anne or Sophia, but only for herself, something which, Sophia reminds herself, she, too, feels when it comes to Harriet.

She pours the last of the water from the pitcher. Of course she can survive, and of course Charles is still intoxicated by her. It is evident in the new room—the new bed, the pillow. Sophia is counting on that, she knows, putting two straggly yellow chrysanthemums in her only vase to make this new home pleasing for his return. She knows what he needs. She will be a good wife. She will be grateful for the food and water and tidy home he has provided. He is a well-meaning man, even though he is twenty-eight years older. Someone whom others might call an old man. But what is she to do if his affections have turned?

She will thank Charles for building this room where she can raise her son the way she wants to. Charles will never know anything is amiss between the wives he has chosen. The second and the third both live in St. Thomas now and are very polite in public except for some of the things Harriet blurts out, almost as if she cannot see past her anguish about being a second wife, a second rather than a first choice. For this separation from Harriet, this small room, Sophia will be forever grateful.

She sinks onto the mattress of her four-poster bed—dressed in her best dress and waiting. Weston has been napping for over two hours. She can't help but wonder if polygamy is part of the Gospel in which she believes. Really?

CHAPTER SEVENTEEN

THE QUESTION

She opens her eyes, having fallen asleep on the bed. She sees him standing in the doorway, bent hat in hands, apologizing for being so late—the one she has thought about for so many months, both good and ill, the man who is her accidental husband. He closes the door behind him and shuts out the life happening in the other room, Harriet and her two children, basically. Thank heaven for those small things.

"Charles," she says loudly with a hint of longing mixed with independence. She pins the strands that have escaped her carefully arranged hairdo and runs to his arms, not exactly sure why she is running to this man except she feels so many feelings about Charles. Push. Pull. Away. Toward. He gives her a welcoming hug though he looks dusty, always dusty, and tired.

She points at the baby who's so close to sleep on the floor. "Isn't he beautiful?" she says as he bends his creaking knees to squat for a closer look.

"A fine son," he says, though Weston Charles is too far gone for a greeting of any kind. Charles stands slowly and carefully and limps to the new rocking chair where he gives all his weight to the seat.

Maybe she will take off his boots and rub his feet. She kisses him again on the top of his hat. She knows he will like that gesture.

"I have missed you, Little Dove." He seems shy, but there is also a boldness about him, a surety Sophia has not always known. "Mail delivery, you know. More and more people out here. Satchel is getting heavier. Letters from home."

"Do you like the rocking chair I acquired with the exchange of two hats?"

"Most definitely. Thank you for that. Eases my bones." He seems older and more tired than she has ever seen before.

Sophia wants him to respond with a celebration of some kind but he has come to her. For that small gesture she needs be grateful. But when she gathers the cooked rice to put it together with the vegetables she still needs to cook, she realizes her thoughts are many-pronged: He loves me, I love him not. Or maybe I love him and he loves me not? But his smell is old. His skin is thin and folds into a thousand lines when his arms are spread out at his sides. His wrists are bony, and there are wrinkles at the base of his hands when he lifts them. There are bruises on his arms that look as though they've come unbidden to Charles, yet he is in his sixties, the likely possessor of thin skin that doesn't clot blood or keep it under control. And he is tired, she observes, as he leans back into the rocking chair, the one that fits his frame and his weight, the one built for both of them—two of Sophia's hats traded to the furniture maker. Charles' beard has grown wilder, barely tamable, and is almost totally white. It is a wonder he can see his way beneath those bushy eyebrows. As she watches out of the sides of her eyes, pretending to be busy, he releases every muscle into the rungs of the chair. A picture of resignation. Uneasy peace, maybe, Sophia thinks. Their time apart has its tale to tell. She excuses herself to the big room to put the last touches on the meal.

"I'll be right back. Close your eyes. Let your arms rest."

Does she want his used-up body over hers, coming inside of her? She divides one half of an onion into ten pieces, chops it fine, and sautés the pieces of carrot and onion over the one burner she has lit with an elongated match, an extension of the fire. Maybe she shouldn't be here, telling Charles she has missed him when she is unsure of her feelings. But she will do what needs to be done to raise her son into a good, honest man, a young boy with a place to belong.

"You are good to me, Sophia," Charles says from the rocking chair in her room, his voice carrying through the open door. "So good to see you again."

"Yes. I say the same to you."

She releases the green peas from the pods. Rice, carrots, peas. A good meal for him, though she cannot help but rerun her thoughts. She can survive on her own if need be. She is used to being alone and to providing her own conclusions, though she wishes she could not hear Harriet rustling about in the room that used to be hers.

Something about Charles has changed. She can feel a shift. Maybe his age or, then again, maybe Harriet, who speaks her mind too easily, not always generous to others. "My, I must say, your son is a stick that bends,"

Harriet had said last Sunday, laughing at her lame joke, glibly announcing Weston's and Sophia's arrival at the Relief Society gathering on their first Sunday at church since returning to St. Thomas. "A willowy, graceful stick, of course." She flapped the flats of her hands in dismissal, "but so much more supple than Charles and his kin. Green eyes, too." Maybe Harriet has caused this change in Charles. Maybe she has made him think about who and what Sophia might be. Maybe Harriet has created a problem when none existed before.

But Sophia is done digesting the snide words Harriet chose to say out loud to the sisters last Sunday. She fills a plate for Harriet, even though she has probably eaten already. She was currently tending to Jonah and her new baby in Sophia's old bedroom. Noisily. Making her presence known. Always in the background hovering like a vulture. Please, Sophia, she reproves herself quickly. Forget Harriet for now. Let her rustle. She is your sister. Your sister. Your sister.

Sophia smiles as she carries two plates back into her room—always happy when she can be near her son, Weston, and now her husband who will be a good father.

During the week, she refolded both hers and Weston's clothes that were wrinkled and misshapen in their travels. She shook and refolded them, ironing some, busy making a one-room home. Before she sets the plates on her makeshift table, she repeats, in a singsong fashion, something from her small book of poems by William Wordsworth, the book her father once gave her:

> Eyes of some men travel far
> For the finding of a star:
> Up and down the heavens they go,
> Men that keep a mighty rout!
> I'm as great as they, I trow,
> Since the day I found thee out,
> Little flower!—I'll make a stir
> Like a great Astronomer.

"Yes, Weston Charles," she whispers out loud to the child on the floor whose eyelids are closed in sleep. "You are my little flower."

"What are you murmuring?" Charles asks, sounding even more road-weary than Sophia has figured.

"You know I love Wordsworth." Her husband sits with his eyes half-closed. "Something he wrote, that's all."

"Trow. That is a word I haven't heard before. What's it mean?"

"To think or believe, I am quite sure. The word is archaic. Something used long ago, though Wordsworth did not write so long ago."

She looks over at Charles in the rocking chair with both love and distaste. He is leaning back and closing his eyes. He is too tired to care about the word "trow" and maybe too tired to lift a fork to his lips. She straightens the antimacassar on the dresser.

But Charles is different, of that she is sure. Maybe the difference has to do with life in general, or maybe with the little boy who is the spitting image of Geoffrey Scott, the long-limbed man with green eyes who has floated in and out of St. Thomas, the salt mines, and Pioche with his camel that frightens Midnight—the horse unafraid of rattlesnakes and scorpions, gullies, ditches, plateaus, and table rocks, whatever, but spooked by a camel. Why is this magnificent horse afraid of a camel, though granted, it has a distinctive smell disliked by not just Midnight, but by a good many horses reacting in much the same way. Nothing else smells like a camel.

Weston is now asleep on the floor, and Charles in the chair, even before dinner has been eaten. Should Sophia wake him or let him sleep? Would that this divided feeling in her disappear, that she may be totally loyal to this man who slumbers in the rocking chair? Of course, he needs his rest for now.

Where is Geoffrey Scott? she wonders as she puts the rice and vegetables in a serving dish. Sophia has been in town for one week and has heard very little about the man from Kansas. Gone north to Pioche, some have said. Or maybe to the north of Elko in Tuscarora or Columbia. Or south of Elko in Bullion City, where every means of transport is not only needed but making men rich beyond their dreams. Gold and silver fever. Spread to Nevada, though rumors have said the strike is over. Maybe he's gone west to California where new lodes are opening up daily it seems, though no one has spoken more than a few passing hellos to the man so why would anyone know? Sophia suspects he has gone somewhere to sell to the miners needing salt for the reduction of the silver ore, a bigger market than table salt alone. Huge amounts of salt wrapped in burlap sacks carried to the mines on the back of a camel or maybe a string of mules to the western slope of the Sierras. Or to Pioche where mining is rumored to be on the edge of something great. He had talked of caravans. Maybe he has found a way to make that happen.

No one knows for sure where he has gone, but, as she leans forward to eat her dinner alone and keep peas from rolling off her fork, she vows to make Charles happy she is back. But for now, he sleeps. Thus she allows herself to think, just one more minute, of the man who has no truck with the Mormons and apparently does not wish further involvement. James Milhaus knows that the Gospel is first and foremost in her life. "And whoso believeth in me, and is baptized," which she does and has been, "shall inherit the kingdom of God… Repent and become as a little child… or ye can in nowise receive these things."

Except, she has also heard that the Indian had ridden Adababa away from the house where Geoffrey Scott stays, ridden away with a stoic look on his face while Geoffrey Scott watched him go, rifle in hand. "Grief-stricken he looked," Portia had reported. "He never lifted that rifle to shoot, but you could tell he was thinkin' about it. Twitchin' the way his finger was. Never seen a mix of anger and grief like that."

Maybe, as she debates whether or not to waken Charles, Geoffrey Scott was perturbed. Using a rifle is not something Geoffrey Scott would do. She knows that.

SPRING 1870

Charles has taken another run and now is back again, hat in hand, crumpled as usual. Having ridden his new horse on a mail run he's not supposed to take because the doctor said to stay closer to home, he collapses into the rocking chair. Sophia uses feathers she's tied together to keep it free from dust and debris, but truth is, he is a sand creature, a man made of grains of the earth, and he won't notice what's in the seat of his chair. He crosses his legs. Then he uncrosses them. He speaks, though not as boldly as he usually does. Sophia can see the pain in his body and in his eyes and pulls beside him in a chair borrowed from the other room.

"Weston Charles is not my son, is he?"

The question is direct, so absolutely direct. Sophia is speechless. She barely recovers enough to make an answer, though she has seen Charles' eyes with their beseeching and questioning. She wants to be careful and not say anything that will hurt him further. He is her husband, after all.

"I can see your white forehead when you're not wearing your hat," she says, teasing him with her fingers brushing across his brow. They laugh, and he, too, touches the band of stark white skin beneath white hair, a sun-tanned face below that, a two-toned face with a stringy white beard with a touch of black. Sophia takes the hat from him and sets it on her lap.

"You have been in too much sun," she says, trying not to stumble with her words even as she wipes one hand on her apron, wiping whatever might be on her hand, which is nothing at the moment. "And yes, he is your son. He adores you, and you make sure he has food to eat, the same as with me. You are his teacher. You are his example."

"But am I the father?"

Again the question is too direct for Sophia. The only words she can speak are pulled out of thin air. "Of course. What kind of question is that?" She turns the hat in her hands.

"It's a question that came to me while riding Midnight when he was alive, though please hear me," he makes certain to say, "this question was not born from Harriet's inquiries. The answer doesn't matter anyway because I've held that little one. I played games with him. I patted his round little potbelly." He straightens himself in the chair, his buttocks having slipped forward on the smooth wood. "Harriet does mention he's not like me, but her words aren't of concern to me."

There is a heavy foot of silence that wants to land somewhere. Sophia waits for his next words, pretending to equanimity, calming herself as best she can.

"That said, he does have sandy hair. Mine was always dark. And…"

Sophia becomes a fireworks display, her hands hitting the air, Charles' hat falling to the floor as she stands, sitting by its lonely self on the floor made of pine.

"Why do you believe everything Harriet has to say, when I am telling you that you are the father? Why should she be able to discern the truth when Weston is our son, yours and mine?"

"But I…I've thought the same thing myself. He's not like me. I told you to stay clear of that no-good fellow with the camel." He leans forward in his chair, his complexion darkening like a thundercloud "I never liked him hanging around. Neither him nor his stupid camel. You know that. Had his mouth open. Salivating over you. I saw that. I'd go after him if he were in town. String him up even. Who does he think he is? And who are you to let him look in the first place? I should say touch, shouldn't I? There's a big difference between me and that son you say is ours."

"What are you talking about? You and your foul mouth. Let me remind you that Weston Charles is young, very little, and in need of you. And you make such statements. You say Harriet has no say in this matter?"

"She has made a few comments, but she…"

Sophia wishes to shout at him, to call Harriet a demon, a betrayer, whatever word she can produce from her vocabulary of strong nouns, but she knows Charles trusts Harriet. She came to St. Thomas when he needed a companion, when Sophia chose Willard to make sure her baby would be born into a safer world. But she also knows that Charles would not be casting doubt in her direction if he wasn't prodded on by someone, that someone being Harriet, of course. She wishes she could yell into the other room and tell the woman to mind her own business. Her beeswax, as that hateful woman would say. She retrieves the hat from the floor, hands it to Charles, an invitation to leave, but then she reconsiders, stands proud, and folds her arms tight against her chest. Indignant.

"Harriet has her sisters in Springville in which she can confide, and besides, she is expecting another child of yours and wants the best for it. How can you let her determine what happens between you and me?"

"You're right. This is our own personal matter, but…"

"But what? How can you let a cloud of doubt come over you and this young boy who needs you. He needs your example to follow. I need you. You are my husband."

"That I am," Charles said, crossing his legs again, cupping one knee with his hands, then putting his legs parallel and placing both hands on his knees. He angles his back forward and points his elbows out, looking as if he is about to stand and leave and escape this encounter with which he is obviously uncomfortable. Escape to his new horse. Take another mail run, which the doctor has told him not to do. Anything to avoid the woman standing in front of him, the accused woman. But he is tired. That shows everywhere on his body—his wrinkled forehead, his droopy eyes, his sagging posture.

Sophia stands with one arm folded across her waist and one hand over her mouth. She can be a formidable opponent when necessary and will do anything to ensure Weston Charles has a father. He needs one. This man who cares about Zion will raise him. No one will get in the way. Not Geoffrey Scott. Not Harriet. In this, she is determined.

Regret crosses Charles' face, which is changing as she watches, changing from thunder to a gloomy, overcast sky. The hurt in his eyes has deepened to regret, to a sadness even. This is something she has never seen before. He was usually so sure of everything he said.

"I don't know what to say," he says to Sophia, not able to speak further. He kneads the hat in his hand and reworks the angle of the crown. He looks down, unable to raise his eyes.

At that moment Sophia sees a tired old man reviewing his life. Maybe a defeated man, though "defeated" is a word she would never choose to define Charles Weston Hughes, a tough old bird if she ever saw one. This man in the rocking chair appears helpless, and she has never seen him this way before: regret on his face, a melancholy in his eyes rather than determination at all costs. A sense of diminishment and a faded past circles him. She can feel its sad music. Suddenly she takes pity on the man who has roared and smoked with fury and been every sort of annoyed with her and the world. She wants to pull him from his chair and waltz with him. She wants to take him backward in time, back to the days when he was vital, more opinionated. At least he was alive when he lost his temper and caused eyebrows to raise, not some sad man regretting his mistakes. She prefers his bluster to this. She wants that Charles back—the one who tussled with the world, who walked big through any and every geography, a man who could tackle life head-on no matter how other people were affected. This is the husband she has married. This one. Not the one moping in the chair.

"I need to check the mail at the post office," he finally says, pulling himself up and out of the rocker, though he is still lame from his fall, the one in which Midnight stumbled into a gopher hole, crashed forward, and broke its leg. The accident after which Midnight had to be put down—his beloved horse wrenching its leg in an unsuspected hole, who had twisted it until it had broken. Now the doctor has advised Charles to discontinue running mail though he hasn't listened.

"Of course," Sophia says, staring out the window, wishing she could say something to make everything all right again though not sorry this conversation is almost over. "The mail. No one has been a finer postman than yourself. No one has been so dependable as you."

"I'm sorry," he says, putting the hat back on his head, adjusting it, then walking through the door to the community room, empty at the moment, though Harriet probably heard their discussion. Favoring one leg, he walks outside where the sky is cloudy for a change. Re-saddles his horse and rides. Maybe there will be rain. Maybe a flash flood. Something in St. Thomas besides the sun and the heat.

* * * * *

It happens suddenly. Nobody planned for this. Nobody saw it coming, except maybe the doctor who told Charles to stop running the mail or be bound for trouble. Nobody suspected his horse would stumble, the same as Midnight had done, and throw Charles through the air—the obstinate man flying to his death, maybe like a bird with no wings, crashing into the ground next to a giant Joshua. Least of all, Harriet, who revered Charles.

The runner comes with the news, breathless with the news. "They found him," he shouts. "Behind one of them hills. On the ground. No breath or nothing. Blood on his forehead. Your man's gone, dead, passed on to another place."

"Charles?" Harriet's face has turned a white Sophia's never seen before. A ghostly white, an unearthly white, a specter. She seems turned on her head, upside down, not the woman she's been, and the baby she holds is crying as if it comprehends the news more fully than anyone else.

Sophia's face is white as well, especially the pale ring around her mouth, but she is not as hysterical as Harriet is. Charles was a man she loved as best she could. And now he's dead? Not here anymore to be who he was? She has thought nothing could take Charles anywhere he didn't want to go, could it? He didn't want to leave this earth just yet, did he? What will Mary Anne say? How will she, Sophia, and Wes survive?

But Sophia is able to rise above her questions. She is partially sympathetic yet partially unbelieving at the way Harriet's carrying on, acting as if life has come to an end, that there is no breathing left without her dear Charles. She is not the only one married to him. There are two others and Charles had held everything together, even the loyalty of three wives as diverse as that loyalty has been.

Harriet sinks to her knees. "Oh, dear God," she says and folds her hands beneath her chin. "This isn't true, this isn't true. Charles will be back tonight. This is just a game. Oh, dear God. Bless us. Bless the children. Charles, oh Charles."

Sophia has no words, only her own shock braided with a realization that life goes on even if one life stops, such as the life she is holding in her arms, her Weston, her baby who brings her such joy even if he's not always easy. Charles was too ornery to die, wasn't he? Too committed to God's plan to be lying there inert, no pulse, no life. Charles. She feels as though she should cry because this is someone who has been such an integral part of her life, but no water comes, no tears spill onto her face. Please, God, she prays inside herself. Please help me feel something for this man, this person who has given so much in his way. He's done his best, he has. Charles. So many miles. So much concern for the Saints to be true to what they've been taught. To what they said they believed. Charles.

There is a pounding on the door, then a hard knock. Two men have carried Charles' body back to the house, a gash on his forehead painted deep by blood, a man who is limp and has nothing left to give.

"Sorry about this, both of you," they say. "We found him lying on the sand after his horse wandered into town and let us know he was missing. Something must've tripped his horse up." They lay him carefully, even tenderly, on the only rug inside the house. A braided one. The colors of autumn leaves, golden colors as if the world is dying, turning to browns before falling from the tree. Charles. A man of action and determination—lying still on the living room floor of his seventh house he's built. Two wives and their babies looking at the man lying there, the man who doesn't speak or tell them something needs to be done.

"I know we haven't talked much, Harriet," Sophia forces herself to say. "We haven't appreciated what the other of us is about, but we're all we have left now, don't you think? We need to decide how to proceed from here."

Harriet's tongue seems tied. She has been off-putting to her sister wife, dismissing her as if she were a bother and an interruption. She doesn't seem to want interchange with Sophia, any talk at all. But they have been married to the same man, have they not? Shouldn't that mean something when faced with an end the way they've been?

"Harriet," Sophia says. "We can help each other, we can. Mary Anne helped birth my child. She did not get clotted up with her feelings, that I have taken something from her. You and I need to do the same thing."

"But you haven't been loyal to Charles," Harriet says, suddenly speaking, tears wetting her cheeks amply. "And you know what I'm saying."

Sophia is taken aback. She has been a partial wife, disillusioned with St. Thomas and with her husband who had such an unpredictable temper, at least when it came to his dealings with her. She does know what Harriet is saying and wishes at this moment she did not.

"Your son," Harriet spits out the words. "Whose is he?"

Now Sophia is the one who cannot speak. She has wondered about Harriet's suspicions but has never heard a point-blank accusation.

"How can you say such a thing?" she says. "Especially at a time like this."

"You know it's true." She's wiping her face with her apron. "Why Charles put up with it I'll never know."

"Who do you think you are to be throwing slander around the way you're doing?"

"I only speak the truth, and you know it."

Sophia could tear into Harriet's skin, she could. Bloody her even. She could rip off her apron and stuff it in her mouth. She could even hit her insolent face with the back of her hand, but that would only be playing to her ignorance. But was it ignorance she was dealing with here, or a simple truth that Harriet could see when everyone else either ignored or pretended? She should tear into herself, into her desires for something other than she's chosen, into her caring about Geoffrey Scott, someone who's not even a part of this community. Who knows the truth of the matter?

"So you are not interested in making any decisions?" Sophia queries.

"Not with you, harlot."

Sophia clenches her fists, bends forward on her toes, and tips her small body toward Harriet and her loose mouth. "What did you call me?"

"I…I shouldn't…" Harriet is exchanging her baby from side to side, as if unable to allow it one place to rest, as if she's grasping for something to say. "I guess I'm struggling to accept what's just happened. We've been through hard times…"

"If I were into name-calling, I'd think of something equally hurtful to say to you."

Harriet is plain as water in mid-ocean, she could say. Ugly as mud. Or she could tell her that her face is obscene, the way it is dotted with girlish pimples. Sightly ruptures. But vanity showing its face once again and being put back in place, Sophia remembers that Harriet has said what she has wanted to say ever since she had arrived. The room is filled with their antipathy.

"You think you're better than me," Harriet says instead of saying she's sorry. "You have airs. You think St. Thomas is the last place on earth. Why should I cotton to that?"

Sophia would sputter if sputtering were something she did. Harriet has stepped way beyond any kind of boundary. She's mean-spirited. Vengeful. Proud of her self-righteous stance. She's all the things Sophia has strived not to be. And yet the woman knows about Sophia's baby just as surely as she knows she's a wife to Charles. The woman knows how to thrust knives into wounds.

"I am sorry," Sophia says carefully, gathering herself, closing her eyes as she does, "that you have such a low opinion of me and my son. I'm sorry that I have caused you this kind of anger, even grief. But we need to work together now, not at odds. It will take two of us to get Charles buried and to move forward. What do we do now?"

"What do we do? What do we do?" Harriet covers her face with one hand, unable to talk for a few moments, overcome with emotion. "I'm thinking I'll go to my sisters' and make my life with them," Harriet finally says, turning her back slightly away from Sophia, still trying to calm her baby and now trying to keep her face out of sight.

"I'm probably going to Willard to be with Mary Anne," Sophia says, "but I guess you have other preferences."

"My sisters are good women." Harriet is walking toward her room, creating a distance that needs to be created. "They'll take me and my two babies in. My three babies when the time comes." She looks over her shoulder and smiles, almost in spite of herself, for this is the first time she's announced she was with child again, though people have been suspicious. Mademoiselle Plentiful, Sophia thinks, happy Weston Charles is in her arms, her baby who is with her through all of this.

He has been quiet, even respectful of the grief for Charles, but now Weston wails. Time to eat. Time for you to remember I'm here, he announces with no hesitation. Harriet and Sophia part ways. They each go to their rooms to figure where their man will be buried and laid to rest. How they will cope with what lays in store for them. How they will digest what has been said between them.

CHAPTER EIGHTEEN

THE DESERT

AUTUMN 1870

Brigham Young, Prophet, Seer, and Revelator of the Church of Jesus Christ of Latter-day Saints, visits St. Thomas, St. Joseph, and the surrounding towns he has never seen, though he is now seeing them. He tours the course of the Muddy and the Virgin. He is told how these rivers join the Colorado south of these settlements. He does not bother to visit Callville, most likely privy to why and how it has failed.

"Who asked the Saints to come here?" he says to the small crowd gathered around him before he speaks to the congregation as a whole. The sun is its usual large self and glares on his skull until he wipes the sweat from his forehead. "This is not a good place for a settlement, forgive me for saying so."

No one volunteers to speak, possibly shocked into silence. Brother Brigham, the colonizer, the prophet who called them to this place, hasn't seen the sites for these towns?

A month later, the Saints of St. Thomas receive a letter from the First Presidency:

> To the brethren and sisters residing on the Muddy:
>
> It proves that the survey of the line of Nevada places you within the jurisdiction of that state… Without your consent [it] imposes upon you the onerous burden of taxation and license and stamp dates with which that state is oppressed.
>
> Your isolation from markets, the high rate that this property is assessed in Nevada with the unscrupulous character of many of the officers of the newly organized regions, all combine to

> render your continuance in developing the resources of the Muddy a matter of grave consideration... When you consider the drawbacks with which you are surrounded, you may think them too great to overcome in view of the advantages to be attained thereby.
>
> You have done noble work in making and sustaining that outpost of Zion against many difficulties amid exposure and toil. We now advise that you gather together...and take consideration of your future course and if a majority [decides to stay]...all abide by the result. But if the majority of the Saints in counsel determine it better to leave the State whose laws and burdens are so oppressive, let it be so done, but it will not be prudent to reduce your numerical strength much and attempt to remain...
>
> Brigham Young, Geo. A. Smith, Erastus Snow

"Your isolation..." This phrase is what she repeats to herself several times, her tongue and lips moving though no sound can be heard if anyone wants to overhear what she's thinking. She's reading the letter posted on the wall of the post office, the place where Charles once picked up and deposited his leather bags filled with mail, fat or slack–the mail must go through. The post office seems smaller than it ever has, almost a four-walled chantey today.

"There's a vote next Sunday," the clerk says, too busy organizing the daily mail to chat about the weather or whatever else needs to be talked about. "See you there." The screen door slams quickly with the help of its tight, new hinges, and she is out the door. A vote. The following Sunday. Should people stay in St. Thomas or leave it behind?

Everyone in town is talking about the letter. The subject of every conversation. But the debate over staying or leaving has already been decided, hasn't it, she can't keep herself from hoping. Brigham Young mentioned the taxes Nevada has levied–all of it to be paid in solid currency: gold, silver, gold bullion. All of which no one has. The people of St. Thomas are farmers, barely hanging on, not miners. They barter. They trade. They barely survive. And they have paid taxes already to Utah Territory, even if the boundaries are always changing and thus confusing everyone. St. Thomas is not a place where anyone will stay much longer.

Charles is not alive to see all of this, she thinks as she walks toward home, waving at whoever's outside tending to their yard. "Good morning. Good day," she says, stopping to talk to a few of the residents, asking how they fare, how their children are doing. But when she reaches the crossroads and turns onto the road that runs past hers and Harriet's home, she can't keep from considering how Charles died five months before the letter from the First Presidency arrived. Brought to the house, that man with no breath left to him, splayed on that autumnal rug, lying still among the colors of pumpkins and squashes. Nothing raising or lowering his chest. Maybe it is best he has died, Sophia allows as she negotiates the road that will never be smoothed or paved now that the Saints will be leaving.

Shoes do not last long here, in these ruts, in this dirt, and maybe she should take them off, undo the laces and pull them out of the grommets. Except there will always be thorns. Stickers, goats' horns, whatever can puncture the skin, so maybe keep them on, which is a devil-and-the-deep-blue-sea choice. No one will be thinking of these roads or how to finish this task, just like Charles will be unaware his efforts have been of no use. Is it right he gave so much of himself for nothing? That St. Thomas will soon be a fleeting memory? He will never know, will he?

She pauses where a recent sandstorm has covered the tracks that one can usually follow on the absurd, half-formed road. The sand is irritating her feet inside her shoes. Where does it come from, so much sand? She stops to shake offending grains out of one shoe because they bother her instep and her toes and both feet, period. Then she wiggles her foot into the heavy shoe again, reties it, and makes her way toward home. But then, before she's taken twenty steps, both shoes fill again, the grains working their way inside no matter what measures she takes.

The truth is, Charles spent more time with Harriet after he asked The Question. A fact. A disappointment. He became more of a stranger to Sophia than he had ever been before, working in both gardens, dutifully, though he paid less attention to the plot Sophia tended, the one where she'd raised beans and a few straggly ears of corn and tied a string to slats around its boundaries. He planted cotton in Harriet's garden per Brother Brigham's request, though his plants were stunted by the sun that grew bolder every day, it seemed, even in the autumn. Sad bolls of cotton, meager, beleaguered. The wrong soil. Not enough water. All in all, a hard year for the Saints of St. Thomas. Cotton in the Muddy Mission did not fulfill its hopes and promises. The last battle of the Civil War had been fought almost five years before and cotton was being sent west again. Soon, the cotton missions would not be necessary. Homespun would not be necessary. The railroad was nearing completion. It would bring converts and cotton to Utah Territory. No river travel necessary. Everything would be different.

"Charles, please," she wanted to cry out when he walked through the outer door on the night he'd asked the question, when she heard him mounting Midnight, when she heard the sound of the horse's hooves dying away. She had sunk to her knees, knelt to pray, and propped her elbows upon the seat of her chair. "Please allow this to pass. Please, God, make everything right. Let him find a place in his heart for me and for Wes."

She has reached her home but pauses on the outside, not yet ready to go in. Truth be told to God and all people, she has failed him, hasn't she? And he has failed her. Has her heart ever belonged to him? Or has his ever belonged to her? Did he love her in particular or was she a mere grain of sand in his grandiose plans, like the sand she's negotiating at the moment?

"It's a good thing he's no longer around to spit his venom," one man said at the wake, though she wasn't supposed to hear his comments. They weren't meant for her ears. Everyone had been dressed in black, black, black. Besides the man who seemed so bitter, most everyone seemed to be mourning, genuinely mourning, though probably not everyone was saying what they thought. The dead become sacred. Beyond the reach of pettiness or cruelty or even truth. She will not think about his disposition. Not now. She will remember him as a good man who kept his word. Her husband. Even if a partial one.

She trips over a cholla cactus almost buried from her line of sight. Removing the right shoe for the second time, she realizes she is weary of lacing these industrial coverings on her feet. She pulls a thorn out of her shoe's sole—black shoes with firm heels. She calculates. It was months ago since Charles asked her if the baby belonged to him. A question that shook her to her soul—the soul of her body as well as the sole of her shoes. She laughs out loud, still a modicum of humor left in her mind, jaded by sun and wind and Charles' passing.

Maybe if he had been a jester rather than a man with such a temper or a man subject to suspicions. He could have poked her in the ribs and tickled her in the armpits, but he should not have asked. No. "A question came to me," he had said. "Riding my horse across deserts, bajadas, and mesas. It was not born from Harriet's inquiries," he made certain to say. "I love you and Weston," he added, but then he asked The Question. And the answer had its consequences, no matter what he promised.

Sophia wants to wake him from the dead and tell him he was stepping beyond his boundaries with that question about the only living child she had. How could he think so little of their time together? She listens to the rhythm of her feet—something constant. Something regular. Something to believe in and hope for. But maybe her time with Geoffrey Scott was one of the panoply of sins she should not have committed. Her vanity was one thing but she had committed adultery. But then, what is polygamy? And why should she not have two husbands if he has three wives?

She should have talked with him more, told him how she was lonelier than she had ever been. Isolated. No family to turn to or care for. Abandoned not only by Charles and his mail pouch, but by God and Nature. She should have looked directly at him, not toward the only window, which she had done that night. She should have told him of her hunger to see something green and bountiful rather than the continuous wind-blowing sand. Listen to me. Between the lines, she should have said. Listen to all of me. My body. My gestures. You are supposed to be my friend.

She should have told him, she scolds herself. She should have said how Geoffrey Scott offered her a ride on the camel. It was only a ride, she would have said, though she won't admit, even to herself, that she had been eager for something to break up the monotony of her days and the mediocrity of the landscape. Most of all, she wishes she could have told him how it was stunning to ride on the back of Adababa, to feel its thick, strangely velvet coat beneath her hands. How it was amazing to be so high in the world and to travel so quickly over the red dirt, to be Queen of the Desert for a few minutes.

"The Queen of Sheba," she laughs, though no one is around to hear. She is often talking to herself, she knows. "The ruler of all her subjects."

But she is hesitant to go inside. Hers and Harriet's house now. The place where she and her son, Weston, live. Gratefully, he is being watched by Harriet while she made the trip to the post office. She has to give Harriet some credit. She is trying to help out, trying just as Sophia is trying. They've reached the bottom of the well together and are trying to scale the walls upwards.

But Charles still bothers her mind. "In the entire scheme of life," she could have told him, "this incident did not add up to much, not really." It did not count, except it does count, she reminds herself. Weston is real. That beautiful son who will be waiting to leap into her arms as soon as she walks up the stairs to the house.

Charles had nothing more to say that day except that he needed to check on the mail. He pulled his well-worn hat down to his ears, mumbled a few niceties, maybe, she cannot remember. She can envision him limping into the other room. Into the community kitchen. The place where she and Harriet prepare food and are now working at being civil to each other. And then he was a shadow in the doorway, outlined by the moon and the light of its full face. And then she heard the hooves until they faded in the distance and she could not hear another sound.

* * * * *

On Sunday next, with everyone except one family who has helped build St. Thomas signing their name to a petition that will be sent by horse and rider to Salt Lake City, Sophia votes "yes." She signs with a flourish. A large signature. A definitive "yes," adding her name to the long list of people who've tried to make this a workable place. While the entire population of St. Thomas watches the process, gathered beneath the bower, gathered to offer prayers of thanks and hope for the last time in this place, she passes the petition, though she wonders if maybe she should have signed Adababa's name, or Geoffrey Scott's. Or Charles' or Kwami's. They lived here, too.

The woman seated next to her votes "yes" as well, signing her name to the petition laid across her lap. She is wearing a limp cotton dress that hangs too loosely on her bovine frame. Wide hips. Caved shoulders, all of this reminding Sophia of Harriet, whom she thinks she needs to learn to love better than she does. Instead she concentrates on the variety of fabric in the dresses, some of the cloth worn so smooth that it would tear if someone pulled hard. Some fabrics are tasteless to begin with, oranges clashing with purples. Some are practical and sensible. But she is surrounded by women who have more important matters in their lives than fancy hats, bustles, and crinolines. Maybe, for today anyway, she lacks sufficient knowledge about things that matter. Maybe there is some humility to inculcate into that small brain of hers that seems averse to lack of pride.

After they have sung "Till We Meet Again," she shakes hands, says good-bye too many times to count, and is ready to leave the settlement with its memories of a too-frail baby girl, its troubles with the Indians, its bad water, its grasshoppers that eat everything the insects can find for a meal, its swarms of mosquitos that spread malaria. And its taxes. Not to forget the taxes. She gathers her belongings and embraces the quilters she has known. Her friends. Then her brothers, too. "Good-bye. We'll meet again somehow. Somewhere."

"Put your marbles in your pocket," she tells Weston when they have gone a ways down the road. "Both of them." Hand-in-hand, they trudge toward the home Charles built for them, for Sophia and Harriet and their offspring. The house that has held two wives and three children. Maybe there would have been more babies had he not passed, but he is gone. Not unlike the blowing sand.

Neither man she has known intimately was present today to cast his vote—one passing through, the other passed away. Geoffrey Scott is a ghost now, gone to who knows where, and Sophia has promised herself she will not think of what might have been. Charles has gone to the heavens with a Savior and with God. She will carry on and be faithful. Diligent. Endure to the end and help Mary Anne in Willard. And after she and Weston finish their trip north and when the trip across the ocean and the continent can be made, she'll hold her very own sister in her arms. Elizabeth Poultney. In Willard. They are destined to make the best of the time left to them.

She feels like singing. The day is bright, the temperature is cooperating. St. Thomas is almost over, this time away from everything she has known. Maybe she can make hats again. Maybe she will meet someone to love, someone like Geoffrey Scott. If only he could be here now. The way his eyes light up when they are together—candles in a dark night, maybe a cliché but true enough. Life will continue. Sisters. Sister-wives. She lifts Weston up high, waggles him back and forth, and lowers him to plant a kiss on his firm cheek before setting him down. He's off and running once again. "Don't run too fast," she tells him. "Come back. Hold my hand, little one."

He runs back and forth, reaching out to her hand when he is by her side. "Two hands," he says when he's next to her, skipping and chanting in his singsong way. "Your hand, my hand." And Sophia tries to keep up with him, skipping to the best of her ability, not a particularly easy task in deep sand nor in heavy shoes.

"That is right," Sophia says, not sure if skipping is something she can or wants to do anymore. "A good thing, though I think that's enough skipping." She stops, doubles over, and jams her hands into her waist and pulls her shoulders back to breathe more deeply.

She follows in the best way she can, sometimes at a clip, sometimes more slowly, wondering if she and Charles will be reunited again in the celestial kingdom with their two children—the one who died too soon and the little boy who holds her hand sometimes. Things will be different in their immortal formulation. All of them will be altered beings, able to tolerate what had not been tolerable in the human condition. Maybe polygamy will work better with an infinite understanding, though there is much living and loving to do in the meantime. Maybe there will be someone… maybe there already is someone, and she can't help that Geoffrey Scott and Adababa are on her mind.

But does an individual matter? she interrupts herself, suddenly world-weary as her son runs back and forth, sand filling her shoes as it always does when she's walking through St. Thomas. Does her name even matter? Sophia Poultney Hughes? Sophia scolds herself for her cynicism, but when she walks more at her own pace while Weston runs, she continues that line of questioning. Are not we all the same thing? Made of the same chemicals? Exchangeable wives? Exchangeable people? Paper dolls? But enough, Sophia. Enough. Exchangeable is not a word to love. We are all children of our God. Each loved for who we are.

"We'll be on our way first thing in the morning," she says after three deep breaths. Weston runs to a bush, tears two leaves off, and throws them in the air. He's a wild man today, knowing, as children know, big changes are in the air. "You'll like the animals at the Willard house," she says to seduce Weston back to her side. "You touched their noses when you were a wee one," and she touches his nose with her finger and wiggles its tip. "Now you can touch them again." But he loses interest and runs to look under rocks and behind bushes.

She is relieved she will be driving her spring wagon on the Mormon Road that has been graded, an expansion of the old Spanish Trail, and that she will not have to cross the unpredictable Virgin thirty-six or forty ways this time. Low water time anyway, so the trip wouldn't be as difficult, but she cannot help but stare at the mountains that appear a pale blue in this light, like islands in a sea of clouds, and at the creosote bushes covered with yellow flowers. Tiny balls of fuzz will overtake the bush soon, edging out the small leaves and the blossoms, but there is a brief brightness. A flare. An impulse of the desert to show off and remind those watching to be patient. "All things come to those who wait," she says out loud to herself. A seemingly forlorn, unredeemed beauty surrounds her in St. Thomas, but on this day that is overcast, no storms threatening, cool even, she can see something she has not seen before. The desert is a land of grace. She can see an elegance in the stillness of the landscape, its immobility, its ongoingness, the way it speaks without words. Its lines. Its structure. It has affected the way she thinks.

Maybe she herself was once like what she imagined a desert to be—a parched place, something people wished to leave alone. But now she's found a quiet strength. One that needs no broadcasting. Yes. Maybe there will be green when she returns to Willard, but something about the desert will go with her. It has worked itself under her skin. The spare, abandoned stretch of sand and hills now seems arresting, even beautiful, in its design. She sees all of this as if for the first time while she and Weston walk a road they've walked many times before. And yet it seems different today.

"There is beauty here," she tells Weston who has returned. "Don't you agree?" He stoops over, picks up a small rock, and slips it in his pocket, not responding to her question, except that, to her, he does. He holds out his hand. "Hold me," he says. She squeezes his fingers as they walk toward home, so small in her fine-boned fingers. Two smalls. She hopes for a bright future for both of them. A full and exhilarating life.

There is no Geoffrey Scott on a white horse, or camel for that matter, and no Charles. If she is honest, and she has promised herself she will be, she cannot make a black-and-white statement about Charles. She has tried to "Love one another, as I have loved you," maybe imperfectly, she tells herself as she surveys the horizon that changes color when the sun moves from its zenith, but she has tried. She cannot help it if Harriet is difficult, her snapping eyes full of judgment and assessment, and yet, there is feeling that resides in the woman. A place where there is softness. Sophia has watched how she cares for her little ones. And somehow, the two women have found a few small ways to respect each other. Small, but something.

"Tomorrow we will go north, Weston," she says to the toddler who's ready to burst free of her hold again as they approach their home. "You will like it. Especially the seasons."

He runs from her, jumps on a wheel of their spring wagon, and climbs its fellies until he reaches the top and flops onto the covered cargo. He finds a place to stand in the loaded bed of the wagon. "Let's go." He pretends there are reins in his hands. He urges the invisible horse forward. He climbs up on the buckboard running between the front and rear axles, runs its length, and lets out a war whoop. The wagon is his new home. He is ready.

"Tomorrow," Sophia says. "Tonight we have a floor on which to sleep. Let me check the house one last time," Sophia says, laughing at his antics. "See if we or Harriet left anything behind." She disappears into the house and finds only the two blankets and pillows on which they will sleep for one more night. One more night of surrender to the desert before the long journey begins. They'll close the doors to keep out the critters though some of them could squeeze through the cracks for sure.

Sophia has been filling the wagon for almost three days, though Harriet left before the petition was passed. She said she had a ride and needed to get to her sister's to leave this all behind. When they had stood outside waiting for the wagon to arrive, the two women shook hands then held each other's fingers a bit longer than they ordinarily would have. Then they looked straight look into each other's eyes. Something behind glass, Sophia had thought. Something for her to remember.

"Why leave so soon?" Sophia had asked, her hands back in the pockets of her apron, a habitual response to keep her chafed hands out of sight. "Are we not sisters?"

"Works when the man's around, but doesn't mean much when he's gone now, does it? I'm going to my regular sister's. I've told you that. But," she says, looking sideways at Sophia, her lips set in a straight line, "we've learned a lot, haven't we?"

Sophia wishes Harriet could have let herself loose into a memorable smile, into some parcel of pleasure. She, however, accepted whatever has passed between them and squatted to put her arms around Jonah, who on occasion called her Aunt Sophia. Then she reached to Harriet's side to pat Anna on the head, the girl who had just learned to walk, and then stood to squeeze Ephraim's cheek—the new baby wrapped in a receiving blanket, its black hair thick around its ears but bare on top. Each child hung onto Harriet, her legs and arms. There was no room left for Sophia, even if she wanted to pat Harriet on the back, something to make a temporary, if any at all, connection.

The second wife climbed into the back of the wagon and tucked her three little ones in wherever they would fit. Sophia had coughed into one hand, bothered by the dust stirred up by the wagon's wheels, and noticed how worn the hand was across the knuckles. Please, Sophia, she coached herself. Not now. Forget your hands. Whether or not they are red or damaged. Be present for this farewell. This woman is part of your family. Harriet, too, is married to Charles, whether you like it or not. It would be good if there were some acknowledgment of this connection, a closure of the gap between them, but maybe they had done the best they could do. Standing in a tail of dust, she and Weston waved good-bye.

"Now is the time," she says to Weston who's waiting on the doorstep, several pebbles stacked high, trying to keep them in balance. She sits beside him. "We will make the journey to Willard and be with Mary Anne, who is frail to the touch and won't last much longer. We will care for her in the same way Mary Anne cared for me when you were born. Y-O-U! And you will love your Aunt Elizabeth when she comes. We'll help her make a new life in Willard."

Willard. The sound of that name excites Sophia, though she still doesn't know what to do about Harriet except she hopes she will be content at her sisters'. Will she ever want to come to Willard? What will happen then? That is too much to think about.

She pats Weston on the head then puts her arm around his shoulders and pulls him next to her. Sweet boy, a young thing, innocent of the frailties. She needs to help Harriet if she needs or wants for anything. Maybe that is what polygamy is about, even though it has always felt like a shoe too small to fit. In any event, it has not fit when it comes to Harriet. Selflessness… giving up the idea of being a woman among women or of being called the "one and only"? Is that what it is supposed to be?

* * * * *

In her nightgown and worn slippers, Sophia makes her way through the darkness, through the everlasting sand, through the large and small pebbles and nettled bushes. After Weston sighs into sleep, she has gone outside to find peace in the quiet night. On her favorite rock where she can sit. She is not far from her son, ever, but tonight, she needs to be outside. To sit on this warm rock that gives her solace. She needs the companionship of the desert, its contours, its silence. She needs to ponder the web she has spun for herself and her son. She needs to think about direction. Weston is safe in sleep's arms. God will watch over him.

The night is cooler than the day but for now the rock still holds the sun's heat. She looks up into the sky and sees a plethora of stars, more than usual because the moon is crescent rather than a full round. A full moon shines almost too brightly in the desert sky, making every little thing, every path by whoever passed through, clear. It makes the desert alive with shadows, both long and short, wide and thin. But tonight, the moon is pale, and millions of stars wander, wherever they come from, whatever they might be. Some constellations, but mostly stars with no name, with no purpose other than to shine in the night and make humans know how small they are. She is so insignificant. So small. Only one of so many beings, and yet she has an incontrovertible allegiance to her singular life.

She did lie to Charles. That is the truth. A bald lie, even, though she's tempted to reassure herself, to repeat to herself, that she knew nothing for sure. Nothing for sure. But she needs to be truthful with herself especially, once and for all. Weston favors Geoffrey Scott. He is her souvenir, what a funny word, of that day, that time in the red rocks. Heaven forbid, she could not tell Charles how she felt so alive in her rebellion. The irregularities of the rocks had meant everything because life was not meant to be predictable or dictated. The time she spent with Geoffrey Scott had freed her from her sense of being stuffed into a tight stocking of third wife and a rigid person who always cooperates. But whatever that was, tonight she is simply full of gratitude for the quiet beauty of the stars and the small sliver of moon. The solitude. Thankful for her beautiful son who lies sleeping on a blanket on the floor of the house that will no longer be her home after tonight.

There is movement on a nearby hill. Slow motion. A strange shadow. It reminds her of Adababa though the camel has been gone for a good while now, Kwami with him, or so she'd heard. But there, on the outskirts of St. Thomas, something has now stopped and is standing on a hill. In profile. Its head high. Its feet buried in the sand. Maybe what she is seeing is the stuff of dreams. Something caught between the real and the imagined.

But then she watches the silhouette move higher on the hill, meandering in the half light of the night. It nibbles at leaves and branches. It must be a camel. Adababa even, if her eyes are seeing the truth. Except, she notices, the camel wanders with a slight limp. What has happened since the last time she saw him? But even as she asks herself this question, she remembers that this desert is where the camel lives. His geography. His home. This is where he eats, drinks, defecates, and wanders. Where the sun heats up the sky and the ground beneath his feet, where the landscape seems painted and imagined, where flash floods change the shape of things, where the land seems both empty and full at the same time.

As he wanders on the hill, he seems at ease with the seasons, the moon, and the sun. Night and day. He seems perfectly at home. At peace with the world. But if someone were to look at this landscape with naked eyes, they would most likely not see this camel who blends with the subtle colors or the monotony of the landscape, nor would they believe what they saw anyway. A camel. She would wager that most humans do not understand what Adababa would and could do for them. *Attah Allah*. God's gift. Geoffrey Scott's words.

Adababa crests the hill. He pauses, tilts his head skyward, his mouth open, swallowing the sky, which has become a cup—pouring itself down, giving all it has to give. Sophia forces her eyes wide open. She cannot see the camel's matted hair—the coat it is probably shedding in chunks by now—or smell its musty smell, but she can watch him holding a pose against the moonlight, almost as if he were standing for a painting.

Adababa. Yes, Adababa. The profile. The camel. The same one she rode behind Geoffrey Scott, sitting at the front, feeling its thick coat with one hand. The animal is regal in the moonlight. All of a sudden, the story of Ali Baba and the Forty Thieves is on her mind. Geoffrey Scott was enamored by that story, by this animal, and she wonders if she fully understands the import of this story and where Geoffrey Scott might be on this night.

Endless stars shower their light, and she reminds herself that she was gone for a long time. Gone to Willard about a year. And besides, she had told him she was not interested in continuing anything between them. She'd been almost hostile in her shame, in her confusion, the closer they got to St. Thomas that day. She wishes she had not been so blinded by her devotion and that she had been able to see his worth even though Geoffrey Scott is an outsider. He is still a person. A child of God, even if he's not interested in people who are busy building the Kingdom, the ones more than attached to the world after this one, ready to shake the dust from their shoes after someone is unresponsive to their message. But then she remembers she believes some of these things, too. She believes in God, in "the presence" Wordsworth has written about. In something beyond herself. In Jesus Christ's atonement and a world beyond this one. What does all of that mean?

She looks back to the hillside. She thinks too much, that she knows. Always thinking. Maybe it is time for her to spring into action and ride Adababa into a new life. Go retrieve Weston from his sleep and ride into the forever sky. But Adababa has disappeared over the hill. Gone. Vanished. And she cannot keep from wondering if he was ever there in the first place or if she has needed him to be there in the moonlight to help her beyond this moment in time.

"Adababa," she whispers. "Animal of mystery. Animal so exotic, and yet animal so faithful. Thank you for appearing to me."

As she stands—her slippers half-filled with sand, her nightgown untwisting and falling into straightness—she leaves a pocket of extra warmth on her rock that is cooling with the change of temperature. Discerning the outline of the house in the dark distance, she listens for any sound of her child and is relieved when there is nothing to hear.

She knows, whether or not the camel is real, she will not escape into a faint blue line on a horizon with him. She has a life to live. A child to raise. Sisters to aid. But Adababa will always be a reminder. A vision even. She must remember to speak the truth, whatever that is, to herself and to everybody else. She must remember not to let fear be her ruler or her guardian. This she believes as she traipses back to this home for the last time—through the sand. She watches the desert sky spin with stars.

* * * * *

AFTERWORD

The military expedition led by Lieutenant Edward Beale in 1858 was the basis for the road built from Albuquerque to Needles, California, later known as Route 66. Camels were brought from the Middle East by the United States government to help explore this dry and mostly waterless route.

St. Thomas, Nevada, was a Mormon-established settlement from 1865, was dissolved in 1870 because of a demand from the state of Nevada for taxes paid in gold and silver that the settlers did not have, and was reestablished in 1880 as a "regular" town, though some members of The Church of Jesus Christ of Latter-day Saints returned to live there. It was finally buried beneath the waters of Lake Mead in the 1930s after Hoover Dam was built on the Colorado River. In the twenty-first century, because of the low level of water in Lake Mead, the site has been uncovered once again.

BIBLIOGRAPHY

100 Years on the Muddy, Arabell Lee Hafner. (Springville, UT: Art City Publishing Company, 1967).

Anson Call and the Rocky Mountain Prophecy, Gwen Marler Barney. (Salt Lake City, Utah: Call Publishing, 2002).

At Sword's Point: A Documentary History of the Utah War to 1858 (in the *Kingdom in the West* series: *The Mormons and the American Frontier*, Series Editor: Will Bagley), ed. William P. MacKinnon. (Norman, OK: The Arthur H. Clark Company, 2008).

Exposé of Polygamy: A Lady's Life among the Mormons, Fanny Stenhouse, ed. by Linda Wilcox DeSimone. (Logan: Utah State University Press, 2008).

A Frontier Life: Jacob Hamblin, Explorer and Indian Missionary, Todd M. Compton. (Salt Lake City, UT: The University of Utah Press, 2013).

The Good Lord Bird, James MacBride. (NY: Riverhead Books, the Penguin Group, 2013).

Handcarts to Zion: The Story of a Unique Western Migration, 1856-1860, with contemporary journals, accounts, reports; and rosters of members of the ten Handcart Companies, Leroy R. Hafen and Ann W. Hafen. (Lincoln: University of Nebraska Press, in association with The Arthur H. Clark Company, Spokane, WA, 1960).

How To Be a Victorian: A Dawn-to-Dusk Guide to Victorian Life, Ruth Goodman. (NY: Liveright Publishing Corporation, a division of W.W. Norton & Co., 2013).

The Last Camel Charge, Forrest Bryant Johnson. (NY: Berkeley Caliber, 2012).

Legends, Lore & True Tales in Mormon Country, ed. by Monte Bona. (Charleston, SC: The History Press, 2015).

A Little Lower than the Angels, Virginia Sorensen. (First Edition, NY: Alfred A. Knopf, 1942. Reprint Edition: SLC, Utah: Signature Books, 1997).

Mormon Convert, Mormon Defector: A Scottish Immigrant in the American West, 1848-1861, Polly Aird. (Norman, OK: The Arthur H. Clark Company, an imprint of the University of Oklahoma Press, 2009).

The Mormon Rebellion: America's First Civil War, 1857-58, David L. Bigler and Will Bagley. (Norman: University of Oklahoma Press, 2011).

Muddy Valley Reflections: 145 Years of Settlement, Virginia "Beezy" Lani Tobiasson and Georgia May Bagshaw Hall. (Mesa, Arizona: Cox Printing, 2010).

Recollections of a Handcart Pioneer of 1860: A Woman's Life on the Mormon Frontier, Mary Ann Hafen. (Lincoln: University of Nebraska Press, 2004).

St. Thomas, Nevada: A History Uncovered, Aaron McArthur. (Reno, NJ: University of Nevada Press, 2013).

Three Caravans to Yuma: The Untold Story of Bactrian Camels in Western America, Harlan D. Fowler. (Glendale, CA: The Arthur H. Clark Company, 1980).

A Treatise on Hatmaking and Felting including a full exposition of the singular properties of Fur, Wool, and Hair (1868), John Thomson. (Philadelphia: Henry Carey Baird, Industrial Publisher; London: E. & F. N. Spon, 1868).

Uncle Sam's Camels: The Journal of May Humphreys Stacey, Supplemented by the Report of Edward Fitzgerald Beale (l857-1858), ed. by Lewis Burt Lesley. Copyright 1929 by the President and Fellows of Harvard College. Second printing 2006 (San Marino, California 91108: Huntington Library Press).

Wagon Road—Fort Smith To Colorado River, Letter of the Secretary of War transmitting the report of Mr. Beale relating to the construction of a wagon road from Fort Smith to the Colorado River, Edward Fitzgerald Beale. Reprints from the collection of the University of Michigan Library. Submitted to the House of Representatives in the 1st Session of the 36th Congress by John B. Floyd, Secretary of War, on March 8, 1860.

The Year of Decision: 1846, Bernard DeVoto. (Boston: Little, Brown and Company, 1943).

Zion on the Muddy: The Latter-day Saints Settle the Muddy, and organize Nevada's Oldest Stake, G. Lynn Bowler, Logandale, Nevada Stake Historian. (Cedar City, Utah: ImagePro Printing & Copying, Inc., 2004).

ACKNOWLEDGMENTS

A special note of thanks to Connie May Fowler for her encouragement of the novel project which I took to the Vermont College of Fine Arts novel workshop in 2016; to Michele Morris and Kathryn Gold for their careful and supportive readings; to Jay Kinney for his professional map making abilities and unswerving attention to getting everything right. Thanks also to Anne Penfield for her expertise regarding horses; to Steve Ivie for an afternoon in Grantsville, Utah, with his camels and the convivial company of Jennifer Librizzi, photographer, who took such charming pictures of me with the camels; to Connie Chard for making the introduction to Steve at Christkindl Markt; to Phyllis Leavitt for a copy of *100 YEARS ON THE MUDDY* when the book wasn't available in hardcover; to Elayne Sorenson for a loan of the history of Moapa Valley; to the many authors who have researched and written about this historical period; and to Hugo Coffee in Park City, Utah, for a responsibility-free environment in which to write.

Special thanks to Sara Hendricksen at the University of Nevada Press, who believed in the book initially and whose enthusiasm was instrumental in the book's publication. And kudos to Alrica Goldstein for her meticulous attention to copyediting detail and efforts to make sure the map was included.

Appreciation also to Curt Bench at Benchmark Books for his guidance on historical books and to the Latitudinarians for their sometimes irreverent yet always insightful encouragement. Finally, thanks to Jonny, Jeremy, and Brad, my living sons, for loving their mother and her efforts; to Geoffrey Barber, my deceased son, for his tender remembrance and the use of his name; and to Bill Traeger, my husband, for his humor, his crazy love, sense of balance, and supportive companionship throughout this process.

ABOUT THE AUTHOR

Phyllis Barber is an award-winning author of nine books, including *Raw Edges* and *How I Got Cultured*, winner of the AWP Prize for Creative Nonfiction. She has received awards for both her fiction and nonfiction and has published essays and short stories in *North American Review*, *Crazyhorse*, *Agni*, and *Kenyon Review*, among others. She has been cited as Notable in *The Best American Essays* and in *The Best American Travel Writing*. In 2005, Barber was inducted into the Nevada Writers' Hall of Fame. She lives in Park City, Utah, and is the mother of four sons.